Reviews for *The H... vest* ... s

'Tony ...chards proves to hav... a strong ... e of ... cterization and plot . . . Recomm... ed'

CHARLES DE LINT

'Man, can this guy write. Hard and beautiful . ... book ... hat has the power to scare yo...

ED GORMAN

'A super... ural thriller with a real sense of me...

RAMSEY CAMPBELL

'A genuinely gripping supernatural thriller . . . ... ng tale ... ith a persuasive cinematic style'

CRITICAL WAVE

'Some ... , like some people, are almost imp... le not to like . . . *...e Harvest Bride* is such a book. Rich... ds spins a web of intrigue and growing horror'

WEST COAST REVIEW OF BOOKS

TONY RICHARDS

NIGHT FEAST

First published 1995 by Pan Books

an imprint of Macmillan General Books
Cavaye Place London SW10 9PG
and Basingstoke

Associated companies throughout the world

ISBN 0 330 33310 0

1 3 5 7 9 8 6 4 2

A CIP catalogue record for this book is available from
the British Library

Phototypeset by Intype, London
Printed and bound by Cox & Wyman Ltd, Reading, Berkshire

To Sean Monohan
wherever you are.
You were right.

And to William & Evelyn Greene.

ACKNOWLEDGEMENTS

I would like to thank the following people for their help, advice, and encouragement during the writing of this novel:

Doug Cates; the staff of the Comfort Inn Capitol, Paris; the staff of the Coral Cliff Hotel, Montego Bay, Jamaica; Jo Fletcher; Leslie Gardner; the staff of the Hotel George Washington, New York, NY; Martin Goldman; Steve Johnson; Reggie Johnson; Robin Kenyatta; Pete and Sally Osborne; Mike and Alison Sitton; Ritchie Smith; Andy Snipper; Simon Spanton; Paul Stewart; the staff of the Victoria Falls Hotel, Zimbabwe; Jason Wilcox; Dave Wingrove; and, of course, Louise.

T.R.
London 1994

PROLOGUE

THE CREATURE

MANHATTAN, 1928

1

Tharman moved into a corner of the penthouse's huge art deco ballroom, high above Fifth Avenue, and watched as the party shifted up another gear. It was New Year's Eve. In twelve minutes' time, 1929 would be upon them.

And what a year that would be. What glories this country would spring to.

Business had boomed, prosperity was flowing like a river in spate. The music was louder, the automobiles sleeker, the parties wilder, and the women . . . the women had changed since those dreary days around the turn of the century. They sniffed cocaine, danced the Charleston till they dropped. And when they dropped, like the petals off a flower, it was always into someone's bed.

They'd been dancing for a straight two hours now.

Sipping from a glass of bootlegged champagne, he gazed at them hungrily, waiting to Feed. He was so engrossed he barely noticed somebody move up behind him.

'Mr Thurmann? Mr Lucius Thurmann?'

He'd been using the name for two years now, ever since he'd arrived in Manhattan. Tharman turned smoothly.

The short, stocky man who'd spoken to him didn't seem to fit in here at all. His suit was old, frayed at the cuffs, and looked as though it hadn't been pressed since the Great War. His hat, brown and battered, was shoved down firmly on to his head. His accent was pure Brooklyn and his face was hard and shapeless, both at the same time. It bore the deep lines and crinkled shadows of someone who had grown weary of life a long time ago. There was a thin, wavery scar across one cheek, and smaller crescent-shaped ones underneath both eyes, the souvenirs of fistfights.

The eyes themselves were a very deep brown, and were studying him intently.

Tharman smiled into them. They could study him all

they liked. They were only human eyes, after all. They would never see the truth.

The man lowered his voice as much as he could above the blare of the music. 'Mr Thurmann, I'm Lieutenant Chayney from the Nineteenth Precinct. I wonder if I could have a word with you?'

'Certainly.'

'Outside would be better.'

The man seemed overawed by his surroundings. He was sweating faintly, and his nostrils were dilated, as though he were drawing in the very smell of wealth.

Tharman broadened his smile, masking his puzzlement. This wasn't a Prohibition raid, and it wasn't his apartment besides. What did the little man want?

'Of course, officer.'

He gestured politely, and then put down his glass and followed Chayney out towards the huge marble-pillared foyer.

The door to the ballroom closed behind him. The brass chords of the Charleston, the high-pitched babble of voices, became muted.

There was another detective waiting out here. He was olive skinned and taller, younger, sharply dressed, with an angry hawklike face. Tharman dug gently into his mind and saw that he was Sicilian. By the Lords, were they letting guineas into the police force these days?

Chayney's expression had changed now that they were away from the jostling crowd. It had become tighter, and angry, like his subordinate's. They both hated the rich, Tharman realized. They both hated him instinctively, without his saying a word or moving a muscle.

He'd better go carefully, if he wanted those pink, petal-soft girls dropping into his bed tonight.

'Mr Thurmann,' Chayney said, 'I'm going to have to ask you a few questions. Personal ones, I'm afraid. Are you acquainted with a young lady called Dorothea Alderstone?'

He'd been acquainted with her extremely well, two nights ago. Tharman nodded gently.

'Were you at her apartment, the evening before last?'

What was this? Her father? Could that old tyrant have found out, and gone on the warpath?

'Officer – Lieutenant – that is a private matter between myself and the lady concerned.'

'Not any more, Mr Thurmann. We've had a very serious complaint from Miss Alderstone. She alleges that you tricked your way into her apartment and then—'

Chayney faltered, coloured a little. He took a notebook out of his pocket, and began flicking through it. By the Lords, for all his tough appearance, the man was something of a prude. Awkward when it came to sex.

'She claims you attacked her,' the Sicilian broke in. 'She claims you held her down on her own bed, and did the deed on her, smiling boy.'

Tharman held himself quite still. He almost liked this young man. Direct. Aggressive. Far stronger than his superior. Yet he was the one to go for. The one to get quickly out of the way. After that, Chayney would be easy.

He said, very coolly, 'I think you're mistaken. Such behaviour may be standard in Palermo, but not on Fifth Avenue.'

The young man cocked his head to one side. 'Is that so?'

Tharman grinned. 'The boys there practise on their sisters, so I understand.'

The Sicilian came at him with both hard, browned fists. He had three sisters of his own – Tharman had seen that when he'd looked into his mind.

Tharman stood perfectly calmly, with his arms by his sides, and watched while the older cop struggled to defend him.

'Grizzo! Cut it out, for Chrissake!' The two men shuffled backwards and forwards like a pair of drunks trying to waltz. 'Simmer down!'

It ended with Grizzo being sent to stand by the main door, at the far end of the lobby. Tharman could feel his piercing glare, even from this distance. He smiled inwardly, satisfied.

The Lieutenant, his jacket lopsided now, his face red with exertion, eyed him coldly.

'Was there any need for that, pal? Can we get back to the matter in hand?' He picked up his notebook where it had dropped to the floor. 'Did anything happen between you and Miss Alderstone that night?'

'Anything . . .?'

'Intimate, mack – anything intimate?'

They'd been intimate from midnight till the hour before dawn. But she'd been mesmerized, he'd used the Voice-that-whispers on her – she shouldn't have had any memory of that long, violent coupling save in her dreams. What in the world had happened? And how had she remembered it as an assault?

He thought back, recalled how her eyes had flickered coldly, distantly, every so often during the act. The eyes of the women he mesmerized never usually did that.

But she was different from the rest, in so many ways. Dorothea Alderstone hung around the edges of the fast crowd, but didn't truly belong. Her father was a scion of the Catholic Church, a major contributor to the upkeep of St Patrick's. Her mother was a founder member of the New York branch of the Women's Temperance League, a strident campaigner against sin of every description. Dorothea herself seemed unworldly, a plaster virgin amongst all the writhing, sweating flesh of the boudoir circuit. That was why he had seduced her, after all.

But those eyes . . . those detached flickers. A part of her had *not* been mesmerized, Tharman realized now. A part of her had clung on to her old self, her upbringing, with its parroted catechisms, its stench of incense and cloisters, its holiness, its fear.

A part of her had known sex, and turned it into violation.

He could have kicked himself. The holy ones, with their solitary, dull, moralizing god, were always the ones to watch.

And how much else, he wondered, did she remember? How much else?

The Lieutenant was waiting for an answer.

'Yes,' Tharman said. 'There was intimacy between us.'

'And would you say there was anything to Miss Alderstone's allegation?'

It was a ludicrous question, the kind asked by someone who would rather go away and forget the whole thing. Detective – pah, what a joke! But the young Sicilian was still staring at him viciously from the far end of the lobby. He could sense the heat in those dark, liquid eyes. And he knew, deep in his bones, he wasn't going to be let off that easily.

'Of course not, Lieutenant,' he replied. 'I can't imagine why she'd say that. If only I could speak to her . . .'

'Not much chance of *that*, smiler,' Grizzo said loudly, from across the foyer.

Chayney waved his hands for silence.

'What my colleague means, Mr Thurmann—'

'Go on, Frank. Tell smiler what I mean!'

'Miss Alderstone is presently resting . . . er . . . in a sanatorium . . . outside the city.'

It was all too much for the Sicilian. He began marching towards them, jabbing his finger through the air at Tharman, yelling. His narrow, dark face was twisted and creased, like molten wax.

'She's in a private nuthatch out in Westchester, smiler! She's in a padded cell! Why don't you tell him the *truth*, Frank? Why don't you tell him where he put the broad?' He spread his arms expansively. 'Oh, you look so cute in your tux and your white gloves, smiler. But Dorothea Alderstone says you turned into an animal that night. A frigging *animal*! And now do you know what she's telling everyone? That she's going to give birth to something. Something inhuman. Because of you. You pushed that sweetie off the deep end, smiling boy. You ruined her for life, and you're going to burn for it.'

Chayney had lowered his head and closed his eyes. Perhaps he was wishing he were somewhere else. Busting drunks, maybe. Beating up on Negroes. Somewhere familiar and comfortable.

But he was here, and staying put. And it wasn't just the younger man who was keeping him here; which meant that the police department was under pressure. Dorothea Alderstone's father was very wealthy, and had friends in every high office New York could offer.

This wasn't going to be easy at all. He could use his powers on these cops, use the Voice – but there were too many people involved by now. Statements would have been taken. Complaint sheets filed. Orders given. And the one thing he couldn't risk was the undivided attention of the human race.

'Mr Thurmann,' Chayney said. 'I hate to do this on New Year's Eve, but you're gonna have to come down with us to the precinct. If you'd like to get your hat and coat?'

And that was the end of it.

He'd been growing a little weary of the socialite scene anyway. It was high time he moved on.

Tharman cast a swift, regretful glance back at the closed door of the ballroom. He could hear the girlish voices, squealing drunkenly as midnight grew ever closer. He could smell them, even from out here. Their expensive perfumes. The delicate sweat on their bodies.

But there were plenty more women in the world, to Feed on.

And there were other pleasures. He felt his sinews tense, bunch. It was so rare, in this milieu, to use your energy for anything but sex.

'I feel less than refreshed,' he said to the detectives. 'Would you mind if I had a quick wash?'

'Sure,' Chayney nodded, before Grizzo could cut in.

There was a bathroom to the right. Grizzo checked it first, making sure there were no other exits. He took the key out of the lock before he left.

The door clicked shut. The bathroom went very quiet. The floor was Venetian tile, and all the pink and gold furnishings had been shipped in from Milan and Tuscany and Rome. This penthouse belonged to Mildred Davritch-Dwight, the widow of the bauxite magnate, and was furnished entirely in character. Here was the exact kind of room in which a Pompeiian whore might bathe.

Over the wash-basin hung a mirror, a great gilt-framed monstrosity ringed with nude cherubs and bulging cornucopias.

He stood in front of it, now. Gazed at his reflection. He was almost trembling. The power was already building up inside him.

He looked exactly as he had done for the past fifteen hundred years. Like a youngish-seeming man in his mid-thirties. Rather thin and gaunt, especially around the face. There was a hint of shadow beneath his high wedges of cheekbone. His mouth was small, thin lipped, his hair an almost impossible black. Midnight black. His eyebrows were narrow, dark crescents.

But it was his eyes that were his most startling feature. They were violet, with very tiny pupils. In this day and age, with eyes like those, he barely ever had to use the Voice to seduce women.

Now, something was happening to them. The violet was bleeding away, the irises widening.

They started to glow golden, as though they were being heated from within.

His lips parted slightly, baring white, even teeth.

What to do now? Where to go?

He slipped off his gloves quickly, flung them aside. Put the plug into the washbasin, filled it with cold water. He was muttering to himself now, chanting ancient incantations he hadn't used in centuries.

The surface of the basin settled. Tharman dipped his index finger into it, and began drawing symbols in the water. They should have disappeared immediately, but they lingered for a while, as though the fluid had thickened.

When they finally cleared, scenes were revealed. Soundless, moving pictures. It was the future, several months from now.

On the trading floor of the Stock Exchange, brokers milled about in a frenzied, terrified panic. On buildings all along Wall Street, businessmen threw themselves from the high ledges of skyscrapers. The banks were closed. Crowds formed outside them, began to riot.

What was this?

Factories stood empty, their gates chained shut.

A war? Invasion?

Well-dressed corpses swept into view. They had committed suicide. Some had their faces twisted in the agonies of poisoning. Others clutched smoking pistols in their hands. One of them was Mildred Davritch-Dwight. Another, his eyes staring amazedly at nothing, blood clotted around a hole in his temple, was Dorothea Alderstone's father.

A Stock Market crash! Tharman threw back his head, stifled a laugh.

Most of the wealth around him was going to disappear! Most of the crowd he'd dined with, partied with, gossiped with, slept with, were going to be ruined!

The scenes in the water were changing again. Now there was real poverty, real suffering. In every city, soup kitchens were at work, their queues stretching for blocks. Children with no shoes, with spindly legs and swollen bellies, gazed up helplessly at the pitiless sky. Stubbly, ragged men grew prematurely old. Young women had their faces dried to bone, their fingers were like gnarled, brittle twigs, the bloom of youth was dead in their cheeks. Their eyes were dry and reddened, lifeless.

Out in the countryside, families were loading their old, broken-down trucks with their pitiful few possessions. Their farms were being dragged out from under them, their roots torn away, their livelihoods destroyed. They were moving on, in the desperate hope of finding something further down the road, in a different county, in a different state. Something. They didn't even know what.

As Tharman watched, the entire face of the nation changed. Where there had been order for decades, there was chaos. Where there had been stability, unquestioned and unchallenged, there was now dispersal, collapse. Entire communities were simply moving on. And a new race of Americans was being born. Gypsies. Drifters. Itinerants. The highways were filled with them.

The scenes faded. The water cleared.

And what better place to hide than amongst all those faceless people? At the vortex of all that motion?

Grinning, Tharman reached out and switched off the light.

He could see perfectly well in the darkness. He could sense the cops waiting outside, hear their shallow breathing.

He raised his arms in front of him. Watched, as they began to change.

It wasn't a metamorphosis. It was more as though two beings occupied the same space, and one was giving way to the other.

The sleeves of his tuxedo, the white cuffs of his shirt, started to fade away like the residue of a dream. The rest of his clothing was doing the same. It grew thinner, more translucent. Finally vanished altogether. For a moment, his bare arms stood out palely against the blackness.

Then, they too were vanishing. And something else was taking their place.

These were arms as well. But different, very dark, even in this lightless room. Like silhouettes. They were much larger than a human's. Longer in the forearm, thicker, bulging with hawser-like muscles. Dangling, matted fur covered them all the way to the wrists.

The hands themselves were enormous. The fingers widened to broad, flat tips. The nails were tiny and blunt.

He could feel his shoulders spread and hunch. Feel his legs bend, shorten. They had a ferocious strength in them.

His eyes grew closer together at the front of his head. His breath deepened to swift, angry grunts.

His lips peeled back from long, savage fangs.

A faint growling from his broadened throat filled the confines of the bathroom.

Someone began knocking on the door.

'Mr Thurmann?' It was Chayney. 'Are you all right in there?'

Tharman grinned savagely. Then, he opened his mouth wide, strained to make his long tongue produce words.

A voice of sorts came out. A broken, husking voice.

'Lieutenant! Help . . . me!'

The door burst open. Brilliant electric light came flooding through. Trapped like a moth in it, Chayney stumbled forwards. Realized it was pitch dark in the room. Stretched out his hands in front of him instinctively.

He never knew what hit him.

Tharman grabbed him by the wrists, yanked him into the darkness. Broke his neck, quickly and cleanly, before the man could make a sound. Tossed him aside, to the foot of the bath.

It wasn't the lieutenant he wanted. It was the Sicilian.

'Frank?' The younger man was still outside, his voice turning sharp-edged with panic. '*Frank?*'

Tharman waited for him to come in. Kept waiting. The Sicilian had more sense. Perhaps an instinct. The older, the more superstitious a people, the more they seemed to sense mortal danger.

'For Chrissake, Frank!'

Tharman eased further back into the shadows. Opened his mouth again. Worked his thick tongue. It was much easier this time. He forced as much of a Brooklyn inflection as he could into the words.

'Got him, Grizzo!'

And the detective stepped in. He was at a crouch, his gun thrust out ahead of him. He squinted, his gaze trying to penetrate the darkness.

Tharman stood motionless, patient.

Grizzo noticed the lieutenant's corpse first, a dark, shapeless bundle on the tiles. He craned his head towards it. Couldn't seem able to tell who it was. Then, he peered further around the room.

He jerked towards Tharman. The muzzle of the gun came up.

He began to straighten.

And never completed the action.

Because suddenly, he realized what he was looking at.

His eyes opened wide and his mouth gaped. The gun clattered from his limp fingers to the floor.

Tharman flung himself at Grizzo, knocking the door shut as he came.

He grabbed the man's lapels with his right hand, slamming him against the wall. Clamped the left over his mouth.

He could feel the cop screaming into his palm. It went on and on, without a pause. The man was quite blind in the pitch darkness. His eyes were rolling helplessly, unable to focus.

Tharman lifted him off the ground. Grizzo's heels kicked spastically against the wall. His hands scrabbled for purchase. His face was slick with sweat, and there were tears in the corners of his eyes.

They always cried. They cried because they didn't understand what was happening to them.

Don't worry, my young, fiery friend. You'll understand soon enough.

Tharman opened his powerful jaws, and ducked his head down, towards the young man's chest.

He chewed through cloth. Then flesh.

Tore aside the breastbone, splashing hot, dark blood across the floor.

Then he plunged a hand inside and ripped out the Sicilian's pulsing heart.

2

He was tracking blood from the soles of his shoes when he emerged, in human form, a minute later.

There was, thankfully, no one in the foyer. He walked along it quickly.

He paused at the door. Gazed at his pale, slim hands. His gloves. He'd left them behind in the bathroom. He'd been very fond of those gloves. But he wouldn't have much use for them, where he was going.

To be so very powerful, yet have to keep on moving.

Always hiding. Always secretive. It infuriated him sometimes. And yet, it was necessary, inescapable. There were so few of his kind left.

The door shut quietly behind him. He hurried down the winding stairs, marched briskly through the building's abandoned lobby.

A chill winter breeze struck him as he emerged into the clear, star-studded night. His hair fluttered, and the hems of his tuxedo stirred.

Where now? Which direction?

He turned his head towards the docks. There were plenty of hobos down there he could relieve of their ragged clothing. He'd burn the good stuff in one of their makeshift fires.

He began to walk away. Then stopped, turned. Had a final look at the life he was leaving behind.

The windows of the penthouse blazed brilliantly with the glow of crystal chandeliers. Jostling figures were clustered beyond the panes, but none of them so much as glanced down.

He could hear their shrill voices faintly, even from this distance. They were counting down from ten.

'Seven! Six! Five! Four! Three! Two! One! . . . Happy New Year!'

Suddenly, the air of the ballroom was filled with streamers, and everyone was dancing again, and the band was pounding out the Charleston for the fiftieth time.

Tharman smiled, lifted his right hand in a parting wave, and strode away downtown.

PART I

THE DRIFTER

MONTANA, 1931

CHAPTER ONE

1

The town of Yewlburg, eight miles from the Blackridge Hills, lay helplessly beneath a July sun as hot and bright as the very eldest in the county could remember. The grazing land was burning flat. The woods off to the west of town, up on Meacher's Hill, were as dry as tinder, and three young elk had been found up there, lost and dying of thirst, the day before last.

Everywhere you walked, fine, powdery dust curled up, smothering your shoes, getting into every nook and cranny of your clothing. If you stirred it up too much, a choking cloud surrounded you.

The old people stuck to the shade throughout the daylight hours, motionless, their breathing laboured and shallow. The babies in the town wailed and squalled until their cheeks turned blotchy red and Dr Petts had to be sent for in a hurry.

And yet, the town survived. Why shouldn't it?

After all, the Depression had barely made a dent here, when it had wrecked so much of the state. Sweeping across the nation like a tidal wave, it had left this humble place unscathed.

Three men were to thank for that: Colville Laveraux, Arnold Kingly, and, greatest of them all, Edgar Linus Danvers – the owners of the cattle-ranches which surrounded the town. They'd put in extra wells and modern irrigation years ago. They'd bought old Petts a bigger house, with room for an extended surgery. They controlled the bank, held the leases on every store in Main Street, ran the Better Business Bureau. They *owned* this town . . . and so long as no one stepped too far out of line, they would continue to run it with a benign, paternal hand until their time was done. Then their sons would take over the job.

They were tolerant demi-gods. They knew that Eddie Strangsom, in his ramshackle bar-and-diner on the corner of Lime, sold alcohol illegally. They knew that the Widow McAlvaney rented out her favours to the young men at the ranches. They knew that Erskine Marchmont – once the town's librarian, and a much learned man – had become a morphine addict a decade ago, when he'd tried to live in the big city for a while, and that Dr Petts supplied him. Such was the way of all humanity. But if a boy got one of the town's young women pregnant, or if one neighbour fought against the other . . . why then, there would be a quiet knocking on doors at night, hushed remonstrations. And if those failed, threats, and action to back up those threats. Luke Dobbs and his family had been driven out of town last year, for screeching atheistic obscenities across the fence at their God-fearing Baptist neighbours. And young Rick Horton, spunky as a jack-rabbit, had had to be beaten practically senseless before he'd agreed to marry Constance Smith.

They were a happy little family now, with a beautiful baby girl, and Edgar Danvers had even been the god-father. That was the point. It worked. Everyone was peaceable and happy. It wasn't such a bad way to live.

2

Walking from the library, a romance novel clutched under-neath one arm, Betsy Whittaker wasn't so sure.

She was eighteen years old, and the whole of her life had already been mapped out for her.

Sure, she loved Joe Danvers up to a point. And yes, it was an honour to be chosen by the son of the great Edgar. She'd be secure and comfortable for the rest of her life.

But she couldn't help thinking about the late *Mrs* Dan-vers. And *Mrs* Laveraux. And *Mrs* Kingly. About how pale and quiet they always were. How distanced. How alone.

When she'd told her best friend, Ellen Krauss, that Joe was sweet on her, Ellen had cried like a person who'd just been bereaved. They both knew the truth. You couldn't keep your friends in town if you became a Danvers. All that stretched ahead of her was evening after grey evening of entertaining the families from the other ranches and a few old Danvers cronies, moving around and around within a closed, unchanging circle.

Stiffen your sinews, young lady, she told herself. It was an expression her mother often used. Stare straight ahead into the far distance and button up your lip. There were worse things in this world, far worse, than being rich.

She gazed along Main Street, past the stores and the T-junction with Jefferson. A rusted flatbed truck, laden with hay, was rattling up to the gas pump next to Eddie's. A small crowd of the town's urchins were playing stickball in front of the hardware store. Outside Eddie Strangsom's bar-and-diner, the three old drunks who haunted the place had moved their chairs out on to the porch and were dozing uneasily.

Soon, everyone would fall silent and the men would raise their hats when she walked past. Soon. It wouldn't be long. Joe hadn't proposed to her yet, but she sensed that he was going to.

She opened her parasol, and had begun to cross Main when she heard the puttering of another automobile engine in the distance.

It was coming from the east end of town, from the direction of the Danvers ranch, and she recognized it as Joe's car immediately.

For a moment, she thought of hurrying home, avoiding him. But he'd catch up with her sooner or later, whatever she did. And besides, there was a part of her that really did love him, in a childlike way.

She withdrew on to the shady sidewalk, waited.

The car – a new Studebaker Commander in two-tone cream, with chrome trimmings – was washed scrupulously each day by one of the servants at the Triple Y and could be seen from a long way off, glittering on the dusty streets of Yewlburg like a brilliant jewel. Betsy squinted painfully as it pulled on to Main. It was so *bright*.

She allowed herself a little smile. In some of the novels she read, there were heroic knights in silver, shining armour. That was what Joe wanted to be for her, deep down. A knight, with her as his damsel.

He was really so sweet. Such an innocent boy. Maybe she even felt a little sorry for him.

That idea faded the moment he arrived. There was a short blast from the horn, and the Studebaker pulled up alongside her, the motor idling like a nest of busy insects. A cloud of dust followed it, smothering her. Betsy backed off a couple of yards, waving her hands, choking.

'Joe Danvers, you lamebrain! What do you think you're *doing*?'

The face behind the driver's wheel looked crestfallen. The pink, full mouth opened to reply. Never got the chance.

'And take off those silly goggles! What do you imagine you look like? Why, you look to me like the abominable Baron von Richthofen.'

'The who—?'

Joe was slim and muscular, nineteen years old, with the demeanour of a happy, healthy kid. He knew little of the world beyond Yewlburg, and if he ever picked up the papers at all it was to read the funny pages. She'd made him read a few paragraphs of *Ivanhoe* out loud to her once, and it had been like listening to a little boy at the church school where her mother did the cleaning.

'The *who*? The *who*?' Betsy mimicked. 'Joe Danvers, you are a prize ignoramus. The Baron von Richthofen was a German aviator in the Great War. A truly vile and evil man. He was also known as the Red Baron.'

Joe looked awestruck for a moment. Then he slipped off his goggles and his smile returned. 'Do I look like him now?'

A patina of dust covered his features, except for two tanned rings around the eyes.

'*Now* you look like a raccoon. I'm not sure which is worse!'

She could hear her voice as she scolded him. Was painfully conscious of it. Why was she always so cruel to him? He didn't mean any harm, and he did love her dearly, in his own puppylike, infatuated manner.

She always felt so confused around him, as though she were being pulled in two directions at once. And then she'd behave worse, to hide her confusion. She just couldn't stop it.

She raised her head sniffily, gave her parasol a twirl, and walked in front of the car, crossing the street.

Joe leapt out and hurried up behind her.

'Betsy, wait!'

She smiled. Turned.

'Betsy, I dunno what this is all about. I just wanted to ask you out this evening. There's a new movie showing in Malvern. *Hands of the Stranger*, with Lon Chaney and Carole Lombard. I was wondering if you'd like to accompany me to it. You see . . .' and, suddenly, he looked uncomfortable, 'I'm gonna be away for a few days.'

Away?

'Maybe a couple of weeks. Wells are darn near dried up. Grazing's almost gone. We're gonna have to move the stock up-country for a while, till things improve, and the Boss reckons I ought to be in charge of the drive. Sort of experience for later on.' He was being painfully apologetic. 'I'll be back as soon as everything's straightened out. I swear it, Betsy.'

'The Boss' was what everyone at the Triple Y and most people in town called Edgar Danvers. Pretty soon, the arrogant old man would be her Boss too, his word unchallenged law. Betsy's insides knotted up tightly at the thought.

Her anger rose. She stiffened, ready to give Joe another tongue-lashing on two counts – that he wasn't master of his own destiny, and that she *hated* creepy thriller movies.

But she stopped herself. Just stopped.

She realized, quite abruptly, that she was going to miss him, more than she'd have believed possible. She'd grown so used to having him around.

She managed to hide it. Smiled demurely. Twirled her parasol again and gave a playful little curtsy.

'Why, sir, I'd be delighted to accompany you this evening.'

'You mean it?' Joe grinned.

'Well, of course I mean it, Joe Danvers.'

He grabbed her wrist delightedly, hurting her a little. 'I'll pick you up at seven. If that's OK, that is?'

'Joe,' Betsy sighed. 'One of these days, *you'll* have to decide what's OK. *You'll* have to make the decisions.'

One of these days, after all, *he* would be the Boss. It was hard to imagine, sometimes.

3

The confused, torn feeling hadn't gone away by the time she got home. It clung to her like a rat hanging on to the nose of a hound-dog. However much she tried to shake it loose it just stayed there, obstructing her vision, causing her pain. Her head was a muddled, tortured whirl.

Did it always feel this way, this endless, grey time before getting married, this purgatory between one life and the next? Did it feel any better once the vows were taken?

There was no one to ask. Certainly not Mama.

Her father, Bertram Whittaker, had left before she'd even known him, when she was one year old. She'd been raised by Ma alone, with some financial help from the triumvirate at the three ranches. The subject of Poppa was forbidden in the house, and not a single man had stepped across the porch since he had gone.

She gazed bleakly at her home. White paint was flaking from the walls. The roses in the front yard wilted crookedly in the heat. The windows had their drapes half-shut, like sleepy eyes. It was all as quiet and dead as a mausoleum.

Out on their veranda next door, the Crawleys nodded to her pleasantly. Betsy forced a smile in return, then let herself in through the clattering gate.

She stopped at the fly-screen, gazing through the open door. Could see the neat, stark living-room from here. The floral patterns on the drapes and furniture must have been colourful once, but their hues had faded away and muddied. The sole concession to an ornament was the huge iron crucifix spreadeagled against the far wall.

It would be the same question, the moment she walked in. *Always* the same question. As though she were a patient in a hospital, and Mama were waiting for news of her decease.

She held herself ramrod straight, just as she'd been taught a real lady should do, and went inside.

'I'm home, Mama!'

'In the kitchen, Elizabeth!'

Her mother was on her knees on the cold stone floor, bent over a washtub. Her sleeves were rolled up, her scrawny arms immersed in dirty water. Damp curls of thin, grey hair drooped across her narrow forehead.

She asked the usual question without even looking up.

'Has Joe Danvers proposed to you yet?'

'No, Mama. Not yet. He's going to be away for a little while.'

'Up in the hills, on a cattle drive. I heard. Just like in the old days.' She frowned. 'He'll propose to you when he gets back. A man sits alone, with nothing around him but cows and other men, and he soon starts to thinking on the comforts of a home and family.'

She always talked about the subject in the same flat, exhausted tone. It was as though she thought of marriage as some form of human sacrifice – awful, but inevitable if you wanted to please God.

'It might be a while till we think of a family,' Betsy said quietly.

'No. You start having young the moment you get wed. Nothing ties a man to you like infants.'

Oh, sure! Betsy wanted to snap back at her. And a load of good that little gem of philosophy did you!

But she bottled in her anger, as always.

'Mama, Joe's taking me to the pictures in Malvern tonight.'

The arms stopped moving in the tub.

'You know I don't approve of that, Elizabeth.'

'He asked me nicely, and he's always a perfect gentleman.'

'They always seem so, at first.' Her mother let out a rattling sigh. 'I can't stop you, I suppose. But remember what you are, and what he is, and don't let him sweet-talk you around it. You want to be Mrs Danvers, not some pagan Jezebel.'

'No, Mama.'

Her mother's head lifted. Red-rimmed, flinty eyes stared up at her.

'Is that another of them romance books you're carrying?'

'Yes, Mama.'

'Shouldn't be reading 'em. I told you that before. They put strange ideas in your head. Life ain't like that, Elizabeth. Men ain't like that, particularly.'

'No, Mama.'

'Now go and get yourself freshed up. Dinner'll be at six.'

Betsy hurried upstairs to her room. Shut the door behind her, locked it.

Almost everything was white in here, with small touches of yellow. The bedspread, the curtains, the dresser with its vase of silk roses on top. The dolls and china clowns. Mostly, she felt safe here, out of reach of the world. But sometimes, the pureness of it irritated her, made her feel like she was drowning in white.

She tossed the novel on to the bed, then crossed to the window and gazed out. She could see the town only dimly. Overlaying it was a scene conjured up in her own head.

A beautiful, glorious scene. And then another. One taking over from the next.

The little houses below became smoking, thatch-roofed huts, surrounding a fairytale castle with high, gleaming turrets. Then, they were waves on the open sea, and a pirate ship swung into view. A Wild West scene superimposed that. Next, the landscaped garden of a great English mansion from Georgian times.

And *she* was in each fantasy. A knight errant rode out of the castle towards her. The captain of the pirate ship snatched her up in his arms. A young milord in a powdered wig bowed and kissed her hand.

The last scene faded, like thin morning mist. The sunbaked, dingy houses of Yewlburg stared back at her. The cross atop the church spire stood there like a reproach.

She suddenly felt angry and upset. It was as though she'd been cheated. As though life had betrayed her.

She snatched the curtains shut and threw herself out full-length on the bed, buried her face in the soft quilt for a while. She felt like crying, but the tears wouldn't come.

After a while, though, something else did. She felt hot and damp inside, as though she were crying *within* her body. It was pleasant and frightening at the same time.

Another fantasy came to her. Not a scene, this time, not a picture. She couldn't even visualize it properly. Just a thought, that was all. An idea.

No! It was a terrible, unchristian thought. But it wouldn't go away.

Mama's words came flooding back to her. You want to be Mrs Danvers, not some pagan Jezebel.

And the anger she'd been holding in finally boiled over. To *hell* with you, Mama!

She sat up quickly, reached for the crucifix above her bed. Turned it around, so that the limp, agonized figure was facing the wall. Then, almost before she knew what she was doing, she was unbuttoning her frock, pulling it over her head, slipping off her petticoats.

She stayed perfectly still a moment, scared. Her skin was prickling with goosebumps, despite the heat.

She forced herself to move. Got up and walked over to the dresser, stood in front of the small mirror. Looked at the curves of her body underneath her lace-trimmed underwear.

The fine cotton had been moulded to her figure by the heat, and was practically transparent. She could make out roseate circles at her breasts and, further down, a triangle of startling darkness.

Betsy coloured. Put her hands up to her face. Her fingers moved to cover her eyes.

Didn't, completely.

She was so *beautiful*. She knew it was a sin, but she couldn't stop looking at herself.

Couldn't stop imagining someone else looking at her. Even Joe. Would it be so dreadful, just for one night in her life, if she could be a pagan Jezebel? Wouldn't sweet Jesus look the other way for just one night? Wouldn't God, in all His wisdom, understand?

Tentatively, she pushed a hand through her blonde, waist-length hair, lifting it to the nape of her neck. She'd seen a picture in a magazine once, of a movie star doing that.

She put the other hand on her hip, bent her knee, striking a pose.

She struck poses in front of the mirror for almost half an hour, until her mother called.

4

Eddie Strangsom watched his bar on Main and Lime fill up to bursting as evening fell. Drovers from the Triple Y and the Kingly and Laveraux ranches were flooding into town for a last beer before the long, hard ride tomorrow. And Eddie found himself working furiously behind the counter, for the first time in months.

He was a small, balding, nervous man, who glanced up frightenedly at the saloon doors every time they squeaked open. His greatest fear of late, the demon of all his nightmares, was the Treasury Agents he'd been hearing so much about on the radio all this past year.

It hadn't worried him till recently that he'd been breaking the Volstead Act, ignoring Prohibition. The only law in town was old, useless Wilkie Gage, who was owned body and soul by Boss Danvers and was nearing his sixtieth birthday by now. And the owners of the three ranches wanted their men to unwind occasionally, and were rich enough to pay off any marshal who came snooping into town. But this Elliot Ness and his small band of agents were supposed to be incorruptible. What if *they* burst in? What would he do then?

The doors slammed open, and Eddie practically dropped the tumbler he was filling. But it was only Jack Hughes, foreman of the Triple Y, with two of the younger drovers in tow.

They grinned when they saw him jump. One of the kids pointed a finger at him, jerking it like a gun.

'Rat-tat-tat! Gotcha, Strangsom. I'm Edward G. Robinson, and I arrest you in the name of the law.'

Their boots clattered on the bare floorboards as they strode in. A table cleared quickly for the tall, white-haired foreman.

Hughes' grin, as ugly as a scar, grew broader in his pockmarked face.

'Three beers, Eddie, my little pal. And don't keep me waiting all night.'

He took a pack of cards out of his pocket, and the three began to play.

Eddie glared at them angrily. Like kids, that was how they behaved! *Rat-tat-tat*. They always teased him, every time they came here. And how did they know what he was so afraid of? He didn't share a bed with his wife any more, so it couldn't be that he talked in his sleep. He'd never told anyone. How had they guessed?

Perhaps it was simply written on his face.

He poured the beers, balanced them on a tray, and carried them across to Hughes' table. He was ignored as he set them down. The entire crowded bar seemed oblivious to him.

Eddie listened to their dull-as-ditchwater chatter. Most of them were talking about tomorrow's cattle-drive. A few were discussing the town's prettier women in crude anatomical terms. And there was the usual small faction whose talk was of leaving Yewlburg, heading to Chicago for some action and excitement.

Mobsters! Tommy-guns! Ho-ho! They'd be lucky to get a job in a slaughterhouse between them.

Most of them had never even seen a big city. But he had. That deserved him some respect, didn't it?

Eddie pushed his way behind the counter, switched on the radio, and tuned it in to the baseball news. The St Louis Cardinals were still storming up their division, and he found himself wishing that he'd put a bet on them.

5

Tharman stopped at the top of Meacher's Hill and gazed across the town, his ragged clothes dusty and his black hat shadowing his eyes.

Was this it? Was this what he'd come all this way for?

For a month, he'd been travelling through the backwoods of Wyoming with a nocturnal band of thieves and tricksters, moving from one small township to the next. There'd been women with them, fiery, hot-blooded molls, and their lust had nourished him well. But then the vigilante gangs with their axe-handles and shotguns had started showing up. And then the police.

It had been time to move on.

He'd crossed the state line into Montana and kept on walking north-west, sheltering in forests and deserted barns by day. And . . . something had kept leading him in this direction. Something like the scent of raw flesh on the still night air.

Now, his nostrils flared, and he could smell it clearly. A hunger, as great as his own.

He'd been thinking for some years of finding a longer-term companion. Someone with a strength, a lust for life, to match his. To nourish him and please him. He missed the prolonged thrill of female company, evening after languorous evening of beauty and intelligence and grace. But he certainly hadn't found it amongst the flappers of New York. Maybe that was what had brought him here.

A 'one true love'. The term amused him.

Are you down there, my one true love?

He tried to reach out with his mind, but he was too weak. He hadn't Fed in two nights.

Aches nagged at him, all over his body. It had been centuries since anything save hunger or a vagrant ray of sunlight had hurt him. How much of his power was gone?

He studied the town carefully. He'd seen its like a dozen times before. Huddled. Isolated. Withdrawn into itself. He'd had an unfriendly reception in such places, in California particularly. But those times, the power had been almost pouring from his fingertips, and he'd coped easily.

Now? What now?

Perhaps, if they attacked him, they could harm him. Maybe even kill him. The idea made him sick and cold. A million soft, feminine bodies stretched out through the centuries ahead of him. Twice that many naked arms reached up to grasp him. How could he risk death?

But he had no choice. It was this town or starve.

By all the Lords, the Traitor Kellesh could not have devised a worse fate.

His sharp eyes picked out men in boots and wide hats strolling along the main street towards a dimly lit bar. More were just arriving on the back of a canvas-covered truck.

And where were the women?

Their aroma drifted up to him. They were hidden, but they were there.

The rising moon wavered in the night heat. Crickets shrieked at it brittlely.

Tharman started walking down the slope, towards the town.

6

'Sic 'im, Gunner! Sic 'im!'

Teddy Turner, thirteen years old, pointed his German shepherd cross towards the ragged drifter approaching the town's edge, and released the mongrel's collar.

'Get 'im! Get that hobo!'

Normally, Gunner would have chewed a leg off the Devil himself. But now the black ears flattened, the tail dropped. The dog backed up between his master's legs, and began to whine.

The drifter walked past without a sideways glance.

7

'Hey, feller!' called Dan Johnson, looking up from jawing with his friends in the doorway of his hardware store. 'You walk real good! Just keep on walking, y' catch?'

'Right through town an' out the other end!' skinny Fred Willis added. 'Don't stop for nothing!'

The drifter pretended not to hear them.

Johnson folded his meaty arms across his apron, said out loud, 'You know, I just got a new consignment of pick-axe handles in! Can't *wait* for the opportunity to try them out!'

'Might be able to, sooner than you thought,' Sam Yaeger agreed.

8

Halfway down Main Street, a darkened window flew open.

'Hey, feller! Hungry feller?' a voice called out from the gloom. 'Then eat this!'

A chamberpot crashed on to the road, spilling its contents across the dust.

Tharman held his anger in check, and kept his gaze fixed on the dim lights of the bar.

CHAPTER TWO

1

Eddie Strangsom nearly had a heart attack when the doors swung open on someone he didn't recognize.

The figure was enclosed in shadow. A wide black hat and dark clothes were all that he could make out. Just like the Treasury men in his nightmares.

Then he noticed the shabby boots, the holes and patches in the pants. He let out a quiet sigh of relief. Reached out gently and switched off the radio.

The entire room fell silent.

There seemed to be something odd about the drifter as he took a step into the bar. Eddie had seen plenty of hobos before – there'd been a big encampment of them by the railroad track outside San Francisco when he'd last gone to visit his son. They'd all had the same look. Like gutted fish, as though life had ripped the innards out of them. Their eyes had been hollow, their cheeks sunken. Their shoulders had been hunched over as though they were slowly deflating.

This one was different. He was hungry, that was for sure. And awfully weak looking. But he held himself very straight. There was a stern nobility about him, a quality that was almost regal.

No one in the room moved. Every eye was fixed on the ragged man.

He didn't seem to notice the attention he was getting. Began walking forwards.

There was the loud grate of a chair as Jack Hughes stood up and blocked his way.

And Eddie did something he'd never dared before. He wasn't sure why. Maybe it was because the drovers had teased him so much. But he suddenly found himself saying, in a quavering voice, 'You got money, feller?'

The man reached into his pocket and pulled out a dollar bill and some change.

Jack Hughes turned his head and glared towards the counter. Eddie met his gaze defiantly.

'Man's thirsty, obviously. Got money, wants a drink. No harm in that. This *is* my bar, Jack Hughes.'

For a moment, Hughes' face looked like a dark storm. Then the grisly smile reappeared. The foreman put an index finger to his temple, wiggled it.

He sat back down, watching the newcomer like a hawk.

'Beer?' Eddie asked pleasantly as the stranger approached him.

Lord, this was an odd-looking specimen! The thin face, the gangling frame, the stubbled chin were everything you would expect. But those weird mauve eyes! They looked like the eyes of some fantastic animal. He'd never seen the like before.

Eddie was aware that, for once, he was the centre of attention in his own establishment. And damn them if he wasn't going to make the most of it.

He'd spit in their eye – *all* of them.

He smiled genially. Made a great show of pouring the beer into the cleanest tumbler he could find. Set it down carefully in front of the man.

'I can fix you some food, if you like,' he chirruped. 'Got some prime hamburg out back.'

'This'll do for the moment.'

The accent was Midwest, but didn't sound quite right. Something else, something foreign, underlaid it.

'What's your name, feller?'

'Herb Tharman.'

He'd heard of *Thorman* before. And *Thurman*. But that was an odd name.

Eddie shook it off.

'Just passing through, Herb?'

'Maybe,' the drifter shrugged. 'I'm looking for work.'

'Best of luck, friend. Not much around here, I'm afraid.'

The man said, 'You look like you could do with some help.'

What was that? Eddie grinned nervously.

'No, buddy. I don't think you understand. The place isn't usually as full as this. Normally, there ain't enough custom to keep *me* busy. It's just these boys are off to the hills tomorrow—'

'Shut it, Eddie!' Jack Hughes burst in abruptly. There was a tone of menace to his voice sharper than Eddie had ever heard before.

And suddenly, he realized what he'd done. Lord, had he lost his mind? He'd just told a perfect stranger that from tomorrow, Yewlburg would be empty of more than half its able-bodied men.

He flushed nervously. Could feel sweat break out on his forehead.

'Just making conversation,' he stammered to the room in general. 'That's all. That was *all*.'

He leaned towards the stranger, to warn the man he ought to leave.

And the violet eyes seemed to glow golden for an instant.

Held him.

2

Amazing! Tharman smiled. *I am at my lowest ebb, and yet this man is so much weaker.*

He reached into Eddie's mind with what little power he had left, sifted the pale contents there, found what he needed.

And then he used the Voice-that-whispers.

I can help you, Eddie. I can heal you. I can salve away your fears. Those Treasury Agents, they'll never come calling while I'm around. These thugs, you'll never need to be afraid of them with me by your side. Never again, Eddie.

Never. People will respect you. Your wife too, yes. There goes Eddie Strangsom, they'll say. There goes a man. And all you need is me by your side.

Me, Eddie. Me, me, me!

3

Eddie shook his head puzzledly. There was a soft, peculiar ringing in his ears. Had the drifter just said something?

No. The guy's lips hadn't moved.

His thoughts were rambling. Now, where were they?

Oh yeah, the man had just asked for work. And Good Lord, he *could* do with some help around here.

He rested his elbows on the counter, beaming.

'OK, Herb. I can take you on.'

'What?' Jack Hughes shouted.

Eddie stiffened fiercely, jabbed a stubby finger at the foreman. 'Now you shut up, Jack! Just shut up! I don't tell you your business, so don't you tell me mine. One more word out of you, and I'll throw you out of here myself.'

Hughes' mouth gaped. He started getting up, then slumped back into his chair.

He folded his arms across his chest, stared narrowly at Eddie like a doctor studying a patient with an unknown, virulent disease.

'Forgive their behaviour, Herb,' Eddie smiled. 'Parochial types, you know. Not me, though. I've visited San Francisco, four times.'

'Is that so?'

'Sure. Four times in the last five years. Now – I can't pay you top dollar, I hope you understand that. But if you put in a good day's work—'

'Night's.'

'I'm sorry?'

'I only work nights.'

'Well, that's fine,' Eddie nodded. 'That suits me perfectly. I can feed you a good hot meal a day. That's thrown in, on top of the wages.'

'And where am I going to live?'

Eddie let out a high-pitched laugh.

'I forgot that. Stupid of me. There isn't a hotel in town, no call for one. But I'll tell you what. My wife and I have a spare room, used to be our son's. And we already have one paying guest, a Mr Erskine Marchmont. I suppose one more wouldn't make any difference. If you go now, I'm sure Alice'll still be awake. You cut through the alley out back, and down Jefferson Street until you reach a pink house with marigolds in the porch. And tell Alice I said to fix you up a meal.'

Something strange was happening inside his head. One moment, he was chattering happily. The next . . . everything began to grow dark, began to whirl. He could see a pair of golden eyes in the darkness. Burning, glowing golden eyes. So bright they hurt him.

It felt like his head was coming apart. He clamped his hands blindly to his temples. Pawed at them.

The whirling stopped.

His sight returned.

The drifter was no longer there.

All the drovers in the bar were gawping at him amazedly.

'Man's cracked!' said someone from the corner.

What had he just *done*?

He whirled around, looking for Herb Tharman.

'He's gone, idiot,' Jack Hughes intoned. 'On his way to your house, with no one there but your wife and that old stick Marchmont.' He chuckled drily. 'Want us to go after him? Like hell. Sort it out yourself, you lamebrain.'

Eddie felt his mouth work numbly for a moment. Then he forced himself, with slow, deliberate movements, to pick up a glass and a dishcloth, begin rubbing at one with the other. As though everything were perfectly fine.

There *had* to be a good reason for hiring the drifter. He just couldn't remember what. He ought to go home and check that things were OK. But something was stopping him. He couldn't bring himself to move away from the counter.

And the pain in his head hadn't completely gone.

4

Tharman limped past the wooden houses and the neat front yards as fast as he was able. It might only be a matter of time before some of those thugs in the bar decided to come after him. And using the Voice had drained him almost entirely of power.

The night's heat was making him sweat. A hot, swirling breeze sprang up around him, throwing sharp grains of dust against his face. They *stung*. His feet hurt and the muscles in his thighs ached.

Now!

He had to Feed now*!*

The woman in Strangsom's house.

The Alice.

It would have to be her. But how? He couldn't use the Voice again. He didn't have the strength.

A sickly pink house with potted yellow flowers in the porch swayed into view. Tharman moved to the front gate and stared at it. It was not entirely pink, on closer inspection. Great swaths of the paint had crumbled away, revealing the greyed-out, splintered wood beneath, till the house looked like it had a skin cancer. The slate roof was ramshackle, and the windows were streaked with dirt. A rusted mowing machine sat uselessly on the dry brown lawn.

The lights behind the floral-print drapes, on the ground floor, were dim and ochre.

Tharman hobbled to the porch, found the bell-pull, yanked on it.

It was almost a minute before the door creaked open. Standing there, in the faint light of the hallway, was a short, blonde woman just the wrong side of forty. Her face was wide, her eyes round and dark blue. There were crows' feet blemishing her pale skin, and her short hair was dry and unkempt. But she still had about her an aura of simple prettiness, the kind you associated more with a teenager than a mature woman.

Tharman glanced at her figure, beneath her thin cotton bathrobe. Nothing childish about that. It was a fine, shapely body.

She seemed to notice his interest, and flushed uneasily. But she didn't appear offended.

Very feebly, Tharman touched the outer edges of her mind. What he saw there made him smile. By all the Lords, she *knew* she was still attractive. And there was a strong, lingering ache in her. Her husband hadn't slept with her in years.

What a mess this little town was, just below the surface. What a dim, pathetic joke.

He explained who he was, and the woman stepped aside and let him in.

This was going to be so *very* easy.

The Voice wouldn't be needed.

CHAPTER THREE

1

On the screen of the Parthenon Cinema in Malvern, a narrow-eyed, sibilant Lon Chaney was trying to persuade Carole Lombard that he was not a deranged killer. He kept making jerky, startling movements closer to the woman, like a jumping spider closing on its prey.

Joe felt Betsy's grip tighten on his knuckles until it was almost painful. He tried to concentrate on the movie, but all he could think of was the girl beside him.

He risked a sideways glance at her.

Her eyes were wide, barely blinking. Her raised face was ghostly pale in the electric glow of the screen.

She looked like a beautiful statue.

Jesus, she made him feel an idiot so much of the time. He wouldn't have stood it from anyone else. But, with her, he was like a little dog, willing to take any amount of abuse so long as she didn't leave him. It was love. You didn't need books to figure that out.

There was another feeling as well, hot and heavy, pressing. He'd done it three times before – twice with Doris McAlveney, and once with a young Chink servant at the house. But this time the urge wasn't simply for release. It was more complex, and it frightened him. When he finally did it with Betsy, he figured, he would somehow, at long last, own her. It would be like owning a precious work of art. The responsibility of it bore down on him like an enormous weight.

But the stirring below his waist wouldn't go away.

Up on the flickering screen, Carole Lombard yelled with terror. Betsy's nails dug savagely into his palm.

Joe barely felt it. He kept watching her, ready to look

away the moment she turned. Very gently, he slid his free hand across until it was hovering just above her leg.

He was finding it hard to breathe.

He settled it, as slowly as a folding flower, on her long gingham skirt. He could feel the warmth of her leg beneath.

There was a shriek.

But, again, it was Carole Lombard.

To his amazement, Betsy didn't move or say a word.

She stared intently at the screen, and let his hand rest there.

2

Eddie Strangsom got home just after ten o'clock.

He paused at the front gate and shook his head like a dog irritated by flies. The pain that had started earlier this evening still hadn't gone. And every time he blinked he could see those burningly bright eyes within the darkness of his head. What the hell was wrong? Was he sick?

He'd been worried about Alice, ever since the drifter had left. Yet every time he'd thought of coming home, making sure that she was safe, the idea had drifted away from him like gossamer on the wind. He hadn't been able to cling on to it.

Cracked, one of the drovers had said. The man's cracked.

Was that true?

God, there was a small part of him – had been for some time, he realized – that simply wanted to curl up in a deep hole and die.

He looked up at the house.

The doors and windows were all closed, despite the stifling heat. There were no lights on, anywhere. Eddie stiffened. That wasn't right. Alice was always up when he got home, sitting in the parlour mostly, staring at the mantelpiece as though the secrets of the universe could be found in the cheap porcelain ornaments she collected up there.

She *never* went to her bed till he went to his.

The pain grew stronger again. And the urge to turn and run away. He fought it desperately, this time.

Keep a clear head, stupid. Think. What's going on here? Think!

He glanced quickly up and down the street. Perhaps he ought to get help. But the drovers had all gone back to the ranches early, for the dawn ride tomorrow. And not a spark of light showed in a window, anywhere in sight.

What was *happening* in there? What had happened to his wife?

That drifter . . . he might have attacked her! *Killed* her, even!

Eddie made his way, as quietly as he could, to the front door.

Not the faintest sound was coming from inside.

He began fumbling in his waistcoat pocket for his latch-key. His fingers were shaking and numb. They closed over the vague sensation of cold metal. Began to withdraw.

The key slipped loose, fell on to the porch with a sharp clatter.

No! Tears were starting up in Eddie's eyes. He felt nauseous, dizzy.

Couldn't he do anything right?

He stooped to retrieve it.

When he looked up again, the door had drifted open.

3

'Alice?' he tried to say.

His mouth moved, but barely any sound came out. He stepped inside. There was no one in the hallway.

'Alice?'

All the doors leading off to the sides were shut, and it was pitch dark beyond the patch of moonlight he was standing in. Eddie strained to catch a sound, glimpse a shadow. He was sweating furiously now, and his jaw was clenched so rigidly it hurt.

He balled his small hands into fists. Took another step inside.

The door swung shut behind him. The lock clattered.

Eddie stumbled. His shoulders slammed against a wall. His fists came up in front of his face. He could hear himself gasping like a fish.

He couldn't *see*. It was like a coalmine in here!

He waited for the attack to come. Waited for the blade, the club, the strangling grasp. Whatever it was going to be.

Nothing happened.

Slowly, he relaxed a little. He began to make out vague shapes in the blackness.

The curled, serpentine form high on the wall was an old gas mantle he'd never taken down. Christ, where were the electric switches? His fingers scrabbled across the wall, but he couldn't find them. He ought to know where they were, but the sick pain in his head was making him confused.

The tall, many-armed shadow in the corner, like an elongated spider, was the coat-rack.

And over by the parlour door, at the far end of the hallway, there was something else.

Something flat and shapeless. Faintly pale against the floor.

Eddie pressed his palms against the wall and slid along carefully until he reached it. He picked it up.

It smelled of Alice's perfume. It was her bathrobe. Tangled in it was one of her cheap, coarse stockings. Oh my God, she *had* been attacked!

He felt the tears start up again, hot and flaming, burning him.

Then he heard it.

The noise.

It was coming from behind the parlour door.

He couldn't make out what it was, at first. It sounded like a wild beast, grunting very gently. It went on and on, at a continuous, rhythmic pitch.

Run. He wanted to. But no, he couldn't do that. Maybe the drifter was in there. Maybe he was still . . . still . . .

An awful image came to him, and he thrust it out of his mind.

What he needed was a weapon.

He cast his gaze around. Propped against the coat-rack, he remembered, was an umbrella with a heavy ironwood handle his father had owned. He scrambled for it blindly.

His hands closed around it. It felt solid in his grasp.

A sudden, surprising elation filled him. Now for it! He'd show all of them down at the bar. He'd prove that when the chips were down, he was braver and stronger than they were. They'd all think differently of him, after tonight.

He gripped the doorknob.

Paused a moment, breathing deeply.

Then he turned it. Shoved the door open so hard it crashed back against the parlour wall.

The scene inside was illuminated by a single guttering candle.

And what the flame revealed . . . Eddie couldn't believe his eyes.

Alice was naked on the floor. Her face was thrown back, her teeth bared. Her thighs were raised, and her body was moving back and forth.

On top of her, fully-clothed, was the drifter. He had one hand across her temples, as though he were holding her head down. But he didn't seem to be restraining her. She was a willing partner.

Eddie felt the umbrella slip from his grasp. It clattered loudly, but neither of the couple on the floor seemed to notice.

Until finally, Tharman's head turned towards him.

The eyes. They were no longer violet. They were a blazing, molten gold.

And the face – it was not the face of a man at all.

Eddie got a brief impression of a snout with flared nostrils, a ridged brow, curving white fangs.

And then the darkness, the whirling, closed over him

again. The drifter's voice began chiming in his head, and all thought was lost to him.

4

He stood like a statue until they were done.

Finally, Alice rose and, naked, hollow eyed, walked across the room, stood beside him.

They watched the drifter as he settled into an armchair and leant back, a grin on his bestial face. Then they knelt down together, placed their hands on their knees.

Bowed their heads to him.

The candle flickered, and went out. All that could be seen were those golden eyes, burning like beacons in the darkness.

5

Thebes, Egypt, AD 391: *He was a simple priest back then, of the moon-god Thoth, administering to a congregation that was dwindling by the year. Rule of the land had passed from the Romans to the Byzantines, and the winds of Christianity had been sweeping the desert for more than a century. The Coptic Church in Alexandria had become the most powerful force in the province.*

And in that year, the inevitable had happened, the one decision Tharman had always feared. Orders had come from Byzantium itself. The Emperor, Valentinian II, had outlawed the cults. Worship of the ancient gods of Egypt was forbidden, upon pain of death.

He, and a few of his acolytes, were in his back-street temple that night, praying for guidance and protection, when the soldiers burst in. The others were caught and slaughtered on the spot. Tharman barely escaped with his life.

He fled, through the narrow, dusty alleys, to the only safe shelter he could think of – the home of a wealthy merchant, up on Silk Street, who was still, covertly, a believer. And there he hid in the darkened cellar, shivering with fright.

His head jerked up, half an hour later, at the sound of marching footsteps, the rattle of chain-mail. Shortly afterwards, he could hear the banging of sword pommels on doors, and voices being raised. He crept to the ornate grille of the cellar's tiny window, peered nervously out. And what he saw in the flickering torchlight confirmed his worst fears. The Byzantines were conducting a house-to-house search. It didn't take much to guess who they were looking for.

'See how he clings to life?' a gentle female voice whispered, behind him. 'See how desperately he wants to live?'

He gasped, and whirled around.

A motley group of men and women, eleven of them in all, were staring at him from the shadows near the cellar door. Who were they? Who in all the heavens? They were the strangest crew he'd ever seen. Their skin was deathly pale, their eyes intense. They were dressed in an odd assortment of costumes – of street vendors, merchants, beggars, mercenaries.

How— *he began thinking.*

'How did we get in here?' It was the same woman who'd first spoken. She stepped forwards from the crowd, now. She was tiny, petite, with dark hair and green eyes and a flattened, heart-shaped face. She was dressed in the fine robes of a Macedonian noblewoman. A curious smile danced on her lips. 'We can do many things. And who are we? "Were" would be a better word. We once were priests, like you.' She bowed gracefully. 'I am Pashta, of the cat-goddess Bast. I worshipped her fifteen hundred years ago, in the reign of Rameses III.'

Tharman backed away, shaking his head. Either this was some kind of trick, or the woman was completely mad.

'Are you not a true believer?' she was asking. 'Do you not have faith in the old tales?'

He had stopped moving, by now. Her eyes were filling up his vision. His head was whirling gently. And yet – for some reason he couldn't fathom – he was becoming calm.

'Tales? I don't understand.'

The others were slowly closing in around him.

'Of the incarnation of the priests,' the woman told him. 'Do you not believe that the priesthood of the true faiths were once gods on earth?'

He clasped a hand to his forehead, trying to make the whirling stop. He knew the legends, yes. And part of him wanted to believe them, especially in these dark days. But—

'That the Lords of the Underworld,' the woman continued, 'once craved presence on this earth? Physical presence? And achieved it, through their servants?'

'I . . . I don't know.'

'Let me show you, then.'

She stepped right up to him – and suddenly changed. Her eyes burned golden. Her face darkened, and the ears rose to tufted points. Her slim, delicate hands gave way to claws. It was all over in an instant, and it should have had him screaming, trying to run away. But somehow, he remained where he was. The capacity for fear seemed to have left him, as though something were interfering with his mind.

'We are Incarnate,' the woman smiled. 'We called the gods to us, and they came out of the Underworld, and they possessed us. All but one, who awaits his turn. Will you join us, brother Tharman? Or would you die at the hands of the Christians?' She brushed her pale fingers against his cheek. 'I do not think you want to die. But there are new rules you must learn, if you are to survive as we have. How you must avoid the sun. The sun is the god Ra, the Lord of Light, Enemy of Shadows. You must shun the Ra, and all of its devices, all its symbols. They can harm you. They can make you powerless. And you must learn to Feed. The god inside you must be Fed, or you will become vulnerable again, mortal again.'

He stared at her bewilderedly. 'Upon what?'

'On the raw life force of the humans. On their souls. You must draw them to the surface, like honey from a bee. It is not a hard trick to learn, dear brother. We each have

our own methods.' Her hands stopped moving, on his face. 'Will you join us?'

The pounding of sandals, above on the parched street, was drawing closer by the second.

Tharman tried to turn what she'd said over in his head, and then nodded quickly.

And the woman glanced at the others. 'Now,' she hissed. 'Hurry!'

They swarmed up the stairs into the main part of the house, and dragged back down into the cellar the merchant, and his wife, and his children, and even his slaves. Sharp knives were brought with them. The sacrifice was worse than any Tharman had ever seen. And all the while the Incarnate hacked and hewed, they muttered a strange prayer. The Incantation of the Door, he found out later it was called.

The bricks crumbled away at the far end of the cellar. A tunnel was revealed beyond it; a tunnel of coldly glowing stone, that seemed to stretch into infinity.

There was something moving in it. A great dark shadow, golden eyed and loping, the god Thoth was coming towards him.

6

The chrome trim of Joe's Studebaker shone coldly in the moonlight. It was parked just off the Malvern road, by the edge of a high, dark cornfield. Every so often, the hot air would move sluggishly, and a ripple would pass through the ears of maize. They made a sound like a dry salt sea.

Crickets screeched, all around the automobile. An orchestra of them, keeping to one high, harsh note, one obsessive, continual rhythm.

Squirming on the front seat, Betsy kissed Joe so hard she thought she'd suffocate. She couldn't see his face. His head was a dark silhouette above her, topped by a gleaming halo of yellow hair. One of his hands was clasping her shoulder. She couldn't feel the other, at first.

Then it closed on her leg again. Below the knee, this time. Near the hem of her gingham skirt.

She could feel his fingers moving. Scrabbling slowly. Drawing the soft, rustling fabric up.

She let herself relax a little in Joe's embrace.

His fingertips touched the flesh of her calf. Her whole body started shaking slightly. Joe was kissing her neck now.

The hand began moving again. Sliding up, underneath her skirt. It seemed to burn, red hot. And yet – strangely – her own skin was burning too, so it didn't hurt. Could we get so hot we'd weld together like two pieces of steel? It felt possible.

The hand reached the crook of her knee. Paused there a moment.

Started drifting further up.

The melting heat surged into Betsy's head. She felt as though her mind and body had come adrift. As though she were slipping into a great abyss. And there was no Yewlburg down there, no Mama, no church, no roses and clowns, no white and yellow room. Only a great pulsing darkness, tinged with red.

Joe's fingers touched the bottom of her lace-trimmed bloomers. Slid quickly across them to the elastic waist-band, hooked over it, began to yank down. One finger probed inside.

It brushed against the edge of the dark, curling hairs there. And suddenly, a painful coldness rushed into her body, usurping the heat.

Betsy shrieked, and pushed Joe away. She scrambled backwards until her shoulders were pressed against the door.

She sat there with the sound of crickets whirring all around her. Wide-eyed. Panting. Shivering like a wet kitten. Wondering what had just happened.

Joe was staring at her in a bewildered, frightened way. 'Betsy—?'

She couldn't find the nerve to answer him. All of a sudden, she'd panicked. All of a sudden, she'd realized what a huge step it was, how much it would change her . . . and she'd jerked back at the brink. Shied away from the unknown. Just for that crucial moment.

'I'm sorry, Betsy,' Joe babbled. 'Honest I'm sorry. I didn't know what I was doing.'

She burst violently into tears. Couldn't stop it.

'Betsy, please don't. Please? I just got carried away, that's all. I'll never do it again. I *promise* you.'

Her whole body was racked with sobs. She couldn't speak. The tears were gagging her.

Stupid Joe! He didn't understand!

She wasn't crying because he'd tried to take advantage of her. She was crying because she'd *wanted* it to happen. And it hadn't. Wouldn't now. The moment was gone.

It was all her fault!

A cold, serious look came over Joe's face. He straightened, cleared his throat.

'Betsy?' he said. 'Will you marry me?'

No, not this way! This wasn't the way she'd imagined it. This wasn't how it happened in the books. He was asking her out of fear and frustration, not love. But she was nodding. What was wrong with her?

He offered her a handkerchief. She mopped her eyes and blew her nose with it, but more tears welled up to choke her all over again.

Perhaps this was the way it was supposed to be. The way it always was. The way it had been for every man and woman since the world had begun. Except in silly novels. Maybe you were supposed to feel dead, and dried-out, and a hundred years old.

She wanted more than that.

It just wasn't fair.

She wanted *more.*

7

The new ranch-house of the Triple Y had been built at the turn of the century by Edgar Danvers' father, and was modelled on the homes the eccentric old man had stayed in when he'd paid a visit to Europe about the time of the Spanish-American War. It was more like a grand mansion than a cattleman's domicile. Set in well-tended gardens, it was high eaved, many windowed, with polished oaken doors. Ivy scrambled up the walls like an invading army towards a weather-vane at the top.

Jack Hughes stood, hat in his hands, in the dim study in the west wing. There was only one blue-shaded light on, over the desk. Beyond it, Boss Danvers' portly frame could be made out. The bald head was a huge globe, shimmering and sweaty. A moustache, too small and thin for the moonlike face, was suspended above thick, succulent lips. A Havana cigar, half smoked, was jammed into one corner of the broad mouth.

'Tharman, you say?'

Jack nodded.

'And Eddie Strangsom hired him?'

'Yes, Boss.'

'Man always was a fool. So was his father, as I recall.' Boss Danvers leaned back, the springs of his leather chair creaking. 'Now, what are we going to do about this?'

'I can round up a few of the boys, drag him out of Strangsom's place, and give him a good whupping.'

'No. Alice would have to see that, and she has a hard enough life as it is. Let me think.'

The cigar tip glowed brighter in the dimness. Smoke floated across the desk in a lazy S.

'Can we spare anyone from the drive tomorrow?'

'Boss, I'd be happy to—'

'Much appreciated, Jack, but again no. I want you there to keep an eye on Joe, make sure he learns the ropes.'

For a moment, Jack felt a surge of anger he had trouble holding in. Here it was *again*. He was expected to play wet-nurse, for the umpteenth time, to the Boss's pea-brained kid. And one day, that dumb kid would own the Triple Y outright, without the tiniest reward for reliable Jack Hughes; without the smallest token of thanks for the thirty-one years of his life he'd put into the ranch.

It made him furious. But he kept it to himself. There was one thing you never did, and that was show your feelings to the Boss.

'Do we have anyone else?' the old man was saying. 'Someone big and strong and not *too* stupid?'

Jack thought it over a moment.

'Lyle Winters.'

'Tall, sandy-haired boy? I know him. His family're trappers down in Colorado, aren't they? Sounds just perfect.'

'You want him to keep an eye on the hobo?'

'A discreet eye. And if this Tharman begins to look like trouble, that would be a matter for discretion too.'

Jack smiled hungrily.

'How *much* discretion?'

'Oh, enough to make that hunting background come in very useful. Enough to show that we in Yewlburg know how to deal with outsiders. I'm sure you understand me, Jack.' The cigar spat out a few red embers. 'Don't let me keep you. I'm sure you have a lot to do.'

8

A peculiar thing happened the next morning, just as the first glow of day appeared on the horizon.

In Pete Gower's house up on Stock Street – where the ground began to tilt towards Meacher's Hill – his mother Elspeth had lain dying for a week. One of the oldest inhabitants of Yewlburg at ninety-two, she could barely walk and was practically blind.

For three days, she'd been motionless on the cot in the back room, her eyes closed, her breathing so shallow it was hardly noticeable.

Now, the eyes came open suddenly. They were opaque, milky with cataracts, but they flickered quickly to and fro.

A deep rattly sigh was drawn.

Elspeth pushed herself up on her forearms, and began to struggle out of bed.

Her daughter-in-law, Cheryl, came awake in the chair by the corner where she'd been sleeping all night.

'Ma? What are you doing?'

She watched helplessly as Elspeth hobbled to the window, raised one dried claw of a hand, pulled back the drapes. The entire town of Yewlburg lay in silhouette beyond the pane.

Elspeth tipped her head forwards until it touched the glass. As though she were staring out intently. That wasn't possible. She couldn't see two yards!

'Who's out there?' she yelled abruptly, her thin voice high pitched with alarm. 'Who's *out* there?'

She collapsed to the floor. Lay still, her blind eyes wide open, staring.

Five minutes later, Pete Gower was running down the street to fetch Dr Petts.

Petts got dressed in a hurry, but felt faintly annoyed. His wife and children had been woken by the commotion. Now they'd never get back to sleep. Distantly, to the east of the town, a rumbling had started. It was deep and continuous, made the floor shake slightly underfoot. Petts buttoned up his shirt and frowned. The drive had started. Upwards of sixty thousand head of cattle were being moved to the high country, and most of the young men in the area were going with.

The rumbling was still audible half an hour later, when he pronounced Elspeth Gower dead.

By eight thirty, the news had spread down to the office of the *Yewlburg Weekly Gazette* on Main. Franklin Chase, proprietor, editor, and sole member of staff, began to set the type for the obituary.

9

All the trucks had gone up-country with the herd, and he couldn't keep his horse standing around all day while he spied on Tharman, so Lyle Winters had to borrow a bicycle from the servants' quarters to make the journey into town. Every so often as he pedalled, he glanced ruefully towards the north. The heat haze was already wavering and powerful. He couldn't even see the hills. But his sharp eyes picked out, about five miles away, a cloud rising against the sky. It looked like smoke, but he knew that it was slowly moving dust, being stirred up by the cattle and the riders. Damn, he wished he was with them. But orders were orders, and you questioned the Boss's at your risk.

When he reached the edge of town, he dumped the bicycle against the wall at the back of Eddie's. Jeez, folks would really laugh if they saw him riding *that* contraption.

He nodded to Dan Johnson and Bob Nyman and Franklin Chase as he made his way up Main Street. Then he turned at the big T-junction which bisected the town, and ambled along Jefferson. Everyone was up and about, kids were playing on the dry lawns. He crossed to the far side of the road, and approached Eddie Strangsom's house.

All the drapes were shut.

Well, he figured, Eddie had no call to be an early riser. He was surprised at Alice, though. Maybe they'd had a ruckus over that Tharman character. With any luck, the man had been thrown out and gone in the night.

Lyle doubled back the way he'd come, went into Norm Sherman's drugstore, ordered a root beer, and sat shooting the breeze for a while.

When he came back to the Strangsom house, an hour later, the drapes were still closed. He took his watch out of his pocket, flipped the lid open. It was a quarter before ten. He squinted at the windows anxiously.

There was an alley at the back of the house. Feigning

a casual air, he made his way along it, peering over the fence. One drape was open, just one, in an upstairs window. The gaunt, shadowy figure of Erskine Marchmont sat there, perfectly still, like a picture in a frame. The man seemed to be staring out at thin air. That old fool with his morphine. The house could be burning down around him, and he wouldn't have the sense to move.

Lyle went back to the street, cursing under his breath. He couldn't just stand around here doing nothing, dammit. He spotted Eric Gillie, weeding his flower border just across the way, wandered over, and started up a conversation. They talked about the drive, and the weather, and sports. When he checked his watch again, it was twenty after ten.

Other people were beginning to notice the closed blinds now. Dot McFee, in the little yellow house to the right of the Strangsoms, kept leaning across her picket fence, stretching her neck like a turkey. Lois Gillie, Eric's wife, came out on to the lawn, stared at the blotched pink façade opposite, and said, half jokingly, 'Are they all dead in there?'

Talk began to pass up and down the street. Soon everyone who hadn't been in Eddie's Bar last night knew about the drifter.

Finally, it became apparent that Dot McFee could stand it no longer.

She hurried out on to the street, paused at the Strangsoms' gate tremulously, then drew herself up straight and marched to the front door. She yanked on the bell-pull, then began hammering with her fist.

The whole street seemed to hold its breath.

The door came open a crack.

Alice's face, pale in the daylight, peered out.

She and Dot consulted for a moment, Dot's head nodding furiously. Then the door slammed shut again.

Dot waddled out of the yard, looking flushed and aggrieved.

'Still in her robe at this hour,' she announced to the

people watching. 'She pretty well told me to mind my own business.'

She went back into her own house, sulkily.

The Strangsoms' door opened again, twenty minutes later. Eddie, dressed in striped pants, a white shirt with no collar, and black braces, stepped out on to the porch. He'd forgotten to put his Homburg on, and was blinking furiously in the sun.

His skin looked almost colourless, and there was something stiff about the way he walked. Something numb. He didn't seem to realize there were dozens of eyes on him. He buttoned up one cuff, where the stud had come loose. And then, his balding head reflecting the sunlight, he marched off in the direction of his bar.

10

Go, Eddie, a voice was ringing in Strangsom's head. *Go now, do my bidding.*

Other eyes were watching him, from the depths of the shifting, colourless blur in his mind. Golden eyes.

11

On Meacher's Hill late that afternoon, Betsy's best friend, Ellen Krauss, turned to her and shrieked.

'You're not *serious*, Bets?' Her hazel eyes widened in her puffy-cheeked, freckly face. 'Joe proposed to you, and you haven't told your momma yet?'

Betsy lifted her skirt to step over a fallen branch, then shrugged.

'She was in such a good mood this morning, half the men being out of town and all, I didn't want to spoil it.'

The pain and misery of last night hung around her still, but she was darned if she was going to let Ellen see. She held herself erect and moved on tiptoe, a demure, ladylike smile plastered across her face.

At last, they found a spreading fir tree and sat down in the shade beneath it, on a carpet of dry needles. Far below them, the town shimmered like a grey-edged mirage.

'I'm happy for you, Bets,' Ellen said quietly. 'I really am.'

'Thank you.'

'But *you* seem upset.'

Lord, she'd been crazy to think she could keep anything from her friend.

'I don't know.' Betsy folded her hands in her lap, shook her head. 'I want to be Joe's wife, in a way. But . . . I just don't feel I've done anything with my life. Anything *exciting*.'

'You mean wicked,' Ellen stated, matter-of-factly.

'Yeah, in a weird kind of way.'

Ellen smirked, pulled up her petticoats, and produced a fat cigar from the top of her stocking. 'Stole it from my poppa. Want a try?'

'I already did, two years ago. Didn't much like it.'

Ellen struck a match against the fir trunk, lit the cigar, and leant back, puffing, for a while.

'Ellen,' Betsy said at last. 'Have you ever had a drink? Like, liquor?'

'Hell, no.'

'Would you like one?'

'Uh-huh.' The girl was barely listening.

'How about . . . we go to Eddie Strangsom's, then? Walk right in and buy a beer?'

Ellen sat bolt upright, her mouth gaping with shock. No respectable woman had ever been inside Eddie's.

'You're crazy, Bets. It'll get back to our folks. Everyone'll *see* us.'

'Not if we go at night,' Betsy smiled. 'There'll be no one there, if we go late. And' – she reddened and began giggling – 'I'll give Eddie a kiss, if he promises not to tell.'

Ellen's eyes darkened just a shade and she gave a disgusted shudder, the way she always did when the subject of m-e-n and t-o-u-c-h-i-n-g them came up.

'And you're going to give that new feller a kiss too, I suppose?'

Betsy looked at her alarmedly.

'*What* new feller?'

CHAPTER FOUR

1

As the sun began to sink behind the roof tops, Tharman shifted in his sleep.

The room he was in had once belonged to Eddie's son. There were baseball pennants on the walls, sports posters, a framed, yellowing school report, and a faded photo of a short, squat blond boy holding up a smallmouth bass.

The bed was a little too short for his gaunt frame. He slept on his side, his knees curled to his stomach.

Just as my forefathers buried their dead, he'd realized, just before dawn had risen and sleep had overtaken him.

No blanket covered him. He'd put it over the window, to cut out whatever light the old dust-smothered drapes couldn't. And he'd cast a Spell of Fixing on the door – it would take a sledgehammer to open it.

His sleep wasn't like a human's. His brain and body rested, but there was no retreat from consciousness. Simply . . . a stillness, perfect as the silence between stars. He could reach out and touch the minds of those around him, if he wished. And his memories marched, in a direct straight line, from that first night in Thebes to the exact moment his eyes had closed.

Every sight and sound and feeling he'd experienced over one and a half millennia was there for him to study, as though each was vacuum-sealed in a glass case.

He turned a few of them over idly.

A Barbary Corsair coming at him with a scimitar.

A piece by Mozart on the harpsichord, echoing through the court chamber of Emperor Franz-Joseph III.

The moment of his fusing with the Lord Thoth. In that instant, the god's own memories had been trapped inside his mind, as though in amber. The coldness of the *Duat*, the Underworld. The grey, dim solitude. The eternal bleakness. And gazing outward, at the short-lived, tempestuous humans. Feeding on their worship, their hot-blooded fervour. And . . . however dreadful their existences were . . . envying them.

There'd been real problems, of course, in the olden days. Travelling far had involved huddling behind the blinds of a stagecoach, or staying below decks on a wooden ship all day, controlling the minds of the coachmen or an entire crew. Brother Es-shamel of Heliopolis, for one, had failed that way, and perished, his blackened corpse tossed overboard by a pack of terrified mariners.

He felt a bitter sadness for all of them who'd died.

He'd never been that good a priest himself. The priesthood of the old gods was supposed to be celibate, and he had sinned frequently with the few young women who visited the temple. But it had been easy enough, after his Incarnation, to choose his method of drawing out human souls.

Another memory came to him, of the years after Thoth had taken him, all those centuries ago. By 641, new and fiercer rulers had taken over Egypt; black-flagged Muslims, sweeping across the deserts in impenetrable waves. They brought with them harsh, demanding laws, and the Incarnate had realized it was impossible for them to stay. They'd left in a caravan, heading south towards the dense forests of Africa. It was a journey filled with the worst imaginable hazards. Two of them had perished before they'd even crossed the Nubian Desert. But the rest had made it, and spent the next two hundred years moving amongst the scattered tribes, Feeding where they pleased. Until one of their number – Kellesh, dour and ugly priest of the crocodile-god Subek – had turned against them. Sided with the humans. Caused the deaths of Shezmu and Anubis. Taught the tribesmen what they were and how to fight them.

And the Incarnate had moved north again, crossing the Middle Sea to Europe, and spreading out across the teeming world . . .

He moaned in his sleep, stirred.

And then recalled the reception the good people of this town had given him last night. He dwelled on it hotly for a while.

The sun finally set. The last burnished bronze ray vanished, like a lamp blown out. A faint breeze eased its way into the streets of Yewlburg, stirring the dust.

Tharman's eyes snapped open, their mauve irises gleaming. His dreamy smile contorted to a vicious grin.

He'd have his revenge. He would tear this ridiculous little town apart.

2

Lyle Winters jerked sharply as the Strangsoms' door clattered open.

Sitting upright in an alley next to Eric Gillie's house, he'd been practically dozing, his chin touching his knees and the brim of his stetson pulled down low over his eyes.

He pushed it back urgently. Christ, when had it got dark? No lights were on in the Strangsom house at all. He could make out the black rectangle of the doorway, but couldn't see who'd opened it.

He wanted to shout out, but he kept very still, very quiet. The way he'd used to as a teenager in the forests of Colorado, when some dangerous animal was close.

Cloud had moved in, blanketing the sky. The moon and stars were hidden. He didn't notice, at first, a figure stepping off the porch. It was Tharman. In silhouette the man looked like a scarecrow, with his flapping hat. He stepped on to the front lawn, stood perfectly still, his head tipped back as though he was searching for the truant moon.

Then the chin dropped. The face began swinging around, directly towards him. Lyle could see the eyes glitter, and got ready for the moment when they spotted him.

But they didn't. They swept past him obliviously.

A massive feeling of relief washed over Lyle. He wasn't sure why. He was a good four inches taller than Tharman and had thirty or so pounds on him. Being afraid of the man made no sense at all.

He watched as Tharman moved on to the street and began heading west.

Meacher's Hill lay in that direction. Eddie's bar was the other way. Maybe the drifter was leaving town after all. The idea of an honest evening's work had probably scared him off.

Still, it was best to be sure. Lyle let the man get out of sight, then clambered to his feet, brushed dried dirt and twigs from his pants legs, and stepped cautiously out of the alley. He took a toothpick out of his shirt pocket, slipped it into the corner of his mouth, and began chewing it as he walked.

He was passing the outskirts of town before long. Every so often, he could make out Tharman's skinny figure bobbing in the distance.

He hung back watchfully as the drifter reached the foot of Meacher's Hill and disappeared into the trees. Was that it? Was his job done?

He remembered what his father used to say. You can't be sure a critter's dead till it's skinned and cooked and eaten. True. Lyle grinned and pressed on.

As he climbed the slope, the branches of the pines started forming angular patterns around him, like brushstrokes on the darkness. He ought to have felt at home up here. But there was no damp, comforting odour of evergreens. The heatwave had burnt it all away. The woods smelled like a tinder pile.

His boot came down on a twig in the path. It snapped, like a gunshot.

Lyle froze dead still. Spat out the toothpick.

Very faintly, he could hear Tharman's footsteps rustling at a slow, unbroken pace, far up ahead.

He let out a sigh. Close. That was damn close.

And then he felt his relief melt away. The footsteps seemed to be getting louder.

He gazed up the track the way Tharman had gone.

The man was coming towards him. Or was he?

He couldn't see a damned thing up ahead. But the noise of the footsteps – it was like the man was already on top of him!

They got louder.

Lyle spun around.

Louder.

They were coming from everywhere.

From the trees. From the shadows.

They stopped . . .

Lyle heard a chuckle from the depths of the woods. He couldn't tell from where.

And then, before he had a chance to move, something had grabbed him from behind, was lifting him off his feet.

Something was tearing at him, ripping at his clothes.

Something sharp clamped across his mouth, piercing his lips. Pinning them together, so that he couldn't even scream.

3

'Maybe he went in the back way,' Ellen shrugged, ten minutes later.

'I didn't even know there *was* a back way. I don't believe this, Ellen. You mean we've been standing here for two hours, and the hobo might already be in there?'

Betsy wrapped her arms tightly around her chest and glared through the darkness at her friend. They were huddled in the shadows beneath the awning of Mack Plouger's tobacco store, just across the street from the bar-and-diner, hidden from prying eyes by the broad-shouldered mahogany bulk of Chief Ugbug, the store's wooden Indian.

Ellen looked as though she was going to burst into tears. For Heaven's sake, the girl was hopeless!

Betsy peeked around the Indian's curving wooden shoulder, on to an empty Main Street.

She'd never seen Yewlburg so quiet before. Without the young men from the ranches, it even looked like a different place. She realized how much the boys dominated it, most evenings. And the more she thought about it, the more she resented the fact. There were plenty of people still here. All the women. Most of the men over forty, the kids and the old folks. Why were they all indoors tonight? Why were they so timid?

Not her.

A hot flush spread from her collarbone to her cheeks.

Not *her*. Not a chance. The town was like a plain canvas waiting to be painted on, tonight. She could be one of the heroines from her daydreams now. One of the feisty, spirited girls that the hero always had to tame.

'Come on, Ellen!' she snapped.

She stepped out from the shadows, started walking towards the kerb. When suddenly, her friend grabbed her by the elbow and tried to pull her back.

Betsy whirled angrily, glared into her friend's round face. Ellen's eyes were huge with fear, her lips were quivering.

'Bets, no!' Her voice had become a childlike whimper. 'Let's forget this, please?'

Her anger changed to amazement. Ellen was so mischievous, so hot blooded, in a lot of ways. It wasn't just the fear of being caught that was making her behave like this. She'd been in trouble plenty of times before, for smashing windows, using her daddy's snuff, stealing from her mother's purse.

But this was far worse. She was terrified of being tarnished in the eyes of the whole town.

There goes Ellen Krauss, everyone would say. She *drinks*. Saw her myself, going into Eddie's Bar. Lord knows what *else* she gets up to. Reckon we've got another Doris McAlveney on our hands.

And if she got that kind of reputation, no decent man would ever marry her.

Betsy had known Ellen long enough to realize the girl was afraid of marriage, of men in general. But the only other route, in Yewlburg, was spinsterhood, and that was like a prolonged death sentence.

'It's all right for you, Bets,' the girl said, as though reading her thoughts. 'Joe Danvers loves you. No one'll say a word against you. But I don't have no Boss's son marrying me.'

She was trembling. Tears were glistening in her eyes.

Betsy wanted to hug her. Comfort her. Take her away from here. She couldn't do that, she realized. Couldn't back down now.

But damn this town to Hell, for making her friend cry.

She pried Ellen's fingers gently loose, stroked her cheek.

'OK. It's OK. Go home.'

Then she turned on her heel, and marched towards the bar.

4

A radio voice was murmuring behind the counter, talking about today's Cardinals game. The Gas House Gang was well on its way to clinching the division.

The doors swung closed behind her, bumping against her spine.

Betsy stood rigidly on the dusty floorboards, unable to go any further. Everything seemed very bright under the glow of the unshaded bulbs hanging from the ceiling. She felt naked and exposed.

If she turned around and walked out right now, if she did it quickly enough, she could cancel this moment, like a mistake on a blackboard you could erase with your sleeve. She could hear the town's voices in her head again.

You know what happened the other day? Betsy Whittaker, her head all full of books as usual, goes wandering right in through the door of Eddie's. Should've seen her face when she realized where she was. Turns round and bolts out of there like a jackrabbit.

And some of them would laugh and add, *Joe Danvers'*

got his work cut out, keeping that girl's head on her shoulders!

What a safe thing it would be, to hide behind people's laughter.

But she couldn't do it. Wouldn't.

Her neck had gone completely stiff. It felt as though an iron bar had been driven through her spine. But she could move her eyes. She forced her gaze across the bar-room.

Surprise seeped into her. It was nothing. Just a big ugly room with dirt engrained into the floor, and plain round tables with a pattern of circular stains on them. There were a couple of baseball pictures on the wall, and a photograph of Eddie's son Charles, who lived in San Francisco now, and never came back to visit.

This was the place Ellen was so afraid of? This was the forbidden place? This was *it*?

Her neck untensed, her shoulders relaxed, and she began to breathe more evenly. She wasn't sure whether to feel relieved or disappointed.

Betsy took another step into the room and looked into the corners. The place was completely empty. Not even the three old drunks were here.

The radio voice kept mumbling on, talking to a non-existent audience.

Do I wait? Betsy wondered. Call out? Go and serve myself? She walked forwards unsteadily and bumped into a chair, practically knocking it over.

Eddie's voice, from a doorway at the back, shouted, 'Hello?'

She felt her cheeks redden as the little man stepped out into the light and peered at her.

Something was wrong with him. He looked sick. His eyes had sunken back into his head so that only the tiniest glimmers of blue peeked out. His bald crown was damp with sweat, his pudgy face white and slick as the belly of a catfish. He was swaying gently, had to grasp the edge of the counter with his pale, maggoty fingers to keep his balance.

It couldn't be that he was drunk. It was common knowledge throughout town that, despite his trade, Eddie never touched a drop of alcohol himself. Betsy swallowed uncomfortably.

'Er . . . hi, Mr Strangsom.'

He leaned towards her, squinting, as though he was trying to see her through a thick layer of gauze.

'Betsy?' His voice was weary, distant. 'Betsy Whittaker? What're you doing here?'

'I'd like a drink, please, sir.'

'Well . . . the drugstore's just along the way, dear.'

She thrust her chin out.

'I'd like a beer, please, Mr Strangsom.'

His face, slack until now, seemed to be trying to work itself into a frown. A question was burning in those tiny button eyes.

'I . . .' He was mouthing each word carefully. 'I don't understand, dear. What did you just say?'

'A beer,' came an unfamiliar voice from the doorway. 'A nice cool beer for the pretty lady, on the house.'

5

Ellen had not gone home. Partly because she was afraid for Betsy. Partly because she felt hurt at being left behind like some silly child. She was still standing in the shadows by the wooden Indian when the drifter came down the street.

She'd caught sight of his gangly silhouette rounding the corner of Jefferson, sucked in a gasp and dove back out of sight behind Chief Ugbug.

The man approaching her seemed nothing to be afraid of. He was as ragged as an old dishcloth, as skinny as a pole. His gait was flapping, loose kneed. He held himself very straight – maybe because he realized what a geek he'd look otherwise.

As he came closer, though, the light from the bar

caught his eyes. They seemed to glow very faintly. A pale, burning yellow.

Ellen hunched behind the wooden Indian, pressing her face against the dark, smooth shoulderblades, until the man had passed. When she peeked out again, she could see his back retreating through the swing doors.

She shivered, chewed her lip worriedly. Betsy was trapped in there with the man. Some folks might say it served her right, but they were supposed to be friends, after all.

She glanced around quickly, making sure she wasn't being watched. Then, she dashed across the street, to a grimy window at the side of the bar.

She huddled there, peering in.

6

Was this the one?

Was this what had brought him here?

By all the Lords, she was beautiful.

She had pale blonde hair which floated as she turned, settling around her shoulders almost to her waist. Eyes the colour of cornflowers. Skin as pale as alabaster. Her face was a narrow oval, with high, softly flushed cheekbones. And her long-legged body, beneath a simple aquamarine frock, had curves which might have been drawn by da Vinci.

Her pink Cupid's bow lips were parted in surprise. Her thin eyebrows were raised to narrow arcs.

Any man, any human, might have looked at her and fallen.

Tharman . . . took off his hat, and made a low, courtly bow.

He reached out with his mind, and could see a flame inside her. Small but very bright. All it would take was the faintest breeze to fan it into an inferno.

He pressed further into her thoughts, quickly. Saw her fantasies. Saw her hatred of this little town. It was stronger even than his.

She was staring at him oddly, not sure whether to be frightened or amused by him. He took a few long strides across the rattling floorboards towards her. Held out his hand.

'Take it, please,' he told her.

She wanted to back away, but her feet were rooted to the spot. Panic started creeping into her expression.

She gulped, shook her head. 'Why?'

'Why not? Are you afraid of me?'

Her eyebrows knitted and she swallowed hard.

'N–o.'

'Then take my hand, please.'

Her gaze hardened. She was trying to be brave. Very slowly, tentatively, she raised her hand and settled it in his. She was watching him very closely, ready to jump back at the first sign of danger. And was just beginning to notice – Tharman realized – the violet colour of his eyes.

'Does that hurt?' he asked her, a faint, mocking tone creeping into his voice.

She smiled nervously. 'No, of course not. Can we stop this now? Who are you?'

'I'm your friend.'

'Oh, that's nice!' Betsy laughed.

She thought he was an idiot.

'I'm going to help you.'

'Oh, *really*?'

She was trying to pry her fingers loose. He tightened his grip a little.

'I can get you all the drinks you want. I can tell Eddie to pour you a hundred, if that pleases you.'

'Say, what's wrong with Eddie, anyway?'

She started to crane her head towards the counter.

'No, look at *me*, Elizabeth.' He pressed down on her knuckles just hard enough to hurt. Her face swung back towards him, her lips tight and bloodless now. 'I can give you anything you want. Can anyone else in this town do that for you? Can Joe?'

It was very quiet for a moment. All that he could hear was the tapping of a moth around a lightbulb.

Then Betsy scowled, and asked, 'How do you know about Joe?'

'It doesn't matter,' he smiled.

'And how do you know what *I* want?'

The words had barely left her lips when he let his eyes turn golden.

7

What the heck was going on in there? Ellen could only hear their voices faintly, but she understood that business with the hand. Bets would never refuse a dare. But how'd the drifter known that?

Her friend didn't seem to be in any trouble, at first. She was handling herself well, staying cool and detached, when suddenly her eyes glazed over and her body went a little slack.

She looked down at herself, gazing at her frock as though it was the first time she'd ever seen it. Tharman released her fingers and she twirled around on the spot, laughing delightedly.

Bets was glancing around now, as though there were other people in the bar. She simpered and nodded to an imaginary few.

Then Tharman leant towards her and said, 'They're all such bores. Can't we be on our own for a while?'

A mischievous grin lit up her face. 'That would be just wonderful.'

They linked arms and walked outside.

Petrified, completely bewildered, Ellen followed them. They were heading back the way the man had come, past the lightless houses of Jefferson, past the Strangsoms', chattering animatedly. Bets kept looking around and giggling as though she'd swallowed an entire cask of backwoods moonshine. Her head craned back every so often, as though she was trying to stare at something high above her.

Ellen thought of running away, getting help. But she didn't want to risk letting them out of her sight.

Betsy, what's *wrong* with you?

She ducked behind a picket fence as they reached the foot of Meacher's Hill. The couple stopped, hugged each other for a moment, kissed.

The drifter said, in a voice she could hear quite clearly, 'Would you like to make love right here, in Central Park?'

And Betsy nodded.

Do what? In where? Ellen stared up at the cloudy hill. Central Park was in New York, the Sodom of the East, as it was called in church. Was this some kind of crazy game?

She watched them numbly as they disappeared into the trees. A shiver ran through her entire body.

Bets was going to do 'it'. The adult thing. S-e-x.

The other girls talked about it a lot. Some of them even claimed they'd done it. But every time Ellen tried to even think about it, she couldn't seem to focus her mind. She felt sick and cold, always. And there was a great, yawning, dark chasm where the dirty ideas ought to be.

She'd never been sure why it terrified her so badly. But it did. That was a fact.

She kept staring at the path where her friend had disappeared. Couldn't quite believe that Betsy had agreed so quickly. Maybe there was a whole side to the girl she'd never seen before.

But – the idea occurred to her vaguely – what if her friend was hypnotized somehow? What if Tharman was some kind of mesmerist? She'd heard of carny men who could play all kinds of tricks on a person's mind.

She couldn't turn back now.

8

She was sorry she'd come, before long. She kept stumbling on roots and stones. The sky, dimly glimpsed through the tree tops, was still thick with cloud. And she'd lost sight of Betsy and the drifter altogether.

Where the Sam Hill had they gone? She almost felt like crying.

A pine branch rustled, not too far ahead, near the crest of the hill.

'Go on, my darling.' It was the hobo's voice, deep and vibrant. 'Prepare yourself for me.'

Ellen felt her heart pounding in her chest.

'You're not coming?'

That was Betsy. But not the Bets she knew. The voice was husky, and it had a vacant tone.

'I'm afraid that I'm distracted. Have you ever noticed how no one in this town is capable of minding their own business?'

Betsy's laugh sounded through the woods. 'A million times.'

No one? He meant *her*. The drifter knew that she was there, knew she'd been following them.

Oh my dear God! Oh Sweet Jesus, help me!

Ellen tried to turn and go back the way she'd come, but her skirt snagged on a root. A shriek swelled up in her throat, and she only just managed to clamp it in.

She struggled, first trying to pull the hem free, then trying to rip the fabric.

It wouldn't budge.

Her breath sounded like bellows. A pulse throbbed in her neck. She hunkered down, praying that the drifter would pass by without spotting her.

And at that exact moment – like a great eye slowly opening – the moon came out from behind the clouds.

Ellen looked up at it through the branches. It seemed huger and paler and brighter than she'd ever seen it before. Almost as though it had moved closer to the world. Almost as though it was falling on her, to crush her, like the shiny head of an enormous hammer.

Why now? Why did it have to come out now?

She lowered her head. A few thin salt tears dribbled down her cheeks.

When she managed to look up again, the drifter was standing between the trees to her left, smiling at her.

Hazel eyes and big tits and puppy-fat, said a voice in her head. *I could chew you up like a chicken drumstick.*

His lips weren't moving. Ellen's mouth formed a slack circle of astonishment.

But why grab a snack when there's a banquet waiting? Let's see what else you're useful for.

She whimpered, but couldn't move. She could feel an odd sensation, now. He seemed to be rummaging inside her head. It was almost a physical thing, like being pawed at. He began reaching into the dark space, the chasm she encountered every time she thought about s-e-x. Began drawing something out into the light.

Her head filled with a chuckling.

Look, drumstick. To your left and upwards.

Her head turned in the direction she'd been told. She couldn't help it. And her eyes widened with terror.

There was a body up there, starkly pale in the moonlight. It was suspended from the ground by a gigantic briar. Black tendrils curled sinuously around the naked skin. There were streaks all over the white flesh where the thorns had drawn blood. The legs dangled limply and the bare feet swayed. The arms were pinned to the sides, helpless.

She knew him! By God, it was Lyle Winters!

Suddenly, his feet began kicking. His eyes sprang open and rolled wildly. No! Oh no! He was still alive!

He was making gurgling noises, but he couldn't speak. A sucker had forced its way into his mouth and wrapped itself around his swollen tongue.

How rude of me, said the voice in her head. *You haven't been properly introduced.*

The drifter waved his hand and, like a living thing, the briar lowered Winters till his feet touched the ground. Eyes bright with fear stared out at Ellen from the bloodless face.

And Tharman pulled the thing out of the dark chasm. A memory. A memory she'd suppressed for years.

It was her second week at school. She'd been kept in late for misbehaving. Walking home through the gathering dark, she'd passed the hardware store, and a smiling Dan Johnson had called her in. He'd led her to a dim room at the back. And then he'd started fumbling underneath her clothes . . .

The shock of it hit her like a speeding train. She'd never remembered it, kept it hidden in the darkness all this time. Ellen began to tremble violently, her face screwing up with agony, her teeth grinding together till they felt like they were going to break.

She wanted to close her eyes, but couldn't.

As she watched, Lyle Winters' body began changing. Swelling. Becoming bloated, with an overhanging belly and a thick mass of dark hair. Just as the storekeeper's body had looked.

It wasn't *real*! She kept trying to tell herself that, but couldn't keep a hold of the idea. It slipped away from her like a bar of soap.

As though they had a life of their own, her hands began moving across the parched ground, scrabbling. They closed on a large rough stone.

Now, the young man's face was altering too. The sandy hairline thinning back and darkening. The eyes becoming small and piggy, the smooth cheeks turning to loose, flapping jowls.

It was Dan Johnson's face staring at her from the briars now. He was trapped, and helpless, and completely at her mercy.

Ellen scrambled to her feet. Felt her lungs fill up with air.

A howl exploded from her. An animal shriek of rage and perfect hatred.

And she rushed towards the man, swinging back the stone.

She smashed it into the side of his face. Stepped back to admire her work – the lump of flesh dangling from the cheek, the shattered teeth, the streaming blood.

And then she struck him again.

CHAPTER FIVE

1

It started to grow light about an hour before dawn, up in the hills. The blackness of the night sky thinned like smoke. The stars became dim smudges, the moon a globe of mist, faintly translucent, and the heavens took on the greyness of a fogged-up pane of glass.

And everything beneath those heavens was in silhouette. A bird might call, or flap from one crackling branch to the next. But otherwise, the world was completely still. A shadow-show. Unreal.

The drovers had found a grassy valley above the dried-out plains. The gigantic herd, the combined livestock of the three ranches, slept there now. They looked, in silhouette, like thousands of closely packed boulders. Occasionally, a tail would flick, a massive head would shift a little. But that was all.

Around the cattle slept the men, with their horses and their tents and their dead camp fires. They'd been forced to abandon the trucks a few miles down the slope, and felt closer to nature now, closer to the old days their fathers and grandfathers had known. They slept in the open, their heads propped against their bedrolls, bathed from head to toe in the pale pre-dawn grey. And they were silhouetted too.

Humans are not night creatures, after all. Only the daylight makes them real.

*

2

Someone yelled out loud, and Jack Hughes came awake with a jerk. The knife under his bedroll was in his hand before he'd even thought about it.

His dark eyes flitted quickly over the drowsing men.

They were all silent at first. There was no sign of trouble. Then one of them thrashed violently, bellowed out loud.

Damn, it was that jack-ass kid!

Joe Danvers had been nothing but a problem from the outset of the drive. Deprived of his precious automobile, he'd come along on a handsome, long-maned palomino, and had spent so much time making the nag strut and prance and do tricks he'd been worse than useless. He'd let a maverick lead a clutch of heifers off the main track halfway through the afternoon, and Jack and his men had wasted two hours rounding them up.

Now the blasted fool was going to rob them all of their final hour's sleep.

As Hughes watched, the boy rolled over again and shouted, '*Betsy!*'

Jack got up, slipped the knife into his belt, and moved quietly between the sleeping men. He bent over Joe Danvers, staring down at him coldly for a moment, then prodded him with his toe.

'Whuh—?'

The boy jerked awake. Bright blue eyes, opaque with sleep, blinked up at him.

'Jack? What is it?'

'You were dreaming, Mr Joe.' Jack Hughes forced a smile. 'About your girl, I do believe.'

Joe raised himself on his elbows. His eyes cleared a little, but became no more intelligent. He shook his head numbly.

'Yeah. I remember now. That was a bad one.' He seemed to be turning something over in his head. 'Jack . . . do you think there's any truth to dreams?'

What the hell was *this* all about? Jack maintained a polite tone.

'My daddy always said there was, Mr Joe. But then, my daddy was a drunken Welshman, and I didn't pay much mind to what he used to say.'

'I dreamed something terrible about Betsy, Jack. I dreamed she was in trouble.'

You couldn't get that girl in trouble if you tried, you dopey jerk, Jack thought. But he kept it to himself.

'And that,' the boy was saying, 'she didn't love me any more.'

Jack wiped his mouth with the back of his hand. 'That doesn't sound too likely to me, Mr Joe.'

'Yeah.' Joe nodded. 'Just a dream, right?' His eyes became almost tearful. 'I'd die if that happened, Jack.'

Jack thought again about the boy inheriting the ranch, becoming Boss.

Then die, you little asshole, he thought. Lord, how I wish you'd die.

3

Maybelline Krauss left her home on Pinewood Street, her clothes rumpled and her face white with exhaustion, and practically ran all the way to the Whittaker house. She banged on the door with the flats of her hands until Betsy's mother came downstairs and answered.

In her room, Betsy awoke and wondered what the high-pitched, anxious voices were babbling about.

She couldn't lift her head from her pillow. Couldn't clear it properly. It seemed filled with shrouds and ghostly outlines. And a thin shaft of dawn light from the drapes was making her squirm for some reason. She screwed her eyes up painfully.

Betsy tried to remember what had happened last night. But all that she could see were vague, blurred images. It was almost as though one of her fantasies had gone badly askew.

She'd been standing in Eddie's Bar and then . . . it hadn't been there any more. Instead, she'd found herself at the middle of a party, in a ballroom in New York City. The drifter, standing opposite her, hadn't been ragged any more. Resplendent in a white tuxedo and bow tie, his hair slicked back, and a glass of champagne clutched in one manicured hand, he'd stared at her mesmerically with those strange violet eyes of his.

And she . . . she looked down at herself. She'd changed too. The aquamarine frock which reached to her ankles was gone. She was clad, instead, in a flimsy silk dress of white and gold. A flapper dress, just like in the movies. It stopped at her knees. Below were seamed silk stockings and smooth, heavy shoes. Her shoulders and arms were completely bare, and the tops of her swelling breasts were in plain view. Everyone could see them.

For a moment, she'd reeled with shock, tried vainly to cover herself.

Then she'd begun to smile. Then laugh. No one seemed to notice. Or, if they did, they didn't seem particularly affronted by it. She'd felt suddenly romantic and daring and desirable.

And free . . .

'*Elizabeth?*' Her mother's voice came shrieking up the stairwell. 'Ellen Krauss was with you all day yesterday, wasn't she?'

Ellen Krauss? She recalled the name, but she could barely remember what the girl looked like. Betsy cleared her throat and called back down.

'Yes, Mama.'

'Then where is she? She ain't come home.'

She paused a moment. Couldn't think what to say. But some kind of answer was needed. Wearily, she made one up.

'She went off walking by herself. I don't know where.'

That seemed to satisfy the old crone. A short while later, the front door slammed and she could hear her mother and Mrs Krauss retreating down the street.

Betsy pushed her head deeper into her pillow, smiling

dreamily, and ran the New York fantasy through her head again.

4

The word of Ellen's disappearance spread through the town like wildfire. Before long, every able-bodied man was putting aside his work and joining in the hunt.

Dan Johnson and his pal Fred Willis were the first to take the route leading to Meacher's Hill. They noticed the circling buzzards when they were only halfway up. They stopped, gazed at the birds, their eyes widening with apprehension. Fred heard Dan swallow uncomfortably, behind him.

'Reckon we ought to go back, get some help?' Fred asked.

There was a silence which annoyed him. Dan was normally such a stolid, well-balanced man, but he'd been acting strangely ever since Ellen Krauss's name had come up. His movements had become jerky; his face grew red with the slightest exertion. It seemed he'd only joined in at all because it was expected of him.

'*Dan?*' He turned and prodded the storekeeper with his fingers.

'Uh – ' The big man's glassy eyes blinked. 'N–no. We'd better go on up. Before them birds start circling lower.'

Not a word passed between them for the rest of the climb.

Every sound around them seemed to be magnified. The crying of blackbirds in the trees. The sharp rustle of an animal, a weasel or a rabbit, pushing through the undergrowth. The crackling of the dead pine needles underneath their shoes was like fish bones snapping. And there was the noise of insects. A June bug clattered past like an aeroplane with a broken propeller. Hornets made a poisonous humming in the darker corners of the woods. Mosquitoes whined around their ears.

The buzzing of flies took over when they were fifty

yards from the crest of Meacher's Hill. It was so dense a sound, they barely realized what it was at first.

Fred's hands began to shake. 'My God, Dan!' His voice was a hoarse whisper. 'I think we oughta get help.'

He started to back away, expecting Dan to do the same. But, to his surprise, the big storekeeper drew himself up very straight and, with a hardened, numb expression on his face, began to walk towards the noise. Fred tagged along behind, mostly because he didn't want to be left here on his own.

He kept Dan's body between himself and the clearing as the man parted the branches and stepped through.

And then the stench hit him. Fred began to gag.

Through streaming eyes, he saw a great black mass of flies whirl up into the air, revealing two motionless figures on the ground, then settle down again, covering them.

5

Boss Danvers was driven from the Triple Y in the jet-black Chevrolet Magister by his Negro chauffeur, Henry.

The car stopped at the foot of the hill, and Henry had to help the gouty old man up the steep incline without *seeming* to help him too much. He'd had the sense to bring some water, and a pocketful of handkerchiefs to mop the Boss's face. It was a slow progress, nevertheless, and took the best part of forty minutes.

A crowd of townspeople were already waiting in the shade at the edge of the clearing, when they finally arrived. They parted respectfully for the old man. Boss Danvers shook his elbow free of Henry's grasp, and nodded to a couple of them, as though he were greeting them in church.

He halted within twenty feet of the immobile figures on the ground.

Holy Jesus Christ! In all his years, and there'd been some rough ones, he had never seen anything like this.

The only person near the boy and girl was Dr Petts.

He'd removed his straw boater and black jacket, and had a handkerchief wrapped bandana-style around his nose and mouth. He was kneeling over what looked like a mass of tiny coals, which lay within a tangled briar. As the Boss watched, he swiped at them, and they hummed into the air for the briefest instant.

It was enough. More than damned enough. The pulped mass of flesh which lay beneath the insects couldn't even be described as human. And the girl, though alive, looked even worse.

She was kneeling, entirely still, at the corpse's feet. And she was covered with flies too. Her hands. Her arms. Her dress. Her hair. Expressionless eyes stared out from the shifting, glittering blackness on her face.

The Boss sucked in a deep breath and then decided to take charge.

'Is no one gonna *help* that lady?' he shouted angrily.

The crowd stirred a little, but no one moved. Petts looked up, blinking, and nodded to his old friend.

'No one's sure if she's dangerous, Edgar. She's still got a rock in her hand. And she sure as heck killed this feller.'

The Boss felt a chill sense of unease growing in his belly.

'Who is it?' he asked.

'Nothing left that's recognizable except the hair. It's curly, and sandy-coloured. I'd say Lyle Winters. Didn't he go up-country with the others yesterday?'

The Boss took a little while digesting that.

'No, Jed. I kept him on at the ranch. Needed him to run some errands for me.'

'And what did those errands include?' the doctor asked, a touch annoyedly.

He didn't like the way Petts was looking at him now. Boss Danvers felt the muscles stiffen at the back of his thick neck. Of all the damned impertinence. Why the Sam Hill was the quack talking to him like this? And in front of half the town, too!

He floundered, whirled around, began jabbing at the air with his ring finger and bellowing at the assembled crowd.

'Are we going to leave that girl sitting there all day?

One of our own? You, Tobe Jugger! And *you*, Wayne Snell! Get over there and help her up. Get her to the surgery. *Carry* her, if you have to! Are her folks here?'

'They haven't come up yet.' It was Franklin Chase, the editor of the *Gazette*, peering from behind his half-moon spectacles. 'Mary Whittaker and Alma Reis are with them.'

'Well, thank the Lord they've been spared this. Go *on*, now!' the Boss yelled at the two men he'd press-ganged. 'You scared of a few flies?'

They couldn't have approached a wolverine more gingerly. Their eyes never left the girl's hands, the tightly clasped stone. Finally, Wayne Snell plucked up the courage to reach out and touch her shoulder.

She didn't move. She might have been frozen in a block of ice.

They got on either side of her, took hold of her beneath the elbows and lifted her very gently to her feet.

The blanket of flies roared up and began to dance and spin.

And the entire crowd gasped.

Boss Danvers found himself recoiling.

The flies had been feeding. And there was plenty for them to feast on. The shifting black had given way to a second layer of flaking, rust-coloured red. Ellen Krauss was covered from head to toe with dried blood.

The two men looked as though they were going to vomit. They almost let go of her, but they didn't dare, under Boss Danvers' gaze. They averted their eyes and, breathing heavily, began to lead her back towards the path.

'Put down the stone, Ellen,' Wayne Snell was whispering insistently. 'Please, just let it go.'

She didn't seem to hear. Her face was as stiff as a painted wooden mask. But her eyes were animated, roving over the crowd, as though she was trying to remember who they were. She allowed herself be hustled along quite calmly until her gaze brushed across Fred Willis' skinny, whiskery features, and settled on Dan Johnson.

Her lips drew back from her teeth and her eyes blazed. Her doughy arms tensed.

She'd broken free of her helpers before anyone could stop her. She lashed out at Dan Johnson with the stone, caught him a glancing blow on the temple. He yelped with pain and stumbled backwards.

A dozen townspeople were on her in an instant, surrounding her, trying to hold her down. She struggled furiously, her voice shrilling.

'He *did* things to me when I was a little girl! In the back of his store! He *did* things to me!'

It took several minutes to subdue her and drag her away. Most of the crowd followed in a nervous, shambling procession, many of them throwing curious glances at Dan Johnson as they passed.

Blood was pouring from the gash on his forehead, but he wasn't even bothering to try and staunch it. He just stood there, gazing straight ahead, as pale and goggle-eyed as a toad caught in a flashlight.

When the rest had gone, he finally hunched his shoulders and slunk away down a narrower path.

Boss Danvers watched the man's retreating back and wondered, not for the first time that day, what in God's name was going on.

He glanced at the few people who were left. Dr Petts had covered Lyle Winters' corpse with some branches by now, and was rubbing at his hands with his bandana, while Franklin Chase looked nervously on from the shade of a pine tree. Henry was standing patiently at the back of the clearing, his cap in his hands, his eyes hooded and downcast.

The Boss waved imperiously at his chauffeur. 'Henry, go back to the ranch-house and fetch a couple of the Chinee. They can help you get this boy's corpse back to town.'

Then, without waiting for a reply, he turned to the doctor and the newspaper man.

'Gentlemen, I'm getting a little too old to play mountain goat, and it's a long way down this slope. So why don't you do me the honour of lending me a hand?'

He was making himself vulnerable to them because he wanted something from them. They knew it – he could see it in their eyes. But they wouldn't dare refuse him.

The three descended in silence for a while, the narrow shadows of the trees growing shorter around them as the day progressed.

'Hell of a way to start the morning,' Boss Danvers observed, at last.

'One I could have certainly lived without,' Petts nodded. There was still an edgy, grumbling tone to his voice.

The Boss smiled wearily. 'You've been touchy with me, Jed. You were touchy with me back there in the clearing, and you're touchy with me now. Any particular reason for it?'

'You don't need Lyle Winters to run errands for you, Edgar. You've a bigger staff over at that ranch house than the King of England. So what exactly was he doing?'

'He was watching that Tharman for me. That drifter Eddie hired. What he was doing up here I can only guess. Can you do any more than that?'

'Yes, sir, I can. I didn't want to say in front of the whole town, but in my inspection of Lyle Winters I found barely any clothing whatsoever. The man was buck naked.'

'*Good Lord.*' The Boss's cheeks reddened and his nostrils flared, but he didn't break his pace.

'In my estimation,' Petts continued, 'he somehow lured Ellen Krauss up there and tried to attack her. Sexually. She must have got the better of him, knocked him cold with the rock, and then gone berserk. Did you notice the smell in the clearing? Flesh doesn't rot that quickly, even in this heat. His guts were burst wide open. Every internal organ in his body's smashed. That little girl pounded him to a fine paste.'

'And what she said about Dan Johnson? Could that be true?'

'Who knows? She might just have been hysterical. But the seed of doubt's been planted now.'

'And that's what I want to talk to you two gentlemen about,' the Boss said, expertly taking his cue. 'Franklin, I can read you like one of your own papers. I can see you, right now, composing a front-page story in your head.'

The little editor blinked up at him worriedly.

'Well, you can forget it,' the Boss snapped. 'None of this, but none, makes the news. And the word's to go around, we keep this hushed up for a while. Lyle Winters is dead, sure, but he was killed in an *accident*. Ellen Krauss is simply going through one of those difficult phases young women suffer, and she's under the good doctor's care. There's nothing wrong in Yewlburg. All's right with our little town.'

'May I ask why?' enquired Petts.

'You may. And for an answer, look at the outside world. At the so-called newspaper men, at the high-and-mighty marshals, at the snoopers and the busybodies and the government officials. And then ask yourself, do you want any of those people interfering in our town?'

'In other words, Edgar, you'd like to keep control of things yourself.'

'My family's done precisely that for several generations, and we haven't made such a bad job of things, now have we?'

The doctor shook his head angrily. 'And if people decide Ellen Krauss *was* telling the truth about Dan Johnson?'

The Boss smirked and came to a halt, leaning against a cracked, peeling tree trunk.

'I'm composing something in my *own* head. Nothing so grandiose as Franklin could manage, just a mental note. *Send a rider out*, it says. *Fetch Jack Hughes and a few of the boys home.* Why, I think their methods of policing would make J. Edgar Hoover bow with admiration, don't you, gentlemen?'

6

About three in the afternoon, Dan Johnson's wife Eunice bundled her weeping fourteen-year-old daughter Clarice into the family's Model-T Ford and drove hurriedly to Dr Petts' surgery. They were in there for almost an hour. A small crowd gathered outside the crimson-draped windows.

When mother and daughter reappeared, Clarice was crying more bitterly than ever, and Eunice was white in the face, except for two small spots of bright red on her cheeks. Her eyes were glassy. She blinked in the daylight like a prematurely woken owl.

She stared at the crowd embarrassedly, and then began shoving her daughter back into the Ford.

'Where you goin', Mrs Johnson?' called out Bob Nyman, as the motor started up.

'Anywhere!' She didn't look back. Her voice was croaky, but had a stern, resolute quality. 'Anywhere in the world, just to get my girl away from that . . . that filthy *monster*!'

The townsfolk watched as the black car puttered down the street, trailing a cloud of dust, and diminished into nothingness.

Around six o'clock, a mob of twenty, led by Dan's old pal Fred Willis, broke down the front door of the Johnson house and ransacked the place, searching for the burly storekeeper. He wasn't there.

'The hardware store's all locked up,' Bob Nyman pointed out. 'You don't think he's cooped up inside?'

The crowd swelled as it made its way to Main Street.

All the blinds were drawn, in the windows of the store, and the wire grilles were padlocked into place.

'Mebbe he's hanged himself in there,' Tobe Jugger suggested, rattling them.

'He's got a cellar down the back,' Eric Gillie reminded everyone. 'He could stay in there for weeks if he's got food.'

'Well, that's just fine,' said Bob Nyman. 'We can wait.'

More than a dozen men were still outside as the sky began to darken.

It was about nine thirty when the blaze started at the rear of the building. Nobody was certain how it happened, except there was the sudden crash of breaking glass, and shortly afterwards a few teenagers, Teddy Turner amongst them, were seen scattering down the backstreets.

The pungent stench of burning kerosene drifted into the night air. Flames began licking up the back and dancing along shingles of the roof. Bob Nyman started yelling panickedly. His own place was directly next door.

The crowd split into two groups. One to get buckets and form a water chain.

The other to fetch a rope.

7

Jack Hughes and the four drovers he'd brought with saw the amber glow of flames against the night sky as they reached the foot of the hills. They reined in their horses for a moment, gaping with amazement as a dense black pall of smoke rose from the centre of the town and began to drift across the stars.

Then they were jabbing with their spurs and snapping their reins. They rode across the flatlands as though Satan himself were chasing them, the hoofs of their mounts thundering on the parched, unyielding earth. By the time they clattered into Main Street the fire had been put out, but Johnson's Hardware had been reduced to a blackened shell, and half of Bob Nyman's grocery was gone.

It seemed the whole town had turned out. The recently bereaved Pete Gower was there, and Iris Yorgeson, the schoolteacher.

At the centre of the crowd, stripped to his undershirt and filthy with smoke, was Dan Johnson. His hands had been tied behind his back, and there was already a noose around his neck. He was pleading terrifiedly, his voice growing higher, becoming a hideous whining.

Fists grabbed at him, shook him angrily. The crowd's whole baleful attention was directed on him. Doris McAlveney, far at the back, was the only one who noticed the riders as they trotted down the street. She looked up at Jack Hughes with relief on her narrow, rouged face.

He pulled up in front of her, leaned over in his saddle.

'What the hell's going on, Doris?'

'Dan was making hay with his own daughter. And with Ellen Krauss.'

'Holy Jesus Christ!' Jack turned his head to the side and spat. 'Sonofabitch.'

Doris let out a weary sigh. 'There weren't no need for him to do that. If he'd only of come to me—'

The man beside her suddenly whirled around. It was Fred Willis, but Jack barely recognized him. His stubbled face was crumpled like a ball of paper. His eyes were folded to thin, deep creases, and his yellow teeth were bared.

'Shut your trap, whore! No one wants your opinion.'

He seemed about to strike the woman. But then he noticed Jack. His jaw dropped, and he edged back into the crowd like a crab retreating beneath a rock.

What had *happened* to this town in the couple of days they'd been gone? Jack thought about the Boss's orders. If there was a lynching, word would eventually spread to the outside world; there'd be no way of stopping it. And that couldn't be risked.

He stood up in his stirrups, towering above the bobbing heads around him.

'All right!' he yelled. 'Everyone stop and *listen* to me!'

The four younger drovers closed in behind him. The crowd fell silent. Sweating, grimy faces peered up at him through the gloom.

'Put down that rope! No one's gonna be hanged.'

'But he asked for it, Jack!' someone protested. It was that big-mouthed bastard Eric Gillie.

'Maybe. But not from you.'

'What—?' Eric started asking.

Jack stared him down, and he faltered.

'What gives me the right? In the first place, Boss Danvers has asked me to keep an eye on things. Keep things nice and calm. In the second—' Jack reached down and patted the gleaming walnut stock of the shotgun hanging in his saddle. 'I've never drawn a weapon against a living soul in this town, but I will if I'm pressed too far.'

He began walking his mount forwards, very slowly, and the crowd parted like water. The only people left in front of him, in the end, were a quaking Dan Johnson, and Bob Nyman, still holding limply on to the end of the rope, as though lost in a dream.

Jack reached down and plucked it gently from his fingers.

'Mr Liffut.' He turned and held it out towards the youngest drover, a tow-headed boy with sharp green eyes. 'We have here what appears to be a dog on a leash. A *sick* dog. Take it to the edge of town and set it loose. And shoot it if it tries to get back in.'

Dan Johnson's gaze flickered back and forth in his scorched, soot-blackened face, but he had the sense to remain quiet. He was running furiously, a moment later, as Liffut's horse cantered away. Jack watched him disappear, his dark eyes gleaming with laughter. Then they cooled, went hard again, and he turned his attention back to the crowd.

'It's over. All of you go home now.'

The townsfolk were dispersing the moment he'd spoken.

8

'Sweet Jesus in heaven, watch over the soul of Lyle Winters. Clutch him to your bosom and forgive him his earthly sins. And watch too over the soul of Ellen Krauss, though she has been defiled and is unclean. And Lord, guard our little town of Yewlburg, which has fallen on dark times. Protect us from the demons in us, and help to make us clean and pure . . .'

Betsy sat in the darkness on the edge of her bed, and listened through the partly open door as her mother prayed downstairs. The old woman had been mumbling all evening, ever since she'd got back from comforting Ellen's family. Without pause, without inflection, the prayers kept pouring out of her in a grey, monotonous river of sound.

They seemed to have no more meaning than the whirr of crickets on a dry summer's night. Betsy pressed her hands to her ears, trying to shut them out.

She'd been in her room all day. What with the commotion around town, it had been easy for her to escape notice. The one time her mother had called up and asked what she was doing, she'd simply claimed that she was upset about Ellen.

She was grateful to be left alone. She couldn't have faced going out into the daylight. The little that had filtered through her curtains, around noon, had made her skin prickle and her head pound. It was as though she'd become allergic to the sun. She didn't know why, and didn't particularly care.

Few thoughts drifted through her head as she sat there. Her eyes barely blinked. She was perfectly motionless, her back straight, her hands folded neatly in her lap. As though she were waiting for something.

My darling.

The voice, inside her mind, made her jump a little. Then she tipped her head to one side and smiled dreamily, listening.

Come to me. Come now.

Betsy rose smoothly and went to the door. She hurried quietly down the stairs, making her way towards the porch. As she passed the living-room, she glanced inside and saw her mother on her knees, facing the crucifix on the back wall. The woman's bony hands were clasped in front of her, and she was rocking as she prayed.

A delighted grin spread over Betsy's face as she slipped out into the night.

9

Jack Hughes and his men fanned out and scoured the streets around Main, making sure that everyone had gone home. By the time they reassembled outside the *Gazette* offices, half an hour later, the foreman was wearing a thoughtful, brooding expression.

'Anyone seen that damned drifter? Anyone know if he's still around?'

The younger men shook their heads puzzledly.

Jack took his watch out of his pocket. 'Well, if he's still here he'll be at Eddie's by now. Let's go see how our newest citizen's doing. I could use a drink, anyhow.'

They ambled their tired, dusty mounts the length of the shadowy street.

As they drew closer to the bar-and-diner, though, the men's heads came up, all weariness forgotten. Their horses' ears began to prick.

Nothing but news and sports broadcasts had ever been heard from Eddie Strangsom's radio before. But now, floating through the swing-doors of the bar, was the solitary wailing of a cornet, high and melancholic on the cool night air.

A gentle breeze began to spring up from the east, stirring the fine, powdery dust. The horses grew more restless still, shuffling their hoofs and rolling their wide eyes.

The men dismounted quickly.

From the bar, the cornet's last note floated into space and burst like a shimmering bubble.

'*Yes, the sweet, sweet sound of Bix Beiderbecke*,' came a radio announcer's voice. '*And now, hot from the studios of New York City, the Fletcher Henderson Orchestra and "Only For You"*.'

'What the hell is that?' muttered one of the drovers.

Jack raised a hand for silence, led the way to the edge of the sidewalk, just outside the doors.

He could see inside quite clearly, from here.

Eddie Strangsom was standing in front of the counter, his hands folded behind his back, like a flunkey in attendance on a duke. His face looked like a white, shapeless balloon. His pale eyes had been reduced to lustreless pinpricks.

In front of him, the tables had been cleared to make an open space. A dance floor. On it, a solitary couple stepped and turned. Gracefully, slowly, as though underwater. One was Betsy Whittaker.

The other was the drifter.

As the men watched, Tharman pulled the young girl to his chest, and they began to kiss.

Paul Tarlton, the biggest of the drovers, started lurching forwards angrily. Jack grabbed hold of his arm and pulled him to a halt. He shook his head, pressed a finger to his lips.

'Leave 'em be, Paul.'

They stood there watching until Clete Liffut came back. Jack motioned the boy over, put an arm around his shoulders.

'Clete,' he whispered. 'I won't need you here tomorrow. I want you to get back to the hills, carry on working with the drive, just like normal. And if you happen to mention what you've seen in Eddie's tonight . . . and if a certain Joe Danvers gets to hear about it, why—' His grin had become a terrible thing, all clenched teeth and squeezed muscle. 'I won't be upset with you at all. Understand?'

10

As the first light of dawn limned the edges of the distant hills, Clete Liffut pulled himself into his saddle on the silent Triple Y, and began trotting his horse towards the horizon as quietly as he could. He waited till he was a quarter of a mile from the big house before he broke into a canter.

He only glanced back once. Behind him, framed against the sky on a low knoll, watching him go, was the tall, broad-shouldered figure of the foreman.

11

Tharman sensed the rider go, as he eased himself into bed. He reached out idly and touched the young man's mind, saw how stupid he was, how puzzled by the foreman's orders. And yet, how eager to please.

Further towards the ranch was Jack Hughes himself, the same brutish hoodlum who'd threatened him in Eddie's that first night. Tharman plunged into his thoughts now. What he saw there, the envy and the boiling hatred, made him stiffen with delight.

He let go and leaned back.

Betsy's perfume still hung richly about his clothes. He idly plucked a long, pale hair from the shoulder of his jacket, grinned. He was so *strong*. Had Fed so *well*. Every human in the town was within his reach, by now. He swept quickly through the clustered houses, could hear their sonorous breathing, see their tawdry dreams.

He could reach much further than that if he wanted to. And now he did want to. It was time.

The first, faint yellow glow appeared beyond the drapes. He settled his head on his musty pillow, closed his eyes, and sank into darkness.

Pashta, and Gorreq of the war god Buchis, were waiting for him down there, the one tiny and slender, the other as huge as an ox. Their eyes burned like hot golden coals.

We greet you, brother. You seem well.

I am. We all appear to prosper.

It is an interesting time. A time for banqueting.

Pashta gave a high-pitched, faintly hysterical giggle. *You are still in the New World?*

In the Americas, yes. In the heart of this land. This heart nourishes me well. And you, my sister?

In Marrakesh. The locals are dull Musselmen. But the rich boys and girls who visit here for the free life! For the opiates, and the smoking hookahs. The dreams they dream! You would not believe . . .

And you, brother Gorreq?

I am in Cathay, that is now called China. The Japanese are here, invading Manchuria. It is a fine country for fear and death.

I am pleased for you.

It is a good country, alas, for misery too. Kellesh was here. He was dogging my tracks these last few days.

The Traitor Kellesh. Kellesh the Betrayer. Tharman felt his teeth grind at the mention of the name.

Go carefully then, brother. He has killed before.

There is no need to concern yourself. He has gone. I had a trap set for him. Planned to finish him off once and for all. But there is so much blood around here, to cast spells with. He chanted the Incantation and escaped, back into the Underworld.

Tharman got a picture, in his mind's eye, of a darkened paddy-field, a sickly yellow moon hanging low above it. The dead-faced, ugly Kellesh draining the blood from a corpse, using it to draw patterns on the dank water around him. Mouthing the Incantation of the Door.

And a portal opening in the fabric of the night. Cold, grey light flooding out.

The Betrayer slipping away into the tunnel beyond.

It will be a long while, Pashta grinned, *before he finds his way out again.*

Good. A fitting punishment. The idea so pleased Tharman he was silent for a while, basking in its perfection.

Together? he asked at last. *We shall be together again, sometime?*

When shall we three meet again? laughed Pashta. *In thunder, lightning, or in rain?*

When the hurlyburly's done, Gorreq replied. *When the battle's lost and won.*

Tharman rolled over in his sleep.

That will be ere rise *of sun.*

CHAPTER SIX

1

Dr Petts wandered down to the Krauss home an hour later to check on Ellen. She was in much the same condition as she'd been since he had sedated her; lying, quite still, on top of the bed, her eyes wide open, staring at the ceiling. She'd been scrubbed clean by her mother and Mary Whittaker, and been put into a long white nightgown. But Petts reckoned he'd never be able to look at her again without seeing caked blood and swarming flies. He doubted anyone in town would.

He made his way back to his surgery around nine, feeling weary and depressed. The heat of the day was rising, the sky bare of clouds. It promised to be another scorcher, and he hated that.

His waiting-room was dim, the blinds drawn, as he let himself in. He dumped his worn leather bag by the empty couch, took off his jacket and hat and put them on the stand in the corner, then walked through into his office.

As he opened the door, something moved in the faint light. Petts jerked back.

'It's only me, Jed.'

Goddamit, it was Erskine Marchmont.

The retired librarian was sitting in the big green chair behind Petts' desk. He remained there a moment. Then he got up slowly, shakily, his long, skinny arms struggling to lift his meagre frame. His skin was greyish, pitted, and his lips, beneath his tattered moustache, trembled like a weeping child's. Sweet Christ, the man looked like a ghost. He was here for his supply of morphine, that much was certain. It was the only reason he ever came. How Eddie and Alice bore his shambling presence in their house was a total mystery.

Maybe, Petts considered drily, they kept him on for the same reason he supplied the drug. Out of a misplaced sense of kindness. Out of respect for the Erskine Marchmont that had been; the wisest, most refined, most knowledgeable man in Yewlburg. Lord, it'd been hard to understand what he'd been talking about, half of the time. But his presence had been valued, almost treasured, in the old days.

A trickle of saliva spilled over Marchmont's lip and ran down to his chin, where it hung ignored, dangling like a pendulum. The old days were well and truly gone.

The man raised his hands – they looked like parched bunches of twigs – and waved them furiously.

'You didn't come yesterday, Jed. I was *waiting* for you.'

'I was busy yesterday. The whole town was.' Petts scowled at the old man. 'Don't tell me you didn't hear about it?'

'About what?'

'Oh, for pity's sake!' Petts started to get angry. He felt a sudden, violent urge to hurt Marchmont in some way, punish him for what he'd let himself become. That only made him angrier still. 'Get out from behind my desk. You haven't been rummaging through it, have you? Come sit down over here.'

He jerked a finger at the straight-backed chair beside him. The old man complied quietly, his eyes, behind his smeared bifocals, taking on a sad, bewildered look. Petts felt his rage give way to guilt.

'Good Lord, Erskine, I'm sorry. I shouldn't speak to you like that. Hold on and I'll fetch the stuff. I got some new in just this week.'

He went to the chunky safe in the corner of the room, next to the filing cabinets, worked the combination, came back with a little bag full of fine beige granules.

'I'll give you the first shot.' He smiled at the man, as though he were treating a kid with chickenpox. 'Roll up your sleeve.'

As he prepared the syringe, his voice took on a light, conversational tone.

'How are things at the Strangsoms'? What do you make of your new boarder?'

'*I'm* the only boarder, Jed.'

Petts shook his head and chuckled. 'No, Erskine. Eddie took on a second guest, a couple of days ago. A drifter called Herb Tharman. It caused quite a stir at the time.'

'I *thought* I could hear someone else moving around, last night.'

'Well, you're gonna win no prizes for observancy, now are you?'

He squirted a little of the morphine solution into the air.

Marchmont cocked his head to one side, thoughtfully.

'Jed?'

'Yes?'

'Jed, is there a second phase to my addiction?'

Petts stopped in the act of twisting a rubber tourniquet around the old man's arm. 'How do you mean?' he asked, cautiously.

'Is there . . . a time when the dreams cease to be beautiful? When sleep gets really bad? Does that happen, after a while?'

'Could be. Is it happening to you?'

'In spades, as the saying goes. Awful visions, I keep seeing. Dreadful nightmares. Great dark places where the sky is like no other. Things moving in it. Strange animals, with blazing yellow eyes. And one walks up to me, very close. It's been the same the last two nights.' Marchmont stopped, gazed thoughtfully into space for a moment, as though he were trying to put two and two together in his addled mind. '*Tharman*, you say?'

2

As the morphine took hold, Marchmont felt his mind clear and the years slough off him. That was the real wonder of the drug. It took him back to his prime, made him feel human and whole again.

He walked home with a light step, glancing avidly from side to side. The whole of Yewlburg seemed to glow around him. The colours were bright and full. The dust on the streets was no longer yellowish grey but a rich, full ochre. The lawns were no longer brown but a strangely vivid green, and every window seemed to gleam with a wonderful bluish-silver hue.

But the darkness started closing in again, as he neared the Strangsom house.

All at once, the clear blue sky grew duller, the sun began to shrink. The beautiful hues started to crumble, as though moths had been chewing at them. Marchmont shivered and wrapped his arms around his shoulders.

He stepped unsteadily on to the porch, paused there. All the drapes were shut, and not a sound issued from behind them.

He didn't want to go inside. There was something about the place that was giving him the shakes.

But there was nowhere else to go.

He let himself in carefully, letting his eyes adjust to the dimness. Not a noise, not a movement, greeted him. Where was Alice? She was always around the living-room, about this time of day. He called her name softly.

There was no answer.

Something else was peculiar. He realized what it was after a while. Not a presence. Quite the opposite. There was something missing. Something out of place.

Through the open doorway, he could just make out the far wall of the living-room. A bare, pale patch, high up on the wallpaper, could be made out through the shadows. A clock had hung there yesterday. A large, brass clock, in the shape of a sunburst. Now, it had been taken down. Why?

Marchmont glanced up the stairs, to the closed door of Charlie's old room. It seemed to waver slightly. Seemed to rock back and forth. Marchmont rubbed his eyes – the motion stopped. It was only the morphine, that was all.

He walked up to the landing quietly, reached out for the doorknob. Tried to turn it.

It wouldn't budge a millimetre.

That was odd. There was no key for this door. Eddie and Alice always kept it unlocked, as though they were waiting for Charlie to come home some day.

Who was in there now? Marchmont glanced around nervously, but there was still no sign of the Strangsoms.

He got down on his knees and pressed his eye to the keyhole, expecting it to be blocked. It wasn't. To his surprise, he found he had a narrow but unobstructed view of the room. It was dark in there, but he started to make out shapes after a while. He could see the edge of the window sill, and most of the bed. And someone lying curled up on it.

A very thin man, dressed in black, apparently fast asleep.

So *this* was the drifter Petts had been talking about. Marchmont pulled his head back, blinked a couple of times, then stooped down for a better look.

This time, the morphine made the scene waver. And change.

Marchmont stifled a yell.

Lying on the bed where the man had been a moment ago, there was now a massive creature. He couldn't make it out entirely, but it was broad chested and muscular, and covered with thick black fur. Its arms were as long and sinewy as an ape's, but it couldn't be a simian. Its face – he couldn't quite see what it was, but it didn't seem to fit.

Marchmont stumbled backwards on his knees. Hit the banister railings and crouched against them, breathing hoarsely and asthmatically.

It was the drug, that was it! It was the drug making him see such awful things.

The old man gave a start as a shadow fell across him. He looked up.

Alice Strangsom was standing above him, peering at him dully. He didn't know where she'd come from, or how she'd approached him so quietly. But her whole appearance startled him. Her hair was tangled and unkempt.

Her eyes were lifeless, and her face was set into an expression of stern, unyielding contempt.

She folded her arms across her chest, and her jaw moved, as though on rusted hinges.

'Mr Marchmont, what do you think you're doing? If you're going to start prying, I'd thank you to leave my house.'

Even her voice wasn't the same. It was slow and dry, bottomless as an echoing well.

Marchmont shook his head jerkily. 'I fell, Alice. That was all.'

She seemed to take a while absorbing that. Her expression didn't change – she didn't believe him. Then, she reached down and helped him to his feet. Her arms seemed very powerful, for such a small, slight woman.

Before he knew what was happening, she was bundling him along the landing like a parcel, shoving him into his room, slamming the door behind him. Marchmont squinted alarmedly in the brightness pouring from his window. Propped himself against a bookcase and allowed his nerves to calm. Caught in the daylight, everything that had just happened seemed utterly unreal.

It *was* unreal. It was the drug. He was remembering the whole thing wrongly.

But he had to be sure of that.

He peered uncomfortably about his room, trying to find solace in the small collection of familiar objects. The narrow, crumpled bed, the coin-strewn dresser. The maps on the walls and, of course, the books. Hundreds of them. They marched like troops in their worn, faded covers, spilling off the shelves and forming tall piles on the threadbare maroon carpet. They were filled with history, geography, literature, and science, and he'd read them all, earlier in his life. It seemed so long ago, now. As though another person altogether had sat poring over them.

Maybe, if he delayed the next injection . . . maybe, if he just rode it out until he could see into the next-door room unhampered by the morphine . . .

You'd never make it, old man, said an amused voice in his head.

Marchmont blinked, amazed. He'd never heard voices before, even in his oddest hallucinations.

Pashta would love you. She'd sniff you up like fine cocaine.

Was it real? Or a new stage of the narcosis, the second phase he'd talked about with Petts?

Oh, it's real, old man. But who in this town would ever believe you?

The laughter started ringing in his skull a short while after that.

Marchmont sat down on the bed, folded his arms around his head, and began to weep.

3

As Betsy Whittaker gradually awoke, she realized she was not in her bedroom. Nor even in her own home.

She was in a parlour, very dim, with the drapes pulled shut. A mantelpiece crammed with gee-gaws, a battered armchair, and a newspaper rack filled with copies of dime pulps could be made out from where she lay. She was on the floor, wrapped in a blanket. It felt rough against her naked skin.

She lay there for a while, puzzled but unafraid.

The faint murmur of everyday noises and voices drifted in from beyond the drapes. The only sound inside the room was a loud, persistent ticking.

Finally, Betsy sat up and craned her head around. There was a grandmother clock against the wall behind her. The time was just gone ten thirty.

She got up, still wondering vaguely where she was, and retrieved her underwear from a pile of clothing by the mantelpiece. Something pricked her finger, and she inspected it carefully. A few dry pine needles were sticking through the delicate lace.

She couldn't remember anything that had happened

last night. Not since Tharman had called to her. It ought to worry her, but didn't.

She picked her camisole clean, pulled it on. And then an idea took her.

Crossing to the drapes, she yanked them back. Sunlight burst in, blinding her.

When she managed to unscrew her eyes a little, she realized she was looking out across an unfamiliar front lawn on to Jefferson Street. She was in the Strangsom house, she registered dully.

A face was peering in at her, leaning over the white picket fence of next door's front yard. It was old, round, with great puffy cheeks, like a badly squashed apple. Small, hard eyes glinted behind tiny spectacles. She struggled for the name. Dot McFee.

As Betsy watched, the woman's mouth gaped open. The eyes widened in disbelief.

Unconcerned, Betsy pulled the drapes shut again and carried on getting dressed.

She slipped her shoes on last, made her way into the hallway. When she glanced up the stairs, she saw that Alice Strangsom was up there, looking down at her impassively. Betsy smiled and nodded to her. Alice returned the nod, but her pale, cold features remained blank.

No matter.

There was a faint mewling noise coming from behind one of the doors up there. A sound like someone crying. But Betsy ignored it.

She went out through the door, shut it carefully behind her, walked briskly on to the street, shielding her eyes from the sunlight. A lot of people were staring at her now. On lawns all along Jefferson, folks stopped what they were doing and gaped as she walked by. They looked shocked, aggrieved, bewildered. It started to bother her.

So did the sun's brightness. It was almost painful, as though it were scouring her flesh like wire wool. She found herself aching for a little shadow, a touch of darkness.

Keeping her face downturned, she hurried to the bottom of the street, turned the corner and headed home.

Eyes seemed to follow her from every cranny, every window.

Why am I being stared at like this? She felt a cold, bloodless anger swelling in her breast. I'm a free person, aren't I?

Aren't I?

4

It had become a mantra, a constant rhythm in her head, by the time she reached her front door.

And her fury practically boiled over when she stepped into the living-room and saw her mother, on her knees again, in front of the ugly iron crucifix. The woman's back was to her. Betsy could see only the worn soles of her shoes, the wrinkled, loose skin of her scrawny neck, the grey hair which twisted across it like clumps of Spanish moss. Vertebrae, hunched through years of praying, protruded through the woman's cheap, worn, printed dress.

She was repulsive. Absolutely ghastly.

A few memories of Betsy's earlier life drifted back.

She wants me to wind up exactly like her, Betsy realized. Dried to a husk and living on my knees. The thought, the horror of it, made her more furious still.

'Mama!'

The woman straightened, her hands still clasped in front of her face, but she didn't turn.

'Mama, what are you *doing* down there?'

When the pinched, bloodless face swivelled around, it looked more hideous than ever. The skin hung about her jowls in exhausted folds. The lips were clamped so tightly they were almost blue. The eyes, veiled by more of that unruly hair, were red rimmed, and the whites were marbled. They were quite dry, though. There were no tears. It was sleeplessness that had made them like that, not crying.

Had she been up all night, praying?

The lips skinned back from narrow, wedge-shaped teeth. The sore eyes flickered up and down Betsy's frock, as though looking for something. Some clue. Some damning evidence.

Betsy drew back a couple of steps.

'Mama . . .?'

'So. Jezebel has returned.'

Betsy's jaw slackened and she shook her head.

'Don't try to deny it.' Her mother got up, raised a trembling finger towards her. 'Don't try to hide your sins from me. Where else have you been all night? What else is there to do all night, except the Devil's work? A man, Jezebel. You've been with a man. I can *smell* him on you.'

Betsy had a brief, flickering recollection of a gaunt, handsome face looming above her. Moving rhythmically above her. Somewhere amongst darkness and trees, in the moonlight.

It wasn't a terrible thing. Wasn't evil. If anything, the memory warmed her.

Perhaps that was what all the attention from the townsfolk had been about? Some kind of peculiar misunderstanding. The anger in Betsy drained away, and she smiled querulously.

'I . . . don't understand. I haven't done anything wrong.'

Her bewilderment only seemed to enrage her mother more. The woman started shaking, as though she was on the verge of an apoplexy. Her hands bent into claws, and made little, furious snatches at the empty air.

'Temptress. Harlot. Whore of Babylon. Get out of my home!'

When she didn't move, the woman turned to the iron crucifix on the wall. She lifted it from its hooks and raised it, brandishing it like a sword. She advanced on Betsy, jabbing it out in front of her, muttering between her clenched teeth.

'Leave! Go!'

Betsy stood her ground. But she couldn't think straight. Couldn't think what to do. The cross was waving inches from her face now, and she tensed, anticipating the first blow.

Her eyelids blinked shut momentarily, and she could

suddenly see a pair of golden eyes, staring at her through the darkness in her head.

Her sight was clouded, when she opened them again. Her mother had been reduced to a shifting, abstract blur. And the confusion she'd felt a few seconds ago was fading away quickly. New thoughts had started filling her head. She couldn't seem to feel her body any more.

Before she knew what she was doing, she had swung out with her right arm, knocked the crucifix aside. It clattered to the floor. Her mother stared at her numbly.

Betsy didn't pause. She reached out and grabbed the woman by the lace collar of her dress. Lifted her off the floor. Then shifted her grip until her fingers were around her mother's throat.

She squeezed, hard. Her hands sank into the wattled flesh. Her mother's face began to turn blue, and her tongue poked out at the side of her narrow mouth.

Harder. *Harder*.

There was a sickening crunching noise. The body in her hands went limp.

She let it go, and it collapsed to the floor.

5

Boss Danvers' study was a good place to be on a hot day like this. It was sheltered by the elms outside the windows, very cool and comfortable. Filtered sunlight drifted through a gap between the half-closed drapes, sweeping across the room like a translucent yellow veil. Motes of dust swarmed in it like a cloud of tiny insects.

It was well into the afternoon by now. Jack Hughes sat opposite the Boss's desk, casually discussing the minute details of managing the ranch. So many yards of fence to mend, so many barns and haylofts to be readied for the winter.

The phone rang. Boss Danvers paused to flick ash from his fat cigar before answering it.

'Jed? . . . What's all across town? . . . For Weeping Jesus' sake, Jed, *tell* me . . .

Jack could tell, by the darkening expression on the man's face, that it was something serious.

The receiver was dropped back into its cradle, after a long silence. There was no 'goodbye', no 'thank you'.

Jack had never heard him omit the usual pleasantries before, except when he was shouting orders. Never seen the man so quiet, so stunned.

The Boss leaned back in his big wing-backed chair, stared at the porcelain chandelier in the ceiling for a moment. Then he closed his eyes, and sighed exhaustedly.

Jack waited, his frustration growing. It was so quiet he could hear bees humming amongst the leaves outside.

What the hell was going on? He wanted to ask outright, but sensed it would be entirely the wrong thing to do.

Goddamit, how much longer am I going to have to sit here? The fingers of Jack's right hand clenched and unclenched on his knee, and his cheeks took on an angry flush. Old man, you've known me for thirty years. I've been your right hand for most of them. Are you gonna speak to me? Or are you just gonna leave me sitting here like some faithful bloodhound?

When the Boss's eyes finally opened, there was a vacuum where the fierce, animate sparkle of life had been. The blue was as pale as faded denim, the whites without lustre. The pupils had shrunken very small, as though they could not bear to look at the world properly.

His mouth dropped open, and he gave out a hoarse, croaking wheeze.

'Jack?'

The voice was so faint Hughes could barely hear it.

'I'm here, Boss.'

'I . . . find this hard to believe. But I see no reason why Jed Petts should lie. It seems Elizabeth Whittaker has become involved with that accursed drifter. Don't ask me how, or why. Did you know anything about this?'

'No, Boss,' Jack lied quickly. 'Nothing.'

The old man looked away, towards the gap in the curtains and the drifting sunlight.

'Should have dealt with the bastard right away,' he muttered, almost to himself. 'Shouldn't have left things so long. Always was a mistake, letting outsiders into town.'

He stiffened as he came to a decision.

'I want the Whittakers, mother and daughter, out of town by tomorrow morning. I'll think of *something* to tell my son – God only knows what. And I want that Tharman dealt with. Permanently. *Tonight.*'

Jack shifted uneasily in his chair, grimaced. The Boss didn't even notice.

'Are you going to sit there all day?' the old man asked, refusing to look at him. 'Shouldn't you be getting the boys together, making plans?'

Say 'please' for once, Jack thought. *Please* do my dirty work. *Please* save my idiot son's face. Look at me, old man!

The Boss was watching something else. A hornet had got in, and was dragging its streamlined, glistening body up the drapes.

Jack rose swiftly, made for the door.

'And Jack—'

He stopped, turned.

'Yes, Boss?'

'Put it around town, and make sure everyone understands. Joe must never know a thing about this. My son must *never* know. I think I'll send him to New York for a while.'

Jack gazed at the back of the Boss's round, bald head and grinned savagely.

Too late for that, old man. Yet again, you're much too late.

6

Joe yanked his palomino to the left, broke him into a gallop, and cut in front of a retreating steer twenty yards from a dense clump of thorn scrub.

The animal stopped dead, gazing at him with its small red stupid eyes. Was it planning to go around him? Maybe it was going to charge? Joe sat up in his saddle, breathless with anticipation.

The beast pawed the dirt with its hoof. Then it turned around, and trotted back quickly towards the herd.

Done it! Joe's spirits leapt, and he whooped for joy. Then, he stood up in his stirrups to see if anyone else had been watching. There were three drovers bunched together just a hundred yards away, and they were all looking in his direction, grinning. Joe lifted his hat, waved it, smiled.

None of them took their eyes from him. But none of them returned the gesture, either. As he watched, one of them leant across and whispered to the others, and he heard them chuckle.

Bewilderment washed over him. Had he done something the wrong way? Shouldn't he have stopped that steer?

People had been acting oddly all morning, ever since Clete Liffut had returned from town. The men had been going into small huddles, their voices hushed, save for the occasional guffaw. He'd only caught one brief snatch of their conversation. 'There must be some attraction in it. Mebbe the drifter's got a better automobile stashed away somewhere.'

The remark had been followed by riotous laughter.

A better automobile? He didn't get the joke.

Joe prodded Diamond gently with his spurs, and began trotting the palomino towards the three men.

But as he approached, they moved apart and quickly scattered.

7

The shadows in the living-room were growing long, as though the house and everything in it were bleeding away into darkness.

Betsy knelt down by her mother's prone body and shook her. There was no response. The woman was face down on the faded rug, one hand tucked under her chest, the other outstretched, thrown across the iron cross. Jesus, in divine pain, stared up at her accusingly.

She pushed her fingers underneath her mother's chin, tried to turn her head. It wouldn't move. The neck had stiffened.

Some of Betsy's old self came fighting back to the surface. What had she done? Lord, what had she *done*? She could barely remember what had happened. It had all been so . . . so fast!

Now, she withdrew her hand, lifted it to her face. It was stained with blood from her mother's lips, dark crimson in the gathering twilight. Betsy stared at it, and moaned. Tears began prickling at the corners of her eyes.

How had she become so strong?

She ran her gaze down the length of her forearms. They were as slim and pale as ever, looked no different from before.

What was happening to her? And what was she going to do now?

It wouldn't be long before someone came by, found out what had happened. Betsy let out a small moan of desperation.

The shadows began overlapping, locking together, as evening fell. Betsy craned her head towards the front door and saw that the street outside was beginning to grow indistinct. Her husky breathing became a little slower, gentler. It was the darkness doing it. It was soothing her, like a velvet glove brushing against her skin. It felt comforting and safe.

Before long, all her fears had vanished. Her old weak

self had disappeared again. Her eyes were wide and bright as she sat, motionless, by her mother's corpse. Every thought cleared from her head, until it was completely empty.

8

How much time had passed? All day, and he'd spent it without moving.

Erskine Marchmont let his gaze drift from the pile of books in front of him to his fly-specked window. Out there, the copper globe of the sun was drifting down behind the rooftops. A last ray stretched up for a moment, then vanished, like a flashlight winking off.

Next door, he could hear the bedsprings grate as its occupant got up.

Marchmont tensed, began to shiver. Maybe if he thought of nothing, maybe if he remained so still he didn't even breathe, maybe then whatever was next door wouldn't bother him.

There was the padding of footsteps. The door of Charlie's room clacked open.

Marchmont listened, terrified. He could hear a quiet, deep voice conferring in whispers with Alice Strangsom, in the hallway outside.

Then, the footsteps started up again. They were coming towards his door.

The knob began to turn.

Marchmont had never been a religious man, had always considered it somewhat beneath him. But he needed some god, any god, to help him now. He began reeling their names off.

O God, Jesus, Holy Lord, help me!

The latch clicked. The hinges of the door started to move.

O Allah, Buddha, Jaweh. O Shinto, Brahma, Jove.

The door began creaking open. There was something

very dark, very black, standing in the lightless hallway beyond it.

O Shiva, Rama, Zoroaster, Krishna.

The door was a third of the way open now. A pair of burning yellow eyes stared in at him.

Gogoth, Imshael, Darggan, Ra!

The door stopped moving. The eyes narrowed, lost a little of their intense brightness.

Ra, Lord of the Sun! Lord of Light! Ra!

The door pulled back a little as the eyes, the creature behind them, shied away.

Why did you only wake up now? Marchmont thought, trembling. Why do you hate the sunlight? The very mention of the sun?

He remembered the sunburst clock, in the living-room downstairs. Did symbols harm this creature too?

The voice he'd heard before started echoing in his head again.

Clever. Very clever, old man. It gave a dry, cold chuckle. *I haven't quite decided what to do with you yet. But I'll think of something. I'll deal with you later.*

The door slammed shut.

And the footsteps padded away down the stairs, towards the street.

9

Jack Hughes, Paul Tarlton, and Howie Kensey stood beside the Boss's automobile in front of the burnt-out hardware store, waiting for the fourth member of their party, Ivan Travis, to return. They'd sent him up to scout the Strangsom house, as though they were on a military operation.

It was very quiet on Main, yet the sidewalks still seemed to echo with the events of last night. Jack Hughes accepted a wad of chewing baccy from Tarlton, crammed it into the corner of his mouth, and looked around. Past the ruined shell of the store, he could see lights in the windows of a dozen little houses. What was going on behind those blinds tonight? Was there a nervous tension, an electricity, where once there had been soporific calm? Despite the fact that he'd barely exchanged a dozen words with Tharman, and angry ones at that, he almost liked the man. He'd stirred things up around here, that was for sure.

But Jack liked something better. The thought of impending violence. It made his pulse beat faster and his blood sing. It wasn't the act itself which made him feel so good. It was the power it gave you. The way a man grovelled and pleaded. The way you could extinguish him, as easily as stepping on a bug, if you wanted to. He'd handed out more than a few beatings on Boss Danvers' behalf, and they had always made him feel like God Almighty.

But this. A killing. This was going to be a hundred times better.

Jack reached inside the long coat he was wearing, felt the reassuring coolness of his sawn-off shotgun barrel.

He spat tobacco juice into the dust, and waited.

10

Ivan Travis came hurrying around the corner of Jefferson a short while later. His pace slowed as he approached. He was a sunburned, hefty twenty-one-year-old who'd been in loads of bar fights in his time, but never taken part in anything like this.

Jack watched amusedly as the young man squared his shoulders and turned his hurried gait into an aggressive swagger.

'Well?'

'He ain't there any more, Mr Hughes. I saw him head off in the direction of the Whittaker house.'

Jack's head shook with silent laughter. 'Two birds with one stone. All the better.' He turned towards the car. 'Let's get going.'

Paul drove. The big, gleaming automobile wove slowly

through the streets of Yewlburg, its engine purring like a jungle cat. It smelled of expensive leather inside, like the drawing-room of a grand house. The men sprawled on the rich, yielding upholstery. They all watched silently as one little house after another slid by.

Every so often, a shadow would hover briefly behind a net curtain, an upstairs drape would lift and flutter. Everyone was watching, Jack noted with a grim satisfaction.

They reached the corner of Spring Street.

'Should I stop here?' Paul asked.

'No. Take us right up to the front door and park outside. An example is what we're giving, and you don't hide an example.'

11

Tharman stood in the darkness of the Whittakers' living-room, listening as the Chevrolet pulled up outside and the motor puttered down to silence. Betsy was kneeling at his feet. Her arms were wrapped tightly around his legs, her head was pressed to his knees, and she felt more warm and perfect than ever.

There was the clack of doors, then the soft crunching of boots as the four men moved towards the house.

The heaviest set of footsteps stalked up quietly to the front door. *Hello, Jack Hughes.*

It was open. There was only the fly-screen between him and the foreman. Very faintly, Jack's silhouette slid across the fine cotton mesh.

Tharman raised a hand, dabbed with his fingers at the air, and began weaving spells. The other footsteps stopped, as the men were suddenly frozen into place. They wouldn't be able to move again until he decided to let them go; and they wouldn't even be aware that they'd stopped moving.

Tharman grinned, lifted his open palm towards the ceiling. There was a crescendo of short, brittle cracks as every lightbulb in the house exploded.

The silhouette outside the fly-screen dropped to a crouch. Tharman could make out the slim shape of a gun protruding from his arm.

Was that gunfire, Jack? No, you'd recognize that sound. So what is going on in here, eh?

Was the man going to creep in very slowly, or hurl himself inside?

It turned out to be the latter.

Jack plunged through the fly-screen, rolled twice, came up on his elbows with the shotgun raised and cocked.

Tharman moved his index finger and thumb very gently. Above the town, the clouds parted. The moon came out. Its light poured in through every window, and the house was filled with a glaring, cold glow, bright and dead as a sheet of platinum.

Jack blinked alarmedly. Levelled his gun at Tharman's chest. Then he noticed Betsy, stopped.

12

Jack felt his skin turn cold, his mouth go dry.

My God, what was happening here? The way Betsy was crouched, clutching Tharman as though in worship; it was like something out of a bad dream. And who was that on the floor behind them? Was that *Mary* Whittaker?

He'd hit them all, using the sawn-off. The pellets would scatter in a wide cone, from this distance. And his orders didn't include harming the women.

He kept the gun aimed at Tharman, and shouted, his throat tight and rasping.

'Let go of him, Betsy! Move away!'

She didn't seem to hear him. Her gaze was fixed on Tharman's tattered boots. The man above her grinned like some benign sovereign.

Jack tipped his head towards the window.

'Paul!' he yelled. 'Ivan! Howie!'

'They can't hear you, Jack,' the drifter said, abruptly.

Jack squinted at him. 'Whaddya mean?'

He wished, suddenly, he wasn't on his belly. The man above him seemed as tall, from this angle, as a redwood tree.

'What I said. I stopped them for a while. It's just you and me.'

'Whaddya mean, stopped?' The man was as crazy as a 'coon. Jack ran his tongue across his teeth. 'You gonna hide behind that girl all night? Let her go.'

In the warmthless light, laughter danced across Tharman's face.

'She doesn't want to go. But if you insist—'

He reached down very gently and brushed a hand through Betsy's long hair. The girl stirred, as though waking, then released her grip and clambered to her feet. She moved to the side of the room, her movements as stiff as a sleepwalker's.

Jack took the opportunity to get up on one knee. He pressed the stock of the shotgun hard against his shoulder.

'How about her?' His gaze flickered towards Mary Whittaker. 'She dead?'

'Yes.'

'You kill her?'

'No. She died in the pursuit of her beliefs.'

What in God's name did he mean by that? And where were Paul and the others?

The drifter was staring at him intently now, quite unafraid of the gun. Jack could see the strange mauve colour of his eyes in the peculiar, filtered brightness.

Damn it, what was the guy trying to do, hypnotize him? He tightened his finger on the trigger. Squeezed.

The cloud of smoke from the discharge swirled in the moonlight like the surface of a luminous marsh pool. When it cleared, Jack saw that the man hadn't moved.

What the *hell*!

He fired again. This time, the tall, ragged figure rocked gently as the pellets tore into him. Jack waited for him to fall.

He didn't.

He regained his balance. Smiled.

And raised both arms in front of him.

Jack felt the shotgun fall helplessly from his grasp.

No man could take two blasts from a sawn-off! *No* man!

But in the moonlight, Jack could see the drifter was changing. Crouching lower, broadening. Darkness seemed to wrap itself around him. It coalesced – and the human shape began to fade.

13

The three young drovers broke out of their trances as Hughes emerged from the house. They stared around, shook their heads bewilderedly and then hurried up to join him. The foreman was striding woodenly towards the car.

'You done it?' asked Paul Tarlton.

'Didn't you hear the shotgun?'

'You just gonna leave him *lying* there?' Paul asked. 'How about the Whittakers?'

'You gonna argue with me, Paul? Just get inside and drive.'

Jack's dark eyes seemed to burn intensely in the moonlight.

CHAPTER SEVEN

1

The ranch house was silent as Jack crept in. There were no sounds coming from the servants' quarters, and the only noise in the big oak-panelled hallway was the ticking of a Swiss clock on the wall by the curving banisters.

Jack closed the door softly behind him and made his way up the huge winding staircase to the bedrooms above. He was overwhelmed, as always, by the sumptuousness of the place. Heavy velvet flock wallpaper swirled around him. Ornate gold-rimmed mirrors hung from the dados. The furniture was American Colonial, all bulky oak and maple. And there were small paintings and little charcoal sketches which the Boss had picked up on his rare trips to the big cities.

A huge vase, with a blue and white pattern of Chinese forests, stood by the door of the master bedroom. Jack had always liked that vase. He wasn't quite sure why. But when he was Boss he'd order a dozen like it.

The door was oiled every week. It didn't make a sound as Jack eased it open.

There was a small light on inside.

Before him was the four-poster the Boss had once shared with his wife. And there, amongst the blankets, the old man lay asleep. He looked surprisingly small in the massive bed. His head was buried deeply in a thick white pillow. His mouth was open wide and, with his rounded face and bald head, he seemed almost like a baby. On the cabinet beside him was a leather-bound accounts book, a pair of gold-rimmed spectacles folded on top of it.

Jack took three paces towards the bed. The Boss stirred, came awake.

The old man peered at him bewilderedly a moment,

then sat up, put on his glasses. He blinked at his foreman, confused.

'Jack? What are you doing here?' His voice was strangled wth sleep. 'Have you done the job?'

Jack smiled.

'Not quite, Boss.'

The old man's stare became uneasy.

'What do you mean by that?'

'There's a little more to this than meets the eye. I don't want to wake the whole house up, Boss. Let me explain it to you quietly.'

He walked smoothly over to the bedside, towered over the old man for a moment. Then he bent down lower, as though to confer in a whisper.

In one quick motion, he snatched up the pillow and shoved it over the man's face.

God, but he struggled at first. Who'd have thought he still had it in him? Those short, pudgy hands kept snatching at his wrists, but Jack simply responded by pushing down harder. The grasping fingers dropped away. The fat old body began to jerk and spasm.

Jack grinned, and shoved down with every ounce of his strength. How strange, to kill someone with softness, whiteness. The Boss's feet started kicking at a furious, staccato pace. The shoulders writhed from one side to the other, trying to escape. Then, every movement slowed, trailed away, like a motor dying down.

Jack kept the pressure up for a full minute more before uncovering the face.

The mouth was open, the lips bright blue. The eyes stared at him, vacant and bewildered . . . betrayed.

Jack chuckled to himself. Plumped out the pillow and set it back behind the limp head.

He left the room as quietly as he'd come.

2

As the night began to turn grey with the onset of dawn, Erskine Marchmont heard Tharman return to the house, stride upstairs, and shut himself in the next-door room. It wouldn't be long now till the creature was asleep again.

The morphine had practically worked its way out of his system by now, and Marchmont had not been idle. He'd spent the night moving softly about his room, first finding everything he could read about Ra and ancient Egypt, then hunting for gold leaf and yellow paper. The only source, it turned out, was in the flyleaves of the books themselves, and it had felt like he was dismembering his own children as he'd ripped the pages out. But what choice was there? Next, he'd spent a painstaking hour tearing with his thumbnail, creating plain gold discs, the symbol of the sun god, Ra. He'd put them up all over his room.

Would they work at all? Would they stop the creature getting in? Only time would tell.

Marchmont sat on the edge of his bed, his fingers knotted together in his lap, and waited for the sun to rise.

When it finally did, it had never looked so immense, so beautiful. He waited until the entire globe was visible, then picked up the largest of the discs and made his way quietly to the door.

He pressed his ear against the wood, listening intently. Nothing could be heard outside. Nor from the next room. But silence wasn't the same thing as safety. He still had to be very careful.

He opened the door a tiny gap. The same dimness there'd been the previous morning waited for him. The same banishment of sunlight from the house, as if it were an unclean thing.

He cupped the Ra disc in his palm, held it in front of him, and opened the door fully.

Jerked with shock.

Alice was standing on the landing near the stairs, perfectly motionless. The dull, grim expression on her face hadn't changed since yesterday. Her arms were folded across her chest again.

And in her right hand, she was clutching a long, broad-bladed kitchen knife.

It glittered faintly in the weak light.

Her eyes moved, sliding towards him.

The hand clutching the knife twitched, then began to rise. The blade flashed and shivered, like moonlight captured on a rippling tide.

Marchmont pushed the disc towards the woman.

And at first, it seemed to have the desired effect. Alice Strangsom's face contorted worriedly, and she edged back until she was touching the banisters. Marchmont was shaking furiously now. Couldn't help it. He began sidling out of the room, keeping as much distance between himself and the woman, the knife, as possible.

Suddenly, quite without warning, Alice set her teeth and made a swift jab forwards.

She only got six inches before stopping. Perhaps the Ra disc was keeping her from following through. But it was enough to make the old librarian let out a cry, pull back. His old, bent spine slammed against the doorpost.

Unconsciously, he clenched both hands.

When he realized what he'd done . . . when he opened his right hand . . . the Ra disc lay uselessly in his palm, reduced to a crumpled ball.

Alice let out a keening noise from between her teeth and plunged towards him.

It was odd. He didn't feel the knife go in. He simply put his left hand to his stomach, and felt something warm and wet there, something shifting, spilling. In a blind panic, he began staggering back into his room.

Alice was following him now. She raised the knife again, ready to strike another blow.

Marchmont could feel his legs buckling under him. He tried to cry out. Nothing came.

He raised his arms, in a feeble attempt to ward off the knife.

The blade swung down across his right hand. The pain

seared up to his shoulder. His palm became slick with dark, dripping red.

Somehow, he got back into the room.

Alice reached the threshold. Stopped dead. Her lifeless eyes wandered across the golden discs, which Marchmont had tacked everywhere. Her expression, at first, became bovine, sullen.

Then she looked at Marchmont's stomach, where she'd stabbed him.

And she smiled delightedly.

He cupped his hands to the wound, followed her gaze. Couldn't understand what he was looking at, at first. Then, the room, the window, the world beyond it all began to spin.

Sliding into his cupped palms, red and shapeless in a froth of blood, were the ends of his own entrails. He'd been gutted like a fish.

The pain began to thud home. Slowly, at first. A dull, terrible ache. Then it uncurled, like a great serpent awakening. It began tearing through his stomach, through his whole body, up into his brain. It ripped thoughts and feelings to a bloody jumble. There was a roaring in his ears.

Everything was disintegrating. Everything was crimson, as though bathed in an ocean of blood. There were dark black slashes running through the red, like the dark slash in his stomach.

Marchmont was dimly aware that he'd fallen to his knees on the rough carpet.

He managed to raise his head, squint upwards. And watched as a grinning Alice Strangsom closed the door.

3

There was a clattering noise on the stairs.

Jack Hughes woke up with a jerk and gazed around blearily. He was in the Boss's study. In the Boss's chair. He'd been sitting in it last night, luxuriating in its softness and the feeling of authority it gave him, and he must have dozed off.

Warm, lemon-yellow sunlight was pouring, now, through a gap in the drapes.

Before he had time to get up, a figure appeared in the doorway. It was Henry, the chauffeur. The man was in his shirtsleeves, and panting furiously, his grey wire-wool hair dishevelled and his face damp with exertion.

He looked at Jack and his eyes widened with surprise. His jaw moved slackly, trying to find the right words.

Jack rubbed his face and stared at the black man coldly.

'What the hell is it?'

He tried to make it sound as if he didn't know. Something was at work in the chauffeur's eyes. A hard, suspicious glint that said, What're you doin' in that chair? What's goin' on here?

'It's the Boss, Mr Jack. You'd better come quick.'

He followed Henry up the stairs.

The old man was in the same position as last night, mouth still gaping and blue eyes staring at the canopy of the four-poster. It was as though he hadn't died, but simply been frozen in a stray moment of time. Jack expected to feel a sense of guilt, here in the daylight. Some twinge of regret. But there was none. It felt so right. He was perfectly entitled to do what he had done. The creature at the Whittaker house had told him so.

He turned the Boss's head from side to side, then straightened up and gazed at Henry evenly.

'Looks like his heart went. Had to happen some time.' He kept his tone low and respectful. 'Get the houseboys together, dig a grave out back. We'll have the burial service 'round noon.'

'*Here?*' Henry blurted. 'Not at the cemetery? I . . . I don't understand, Mr Jack.'

'He'd've wanted to be buried here, on his own land. And in this heat – Christ, do I have to stand around explaining everything to a nigger? Who's in charge here, Henry? Now that the Boss is gone, who's in charge?'

He'd expected the man to cringe, recoil. But instead,

the ageing chauffeur drew himself up very straight and gazed at him with an incredible stony dignity.

'Will somebody be sending out for Mr Joe, suh?'

There was not a hint of impertinence in his voice. It was there, but it was all hidden below the surface.

'I'll take care of that,' Jack snapped. 'Now do as you're told.'

He turned on his heel and marched out of the room.

Henry waited sullenly, watching him go. Then, he bent over his old employer. Something caught his eye.

It was a crescent pattern of toothmarks on the upper lip, faintly lined with dried blood, where the Boss had chewed into it just before he'd died.

He wasn't quite sure what it meant, but heart attack like hell. A man didn't do that, when he was having no heart attack.

4

The sun rose higher, blazing through Marchmont's window. The air was stifling. He couldn't breathe.

Why don't I faint? Why don't I die?

That would come, he knew. There was nothing that could stop it. But when?

The unbearable pain continued to savage him. It felt as though wild dogs were chewing at his body. He would welcome unconsciousness, death.

Neither of them came.

How much longer do I have to wait? How much longer do I have to endure this?

The sun, rippling behind the warped glass, seemed to be gazing down at him passionlessly. It couldn't save him now. It might be proof against the forces of darkness, but it couldn't heal a knife wound.

He curled into a foetal ball, blinking tears of pain. If only it would end. Marchmont tried to think how long someone with a severed gut could survive. He'd no idea. All he knew was it was too long by far.

Blurrily, he remembered the twist of morphine in his jacket pocket. It was his only possible escape.

He managed to raise his right arm – it made a ripping noise as it pulled free of the blood-soaked carpet – and worked his fingers into his pocket. They had almost no feeling, as though some parts of him were dying ahead of the rest. He pinched them together, forcing them to move, and then eased them deeper.

Still, he could feel nothing. All the nerves in his fingertips were dead.

Finally, he just closed his hand and hoped for the best.

When he drew it out into the light, he gave a bubbling gasp of relief. He was holding the twist of paper.

It began to shake in his palm, tremor violently, as he watched. The numbness had worked its way down to his wrist, by now, was seeping into his elbow like a trickle of ice water.

He couldn't risk unwrapping the crystals. Couldn't prepare a syringe.

He put his hand to his lips. Crammed the twist in, and began to chew.

The sharp, bitter taste of the morphine flooded his mouth. He swallowed carefully. Waited for the overdose to finish him off.

His throat began to burn.

For the briefest instant, he fancied he was floating above the ground, leaving the world behind. He came down sharply. The pain returned for just a second. Then it started to transform itself.

Into colours. Pouring out of his stomach. Colours so bright, so iridescent, he could barely stand to look at them. A geyser full of rainbows. It was so beautiful he *had* to look.

The rainbows sputtered out. He could see his intestines again. Except, this time, they were moving. Like snakes, bloody, skinned, and raw. They began to writhe.

Marchmont's eyes widened and his eyebrows arched, his mouth gaped open in his rigid face.

Let this be over! Please!

They seemed to grow longer as he watched. Their severed ends made rapid jerking motions towards his eyes, hissing, spitting bright green poison.

He was screaming. But it was all inside his own head.

They vanished.

His body was spasming violently now. His back was arching like a longbow. His mouth flapped open and shut, and his eyes blinked violently. His hands made spastic, grasping motions at his sides.

He could hear his heart beating. Heavy thumps. Completely erratic. But faster and faster until they blurred together.

They stopped, abruptly.

Marchmont felt himself rise again. Stared down at his own body on the floor.

And then something was tugging at him violently. Pulling him away.

And he was falling . . .

5

He seemed to be dropping through an enormous tunnel, as wide as the Grand Canyon. The distant walls, blurring as he plummeted by them, were of rough, unbroken rock. But far paler than any mineral he'd ever seen. They glowed with a cold, dead, grey light. Seemed to grow ever brighter, the faster he fell.

Marchmont tried to shield his eyes.

But he couldn't move. Only twist and tumble. He couldn't feel his hands or his arms, couldn't even see them.

A wind was screeching around him now, freezing his skin, ripping at his hair. He wasn't breathing any more. There didn't seem to be the need.

He waited for something to change. But the fall, the tunnel, appeared endless.

There was no sense of time passing.

He wasn't sure how long it was before he saw the

ground rush up beneath him. He prepared himself for the shattering impact, but it never came.

Abruptly, he was lying on a cold, hard floor of faintly glowing stone.

Without raising his head, he looked around. He was in a complex of vast caverns, a dozen passages leading away from him into the darkness. A silvery mist floated on the chill air. Faint shadows seemed to move, at the corners of his vision.

A pair of mud-stained shoes moved over to his head, and stopped.

He found himself looking up into a flat, warmthless, ugly face, a pair of glowing yellow eyes.

'Wh-where am I?' he asked.

'This is the *Duat*. The Underworld,' the creature said. 'I brought you here.'

'And . . . who are you?'

'I am Kellesh.'

6

The sun rose towards noon. The town carried on almost as normal. On Spring Street, people went about their daily routines a little more subduedly than usual. Men tended their lawns at a stately progress. Children climbed trees, and played at being Red Indians, but there was a sluggishness to their movements, a dulled edge to their shouts, as though they hadn't woken properly.

Wives brought pitchers of lemonade to their husbands on the porches, and the husbands drank slowly, without pleasure. Wordless glances passed between each couple.

Hadn't there been a commotion last night? Gunshots? And Mary Whittaker and her daughter ought to have put in an appearance by now. Shouldn't someone go and check they were OK?

They weren't sure. It all seemed like a dream.

Dogs scuttled from the shade of one tree to the next, gazing anxiously at their masters.

7

Betsy sat on the living-room floor, her legs tucked beneath her, her hands wrapped around her pale shoulders. Her face wore a gentle smile, and her eyes were dreamy.

Outside, she could hear the townsfolk go about their business. The noises seemed softer than usual. That was good. At least they weren't bothering her, now. At least they weren't staring at her.

She gazed about the room, and barely recognized it. Something at the back of her mind told her that she'd lived here all her life – but that seemed ludicrous.

She tucked her chin against her throat, closed her eyes to shut out the few rays of sunlight streaming in.

A humming, scuttling noise rose, as insects began to swarm around her mother's corpse.

CHAPTER EIGHT

1

Joe had been in a daze all day. He'd had a restless night, tossing and turning like a sick man. The nightmares about Betsy had come again.

Now he found himself growing angrier as the afternoon progressed. The whispering and the huddled backs of yesterday had stopped, but they'd given way to something far worse.

The drovers were shying completely clear of him, as though he had some kind of plague. Every time he managed to get close, talk to them, they'd reply quickly, without meeting his eyes, then canter away. And each time, as their faces turned, he'd catch a glimpse of sneering grins, laughter in their eyes.

He couldn't work out why. And he couldn't take it any more.

It was all down to Clete Liffut. This craziness had only started when the tow-headed young man had come back from town. Joe sought him out, spotted him at the rear of the herd, beyond a forest of curving horns.

The man saw him coming and began to back his horse up in the act of turning. Joe sped up, reached over in his saddle, and grabbed hold of the drover's reins.

'Want a word with you, Liffut.'

The face which met his was gloating and arrogant. The sharp eyes looked him up and down as though he were something pitiful.

'Uh-huh, Mr Joe?'

'What the hell is going on here? Why the hell are people avoiding me? Laughing at me?'

'Laughing, Mr Joe?' The tone was one of feigned surprise, but it couldn't hide the mockery bubbling just below the surface.

'That's right. You think I'm dumb or something?'

'Of course not, Mr Joe.' A grin started breaking out on Liffut's face. 'Now if you're finished, I'd like to get back to work. That *is* what your daddy's paying me for.'

He snatched the reins free of Joe's grasp, so sharply that the young man almost overbalanced in his saddle. Liffut began wheeling his horse around.

Joe stared at him amazedly for a moment, unsure what to do. Then blind anger took over. Before he knew what was happening, he was letting out a yell and stretching out, wrapping his arms around Clete Liffut's shoulders.

The world slid sideways sharply. They hit the dirt and rolled, and Joe found himself on top. His hands sought the drover's throat, squeezed.

The horses reared and shrieked around them, their hoofs stamping furiously at the dust. Joe barely noticed. He stopped just short of throttling the drover, then shook him until his eyes popped.

'What's going on? Tell me, you sonofabitch!'

Liffut shook his head groggily.

The fury Joe had bottled up all day spilled over. He swung his fist back, slammed a punch into the drover's mouth. Blood splattered down Liffut's chin, and his eyes went glazed and faraway.

'*Tell me!*'

The drover was limp in his grasp now, all resistance gone.

'It's your girl,' he whispered. 'Betsy. She's with that Tharman. That drifter who came in a couple nights ago.'

'Bullshit!'

Joe's face contorted and he raised his fist again.

Liffut didn't flinch. Didn't even try to protect himself. Just gazed up at him dully.

'It's the truth, Mr Joe.'

Joe rocked back, released his grip. A black, swirling numbness began taking him over.

And at the centre of that motion was a vortex of icy

fear. He'd never been enough for her. Deep down, he'd always known that. She'd wanted the romance and excitement of her story books, and he'd never been able to give it to her. He'd always been terrified that she would find somebody else.

But a hobo? He couldn't take it in, it was so insane.

2

Jack Hughes was sprawled out in the study when he heard the Chevrolet growl into life. Who the hell was using the Boss's car?

He swung his boots off the leather-topped desk and hurried to the front door, only to find he was too late. The automobile was purring down the drive towards the open road, a dark figure hunched at the wheel.

It wasn't Henry. The old black man was standing by a huge clump of rose bushes, his wife by his side. The entire household staff seemed to have turned out. The Chink maids and the Niggrah stable boys, and even Kobi, the Filipino cook. They jerked around as his boots clattered on the veranda, and moved together, clustering around Henry. Their fists were clenched, their eyes defiant.

'Who the hell's driving that car?' Jack demanded, his voice rising to a yell.

'My son, suh. Elias.'

Jack stared wildly at the plume of dust the automobile had left trailing in its wake.

'Where's he going?'

'To fetch Dr Petts, suh,' Henry replied, firmly. 'It's right and proper the doctor should be here. You can't bury the Boss without him. There's documentation and such to be done.'

Jack felt his anger seethe and bubble like the surface of a cauldron.

'Who the hell do you think you are? I want the burial done, and I want it done now!'

'*No*, suh.'

The noise of the automobile had drifted away by now. Jack banged his fists at his sides impotently, trying to think what to do next.

There was the clatter of footsteps coming around the side of the house. It was Paul Tarlton and the others and, as they hove into view, he could see that they were all carrying guns.

Jack looked at them, then back at the servants, grinning fiercely.

'Let's hear you say "no" again, Henry.'

He turned his head, and watched the plume of dust as the Chevrolet headed towards town.

The sunlight burned his staring eyes.

3

For the first time since she'd been brought down from Meacher's Hill, Ellen Krauss was showing signs of life. A little colour glowed from her pale, scrubbed cheeks. Her fingers moved every so often, curling and uncurling like sea anemones. And, less often, her rosy lips would part and a tiny moan would escape, like a dark, humming bumblebee. Other than that, there was no sign that she was aware of the outside world at all.

Dr Petts sat down on the edge of her pink, lace-edged bed and took her pulse. Then he brushed his hand across her temples soothingly.

The girl's parents moved in behind him, peering over his shoulders.

Ellen shifted a little beneath his touch. Let out a faint sigh.

'There it is again,' shrilled Maybelline Krauss. 'Do you think she's getting better, doctor?'

'I know one thing,' Petts said testily. 'I *cannot* examine my patient properly with you both hovering over me like a couple of ghosts. Saul, would you take your wife downstairs for a few minutes, and shut the door behind you?'

His shoulders tensed as the latch clicked and the footsteps retreated down the stairs. He felt uneasy, being left alone with the girl. He still couldn't get the image of the flies out of his mind. His skin crawled every time he thought about it.

He looked at Ellen carefully. Every freckle on her face, even the thin lines of her eyebrows, seemed to shift a little, as though they were taking on an insectile life of their own.

He tried to steady himself. This is ridiculous! You're a medical man, for Pete's sake!

He reached for her face again, to ease back one of her eyelids.

Ellen's eyes snapped open of their own accord, making Petts flinch back. Was she awake?

The pupils were tiny, shrunken to minute black specks. At first, they gazed straight up at the ceiling.

Then, they swivelled around till they were looking directly at him. The smooth, rounded face behind them was totally impassive.

Gingerly, Petts lowered his hand towards her again. Found he couldn't move it all the way. He tried to raise a faint, professional smile, felt his brows knit with curiosity. What was happening?

He cleared his throat softly.

'Ellen, can you hear me?'

She didn't move, or even blink.

'Ellen, do you know who I am?'

There was something strange happening to her eyes. The irises were their usual hazel green, striated with amber. But as he watched, tiny sections of the amber webbing seemed to dislodge themselves. Brighten to gold. And spin.

Petts watched them, dumbfounded. His mouth grew dry. Had the strain of the last few days been too much for him? Was he cracking up?

The golden dots seemed to glow incandescently. They whirled like microscopic planets circling two tiny, jet black suns.

And, before he realized what was happening, he was being drawn into them.

He jerked back, glanced fuzzily at the little cat-shaped china clock on Ellen's mantelpiece. Hardly any time had passed since her folks had gone downstairs. It seemed to have been for ever.

He shook his head, trying to clear it, and then looked back at the girl.

Her eyes were shut now, the lashes quivering gently. Her breathing was slow and rhythmic.

Tiredness on my part, Petts thought. That's all.

Then he saw the largest freckle on her cheek begin to bulge. The dark skin shifted, as though something were trying to push its way out from underneath.

It split, and a tiny head, all bulging red eyes and feathery antennae, poked out.

Petts gave a small cry.

It wriggled clear, scuttled across her face.

A *fly*. He was *seeing* things.

Another joined it, from the same burst freckle. Then a third. A thirteenth. A twenty-third.

Before his horrified gaze, the whole of Ellen's face became obscured in a black swarm of the creatures, just as it had been smothered up on Meacher's Hill. The insects scurried down her throat, and began to cover her entire body.

All reason fled Petts. He let out a horrified yell and began to slap at the things. They didn't try to get out of the way. More and more of them were coming, clustering ever deeper around the girl, their crystalline wings humming furiously.

He kept on slapping. Ellen began to scream with pain.

There were hurried footsteps on the stairs. The door burst open behind him. He didn't look around. Didn't dare turn his back. The flies would get him too!

Something slammed, very hard, into the back of his head. There was a dull explosion inside his skull. A slow, thunderous roaring.

Everything went dark with an absolute finality.

4

Saul Krauss let the candlestick hang limply from his grasp and stared down at the doctor, amazed at what he'd done. There was a dent in the back of the man's skull large enough to put your whole fist into.

Dark blood began to ooze down the quilt on to the floor. The doctor's thin, strong fingers gave a couple of spastic twitches, and then went completely still.

Why'd he attacked Ellen? What the hell had the damn fool been doing?

A minute later, the doorbell rang and the voice of Elias, the chauffeur's son from the Triple Y, floated up the stairs. He was asking if he could see Dr Petts.

5

'Ashes to ashes . . .'

Jack Hughes stood at the head of Boss Danvers' grave, reading from the prayer book in the study.

'Dust to dust . . .'

Half the afternoon was gone. The sun had shifted over towards Meacher's Hill. It felt like a branding iron that was being held inches from his skin. He squinted uncomfortably as he read the tiny print.

On one side of the grave were the drovers, Paul Tarlton with his shotgun still draped across his shoulder. On the other, their heads tucked low and their hands clasped in front of them, were Henry and the servants. They had an enraged, helpless air. But they were listening to the final rites respectfully enough.

Boss Danvers wasn't even in a coffin. His corpse lay, at the bottom of the rectangular hole, wrapped in a tarpaulin, for all the world like a discarded sack of potatoes.

'The Lord giveth,' Jack intoned, 'and the Lord taketh away.'

Except he had a new lord now. Far stronger. Infinitely more powerful.

Every time he blinked, he could see those golden, glowing eyes staring at him through the darkness.

He peered towards the town again.

And suddenly, like a bright flash of lightning, he *knew.*

Knew that everything was solved. Knew that the matter of Dr Petts had been taken care of. Knew that his new lord had watched over him, provided for him.

A dry smile crept across the big man's lips. He snapped the prayer book shut.

'OK,' he told Henry. 'That's enough words. Fill the grave in.'

He strode away towards the ranch-house, the baleful stares of the servants on his back.

6

As the afternoon wore on towards evening, all life seemed to drain from the people of Yewlburg. Their movements became as sluggish as tired beetles' in the heat. Even the noises of the children playing faded gradually away.

The sun dropped towards the roof tops. Folks, for no reason they could think of, started to drift indoors. Porch swings were left deserted, picnic tables bare.

The final rays of sunlight disappeared, one by one, and the soft grey veil of dusk began to wrap itself around the streets, the houses. A cold wind started to blow, chill and shrieking, as though it were a live and hunting thing.

Lights began winking on in curtained windows, but no shadows moved across them.

In the Strangsom house on Jefferson Street, Tharman stirred.

CHAPTER NINE

1

Joe arrived at the Triple Y half an hour after dusk, found a gap in the fence, and galloped his sweating, dripping palomino over the dried-out yellow grasslands towards the dark bulk of the ranch-house.

Something struck him as odd about the place. At first, he didn't realize what it was. He was too confused, too angry. Then it hit him.

There was not a light on anywhere.

He pulled his horse up to a stop about a hundred yards from the back porch, scanned the windows with alarm. Most of them were open. Their curtains trailed out like sheet-clad phantoms in the cold, rustling breeze. But there was not a soul in sight.

It was obvious his horse wouldn't make it any further. The creature was practically lame already.

Joe patted its head gently, then dismounted. He walked quietly to the rear of the house. Thought of calling out, but every instinct rebelled against it. The place was *never* dark like this. Where were the servants? Where was Pa?

Short hairs prickled on the back of his neck. The breeze was raising goosebumps on his skin.

A sudden noise from inside made him jump. But it was only the chimes of the grandfather clock in the hallway, ringing out the hour.

As the last brassy echo faded, silence crept over the house again. Very cautiously, aware his every footfall could be heard, he walked across the back porch.

The sun-bleached boards clacked beneath his heels. The two windows nearest him gaped blindly. The french windows to his father's study were open too, but there was no movement inside. He ignored them.

He made his way around, as quickly as he dared, to the front driveway. The shadows of trees hung all around him, under the rising moon.

He glanced towards the lights of Yewlburg. They glittered in the darkness like ochre stars. And seemed just as distant.

Betsy's face swam into his thoughts again, but he pushed it away. He couldn't afford to worry about her now.

He gazed across to where the Chevrolet was usually parked. It was gone. There were heavy, skidding tyre tracks in the gravel, as though whoever'd taken it had left in a hurry.

Perhaps that was it. Perhaps there'd been some kind of trouble in town, and everyone had gone to help, leaving the place abandoned.

Joe turned to the tall windows out front. Tipped back his head.

'*Pa?*'

He waited.

'*Henry? Jack?*'

Then he hurried towards the barn off past the east wing, where his precious Studebaker was kept.

It was almost pitch dark inside. The only illumination was provided by the few pale strands of moonlight that had managed to force their way in through the knotholes in the walls. A couple of them struck the chrome trim of his car, and made it glint. But something seemed wrong again. He stopped, just inside the doorway, and let his eyes adjust.

There was the motionless figure of a large man sitting in the car, in the driver's seat, lounging back against the cream upholstery, his feet up on the door.

Joe grunted with alarm. And in response, a white smile broke out on the silhouetted darkness of the man's face. A pair of gleaming eyes studied him amusedly.

Joe's hand scrabbled along the wall, where the tools for the motor were kept. There had to be *something* he could use as a weapon.

The figure straightened in its seat.

'It's me, Mr Joe.'

He let out a wheezing sigh and clutched his chest.

'Jesus Christ, Jack Hughes! You scared me out of my skin!' Then he frowned and looked up. 'What're you doing in my car, anyway?'

He watched as Jack reached out and flicked at the rear-view mirror with his fingertips. It made a tinny, pinging noise, shivered a little.

'You know, Mr Joe.' The foreman's voice had become a lazy drawl, mocking and unpleasant. 'I've never rated this automobile very highly.'

What? Who in God's name did he think he was talking to?

'Looks cute enough,' Hughes continued. 'But there's nothing much under the hood. Pretty much like its owner.'

Joe felt dumbfounded and flustered. He couldn't work out what was going on here. Jack didn't sound at all drunk, and that could be the only possible explanation for the way he was behaving.

'What the hell are you talking about, Jack?' He threw a quick glance through the door towards the darkened house. 'Where *is* everyone?'

The silhouetted head wagged boredly.

'Oh, I let the boys have the evening off. They went into Malvern, so I believe. The Niggers and the Chinks? They've all gone.'

'All the servants? *Why?*'

'Oh, you know how those types are. Some peculiar mood gets into them, you can't do nothing to talk them out of it.'

This was getting crazier by the second. Joe peered agitatedly at the big man.

'What did Pa have to say about all this?'

There was a deep, throaty chuckle from the foreman. And yes, the tone of mockery was unmistakable now.

'Ah, Joe boy. My poor little Joe. Your Pa don't have nothing to say about nothing, no more.'

And before Joe had time to understand what he meant,

Jack Hughes had opened the car door and was getting smoothly to his feet.

2

Betsy blinked, and her chin rose a little as she awoke from her trance.

The only light in the room came from the windows and the doorway, the faintest grey glow outlining the wooden frames. Clouds were drifting back across the town again. That was sad. She felt happy and fortunate, these nights, under the warming glow of the moon.

But where was Tharman? Where was her beloved?

She looked around the room frantically and a soft keening whimper pushed its way out from her throat. Her hands jerked up, her fingers scrabbling at the air like crabs' claws.

Then suddenly, she stopped. She tipped her head to one side, as though listening to something. Closed her eyes again.

When they reopened, she was calm. She smiled hugely and got to her feet.

Around her, the room began to change.

She could no longer see the outlines of the dingy furniture. Nor a fancy penthouse in New York.

She was surrounded by pink marble now, veined stone walls carved into swirling, ornate patterns and hung with flowing silks. A fountain tinkled, in the middle of the floor. Peacocks called beyond the arched windows.

She was in a palace in ancient Egypt. She glanced down at herself, saw that she was wearing gold bracelets and fine robes of white and purple. There was a strange weight on her head. She raised a hand to it, felt the smooth, cool outline of a jewel-encrusted tiara.

Her sandalled feet clattered as she hurried outside. A city of marvels was stretched out before her. Chariots were moving along a great dusty road, between sweeping mansions and high-pillared temples. The silhouettes of the Pyramids loomed, beyond.

Overhead, the clouds parted slightly. A single bright shaft of moonlight poured through, striking her, making her pale skin luminous.

Betsy hurried down the street, to find Tharman.

3

The light from the barn door revealed a Jack Hughes who looked like a demented caricature of a man. His eyes were wide, unblinking, staring madly. His lips were drawn back from his teeth, and Joe couldn't tell if he was grinning or snarling. There were deep, dark furrows on his brow and chin, as though his face was a rubber mask which had been pulled at till it had lost its shape.

In his right hand was the Studebaker's crank handle.

Joe floundered back alarmedly, nearly tripped over his heels. His shoulder slammed against the barn wall, making the slats resound.

'*Jack . . .?*' He fought to steady his voice. 'Jack, what in hell are you doing?'

Jack moved away from the car and, crouching slightly, circled around, cutting him off from the door.

Joe drew back from him, sliding along the wall, shaking.

Darkness started to envelop him as he moved further back into the barn. The foreman's silhouette followed him smoothly, patiently.

A weird noise was issuing from Jack's throat. It was barely human. Something like a purr. Something like the rumble of a large, bloodthirsty carnivore.

Then the voice camc. Strange too. Almost a whisper.

'Gonna get you, little boy. Gonna get you. You ain't never gonna be *my* Boss.'

'Jack! Please!'

Joe's panicked yell was answered by a cold, dirty laugh.

His hand slipped down, and brushed against something. A handle, thick and smooth. A pick-axe handle, maybe.

He tried to grab hold of it, but it slithered out of his grasp, banged to the floor.

A despairing moan began welling up in his throat.

He fell to his knees and scrabbled. Found the wooden shaft again. As he started lifting it, he realized from the weight that the pick head was still in place.

He peered over his shoulder.

Could make out a great darkness looming directly above him. It didn't seem like a man any more. Just a great, hulking shadow. Its right arm was raised, ready to bring the crank handle plunging down.

Joe yelled at the top of his lungs.

Span and swung at the same time.

The pick thudded into Jack Hughes' chest, and the foreman flailed back, spraying blood, and crashed into the wall. He clawed at the sharpened wedge of steel for a moment, trying to pull it free.

Then he slithered down the barn wall and lay still.

4

A hole seemed to have opened in the high pale ceiling of the Underworld. No, not *quite* a hole. More, a mirror, a rippling pool, suspended up there against all the laws of gravity. In it, Marchmont could see tiny figures moving. Betsy Whittaker, running towards Main Street. Joe Danvers and Jack Hughes, fighting in the light and shadow of the barn.

He squinted uncomfortably as the pick-axe sank into the foreman's chest. It reminded him too much of his own death.

Above him, the creature that called itself Kellesh hissed with satisfaction.

'You see? You see? His work *can* be destroyed!'

The words were sibilant, misshapen. The flat rectangular face had changed now. It had bulged, below the golden eyes, into a kind of snout. Sharp jagged teeth protruded from the tight hardened lips. The grey skin had given way in places to a layer of rigid scales.

But Marchmont was not afraid. Fear seemed to be beyond him, now.

'This Tharman? Is he one of your kind?'

'Yes, to my shame. And theirs. They call me Traitor, Betrayer.'

'Why?'

'It is too long a story. You will have to take my word for that.'

Marchmont looked back at the ceiling.

'Can the boy stop him?

'No.'

'Can you?'

'Alone? No again. I'm trapped here for the while, and I am far too weak. Tharman would crush me like an insect, if I got too close to him.'

The scenes in the mirror were fading. Another was taking their place. It was a view of Marchmont's room, and looked like a still-life painting. His own corpse lay, in a pool of dried blood, at the centre of it.

'Can you get help?'

'It is there. I am looking at it.' The creature's mouth twisted into a hideous snaggle-toothed grin, at Marchmont's surprise. 'Yes, old man. You can help me. Even in death.'

5

Alice Strangsom stood like a waxwork on the darkened landing of her home, the knife still in her hand. She hadn't moved all day. Didn't feel any discomfort. Didn't feel anything. There was no boredom any more. No thought, no pain.

Her heart beat very sluggishly. Her eyelids only blinked once in a very long while. The woman was no more. Nothing was left but an empty shell.

There was a soft, scraping noise from Marchmont's

room. Her head turned stiffly towards the door on her rigid neck.

The sound of crashing glass came a moment later, and she suddenly sprang to life. She trundled across the landing, the knife raised. Her free hand reached out and grabbed the knob, turned it.

The door swung open.

Alice stopped dead. Moonlight glittered on the Ra discs the old librarian had plastered across the walls. She could go no further.

She let out a whine between her teeth. Stared with dumb puzzlement at the window. It was shattered. Broken glass lay all over the floor. And in the middle of the carpet was the dark shapeless bloodstain where Marchmont had lain.

But there was no sign of the old man's corpse.

Her head swivelled around, as slowly as a buffalo's. The hand holding the knife dropped gently to her side.

She didn't have time to raise it again, when she noticed a movement behind the door.

A thin shadow rushed towards her.

A cold dry hand gripped her tightly around the throat, lifting her off her feet. Simultaneously, something plunged into her stomach.

There was no pain. Only a sense that her life had begun ebbing away.

She looked down, and saw what she'd been stabbed with. It was a daggerlike shard of glass from the window.

6

Betsy ran in through the swing doors of Eddie's, and stopped. Her eyes widened, and her hands clasped together on her pounding chest, as though she was going to swoon.

She couldn't see the dingy bar. Instead, she was in a temple.

Fluted pillars, as wide as tree trunks, flickered in the

light of blazing torches. The stone idols of ancient gods gazed down at her from every side. There was an altar draped with damask at the centre of the floor. Incense burned on it in silver bowls.

Standing before it was Tharman. His head was shaven to a gleaming smoothness. There were smears of blue around his eyes. His robe, trailing to the floor, was pure crimson, and he wore all the regalia of a high priest. At his feet, his brow pressed on the ground, knelt Eddie Strangsom. Not a barman now but an acolyte. A worshipper.

Tharman's glowing eyes met Betsy's.

She thought she'd faint. She had never seen anyone so beautiful, so magnificent, in all her life. It was what she'd always dreamed of, always fantasized about. Love swelled in her till she felt she'd burst.

'My Princess,' Tharman smiled.

He extended a hand towards her. There were heavy golden rings on all the fingers.

Betsy walked forwards almost shyly and took hold of his fingertips.

'Your old suitor comes. The callow boy, Danvers. We only have to rid ourselves of him, and we can leave here, and be together for all time. Is that what you wish, my love?'

Betsy felt her cheeks flush as she nodded.

Tharman drew her closer.

He waved dismissively at Eddie. The little man clambered quietly to his feet and hurried away.

Then, clasping her hand with incredible gentleness, he led her out of the door and along the street, towards the hill.

7

Joe's Studebaker rolled on to Main Street in a cloud of billowing dust. He switched off the engine and stood up in the front seat, gazed around.

The chill wind had grown fiercer, whipping dried pine needles down the road. A sheet of the *Gazette* flapped by like a tattered flag.

Overhead, the dark clouds rolled and tumbled. Gaps between them were opening and closing, the moonlight pouring through them like a cinema projection – vanishing, only to reappear a moment later somewhere else. Whole sections of the town would glow coldly, then darken.

The street was completely deserted. The only vaguely human figure was the silhouette of the wooden Indian, gazing at him from beneath the awning of the tobacco store.

Joe glanced towards Eddie's, but not even the three old drunks who usually hung out there were in sight. The lights were on, though. And a voice was coming from inside.

8

'. . . *More good news for Cardinals fans! The Gas House Gang continued their romp towards the divisional championship today with home runs from Chick Hafey and Pepper Martin, hammering the Cincinnati Reds into a 7–2 defeat* . . .'

It was the radio, that was all. Joe stood at the doorway and gazed into the bar bemusedly.

Why'd a space been cleared in the middle of the floor? The tables and chairs had all been pushed aside, so that no one could sit down.

He took a careful step into the room, his tread echoing on the bare floorboards. The radio announcer was still chirruping away, but there was no other sound.

Joe sucked in a deep breath, and marched through to the back room. Searched it. There was not a sign of life.

He went back out into the bar. Clicked off the radio and tried to think. It was difficult. He was finding it hard to make any sense of this at all.

Eddie Strangsom's house. That was the next place to go. That was where this Tharman lived.

He began moving back towards the door. Stopped. Bent down, as something by a tilted chair leg caught his eye.

Joe picked it up carefully, as though it were a butterfly, alive and fragile. It was a tiny lace handkerchief. The kind a woman owned. It smelled of jasmine when he lifted it close to his face. And when he unfolded it, there were little pale blue monogrammed initials in one corner.

E.W.

Elizabeth Whittaker.

He ran out through the swing doors and leapt into his car.

9

Eddie Strangsom was kneeling on the landing beside the corpse of his wife when Joe arrived.

His small balding head turned as Joe hurried up the stairs. The face that was revealed was completely colourless, the lower lip thrust out like an unhappy child's. The snail track of a solitary damp tear glittered on his cheek below his lifeless eyes. He didn't make a sound as Joe walked up to him.

Joe felt bile pushing up into his throat. He clenched his teeth, managed to hold it in. Tried to avoid looking at the dead woman, at the ruin of her stomach.

'Eddie? Who did this to her?'

Eddie was still watching him dumbly, his round eyes watery in that pallid circle of a face. But he made no attempt to answer.

All that Joe could hear was a faint whimpering, coming from the barman's throat. It was as though the man's mind had gone.

He glanced into Marchmont's room. Saw the broken window, the pool of dried blood.

'Did *Tharman* do this?'

The whimpering noises became louder.

'Where is he, Eddie? Where's the drifter? And where's Betsy?'

Eddie seemed to think about it, slowly. Then, he started getting to his feet.

Joe followed him nervously as he made his way into the room, past the large glossy bloodstain, to the window. Eddie leaned out of it and gazed west, towards the high, dark bulk of Meacher's Hill.

There was a patch of moonlight at its foot. As Joe watched, two small dim specks moved up the path and disappeared into the trees.

Beside him, Eddie suddenly tipped back his head and let out an anguished howl.

10

Tharman swung around as the thin noise drifted to his ears. He reached quickly across the darkness, touched the barman's enfeebled mind.

There is blood here, master. Death has come.

He saw the boy standing at the window. Saw Alice's corpse in the corridor beyond. Puzzlement overtook him for a moment.

And then, his golden eyes brightened with anger.

Kellesh was somewhere near by! But Gorreq had driven the Betrayer from this world. He didn't understand.

He scented around, trying to find the sombre priest. Little came that he could pinpoint. There was a strange feeling to the Betrayer's presence. Something muted and cold he'd never encountered before. Something neither human nor Incarnate. He couldn't tell what it was, but he realized he was in danger.

He hadn't Fed yet. Not since the sun had set. And controlling Betsy's mind and Strangsom's, subduing the whole town, had drained him a good deal. He needed to be at his strongest, if the dark storm of battle was drifting towards him. He needed to Feed to his capacity, gorge himself.

His grip tightened around Betsy's wrist. Her dreaming smile faded a little, and she gave a small, shrill whimper as he began dragging her up the slope.

11

Treading softly, his breathing short, Joe moved upwards through the speckled criss-crossed shadows of the trees. The pressing sensation of fear in his chest wouldn't stop growing. He'd no idea what he'd be facing up ahead. He'd never even *seen* this Tharman.

The car – he'd left it with its engine running – finally puttered into silence far below him. The wind was still blowing, drawing a thin, reedy singing from the branches of the pines. As though the trees were somehow alive. Somehow aware what was going on, and keening with fear, or mourning.

That apart, he could hear no sounds at first. Even the usual noises of the insects and the nightbirds seemed to have vanished. He strained to catch a footstep. A crunching twig. Anything.

Drifting like a thin mist on the breeze, he caught the faintest murmur of voices, too far away to recognize.

His legs found renewed strength, and he continued pushing on towards the top. Dammit, why hadn't he thought to bring a gun from the ranch-house?

Not far from the clearing he inspected several fallen branches to see if they'd make suitable weapons. They had all rotted away from the inside, and crumbled to pieces in his hands.

This was crazy! He'd seen drifters before. They were almost always ragged, exhausted matchstick men. He didn't need a weapon. He could do the job with his bare hands.

He pushed on so quickly that he practically stumbled

into the clearing. He checked himself just in time, drew back into the shadows of the branches. Looked around.

He was at the top of Meacher's Hill. Strangely, the wind didn't seem to reach up here. Nothing moved except his own trembling arms. The scene around him, the pale, flat grass and the surrounding wall of pines, looked suspended, frozen, like an aged photograph.

He glanced down, looking back the way he'd come. The tree tops below him were still churning frenziedly. *More* craziness!

Joe ran a thumb across his brow, wiping away sweat, and then stared up at the moon.

Maybe he was going nuts. He could only see fleeting glimpses of it as the clouds swept across its face, but it looked huge. Far larger than was possible. The altitude couldn't account for that. Meacher's Hill was no more than a couple of hundred feet tall.

But it seemed as though the bloated, pock-marked globe was close enough to touch.

He was almost tempted. Thought of raising his fingers towards it. But that would be a childish, foolish thing to do. And he'd wasted far too much time being childish and foolish.

He hunkered down beside a thin, gnarled trunk and listened. Was rewarded with the sound of movement in the trees on the far side of the clearing. The rustling of people, moving very gently.

And then a voice. He could identify it, this time, as a man's voice, though it spoke so softly he couldn't make out what it was saying. There was a tone to it, though, which made his scalp prickle. This was no whiney, alcohol-harshened timbre. It was calm and even, and entirely authoritative.

Then he heard Betsy. One gentle word.

'Yes.'

She sounded faintly uncomfortable as she said it.

Joe began edging sideways, moving Indian-style from his squatted position, his elbows out for balance, his toes pointed to the sides. He was breathing so heavily now he was sure the drifter would hear him. It was only loud inside his own head. He had to keep telling himself that.

Overhead, the clouds churned furiously, and then opened up completely.

And his beloved Betsy stepped out of the trees, and stood in the spotlight of the moon, like an actress walking out on to a stage.

Her feet were bare, her clothes were dishevelled. Her long blonde hair hung in vagrant wisps around a pale face that was smeared with grime. And there was something dark staining her fingertips.

But it wasn't any of that that made him tense up and hold his breath.

She'd always stood straight, but now it was exceptional, what people called 'ramrod' straight. Her beautiful face, so wan it almost glowed in the moonlight, wore a far-away expression, and her eyes were wide, unblinking. She raised her chin, and gazed into the night sky, as though she wanted to drift up there and sail away.

Then, she moved across the grass, towards the centre of the clearing.

As he watched, one of her hands came up to the neck of her frock. To Joe's horror, she began undoing the top button.

A sudden rage filled him. He wanted to leap forwards, stop her. Maybe even hit her. But he couldn't do that, right now. He *had* to stay put, find out exactly what was going on.

A third and then a fourth button were eased free. As the final one came loose Betsy reached up and slipped the garment off her shoulders, let it drop. She watched it fall blankly.

Joe's throat tightened so sharply he thought he was going to swallow his tongue. He couldn't believe what he was seeing. A memory rushed back to him. Of that time in the car, after they had gone to the movies, when she'd tensed up and almost screamed as he'd touched her. Pulled away from him. Burst into tears.

She began to work at her petticoats, now. Joe felt blood pounding in his ears.

He oughtn't to be watching her. He ought to be looking out for Tharman. The hobo might be circling behind him right now, to cut his throat. But he couldn't stop.

The pain flooding over him was almost unbearable. Part seething jealousy, part loss. Why had she betrayed him like this?

Her bare arms and legs shone like fine white china. Even now, his eyes prickling with tears, Joe was staggered by the beauty of the sight.

Betsy suddenly raised her hands towards the moon, as though in an act of worship.

And the trees on the far side of the clearing parted.

Joe came to his senses quickly, snatched his gaze from the young woman.

His muscles bunched. He knew perfectly well what he was going to do now. He was going to spring out and kill Tharman. Tear the drifter limb from limb. There was not a soul in town who'd hang him for it.

Why couldn't he *see* the man?

It had to be a trick of the light. But all he could make out, at first, was a huge misshapen shadow. Joe swallowed and drew back involuntarily.

Realized, as it moved further into the clearing, that it wasn't a shadow at all.

He couldn't understand what he was looking at.

The dark mass was a figure. But it wasn't a man. Wasn't human in any way. It had to walk fully into the moonlight before he could see it clearly. And even then he wasn't sure what it was.

An ape. That was the first thought that came to him. A massive ape, as tall as a fully-grown man. Like one of those African gorillas you saw in the dime adventure papers.

Hair trailed from its long arms and broad shoulders. There was a ridge of thick fur on its back. Its knuckles scraped the ground, and it moved at a heavy shuffle on thick, bowed legs.

But the face wasn't right.

Didn't fit.

Smooth-furred, with drooping ears and a long, flat-ended muzzle from which glittering fangs, as long as Bowie knives, protruded . . . it was the face of a dog. A great hound, like a mastiff. Its brow overhung the muzzle as though someone had pushed the top of its head flat.

And in the shadows beneath that brow shone golden, glowing eyes.

Joe's teeth locked in terror. What the hell *was* it? He was frozen with shock. Couldn't move. His gaze flickered back to Betsy.

He expected her to try and run, as the creature moved towards her. But she didn't. Her arms fell to her sides, and all she did was turn around and face it.

It snorted, its breath turning to vapour on the cold night air. Stopped no more than a yard from the girl. Reached out, touched her shoulder with one massive paw. And as Joe watched, she began to lie down on the grass.

A little life had come back into her face, by now. Her eyes were glistening with a pained wetness, and her lips drew back from her teeth, quivering. It was as though she wanted to shout out a protest. But she couldn't stop herself from moving.

She was down on her elbows, her body spread across the grass, the creature towering over her, before Joe recovered his senses.

He gave a yell.

'*No!*'

And he leapt out from the cover of the trees.

His hand swept along the ground, as he moved. Closed on a rock. He hurled it, but it curved away, as though it had been knocked aside by an invisible wall. It dropped short of the creature.

The doglike face swung towards him. Joe staggered to a halt. There was something which, even now, he hadn't expected. Something which took his breath away.

There seemed to be a calm, gloating intelligence in those searing golden eyes.

They blazed like tiny furnaces – so bright, so intense that they seemed to burn holes through the night air.

There was bubbling laughter in them.

The beast parted its lips, bared its teeth. Almost as though it were trying to smile.

Joe's eyes swept the trees beyond. Where was the drifter? Where the *hell* was Tharman? It was almost as if the man had gone and the beast had taken his place.

It turned towards him, shuffling on its splayed feet, leaning on its knuckles. He could smell its breath as it drew closer. It was fetid, like the breath of something that had been dining on rotten meat. Dank billows of steam hissed out through its nostrils.

The heavy brow became furrowed with deep creases.

It stopped a mere arm's reach from him. The mouth stretched open wide, revealing a pink, cavernous maw.

The burning eyes held him.

There was suddenly a chuckle in his head. Then a voice. The same one he'd heard minutes before. The voice of the drifter.

Where's that hobo, boy? Where's Tharman?

He couldn't move at all, now. Couldn't think. Couldn't breathe. He felt as weak, as pathetic, as a child.

Look! Look quickly! You might miss him!

The laughter fluttered through his head again. Then, the golden glow dimmed slightly and released him.

His gaze swam across the clearing. There was no one else in sight.

Except for Betsy. It was crazy . . . but if these were going to be the last few moments of his life, he wanted to spend them looking at her.

Something about her had changed.

The blankness was fading from her expression. The corners of her mouth had drooped, her face seemed less transfigured. The glow had disappeared from her cheeks, and a sick, yellow pallor had taken its place.

Her eyes had lost their drowsy sheen. They were the eyes of someone who was just coming awake.

The creature started raising a hand towards him, the

long, dark fingers outstretched. Blunt claws glittered at their tips. They looked strong enough to tear a bull in half.

Still, he couldn't move.

On the ground, Betsy's mouth worked numbly. She mumbled something he couldn't hear. And she began trying to get up.

The creature didn't seem to notice. All its attention was focused on him. It was grinning hugely, its massive curved fangs gleaming. Its hand kept moving towards his throat. Very smoothly. Very slowly. As though it were savouring the moment.

Joe watched out of the corner of his eye as Betsy made it to her feet.

She stumbled groggily, then lurched towards the beast, her arms thrown out in front of her.

Screamed, 'Stop it!'

And tried to grab the creature's back.

It snarled with surprise and rage. Reared up to its full height, swung around. Struck out at her with one great hirsute arm, knocking her off her feet.

There was a crash as she fell back into the undergrowth.

Joe broke free, flung himself towards her. But he couldn't dodge around the beast. A hand grabbed him by the collar, flung him away from the trees, into the clearing. He hit the ground on his shoulders, and pain slammed through his body.

The creature bellowed, so loudly the trees seemed to shake. Joe blinked sweat from his eyes and looked up at it. It was moving towards him quickly now, a swift, expanding shadow, blotting out the moon.

His hands scrabbled futilely. His feet kicked, but couldn't find purchase. He couldn't get out of the way in time.

The beast was on him again. It snatched hold of his shirt front, raising him aloft like a rag doll. For a moment, he was being held above its head. The clearing span around him. His arms and legs flailed helplessly.

Then, it threw him for the second time, pitching him

through the air as though he weighed nothing at all. He hit the sun-hardened earth at the centre of the clearing.

Everything went dark for a moment. An electric storm seemed to flash inside his head.

It was gone as soon as it had started. But this time, the pain took longer to fade.

He couldn't move his neck properly. Tried to raise himself on to his elbows – he only managed one.

Looked up again.

The creature was hunched directly above him, its mouth wide open, triumph filling its incandescent gaze.

It reached towards his throat with both dark hands.

When suddenly, it stopped, turned its head.

Joe followed its gaze.

12

At the far edge of the clearing, in a space between the trees, was a large clump of sagebrush. And moving through it was a figure Joe thought he recognized.

He managed to catch his breath, and swallowed.

Tall and skinny, silver edged in the moonlight, the silhouette of Erskine Marchmont was moving through the rustling undergrowth.

He'd lost his spectacles. His tiny, weak eyes glittered in his darkened face. He was walking unsteadily, practically falling every couple of steps. Joe wondered how he'd gotten up here. What he was doing here? Perhaps the old man was out of his mind with drugs.

There was a huge, black stain covering his shirt. And something loose and shapeless flapping around his waist. No telling what it was.

Joe thought, even now, of shouting out, warning him to get away. But he couldn't find the strength.

His head fell back against the grass. His senses blurred as he started to black out. But he wasn't giving up. Not yet. He fought his way dimly back to consciousness.

And was rewarded by the sight of the ape-creature backing off, and circling away.

13

The old librarian! But Marchmont was dead. Tharman had felt Alice stab him, felt the man's life start draining away.

He snuffled curiously and peered at the advancing figure.

And could feel Kellesh's presence strongly.

It took him a few moments to realize what was happening.

The Betrayer was playing at puppeteer. Had reached out from the Underworld, taken hold of this destroyed, limp corpse, and was controlling it. The thin arms flapped like the hay-filled limbs of a scarecrow. The gait was shambling and nerveless. The mouth gaped open dumbly, and the dead eyes were filmed over, staring at nothing.

For a moment, Tharman felt an entirely unfamiliar sensation. An icy prickling of fear. Kellesh had never done anything like this before. Not in all the passing centuries. Not in all the time since that first betrayal in Africa.

Then, his mood hardened, and amusement started to fill him.

This was *nothing.* A pathetic trick. A hopeless, desperate attempt to thwart him. What could this brittle, feeble old corpse do?

He leaned forwards, his knuckles brushing the ground. And then leapt towards the figure.

He wrapped his massive arms around it. Crushed its ribs and snapped its spine.

But it kept moving.

It grabbed two thick handfuls of his fur, and its stiffened fingers clung on tight.

Tharman tried to push the thing away from him, but it was like trying to remove a leech. It wouldn't budge.

He lunged savagely at its head, raked his claws down the lifeless face. Its eyelids ripped. Its blue lips split wide open, and half of the lower jaw was torn away. But it felt no pain. It hung on to him still.

Tharman howled. Span around on the spot, trying to fling the body from him.

Its head was turning now, towards the boy. Its shattered remnants of a mouth were moving slowly. A voice, as dry and cold as a graveyard wind, slid up from its throat.

'*Run—*'

He tried one last time to break its grip. Shoved at its chest with all his might. One arm tore free of its socket, the flesh ragged, the stump jerking.

The severed arm clung on, though, the fingers twisting ever deeper into his thick fur.

The lifeless eyes were looking at Joe Danvers now. The voice came husking out again.

'*Run, boy! While you have time,* run!'

14

Joe didn't need telling twice. But he wasn't going without Betsy.

All his pain was forgotten as he scrambled to his feet, hurried to the edge of the trees, where she'd fallen. Shadows overlaid her. He couldn't see her properly. All that he could make out was the pale glow of her skin, a vague impression of her slender shape. She was entirely motionless.

He scooped her up in his arms. And then he was running, not daring to look back.

Running away from the noises of the beast howling, and flesh tearing, bones snapping.

He crashed down the slope. The lights of the town ought to be visible by now, but they weren't. He'd gone down the opposite side of the hill, away from Yewlburg. That didn't matter. Anywhere would do. *Any* direction. The chill wind shrieked around him. The branches of the pines lashed at his face, his eyes. He was stumbling blindly now. Shattered fragments of moonlight rushed past him.

He fell, a few yards from the bottom of the hill. Rolled several times, still clutching Betsy. Got up in one fluid motion and kept on, ploughing through the woods behind the town.

When he reached their far edge, and an open pasture stretched before him, he finally dropped to his knees. His legs were shaking and his lungs felt as though they were on fire. He lowered Betsy gently to the ground, collapsed beside her. He just couldn't go on any longer. The top of his head felt as though it was wobbling loose, and he realized he was close to fainting.

The wind had stopped. The coldness was fading quickly, the enfolding, damp heat of a July night returning. All of a sudden, he could hear the familiar sounds of crickets in the long grass, insects in the air.

Up above, the moon glowed hugely. It was the last thing Joe saw before his eyes fluttered shut.

CHAPTER TEN

1

It was dawn when he woke. On the distant edge of the pasture the sun was pushing its way up towards a cloudless canopy of pale blue. Saffron rays were drowsing across the stiff, brittle grass. Birds were singing in the trees behind him.

Joe blinked, and rubbed his eyes groggily, half convinced that he'd just had a nightmare. Except that he was lying in a damned field, there was nothing to convince him otherwise.

But . . . *Betsy*! She'd been in the dream too.

He rolled on to his side, and was looking at her.

Her mouth was open wide, the tips of her teeth showing. Her eyes reflected the sky.

Joe staggered to his knees, crouched over her. Reached out very gently and took hold of her chin. He carefully tipped her head from side to side. It moved with an awful slackness. Her neck was broken.

He remembered her jumping at the creature, and the beast slamming her away with one fierce swipe of its arm.

Her skin was pure white, bloodless, her face slack and placid. She was still the most beautiful thing he had ever seen.

Tears were already starting to blind him. His nose was blocked, and he couldn't stop shaking. He kept brushing his fingers down her cheek. She was stone cold beneath his touch.

She didn't feel like anything human. Rather like a model which had been created life sized and complete and perfect, but which had never moved or breathed, spoken or thought.

As though she'd never lived.

But she had lived. His memories told him that. They welled up like a tidal wave and crashed over him. Drowning him.

2

He picked her up, ever so carefully, after a while. And began walking away from Yewlburg. He didn't know where he was going, but it wasn't back there.

After a while, he found a track, which broadened to a winding path.

And he walked and walked, not altering his stride, not tiring. His mind was blank now, save for the memories. His eyes were glazed, as though he were blind. He just kept on moving away. Far away. Hugging Betsy to his chest.

3

The sun drew higher. He barely noticed.

Birds circled overhead. A crow with a field mouse in its beak flapped out of his way. A jack-rabbit sprang across his path in a flash of brown and white, was gone.

There were no other people in sight.

He wasn't sure how long it was before he reached the highway. It must have been hours.

There, he stopped.

Just sat down, on the edge of the road, with Betsy sprawled across his lap. He lowered his head and, gazing down at her, became as still as granite.

About ten minutes later, he was vaguely aware of the sound of a car drawing up. He raised his head just enough to see a green Packard slow down in front of him, a bearded old man lean out of the window.

The man got out, took a step towards him. Then saw, properly, what he was holding in his arms.

He wheeled around, and began scrambling back into the vehicle.

'Stay inside, Emily!' he was shouting. 'For Pete's sake, stay inside!'

The motor revved, shortly after that, and the car hurtled away down the road.

4

It must have been another hour when the second car approached, coming from the direction the Packard had disappeared. It slowed down smoothly, stopped about ten yards to his left.

There was the slam of metal doors. The heavy crunch of boots progressed towards him.

Joe tipped his head just a little to the side. Just enough to see two pairs of identical beige pants with turn-ups and yellow stripes down the sides.

They stopped, a short distance from him.

'Who's the girl, son?' a voice asked, cautiously.

Joe smiled bitterly, but didn't look up.

'My fiancée.'

'Uh-huh? Where you from?'

'Yewlburg.'

'Jesus, that really is the backwoods, ain't it? Don't think I've ever been there. Tell me, what exactly's happened to your fiancée?'

'She was . . .' Joe murmurred. He stopped, and thought about it. 'She was with some kind of animal.'

The voice above him remained calm, remote.

'Is that so?' There was the click of a holster being unbuttoned. 'Well, son, you can't sit out here all day. Why don't you come into town with us?'

*

5

Three patrol cars were in Yewlburg by evening, sitting like great huddled insects by the storefronts of Main. The sheriff and his deputies were moving from house to house, trying to make some sense of the stories the dull, drugged-seeming inhabitants were telling.

'So his girl picked up with this drifter, right? And where's this drifter now? No, he ain't at Mr Strangsom's, we already checked there. Looks like he lit out in the night.'

'Where's everybody at the ranch-house gone? You know there's a corpse in a fresh grave up there?'

High in the clearing on Meacher's Hill, the mangled remains of Erskine Marchmont lay where they'd been dumped. The head was practically severed from the neck. The legs were attached to the torso only by a few thin threads of skin, and the chest was completely smashed, caved in, the ribcage sticking through.

No animals had touched it all day. Nor had any insect crawled across it.

Suddenly, the eyes sprang open. The heart began to pump, forcing thick, viscous liquid from the veins. It began to form strange patterns on the ground.

The shattered mouth moved gently, whispering the Incantation of the Door, to open the tunnel to the Underworld.

PART II

HANGED MAN BLUES

NEW YORK, 1958

CHAPTER ELEVEN

1

Bee Boopa Looly. What kinda fuckin' song was that? And *Peggy Stew.* Barney Holly and the Crickets. Jesus!

Tommy Brodski pursed his withered lips and sat down in the alley behind Buffalo's Greyhound station.

His eyes blazed angrily and he rubbed at his stubbled chin, then took a swig from the bottle in his right hand, the brown paper bag scratching against his cheeks. They'd had real songs back in his day. He couldn't remember precisely what they were, but they'd been real good songs, he knew that for sure.

He wiped at his nose with a ragged, filthy sleeve, gazed up at the rectangle of sky between the buildings. The moon was peeping over the edge, as though it were watching him. Hey, maybe there'd been a song about *that.* Moon over fuckin' Buffalo. Ha ha! Moon over the bus station.

He spent a while trying to make one up, then finished off the remains of the bottle and sank into a partial torpor, resting his head against the mossy stone behind him. He stared at the opposite wall.

After a time, the bricks started to glow.

Jesus H., he'd never seen that before! His eyes widened curiously.

The wall started to shake, loose flakes of mortar dropping to the ground. A dead grey light shone through the gaps.

Tommy began to grow uncomfortable. He'd had spiders crawling all over him before, and green dogs chasing him, and once his Johnson had turned into a snake. But this was something far worse.

Realler.

Bull! He shook his head and blinked his eyes, trying to make the grey light go away.

The bricks were falling now. Revealing a tunnel of shiny stone. And a man was stepping from it, into the alley. A large man with square shoulders and a flat, ugly face. He had a jaw far too big for the rest of his features, a pointed nose that jutted incongruously from between his plane-smooth cheeks, and eyes so dark they almost seemed black.

Tommy whimpered and lifted the empty bottle, ready to defend himself.

Stopped, suddenly.

The man was dressed in the smart clothes of thirty years ago.

A genuine, ironclad memory came flooding back to him. *He'd* owned clothes like that once. In the days when he'd had a wife and a family, and a job and a house.

It all came pouring over him and, still gazing at the hulking figure, Tommy began to cry.

2

Kellesh studied the weeping man for a moment, then looked around, puzzled. This wasn't Meacher's Hill, and neither was it 1931. The world had moved on since he'd been trapped in the Underworld, the axis of time and space had shifted. But why had the tunnel brought him out here and now, wherever here was, whenever now?

He stooped over the wino, touched his mind. Realized that twenty-seven years had passed and Montana was far away. There had to be a reason for it. But what?

He was too weak to think about it now.

Hunkering down in front of the old man, he put his hands to the wrinkled, grimy temples and began to Feed. There was plenty in the wino to sustain him.

He'd never been as strong as the other Incarnate. He'd never, even as a priest, had their vices, their greeds, their hungers. And it was as though his melding had gone slightly wrong, as though he were still more human than god. He vaguely remembered drawing back terrifiedly from the Lord Subek, trying to push him away, at the moment of his Incarnation.

Maybe that was why he'd sickened of their cruelty, finally betrayed them.

Or perhaps it was because he Fed on misery. He felt it surging from the old man now. Dine on fear, or lust, or the wild emotions of drugged minds, and you could despise humans for ever. But Feed on their inner pain . . . and over the passing centuries it became a part of you. They suffered quite enough, throughout their fleeting lives. He couldn't bear to watch them hurt more, in the end.

He remembered the first time he'd acted, more than two hundred years after they'd fled Egypt. He and Anubis and Shezmu the lion had descended on a village, in a part of Africa now called Southern Rhodesia.

3

They had both been fear-feeders, like Gorreq. And because the village was alone within the wooded hills, they'd decided to stay until the last human was finished.

They'd slept in a nearby cave during the day, prowling amongst the mud-and-wattle huts by night. They concentrated on the children especially – an easy task, since all the boys and girls under the age of ten slept in one huge wooden shack, raised on eight-foot stilts, near the centre of the village. A double banquet, then. They could feast on the horror of the mangled, dying infants, and on the shrieking terror of their families. When they were done, as the pale-red crescent moon was dropping towards the dark outline of the forest, Kellesh would move amongst the tribespeople, Feeding on their sorrow.

Each night, he Fed more reluctantly. Each night, the sickness grew inside him.

The villagers ought to have fled after the first attack. But they had an old half-mad shaman, who told them they were being punished for some unknown sin, some unconscious transgression. When enough blood had been spilled, when the gods had been appeased, the creatures would leave. He promised it, and they believed him.

On the fifth night, the cold sickness inside Kellesh had turned into a screaming pain. He didn't go back to the cave with the other two, as dawn approached. He waited until they had padded away, then sought out the shaman's hut. The moon had disappeared altogether, by then. The stars were fading, and a faint blue glow was starting to light the eastern horizon. Black-faced monkeys had begun their morning chorus, and the uglibirds were wailing in the tree tops. The sun rose within minutes here. He had to move fast.

The shaman was down on his knees and elbows in the centre of the evenly swept floor, his masked face pressed to the compacted earth. He was mumbling a series of staccato prayers, and Kellesh could hear that he was choked with tears.

The old man's shoulders jerked. The mask came up. Eyes stark with terror glittered behind it.

He started backing away, still on all fours.

'No,' Kellesh said. 'I won't hurt you. Listen to me.'

But the old man was waving his arms in strange patterns in front of his chest, shaking his head and gibbering with fear.

Kellesh had to use the Voice-that-whispers, in the end.

When it was done, he crawled under a blanket in the deepest corner of the hut, just in time. Sunlight had started pouring through the narrow doorway.

He'd have to sleep here through the entire day. It was the greatest risk he'd ever taken, but he had no choice. In his sleep, he reached out with his mind, and felt the tribespeople gathering at the centre of the village.

Felt the shaman talking to them slowly, in a quavering voice.

Felt the warriors daubing their foreheads, their chests, every part of their bodies with symbols of the sun, the Ra.

Felt them painting the same image on their wooden shields.

They picked up their spears, and began to move in single file through the trees towards the cave.

For a moment, Kellesh felt a surge of panic. Felt the urge to stop them, bring them back. It was too late, by now. He watched, through the eyes of the tribesmen, as they burst into the cave, and pinioned his screaming brothers with their spears. Dragged them out, shrieking and writhing, into the sunlight. Watched them blacken and burn. Watched them die.

4

The old wino was smiling at him now, the tears drying on his wizened cheeks.

Kellesh snatched his hands away. He'd Fed until the man was drained of sorrow. That didn't really matter. There would always be plenty more where that came from.

He stood up, looked towards the street beyond the alley and, again, wondered why he'd come here.

His power was at its full. He could almost feel his skin tremble, trying to contain it. He cast out with his mind, as far as he could, and sensed two things. Almost smelled them.

The first was the odour of a great city, all concrete and petrol fumes. It was coming from the south. New York City itself.

The second, deep within the first, was a sharp, unmistakable feline smell.

It was Pashta.

He hurried out on to the street.

He was rounding the corner of the station as a bus pulled in. There was the clatter of the doors opening, moments later, and the stentorian bellow of the driver.

'New York City, boarding now!'

The small, tired crowd of people filing on looked odd to him. Many of their strangely cut garments were of a cheap-looking, shiny fabric. All the women wore wide, pleated skirts, and none of the younger men wore hats.

He quickly realized why. Their hair was barbered into peculiar styles, slicked back and duck-tailed or cropped into upright brushes. Hats would only hide it.

Kellesh smiled querulously. Were men becoming vain once more? He almost welcomed the prospect.

And *that*, he finally realized, was why he'd turned against his own kind, sided with the humans. In all the decades of his priesthood – in the great temple of Kom Ombo, during the reign of the Ptolemys – he had existed so separately from ordinary men. Religion in his time had not been for the common herd, but for kings and nobles, for the very rich. And he, amongst the vast, shadowy pillars of his home – the last temple on the Nile before Aswan – had lived as though in a cold, bloodless dream. Every morning he'd woken and bathed in the Holy Lake, the pool of sanctified water at the centre of the temple. Every morning, he had been dressed in finest linen by his acolytes, been handed the implements of worship. He had burned incense, taken the figurine out of its shrine, washed it, clothed it, prayed to it. Normal life, everyday people, had been unknown to him.

Now, he'd been moving amongst them for two thousand years. And he'd come to love them.

Music was drifting from a radio inside the station. The rhythm was black, but the singer was white. These seemed to be confusing times.

The song trailed to an end, and an announcer began screeching in an argot Kellesh could barely understand.

'Yeah, daddio! It's a bea-utiful October evening here in Noo Yawk City. And it promises to be an even more beautiful night. Dig this, all you jazzbo hep cats whose ears only hears the sweet sounds of be-bop! Get down to the Blue Horn on Bleeker and expand your cultural horizons. For elbowing aside the axemen there tonight, and for the next four nights, you're gonna find première blues artiste Washington 'Jailbird' Davis, telling, through words and music, of his life 'on the road'.

'And here's a few cool chords from his latest platter . . . "*Hanged Man Blues*".'

A needle hissed on vinyl. An old, fierce, weary voice came groaning out.

Kellesh turned away. He didn't pay the driver as he got on board the bus; the Voice-that-whispers saw to that. But as he settled into a seat near the back, a few of the other passengers darted glances at him. They were looking at his grey fedora, his Savile Row blue worsted trenchcoat. A change of clothes was needed, as quickly as possible.

He touched their minds, made them forget him.

The bus growled into life and rolled out into the darkness.

CHAPTER TWELVE

1

He wasn't wearing his wristwatch, so Jailbird glanced at the clock on the damp-stained brick wall back-stage of the Blue Horn club. It was ten twenty-four. Six minutes till he was on. And for the very first time in his eight-year singing career, he was nervous.

That astonished him. My God, he'd been a burglar, a thief, since the age of twelve. He'd stolen cars, dealt drugs. He'd been in fist-fights, and worse, with men who would've given John Henry a bad time. He'd been shot at, and beaten up by cops. Had dogs set on him. Been in jails, all over the country, that frightened the guards, let alone the inmates. And he'd been scared sometimes, and angry others.

But nervous?

He moved through the back-stage gloom to the curtains, pushed them open a small gap, and peered out at the source of his discomfort.

The club was packed with the weirdest mix of white folks he had ever seen in his fifty-nine years. The dim, recessed lighting in the ceiling was blue tinged, and underneath its glow the audience looked like a group of space creatures from the cover of *Planet Stories*.

Mostly they were beatniks – the ones who'd read that *On The Road* book. He'd read it too, and it didn't sound like any road he'd ever known. His roads had been dirty and monotonous, filled with exhaustion and fear. Still, it seemed to mean something to these folks. They were mostly dressed in black, the boys *and* the girls, as though they were trying to wipe out any difference between them. Black turtlenecks. Black pants. A French beret, in some cases. A few of the men sported goatees, while the women favoured kohl around their eyes, and earrings the size of hubcaps, their hair cut to a straight fringe at the front.

It made them look like ancient Egyptians. He didn't have much formal education, but he knew about these things. The last penitentiary he'd been in, eight years back, had been run by a progressive governor, and in between practising his guitar and writing songs Jailbird had spent a lot of time in the library.

If the whole audience had been composed of beats, he'd've had a fit. It would've been like playing to a secret army, with its own uniform and covert language. But there were others.

They were worse.

There were a few aggressive-looking weirdos at the edges of the crowd. A tall, painfully thin boy with glasses and a lantern jaw, who kept hopping from one foot to the other, out of rhythm with the combo up on stage. And a prodigiously large girl in a dress like a polka-dotted tent, who sat with her face twisted into a grimace, peering up at the lights fixedly and winding a napkin between her fingers, as though in a religious trance.

There were some college professor types, who wore tweed jackets with leather patches at the elbows and expressions of profound concentration. And then there were the squares. Guys in suits and short haircuts, who'd brought their girlfriends here to show them how hip they were. And God only help them, Jailbird grinned, if their wives ever found out.

Everything, from the floor to the chairs to the crowded bar at the rear, was painted navy blue under the blue lights. He ought to be grateful they hadn't painted him as well. The only black faces in the club were up on stage, where a new saxophonist called Jerome Baker Klane was winding up his set. He was playing be-bop. It'd been around for a good few years, and Jailbird quite liked it, but it had only enjoyed this kind of resurgence, coast to coast, since the Kerouac book.

The air was filled with smoke, and a lot of it wasn't tobacco. His head reeled faintly. He hadn't touched anything like that since he'd gone in the pen the last time. And before, he'd only bothered with much worse stuff than reefers. Much harder stuff. 'Horse'. 'White Lady'. Heroin.

He had a dense pattern of needle-track scars on both his arms to prove it. Grey wormlike atrophied veins crawled beneath them.

He scratched at them worriedly.

Someone tapped him on the shoulder, and he whirled around.

He found himself looking at a skinny woman, no more than twenty years old, who was dressed in the same black uniform as the audience. She had horn-rimmed spectacles and lank dark hair tied back into a pony-tail, and was holding a clipboard.

She smiled, with what seemed to be enormous difficulty.

'Mr Davis?' Her accent, contrary to her appearance, spoke of wealthy parents. 'I'm Margie Hampton and I, like, I announce the acts. I understand this is your first time in New York?'

She seemed stiff. Almost frightened. He made some people nervous, he knew, with his wrestler's build and his huge bald-shaven head. The scar above his left eye didn't help much either. So he grinned at her reassuringly.

'That's right, honey.'

'Er – cool.' She relaxed a little. Looked down, fascinated by his appearance. The leather waistcoat open to his naked chest. The tattered blue jeans, the bare feet. 'Um, did you come all the way from your hotel like this, Mr Davis?'

This girl was one dumb dodo. Jailbird kept his smile fixed in place as tightly as he could.

'No, honey. This is what I wear on stage.'

'Oh, I see.' She seemed faintly disappointed. Glanced at her clipboard quickly. 'I'll be introducing you in a minute. Is there anything special you'd like me to say?'

'Just get my name right, sweetheart,' he told her. 'That's all.'

She blurted 'cool' again, and bustled off into the wings.

A few moments later, after some drunken applause from the squares and murmurs from the beatniks, he could hear her again out front, talking through a microphone.

'And now the Blue Horn is very honoured to present a man who's really known suffering and oppression. Who's truly seen the dark side of life. And who tells about it in his songs. Washington "Jailbird" Davis.'

Jailbird almost groaned. But what the hell, that was what they were paying him for. The chance to hear a man who'd lived some Kerouac kind of existence. Who'd been out there on the asphalt strips between the cities.

As he clasped the neck of his guitar and walked on stage, a woman he hadn't noticed before moved to one of the front tables and sat down.

2

There hadn't been an empty seat there, half a minute ago. Now there was. As though it had cleared for her.

He didn't understand why she'd caught his attention. She was dressed in the same uniform as all the other beats. But once his eyes had fallen on her he couldn't draw them away.

It wasn't because she was beautiful, though she certainly was that. She was petite, no more than five foot tall, with a wasp-waisted figure like a slender hourglass. Her hands were small and pale, the long fingernails painted a dark colour – either green or black, he couldn't tell which under this light. Her hair was thick, black, lustrous, and was tied into a neat bun at the back of her head.

Her face was tiny, a broad heart shape, with high, straight cheekbones, and a nose so small it was barely visible. Her lips were full but delicate. A wan smile flickered across them.

And her eyes . . .

They caught the golden footlights.

Huge eyes. Barely blinking.

A brilliant emerald green, with little flecks of yellow in them.

Only one thing looked wrong. The pupils didn't seem entirely round.

They looked a little distended. A little oval. Almost like a cat's.

3

In the offices of the Injustice Group, four storeys above Vandam, Martin Rosen – 'Marty' only to his very closest friends – was trying to change the ribbon in his much abused Remington. He hated the chore, but he worked at it, as he worked at everything, with a grim, stony persistence, his jaw grinding as he struggled. He only stopped when he heard Lana slam the front door, far below, and begin making her way up the uncarpeted stairs.

He screwed up a sheet of typing paper, tried to wipe some of the black gluck off his fingers. Then he gazed morosely around the cramped office he and Lana and Denny Price had occupied for the past three years.

There was only one bare lightbulb in the ceiling, and beneath its ochre glow the aged off-white paint on the walls was flaking away scabrously. The floor was covered with a cheap industrial carpet in a disgusting shade of green, but fortunately you couldn't see much of it. What with the cluttered desks, the filing cabinets, the stacks of mimeographed hand-outs, and the back copies of their news sheet, there was barely room to move around. The only attempt at decoration had been Lana's. She'd arranged a dozen little flower pots along the window ledge. She'd tended the plants lovingly, and they were all blooming.

And there was, of course, tucked into the corner, an old gramophone player. That had become important, of late.

Thumb-tacked to the walls were a selection of the posters Martin had designed. There was *Reform Prisons Now!*, with a miserable, haggard face peering from behind iron bars. And *How Many Are Victims of Courtroom Corruption?*, which showed an immense demonic judge pounding a tiny cowering defendant with his gavel.

And, naturally, a score of posters calling for an end to the death penalty. Oh yes, especially those. Their work was to expose every miscarriage of justice they could dig up, especially when the victim had been executed. They were part of a nationwide coalition of small groups, dedicated to the reform of the penal system and the end of capital punishment. The HUAC witch-hunts of a few years ago had shaken things up quite badly; no few of their affiliates had socialist connections. But their support was growing again, slowly. They had a few politicians on their side. And they were currently compiling a dossier of wrongful, and possibly wrongful, executions, to support their claims.

The cops had raided the place three times in the last six months, on a variety of pretences. But Martin was used to that. When he'd still lived at home, his father – an English professor at Columbia – had come to the notice of McCarthy, and Federal agents had crawled all over their Central Park West apartment on a regular weekly basis. His folks lived in London, England, now. And sometimes Martin thought of joining them.

But there was Lana to consider. She loved New York with a passion that astounded him. But then she was passionate about everything.

There was a clatter from the landing. Not the least bit out of breath from the long climb, Lana bounded into the room like some crazy red-headed cheerleader. She threw her gangling arms around his tubby frame and kissed him all over his face, working her way down to his thick beard.

He disengaged her carefully, smiled into her sparkling eyes.

'Have you got it?'

'Yeah,' she grinned, delighted with herself. 'It took a lot of doing. Those creeps down at the Horn are like gods in their own little universe. Or a secret society. Or both. I can't figure out which.'

She handed him a scrap of yellow paper with an address hand-printed on it.

Johnston Hotel. West 125th Street.

'Harlem?' Martin grimaced angrily. 'It makes me sick – the man's a goddamn artist, and he has to go all the way uptown to find a hotel that'll take him.'

'That's the world we live in, Marty.'

A large brown moth started banging around the light-bulb, casting huge flickering shadows across the room. A police car went by with its siren wailing, on the street below.

Lana turned away and started fiddling with the gramophone player.

'You can always catch him at the Horn,' she said. 'That's if you can stand that bogus crowd.'

'No, let the man work. If he's staying uptown, I'll go there too.'

He opened one of the files on his desk and shuffled through it till he found the piece of paper he was looking for. An aged, crackly news cutting that a sympathetic lawyer – a J.C. Irving of Butte, Montana – had sent him. Denny had set off there in the bus this afternoon, to see what more he could dig up.

It was from something called the *Malvern Mercury*, dated July 1931. The headline was: MULTIPLE SLAYINGS SHAKE LITTLE TOWN OF YEWLBURG.

He fingered it absently.

'Do you think Davis'll help us?'

'All you can do is ask,' Lana smiled.

She put a record on to the turntable and set down the needle gently. The hoarse, booming voice of Jailbird Davis floated out into the room.

Got jailed in Montana,
Got throwed in the slam,
Met a kid called Joe
An' that kid was gonna hang.

Oh please, Mr Governor,
Turn that poor boy loose,
'Cause that kid is crazy,
Don't show him no noose.

Martin shook his head amazedly and clucked his tongue. Sometimes it struck him that they were going about things completely the wrong way. They worked their butts off trying to get people to take notice of these cases – and here was a man who made everyone sit up and listen with nothing more elaborate than a song.

4

'*Lawd, I'm so lonely*
Walking down this big ol' road.
Law-aawd, never see my home again.
Law man gonna get me,
Gonna shoot me if he can.'

The set was going fine. Even the most morose of the beatniks were taking a polite, respectful interest. The noise from the floor had diminished to the faintest hum of whispers and shuffling furniture, and Jailbird was getting into his stride beautifully, feeling big and loud and confident.

Just so long as he didn't look at the woman with the cat eyes.

Once in a while, though, his gaze flicked towards her. He couldn't help it.

There were six other people sitting at her table, three of them passing a reefer around. They might as well have been a hundred miles away, so far as she was concerned.

She was . . . it was hard to describe her posture. She was *lolling perfectly straight*, if that made any sense. Her legs, crossed at the ankles, were kicked out in front of her. Her backside was barely touching the edge of the seat, and she was leaning back against the table's edge, supporting herself on one elbow. It should have looked like a deadbeat's nerveless slouch. But it didn't. Relaxed, yes. But there was nothing feeble or lazy about it.

Jailbird came to the end of 'Big Ol' Road', and fumbled the last chord badly. No one seemed to notice. They all broke into wild applause and hooted with approval. Even the skinny, jumping kid. Even the college professors.

Jailbird nodded to them. Took great care to temper the warmth of his smile, look a little rebellious and indignant. Just enough to convince them of his seriousness without frightening them. Then he settled his fingers back on to the thick steel strings, and launched into 'Gaol Bars'.

> '*Gaol bars, you can hold me,*
> *But you can't hold my soul.*'

The reefer smoke was still making him dizzy. Christ, why did he have to be subjected to this stuff? He hadn't even touched *liquor* since he'd got out of the pen.

As he shifted up an octave and began the wailing chorus, he fancied that the needle-tracks in his arms throbbed, just a little.

It was his imagination. That was all it could be.

His gaze slid back to the woman in the front row. He was playing and singing automatically now. This was a number he'd performed a thousand times, and he didn't even need to think about it.

And thank God for that, because the dame was unnerving him completely. Didn't she ever blink? She was entirely still, a statue made of flesh.

Her huge eyes were staring directly at his face. And their greenness seemed too perfect, like the cold hue of a precious stone. Her pupils, if anything, looked more slitted than ever.

A trick of the light, that's all it was.

A guitar string nicked Jailbird's third finger, and he found the mild pain vaguely reassuring. That, at least, was real. Everything else around him seemed to be grainy, blurred and dreamlike.

Dammit, lady, stop *staring* at me like that!

He tried to look away, but couldn't. Maybe she had the hots for him. Maybe she wanted to play Chan to his Charlie Parker. He'd met ones like that before, and they'd usually turned out to be nuts, but only dangerous to themselves, by and large. Usually, they either tried to seem aloof at first, or fixed him with an enormous come-hither smile. Much larger than the winsome little smirk this girl was wearing.

C'mon, lady! Jailbird thought angrily. Try harder than that. Let's see a nice big grin.

As though she could read his thoughts, her lips parted abruptly.

And . . . he couldn't put his finger on it. But there was something terribly wrong about that smile.

Jailbird closed his eyes, turned his head away. Shuddered.

He tried to pick up the thread of the song. Where was he? Which verse? Which bar? There wasn't any sound inside his head except his own breathing. His fingers were motionless on the guitar strings.

He'd stopped.

Just *stopped.*

Carefully, he unscrewed his eyelids and peered at the audience. They were all completely still, entirely silent, staring at him open-mouthed.

He felt his cheeks start to burn with embarrassment.

One of the college professor types jumped to his feet, began clapping loudly. A small group of beatniks followed suit. Then more, until the entire club was filled with applause and shouting and stamping.

He realized what was happening, after a while. They thought that he'd been overcome with emotion at the mournfulness of his own song.

Jailbird breathed out a sigh of relief, and smiled, and nodded to them appreciatively.

' "Hanged Man Blues"!' someone shouted from the back.

Oh Lord, it was request time.

'Yeah! "Hanged Man Blues"!' someone else bellowed.

A few more of the audience took up the cry.

He was on a high now. He was on a roll. He could do nothing wrong. Man, maybe New York wasn't such a bad scam, after all!

This wasn't a song he knew automatically. He'd only recorded it last month.

He picked out the first chords slowly. Filled his lungs.

Jailbird, you can do anything you like.

Except look at that woman again.

5

'This song is a true story, from a time when I wasn't much older than you people. 'Cause you see, my early life was very different from yours. At least I *hope* so.'

That got a laugh.

'It's about a boy I met when I was a trustee in prison once. He was on death row, and I've never once forgotten him. And this is how the song goes.'

He launched into it, in the deathly silence that had fallen over the club.

'*Got jailed in Montana.*'

A fat salty drop of sweat ran down his nose. Which was odd, because he suddenly felt cold all over.

'*Got throwed in the slam.*'

What was happening now? He'd felt fine just a moment ago. More than fine.

But as soon as he'd started playing, started singing again—

He didn't dare look at the woman. But he could feel her bright, insistent gaze boring into him. He blinked, and could see her strange eyes, her unpleasant smile, as though they'd imprinted themselves on a dark screen behind his eyelids.

And something, quite out of the blue, started to go wrong with his right arm.

It was beginning to feel numb and heavy, distant. As though it wasn't his own arm at all. As though it had been grafted on. He remembered that feeling quite distinctly – that was what worried him most. He'd felt that lifeless, disembodied sensation a thousand times or more.

In the part of his life, the long, hopeless part, when he'd been a heroin addict.

That wasn't right. Couldn't be! It didn't come back. Not unless you took the drug again. The sensations didn't return all by themselves.

His fingers felt like strands of dead meat. He forced them to work the strings. Where had he got to, in the song? Time seemed to be going so slowly.

'*Met a kid named—*'

And suddenly, he halted.

Couldn't move his arm any more.

Couldn't get a sound out of his throat.

The audience gawked at him. He tried again.

'*J–jj—*'

Only a croak came out.

He looked down, groggily, at the crook of his right arm. At the distended, grey veins leading away from his needle-tracks.

And as he watched, they seemed to writhe.

Nausea swept over him. He clenched his teeth, tucked his head down. The stage, under his feet, seemed to be rocking like a ship at sea.

Vaguely, he was aware of a few people in the audience murmuring discontentedly.

He tried forcing himself to sing, harder than he'd tried anything in his life. But the word 'Joe' just wouldn't come.

Goddamit, man! You're a professional! If you can't sing this, sing something else!

The next tune came pouring out. And then the next. He immersed himself in each one.

But he gazed at his shoes for the rest of the set.

When he'd finished, and the crowd was on its feet and cheering him, he finally dared to look up quickly.

The woman was gone.

6

Pashta made her way through the Village towards the Lower East Side. It was a cool night, with a hint of frost on the air. But, this being New York, the sidewalks were still crowded, every café and restaurant was full. If this were drab, sleepy London, where she'd been last month, the population beyond Soho and Notting Hill would be tucking themselves into their austere beds by now.

She moved fluidly past the little stores, the barber shops with their advertisements for razor blades, the crowded delis. *Hero sandwich, a complete meal*, read a placard. Cars bustled and roared along the streets, all of them big. Pontiacs, and Dodges, and Lincolns, and Cadillacs. The stench of their exhaust filled the air. It was an odour that was permeating the entire world these days, like incense smoke clinging to fine linen. Burning oil. Billions of gallons of it. Who, in her time, would have believed that the barren desert lands beyond the Nile, fit only for nomadic tribes of heathens, would have yielded up such riches?

It still bothered her sometimes, even after all these centuries – the way her own empire had faded away, and others had taken its place. Being one of the most powerful women in Egypt, in her day, had meant she'd been one of the most powerful women in the world.

As she paused to cross Broadway, three tall kids with black leather jackets and greasy, ducktailed hair appeared in a doorway about twenty yards to her left and gawped at her. Pashta wondered amusedly whether they would have been quite so keen if they'd seen her as she had been, as a priestess, her skull shaven, her face painted to resemble a living figurine.

'Hey, babe!' the one who was obviously the leader

shouted. 'Come over here! Wanna good time? Want some fun?'

Ignoring them, she walked smoothly across the road, between the traffic. When she reached the far side and glanced back, she saw that all three boys were still in the doorway. They'd forgotten about her and were feinting punches at each other, giggling inanely.

What a shame. She'd almost hoped they would follow her. Want some fun? Yes. But not the kind of fun they had in mind.

Her fun was waiting for her at home.

The area began to change dramatically. And the pedestrians around her, too. She glanced down a side-street. The only people in sight were two men in black robes and huge flat fur-trimmed hats, eighty yards away at the next corner. They looked up and regarded her coolly for a moment, and then one of them shook his head. His lips pursed with disapproval, and they turned their backs on her.

They were Luboviches, in the costume of eighteenth-century Poland. She was passing by a Jewish quarter.

And Lords, how that clothing brought back memories. How she'd hated middle Europe. There was precious little Feeding for her, in that part of the world. She remembered the last time she'd been there, four hundred years ago. In a village in Slovakia, forty miles south of Bratislava, a mob of peasants had confronted her one night, brandishing crucifixes. She'd torn them apart like cattle at a slaughterhouse, still recalled their amazed, hollow-eyed expressions.

A few blocks further on, the whole mood of the street changed as she found herself in an Italian district. That was one of the things she loved about New York – the patchwork quilt of different cultures. The men she was passing, now, did nothing to avert their gaze at all. A low wolf-whistle followed her down the sidewalk.

Finally, the streets quietened, the lights grew dimmer. Her surroundings had changed again. Here was another early sleeping population. Storefronts with tangled cryptograms stretched out before her. She was on the edge of Chinatown.

Pashta glanced upwards. A full pale moon was floating beyond the tops of the skyscrapers.

She smiled, then walked to the entrance of an unlit garbage-strewn alley and stepped inside.

Only two windows overlooked her. One was boarded up, and in the other there were filthy curtains that never moved. The short flight of steps at the end, leading down to a small iron door, couldn't be seen from the street. A perfect hiding place, during the day. Pashta walked to it, her step a little urgent now.

She'd leaned a rusting, discarded refrigerator against the door, as an additional precaution. If anybody wanted to get past that, it would take two men to move it.

Pashta lifted it easily, and set it to one side. Then, she pressed her hand to the large, cumbersome lock, and made it open.

She wasn't sure what the cellar had been used for originally. Probably a storage space. But whatever, it suited her needs to a tee. It was completely undisturbed, and it had no windows at all. As she closed the door and shot the bolts, absolute darkness enfolded her. Pashta leaned back against the wall, stretched her arms out, arced her spine, wallowing in the blackness, almost as though it were caressing her skin. She breathed in deeply of the dank, fetid air. It was perfect bliss.

Except . . . she would have to light the candle soon. Damn. *Damn!*

The room she was in was about ten foot by seven. There was a broken light fixture in the stained, crumbling ceiling. The walls were bare brick, veiled with moss and slowly powdering to dust. The uneven concrete floor was filmed with a layer of grit.

There was a honeycomb of rat-holes, but the rats had gone away the moment she'd arrived, except for one she'd caught and teased for a few hours before killing. The sole concessions to furnishing were a pile of rags on one side of the floor.

And, in the centre of the room, an upturned packing crate. On it were a candle in a saucer, a box of matches, a teaspoon, a syringe. A small bag of pure white heroin.

At the far end was another door, again of iron, and even smaller than the first. It too was locked. Beyond it, Pashta's sensitive ears could hear an occasional, faint scrabbling noise, and a soft, piteous whimpering.

7

Darkness was fine. Beautiful.

But it could only soothe her. It couldn't Feed her. And she was growing hungry.

Pashta straightened up and walked across to the packing crate. She lit the candle – her pupils contracting in the bright glow of the flame – and began preparing the syringe.

Done, she tapped the needle idly with her fingernail, gazed intently at the fluid in the stem.

What, she wondered, would it be like to pump it into her own veins?

In the old days in Egypt, when she had been fully human, she had lived her life in a mist of drugs. Hashish, and hemp, and opium from the Oriental caravans. And other, stranger things, made from plants and roots only the priesthood knew about. Her word had been law, back in the city of Bubastis; her anger terrible if she was disobeyed. The nobles of the town had brought her everything she'd asked for.

She had been trying to get – she smiled to think of it now – closer to her god. She'd been trying to see the far side, through her visions.

But now? If she plunged the needle into her arm right now? What dreams would she dream?

She tipped back her head and laughed, her teeth bright as knives in the candlelight.

The whimpering from behind the door grew louder.

She loved this part almost as much as the Feeding. It was so much more fun teasing a human than a rat. They got so terrified it was a shame she and Gorreq didn't hunt together any longer.

She took the syringe carefully in her left hand, her thumb on the plunger, and went to the second door and opened it.

The next room was only six foot by five, and a complete dead-end.

But running down the back wall was a sturdy wastepipe, and Pashta had chained the young junkie to it by his ankle.

She didn't even know his name, or where he came from. Didn't care. He'd sat down in the alley yesterday evening, already in a morphiate daze, and leaned his head back against the wall, ready to doze off. And there was nobody around, so she'd simply snatched him. Grabbed him by his greasy, matted hair and his filthy denim collar, dragged him to his feet, and hustled him quickly down the alley and in through the door before he'd had time to cry out.

Usually, she had to coax her victims. This had been far more immediate, and enjoyable for that.

So tranquillized was he, he hadn't struggled or made a sound. Just stared around the cellar numbly.

And she'd Fed well, that night.

Now, the drug had worn off. His head jerked up blindly as the door came open. He was shivering furiously, and the stench of his sweat drifted to her.

Should I talk to him? Pashta wondered. No, better not. He couldn't see a thing, she knew. Not his hand in front of his face. *Certainly* not her. And fear of the unknown was the most delicious kind of terror.

He couldn't make a lot of noise, either. She'd cast a spell on his voice. He couldn't scream, nor shout out for help. Only whimper. He sounded exactly like a small creature in pain.

Pashta gazed down at him coolly. He was as skinny as a rake, dirty from head to toe. His mouth gaped, his lower jaw shuddering. His eyes were bugging from his head.

She took a step towards him. He didn't even notice it. Her feet made no sound on the damp floor.

He was trying to form words, now.

Nothing would come out but a faint, 'Nuh-nuh-nuh-nuh. Whuh-whuh-whuh-whuh . . .'

And she felt the power swell and fill her, until her human side was overwhelmed.

The junkie flattened himself against the wall and began making a suppressed, continuous whining noise, no louder than a fingernail scraping down a blackboard. He *could* see something now. Her eyes. Her golden eyes. Huge and burning, with narrow horizontal slits for pupils.

It must have seemed to him that they were floating in midair.

She padded gently towards him. His wild gaze followed her. The muted wailing didn't stop.

Then she lunged at him quickly with the syringe, drove the needle into his arm. His head jerked back. His eyes went glassy, and his body slack.

She left the needle dangling from his skin. Knelt down beside him, smiling.

He let out a sigh, and a translucent bubble of saliva swelled to his lips, popped. The swirling hallucinations were taking hold.

Later, I'll kill him. With an overdose, perhaps. The visions at the moment of death are so intense.

But not now.

Pashta put her soft fur-covered paws to his temples.

And Fed.

CHAPTER THIRTEEN

1

Jailbird came awake in his lumpy hotel bed, just before dawn. His eyes opened suddenly, sharply, and he remembered what his ma back in Louisiana had always said, that when people were retreating from a bad nightmare they always jumped out of it.

But he couldn't remember any nightmare.

He lay perfectly still on the sagging mattress, beneath the worn, crumpled blankets. And realized he was shivering. His hands trembled, and his teeth were clenched. And what with his sudden loss of voice at the club last night, perhaps he was coming down with something. Influenza, maybe. Sonofabitch.

He got up, padded across the cracked linoleum to the washbasin, and ran himself a glass of brownish water. Downed it slowly. The hotel room, around him, was a small monochrome box of indefinable shapes, all washed a pale ochre by the streetlamps below. Through a gap in the tattered curtains he could make out the city's skyline. There was a faint mauve tinge to the edges of the skyscrapers. Sunrise was not far off.

The trembling wouldn't go away.

Jailbird sighed faintly. If it was a virus, there was nothing much he could do about it, except . . .

A thought took him.

There was a woman he'd known, back in New Orleans. A woman who'd been pretty old even when he was young. And this old lady had dabbled in all kinds of strange magic. She'd had potions for everything that ailed a man, from lovesickness to ulcers. Madame Lapotaire had been her name. Last time he'd heard, she had moved here to

Harlem to be with her granddaughter, after the girl's husband had died in an automobile accident.

Maybe he'd try to find out where she lived, later today. Maybe she'd have something that could cure him.

He could hear the occupant of the next room turn over in bed and begin snoring. It reminded him of a cat's lazy purr.

Jailbird grinned, walked over to the window, and pulled one of the blinds back. He gazed down on 125th Street. It was pretty well deserted, down there. A garbage truck and its crew were at work, a block along, clattering their bins. And, as he watched, the steel grille slid up from the front of a grocery store, and a bald man in an apron began carrying a box of vegetables out on to the sidewalk. But at this time in the morning, New York could have been a sleepy little town anywhere in the States, if you made the buildings smaller and the roads a good deal cleaner.

He was just about to turn away when a figure moved out of an alley. A man, tall and well built, dressed in a blue trenchcoat and a wide-brimmed hat that hid most of his face. He crossed the paving stones.

And Jailbird couldn't be quite sure, from this distance and in this poor light, but he thought for an instant that he caught a flash of white skin.

The man stopped on the opposite kerb, his head tucked down and his hands shoved into his pockets. He crossed quickly, as though he were avoiding nonexistent traffic. His gait, Jailbird noted, was stumpy, ungainly. He hurried out of sight a moment later.

Jailbird let the drape fall back. Put the empty glass on the dresser. Sat down on the edge of his bed, rested his head against the wall.

The catlike snoring from the next room hadn't stopped. It put Jailbird in mind once more of that strange-looking woman in the club. Why'd she bothered him so much? He couldn't figure it, now that she was gone. He'd seen far stranger things than that, in some of the audiences he'd played to. It went with the territory of any performer.

He started to fall into a doze.

Beyond his door, far away down the corridor, footsteps began clattering up the stairs.

2

Pashta, in her human form, lay asleep beside the dead figure of the junkie, one long-fingernailed hand still resting on his brow.

Her thoughts, in sleep, were as clear and geometrical as a crystal. She was remembering quite perfectly her short stay at the home of the painter Dante Gabriel Rossetti. The river beyond the Chelsea Embankment had stank, and so had the menagerie the artist kept in his back yard. His deranged sister Christina had been staying in the room next to hers, and both of them had wanted to make love to her. 'Not I,' she had told them, smiling. 'But I have a friend who would just adore to.'

The memory faded, and she suddenly shifted uncomfortably in her sleep, her nails dragging across the junkie's skin, leaving bloodless scratches on his face.

Sister? What disturbs you? It was Tharman.

He is here. He has come to this city. I can feel him.

The Betrayer?

Yes.

He is a weakling. This was Gorreq. *He cannot harm us, only hinder us. Is that not the truth?*

I hope so, strong brother. And she giggled. *He approaches my little song-bird now. I shall put obstacles in his path.* The giggle became a high-pitched laugh. *Oh, but this will be a* fine *game.*

3

Jailbird lurched back to alertness as the footsteps grew louder in the hallway and stopped outside his door. He'd shot the bolt and put the chain on before going to bed, and he suddenly felt very glad of it.

Mr Davis? said a voice.

It was a white man's accent, middle aged and gravelly, tired sounding. But it didn't seem to be coming from behind the door.

It seemed to be coming from inside his own head.

Jailbird sat bolt upright, scowling confusedly.

Mr Davis, I've spent all night looking for you. I have to talk to you, and there isn't much time.

He tried to keep perfectly still, but the trembling had got worse. His left hand was clutching a fistful of blanket, and tremors were running right along his body.

Mr Davis! came the voice again. *I only have a few minutes. I'm here to help you.*

'Who is that?' Jailbird blurted out. 'Help me with what?'

You're in danger. The doorknob turned abruptly, and the wooden frame rattled. *I'm not going to hurt you.*

Plenty of people had told him that before. Cops. Warders. They'd always been lying.

There was an old brass-based lamp on the cabinet next to his bed. Jailbird picked it up. Then he got carefully to his feet, went to the door as quietly as he could. Waited, listening.

There was no voice any more, outside or inside his head.

But, suddenly, something peculiar was happening. His vision was blurring, his thoughts spinning. A pair of golden eyes seemed to blink at him, from the darkness inside his skull. Before he knew what he was doing, he was unfastening the chain and sliding back the bolt.

He stepped back two paces.

The knob turned again.

The door rattled, but didn't open.

The man outside slammed at it furiously.

'Cut that out!' Jailbird yelled, stumbling backwards till he hit the bed. 'It's unlocked, man!'

She knows I'm here. She's fixed it shut.

'Who has?' Jailbird regained his balance, raised the

lamp fiercely, and adopted a splay-legged fighting stance. 'What the hell're you talking about?'

Christ, it was another nut! He'd been warned New York was full of them, and now he was finding out the hard way.

The room had become a little brighter. He didn't like taking his eyes from the door, but he glanced at the window quickly. Beyond his drapes, the purple tinge of the night sky had become silvery, the darkness was giving way to faded greys and blues.

Listen to me carefully, the voice said. It had become hoarse and uncomfortable. *Stay away from the woman with the cat eyes.*

Jailbird stiffened. How'd this lunatic know about her?

Don't get caught on your own at night. Stay in the sunlight, Mr Davis. Look to the sun.

'What the hell does that mean?' Jailbird rasped.

I have to go. I'll meet you tonight. I can't come into the club, because she'll be there. But I'll find you. Promise me you'll see me, Mr Davis.

A freezing chill seeped into his body, making his skin crawl, locking the breath in his throat. God Almighty, this maniac was scaring him to death.

Suddenly, Jailbird was furious. He lunged towards the doorknob and grabbed it and yanked.

The door came open smoothly, easily. There was nothing keeping it shut.

And there was no one outside.

Puzzledly, Jailbird stepped out into the hallway, still clutching the lamp. Gazed up and down it.

No one was around at all.

There was another clatter, and the door of the room next to his swung open. A huge bearded mulatto in his thirties, clad in underwear with holes in it, peered out at him sleepily. Saw the lamp in his hand and blinked twice, coming sharply awake.

His eyebrows bobbed enquiringly. 'Problems, man?'

Jailbird fingered the lamp embarrassedly and shook his head. The mulatto kept on staring at him, bemused.

'Who were you talking to, just before?'

'Uh . . .' Jailbird's head spun again. He felt like he was dreaming all this. 'No one.'

The mulatto looked annoyed for an instant. Then, his eyes flickered to the needle-tracks on Jailbird's arms. A sly, knowing smile crept across his bushy features.

'Oh, right, man,' he grinned. 'Sorry to intrude. How stupid of me.'

4

All Martin's life seemed to have been lived in cramped rooms, these past few years. First, the Injustice office. And now, the place he rented two blocks away on Dominick, which was even smaller.

Turning over carefully to avoid disturbing Lana, Martin reached across and picked up the alarm clock on the bedside cabinet. It was just gone seven. Beyond his window, the city air was filling with the monotonous thrum of traffic. The waterpipes behind the wall were gurgling loudly, and the elderly Romanian couple were shouting at each other in the apartment upstairs.

Martin remembered his parents' spacious plant-filled home and, for a moment, he felt a sharp pang of regret. He was being bourgeois, he knew. But he couldn't feel as guilty about that as he ought to. There was a lot to be said for comfortable living.

There *were* compensations, though. If he hadn't founded the Group, he'd never have met Lana. And if he'd been well off and living with his folks, she wouldn't have been interested in him anyway. And if his bed wasn't so damned narrow, her body wouldn't be so tightly pressed against him now, her arm across his chest, her damp forehead brushing his shoulder.

He pecked her on the cheek, then nuzzled her hair absently.

She came awake, smiled up at him, her sea-grey eyes wide and bright.

She always did that, and it still amazed him. She seemed to have no midway period between sleep and wakefulness. One moment she'd be unconscious. And the next, alert and chirpy and rushing headlong into the new day.

She sat up and gave him a big, wet kiss.

'Hi! Been awake long?'

'No,' he grinned. 'I'm still not sure I am awake.'

'Coffee?'

'That's a good idea.'

She bounded out of bed, stark naked, went into the kitchenette and began rattling around with the percolator.

'You going to see Davis today?'

'Yeah.' Martin spread out across the bed, his head propped up against the pillow. 'With any luck, I can catch him at his hotel. I shouldn't think he's an early riser.'

'Denny be in Montana by now?'

'He should be, if he hasn't got sidetracked. You know Denny.'

He was just about to close his eyes when the telephone, on the floor next to the window, started ringing.

'*I'll* get it!' Lana yelled.

She hurried out and snatched up the receiver, listened, and nodded for a few moments. Then she held out the phone towards him.

'Speak of the devil,' she grinned. 'Denny. He's in Butte.'

He took it.

Denny's voice came squawking out at him, without any kind of preamble. 'Marty, you're not going to believe this. We've been going through the old trial records, and the DA's case against Danvers was completely full of holes. Some of the worst I've ever seen.'

Martin scrabbled under the bed for a pad and a pen, and began taking notes.

5

Somehow, as the sun continued to rise beyond the skyscrapers, Jailbird had managed to drift into a doze, a dreaming half sleep. He was sitting upright on his bed, propped against the headboard.

A huge black panther was chasing him through his dreams. It followed him down Bleeker. It seemed to be padding along very slowly, but however fast he ran it never seemed to get any further behind him. He stopped, wrapping his arms around a lamppost, gasping for breath.

It sprang towards him, claws outstretched . . .

He woke, for the second time.

New York was in full voice, a raucous snarl. It wasn't just the traffic. Beyond his window, people were babbling, shouting. There was music from radios. The rattle, somewhere, of a pneumatic drill. The clatter of trucks being unloaded.

Closer, there was a jumble of noise from the other hotel rooms. Someone coughing. Someone running a bath. Someone humming tunelessly. Someone practising, badly, on a trumpet.

Goddamn!

Jailbird rubbed his eyes and sat up properly. His back was stiff and his shoulders sore.

He'd be glad to get out of this place. Out of the whole city. His skin was clammy and cold, and his hands were still shaking. Influenza, sure as shitfire.

But then he noticed something else. Another sensation. Very faint, but real.

A gnawing, somewhere inside him. Where, he was not quite sure. In his belly, maybe. Or in his bones. Perhaps his muscles. Maybe . . . everywhere.

It was like a hunger. But it wasn't for food.

Jailbird recognized it almost immediately, though he tried to deny it, tried to push it out of his mind. He *ought* to know what it was. He'd felt it often enough, before the Demerol cure in that last penitentiary.

The gnawing felt exactly like the first mild stage of heroin withdrawal. The shakes, too.

The hunger was for a fix.

'Dammit. No!'

He clenched his fists and banged them together. Then he folded his thick arms around his belly.

The pain, the trembling wouldn't stop. He couldn't understand it. That part of his life was long gone. He wasn't an addict any more. Hadn't felt the slightest desire for the stuff in years. Maybe there were things the doctors hadn't told him, and he was getting some kind of long-delayed craving, the way people did who gave up cigarettes. Or perhaps all the craziness of the last twelve hours had brought it on.

Black coffee, that was what he needed. And plenty of it. That had always helped. He got up quickly, washed all over with cold water from the basin, dried himself with a small, scratchy towel. And, with fingers that felt numb and leaden, he started to get dressed.

He chose a dark blue silk shirt imported from Italy, his Harris tweed sports jacket, and a pair of sky-blue plaid pants. He was just about to top it off with his bottle-green Homburg, when somebody knocked softly at the door.

His head jerked around alarmedly.

'You awake, man?' came a voice.

It was the mulatto from next door.

Jailbird let out a sigh of relief, then undid the bolts and chain, opened up. The big, pale man favoured him with an enormous grin, and took a step inside without being asked. He leaned casually against the door jamb.

He was chewing a matchstick, working it between his teeth. The yellow tip kept brushing against his thick beard, as though he were trying to strike it.

His eyes were narrowed and had no brightness in them. No smile up *there.*

'Mornin', my friend,' he said, extending a hand. 'Thought I'd be a good neighbour and introduce myself. Calvin Watkell. Everyone calls me Cal.'

He waited, expecting a handshake in return. He could

wait all day, so far as Jailbird was concerned. This man was trouble; the signs were unmistakable. He folded his arms across his chest and stared.

Watkell's eyes blazed annoyedly, but his grin simply grew broader – as though his mouth and his eyes were being operated by different parts of his brain.

'Don't mind me, man. Just thought I'd drop around and see how you were. Sounded to me like you had a rough night.'

Jailbird looked him up and down angrily.

'I'm fine, *thank* you. Now if you'll just excuse me—'

He started to push the door shut.

Watkell's left hand – it was enormous, just like the rest of him – came up quickly, palm flat, and stopped it, holding it open.

'Don't be so hasty, bud.' He worked the matchstick into the corner of his mouth. 'I'm just being friendly. That's all.'

Jailbird felt his muscles bunch. For all the younger man's superior size, he could beat him to a pulp any time he wanted. He knew that. He'd have to be quick though, if push came to shove. If this character wasn't toting a knife, his name was Theodore frigging Roosevelt.

Watkell glanced quickly, guiltily, down the hallway, as footsteps went past on the stairs. Then his voice lowered to a conspiratorial whisper.

'You see, man, I can supply *needs.* That's what good neighbours are supposed to do, ain't they? You drop around to them, you borrow a cup of sugar. They're always happy to oblige. Same way with me. Except you don't want sugar, do you, friend?'

'Get outta here, low-life!' Jailbird snapped.

Watkell didn't move, except to let his gaze drop. He shook his head gently.

'Oh, my poor brother. You're a man on the deluded path of self-righteousness. A man who does not know his own soul.'

Jailbird raised a fist.

'I *said*, get outta my face.'

Watkell straightened quickly, and smirked at him.

'OK, I'm going. But I'll be back. And you'll be pleased to see me. I know the signs, man. Look at your hands tremble. I know you better than you know yourself.'

6

Martin took the IRT uptown, his head still buzzing from the talk with Denny on the phone. He and the Butte attorney had dug up some frightening facts. Such as, the boy's father had died the night *before* the other murders. And Joe Danvers had mumbled so insensibly in court there was barely any record of what he'd said. Which meant that 'Jailbird' Davis was probably one of the last people ever to talk to him.

He reached the Johnston Hotel around ten o'clock, stopped on the kerb's edge, and peered up at the grimy, crumbling façade. It looked as though it hadn't been painted since World War I, and hadn't been checked for infestation in twice that long.

The front door was open, the lobby dark and deserted.

A group of kids on the neighbouring porch stoop were gazing at him curiously. Martin straightened his shoulders, self-conscious under their gaze, tucked the manila file he'd brought with underneath his arm, hurried up the steps, and went inside.

It smelled of mildew. There was no furniture, no pictures on the walls, and the dark crimson wallpaper had greasy patches on it. The sound of someone running up and down the scales on a trumpet floated down the shadowy stairwell. A tiny Victorian elevator cage at the far end of the hallway stood with its gate half open, the light inside flickering dimly.

To his left, a hatch was set into the wall, with two frosted-glass panes, both shut, and a shelf with a bell on it. Martin banged his hand down on the plunger. Waited for half a minute, tried again.

One of the panes slid open.

A portly black woman stared out at him. She wore a strap-shouldered print frock, and had bracelets of pink beads on both wrists and a matching necklace around her wattled throat. A dead cigarette stub was jammed into the corner of her mouth.

Her eyes were angry, and she looked as though she was going to say something unpleasant.

That was before she looked at Martin properly, saw that he was white. Her mouth snapped shut. Her face went dead-pan, impassive.

'I – er—' Martin forced a smile. 'I understand Washington Davis is staying here?'

The woman's blank expression didn't alter.

' "Jailbird" Davis?' Martin tried. 'The blues singer?'

'I know that,' the woman snorted. 'He's out.'

'Ah. He wouldn't have mentioned where he was going?'

'What am I? His mother?'

The window slid shut with a bang. Martin gazed at it a moment, forlornly, and then turned away.

He'd almost reached the front door when he heard the grating of the hatch again. The woman called out, 'Hey!'

She'd stuck her head out of the hatch and was peering at him suspiciously.

'You ain't giving him no trouble?'

Martin smiled.

'Far from it.'

'OK, I'll tell you this much. He ain't got nothing to do till this evening 'cept drag his ass 'round town. And musicians ain't the greatest sightseers in the world. If you want to find him, he'll be in a diner, or a bar. And he won't have gone more than a couple of blocks.'

7

A man who does not know his own soul.

Sitting by the window of a diner on the corner of Lennox, with a half-finished breakfast congealing on the plate in front of him, Jailbird kept running the pusher's words through his head.

. . . *does not know* . . . And since the set last night, that seemed to be the truth.

It puzzled him. The last eight years had been good ones. He'd finally found a career they couldn't jail him for, that earned him some respect, put some money in his pocket and good clothes on his back. He'd always played guitar and made up songs, even in prison. Why hadn't he thought of it before? Now, he'd lived confident and proud for almost a decade. Been able to look people in the eye without wondering if they were hunting him. Been able to walk tall.

And today?

He picked up his coffee and swallowed the last dregs.

The shaking hadn't stopped. The chill in his bones simply would not go away. The ache, the craving, was growing stronger.

The diner was packed and busy, steam pouring from the kitchen at the rear, and the plate-glass window was heavily fogged up. On the street beyond it, the people walking by looked like ghosts.

The dim figures hurried past. Everything moved so *fast* here. As though this place worked on a different time scale to the South. No one ever hurried anywhere in the little shanty town where he'd grown up.

Three tables behind him, a group of old men, drunk even at this hour, were engaged in a heated argument.

'Whatchou talking 'bout, we should bomb them Russians?'

'We should bomb 'em now, 'fore they send their space-ships over!'

'Whatchou talking 'bout, space-ships?'

'They got damned great flyin' saucers! With ray-guns! I sawed it in a movie!'

'That weren't Russians, you asshole! That were *Martians*!'

On and on. The racket was making his head throb. And maybe that was what was wrong with him. This city.

As simple as that. Crazy ladies with cat eyes. Lunatics banging on his door at five in the morning. Everyone here was righteously loony-tunes.

Jailbird clutched his arm. Cold sweat broke out beneath his fingers. He thought he'd just felt the needle-tracks move again.

'Are you OK?' said a voice above him.

He squinted up. It was the thin, pretty waitress, no older than fifteen, who'd been bringing him coffee.

He forced himself to smile. 'Yeah, honey. Thank you. I've just got a cold or something.'

He could tell, by her eyes, that she didn't believe him. But she shrugged. It was none of her business.

'Have you finished with that breakfast?' she asked.

'Yep. Thanks. It was fine. I just ain't hungry.'

'You paid for it. You can do what you like with it.' She began clearing the table. 'Any more to drink?'

'No, thank you.' A thought came to him. 'Honey? You wouldn't happen to know an old woman from New Orleans, lives 'round here with her granddaughter? Her name is Lapotaire. The granddaughter's name is Charlotte Colston, I think. Or Causton.'

The girl's brow creased, a moment.

'I don't know them. But hold on right there. I'll just go and ask my mama.'

She bustled away towards the kitchen with the remnants of Jailbird's breakfast.

When she returned, half a minute later, she was smiling.

'The granddaughter's name is Coulston.' She spelled it for him. 'And they run a store up on the corner of Second and 128th. Houngan's Herbs. It's a kind of medicine store.' She beamed at him warmly. 'Maybe they'll have something for your cold?'

'Maybe,' Jailbird nodded.

He left a good tip before going out on to the street.

8

The air, between the tall buildings, was filling with exhaust smoke. Christ, he'd never seen a town so dirty. The throbbing in his head was reaching migraine proportions, by now. And he couldn't stand up straight – as though the folds of his belly had been stapled together. Jailbird hobbled slowly up Second towards 128th, the tightly packed buildings swimming around him.

A green-and-white bus hurtled by, with an advert for *Chlorodent with miracle chlorophyll* down its side. As he tried to cross the intersection at 127th, a strawberry-red open-topped Chevvy blared at him, nearly mowed him down in a swirl of white-walled tyres. Three hefty pug-nosed Irish cops on the far corner turned and stared at him fiercely.

Jailbird tucked his head down, avoiding their eyes, and increased his pace.

He almost walked right past the shop. It was over on the far side of the street, and its frontage was tiny. A dusty window with a plain black curtain drawn behind it, and a narrow door next to that, the cream-coloured paint chipped and battered, were all that was on display. An awning was folded back into the wall. Above that, the name of a previous owner had been removed, leaving the ghostword SMITH's standing out palely against the grimy façade.

Jailbird crossed the road shakily and took a closer look at the door. The legend *Houngan's Herbs* had been painted in narrow red script over the letter-box.

A bell rang, just above his head, as he stumbled inside.

9

How is life in Buenos Aires? Pashta asked Tharman.

As good as life can possibly be, sister, Tharman replied from the darkness. *The nights are warm and fragrant, and so are the women.*

And Leningrad, brother Gorreq?

I am shocked. Truly. I was led to believe there was no crime in this country. And yet every night, since I arrived, someone has been murdered. Torn apart horribly. The Butcher, they're calling the maniac who's done it. He chuckled. *The dull-witted Russian police are simply not equipped to find such a monster.*

And how, more importantly, is your bird? Tharman broke in. A note of impatience had crept into his voice.

Pashta smirked. *He goes to his own kind for help.*

10

The shop was as small as it looked from outside, no more than a hole in the wall, and very dim. There was a small brass chandelier in the ceiling, with three flame-shaped lightbulbs, but it wasn't in use. Instead, the narrow space was lit by candles of black wax, set beneath multifaceted glass covers. The dusky yellow glow they cast was fluttering, uneven. Jailbird glanced down, and saw faint silhouettes of himself trembling across the floor.

The walls were lined with warped mahogany shelving. There were bunches of dried herbs neatly lined along some of them. And boxes and calico bags with handwritten labels. These were the medicines. But there were other items, too. On the opposite side to the door were artefacts of *obeah* magic. Scowling African-looking wooden masks. Rattles and grass switches. Corn dollies and plaster models of a black-skinned Virgin Mary. A frog drifting in a bottle of cloudy fluid. The saurian, parched white skull of a baby alligator grinned at him, as though its own early demise were an enormous joke.

The air was cloying, thick with strange intermingled scents. At the far end of the store was a glass-fronted counter with large baskets – the kind vegetables were kept in – lined up in front of it, each of them filled to the brim with bizarrely shaped roots. Jailbird recognized one of them. Mandrake. And behind the glass itself were small neatly ranked bottles filled with liquids, all the colours of the rainbow. He recognized these too. They were Madame Lapotaire's special potions.

People didn't just come here seeking cures for croup or rheumatism, he knew. They'd come to ensure the child they were expecting was healthy. Or that the man they loved would marry them. Or that death wouldn't cast its long shadow over their house.

Jailbird doubled over a little more, as the hunger began to chew into the lining of his stomach. His face was awash with sweat now, and his breath was coming swift and ragged.

A curtain in the wall behind the counter moved. From behind it, a tall, beautiful woman in her early twenties stepped into view.

She was wearing a long red dress. Her skin was smooth and light. Her hair was tied into plaits and bound up tidily at the nape of her neck. There was a delicate peach tinge to her high cheekbones, and she held herself regally erect, her chin tilted upwards gracefully.

As she looked at him, her dark eyes became cautious. She remained behind the counter, with one hand on the curtain.

Jailbird tried to straighten himself up, but he couldn't manage it. He took two teetering steps towards her.

An angry scowl creased her gentle features. She obviously thought he was a drunk who'd wandered in off the street.

'Charlotte—?' Jailbird said. His voice had become a pained croak.

She looked puzzled.

'How'd you know my name?'

'You – you wouldn't remember me. You were a little girl, three years old, last time I saw you.' He extended a trembling hand towards her. 'My name's Washington Davis. I used to know your grandma, back in N'Orleans.'

The woman didn't relax any. But the bridge of her nose wrinkled thoughtfully for a moment.

'You're the blues singer?'

'That's right.'

'Grandma mentioned you,' she nodded. 'Said you were in town.'

Despite the shaking and the pain, Jailbird managed to force a smile. 'I'll bet she said she'd never thought I'd amount to anything, huh?'

He got no reply.

He stumbled to the counter, clung on to it. Charlotte flinched back.

'Honey, no need to be scared of me,' Jailbird muttered. 'I'd just like to see your grandma.'

She shook her head nervously.

'You can't.'

'Why not, girl?'

'She's in New Rochelle all day, in one of the big houses out there. A rich old lady sends a car for her every week. She won't be back till evening.'

'That long?' Jailbird gazed at the young woman bleakly. 'No way to get in touch with her?'

'None.'

'Well, could you tell her I called? And that I'll be back this evening. Washington Davis, make sure you tell her that name. Tell her I need to see her bad.'

The woman looked unhappy, but she nodded.

Jailbird thought he ought to add something more, try to explain what was wrong with him, but she was frightened of him. She wouldn't listen properly, whatever he said.

And he needed, *badly*, to get back to his hotel room and lie down.

He turned, and began shuffling back towards the door. He could feel Charlotte's cold gaze on his neck.

Lord, how was he going to make it through until tonight?

The sunlight dazzled him as he stumbled out on to the sidewalk.

He only got a slow, excruciating half-block before his view of the street started tilting sideways. Then, he was falling, and hitting something, and there were noises like crushed matchwood all around him. He'd fallen into a pile of crates outside a grocery store. Faces spun around him, gawping. An angry voice was bellowing something about 'damned drunks'.

None of that seemed to matter. All he was really aware of was that the skin of his right arm, around the needle-tracks, was writhing furiously again.

A pair of white hands suddenly reached down and took hold of his shoulders.

A voice said, 'Mr Davis? Oh my God, are you all right?'

Jesus, why did white folks always ask such stupid questions?

11

Somehow, Martin struggled back with Jailbird to the hotel, curious eyes following him all along the street. There wasn't anyone in the lobby, and the woman he'd spoken to didn't answer the bell when he rang it again. So somehow, somehow, he got the trembling singer into the cramped, rattling elevator, and up to the third floor, and into his dingy room.

Jailbird kept staring up at him feveredly and mumbling, 'You here this morning, boy? You the one who was knocking on my door?'

He didn't have the faintest idea what the man was talking about. Perhaps he was high on something. Hadn't he been jailed for drug abuse, a couple of times? Well, maybe he had slipped back into bad old habits.

Martin helped him out of his jacket and laid him out on the crumpled yellow-grey bedsheets, the exertion making his shoulders sear with pain. Then, sweating and huffing, he drew up a battered chair next to the bed, and sat down with a thump.

Jailbird was quiet, now. The old singer had closed his eyes, curled up his fists, and was lying entirely still, feeble grunts pushing their way out from between his teeth. Martin waited till his own breathing had steadied and his pulse had slowed, then leaned forwards and sniffed the man's breath. He definitely couldn't smell any booze. It would have been better if he had. He started thinking, sadly, of all the great musicians who'd been drug addicts. And here, for God's sake, was another one.

It was hard to stop the sadness turning into anger, though. He felt sorry for the man. But after all the work he and the others had done, after all their dreams . . .

A great cause was about to be set back by one exhausted old junkie.

It was as though he'd said it out loud. Jailbird's eyes snapped open abruptly. They were blazing fiercely, and his expression had become taut. The shivering and the sweats seemed to have subsided a little.

'I don't know what's wrong with me, man,' he croaked. 'I haven't touched drugs for eight years. I don't . . . I don't know what's *wrong* with me.'

'Would you like me to call a doctor?'

Jailbird's gaze became damp and uncertain. 'No. I don't think he'd believe me.'

The singer closed his eyes again, let out a sigh. A faint smile twitched the corners of his lips.

'Sorry to be such trouble, man. Things've just been weird since I got to this burg.' He put his fingertips to his mouth; it was the kind of gesture a child would make. 'Can you get me a glass of water?'

'Sure. Of course.'

There were flecks of rust in it, however much Martin ran the tap. Damn, and he'd thought his own place was bad. He returned to the bed and pressed the glass to Jailbird's lips, held it while the man took a couple of gulps.

'Thank you. I feel a little better now.' Jailbird's gaze drifted to the half-closed drapes. 'I don't seem to be so bad, in the dark. I think I'll be OK on my own. Many thanks for your kindness.'

'Perhaps it would be better if I stayed a while?'

'Don't be dumb. You've done enough already.'

'I'm afraid we didn't meet by accident,' Martin said.

Jailbird peered back at him tiredly.

'I was looking for you, Mr Davis. I work for an organization called the Injustice Group, and we've taken an interest in a song of yours—'

His words dried up as the exhaustion in Jailbird's face gave way to something else. Something close to outrage. The lips parted to reveal a scowl. The dark eyes flickered.

'What're you talking about, boy? Can't you see I'm sick? What is it with this city? Does *everyone* want a piece of my hide?'

He felt for the man. But he wasn't just going to turn around and walk away. Not now.

'Look, Mr Davis. I just *helped* you. I didn't need to do that. I could have walked by just like everybody else and left you lying there for the cops to find. You're a convicted felon – if anyone wants a piece of your hide, they do. And now I'm asking you to spare me a few moments of your time.'

He explained quickly what the work of Injustice was. Then, he took the newspaper cutting out of his file, held it in front of Jailbird's face. The singer peered at it blankly.

'It's about Joe Danvers. "Hanged Man Blues"? Your song? How does it go? "*Head all full of demons, with eyes like devil's fire*"? He was clearly insane. He should have been put into a mental institution. But they railroaded him through court and strung him up instead, just to keep things nice and tidy, I'd imagine.'

Jailbird blinked up at him wearily and shook his head.

'That was twenty-seven *years* ago, man. You ain't going to save that kid now.'

'No. But we can stop the same thing happening again. We have cases going back much further than '31. Hopefully, we can hit Congress right between the eyes, with a dossier so large they'll have to take some notice of it.' He put the slip of paper back into the folder, rested it on his lap. 'You met that kid, Mr Davis. You know the truth. Will you tell me about it? For the record?'

The singer pressed his eyes shut, sucked in a breath. Nodded.

12

It had been September of that year. He'd been passing through Montana the previous August, stolen a car in Billings, got stopped by the sheriff a mile down the road. Netted four years for grand theft, auto.

The shakes and the cold clamminess were returning gently, but he ignored them. Martin had taken out a pen and was making notes. The boy could do what he liked, so long as they got this over with quickly.

It was all so clear in his head, though. That was the thing that surprised him. Jailbird could remember it as though it had only happened yesterday.

He was always careful to stay out of trouble while he was serving time, so by the spring he'd been made a trustee. His job had included taking meals to the cells on death row. And the guards had warned him about Cell 2. 'You'd better be careful when you're in there,' they'd said. 'That's one of the worst killers we've ever had in this state. Massacred practically half the folks in his town. His pa, girlfriend, her ma, some ranch foreman, a bunch of other people. Tore 'em to pieces, some of 'em. Probably ate some of 'em, too.' He was shaking as he got nearer the cell. He was expecting some kind of drooling monster. But all he saw, when he looked inside, was a handsome straw-haired white boy about twenty years old, just sitting there. Just . . . sitting.

'He didn't even move when I opened up the door and put his food in. But I got out of there real fast.'

The next day, he'd been going through the same routine when the boy had suddenly looked up at him. Jailbird had jumped back as though he'd just heard a rattler underneath his feet. And the boy had smiled. 'It's OK,' he'd said. 'I ain't going to hurt you.'

And Jailbird replied, 'You sure about that, buddy? What I hear, you've killed a lot of people.'

'His expression suddenly got tearful. He stared at his knees and began rocking from side to side. "It wasn't me," he said. "It was the creature." Then he clammed up again. But over the next few days, he opened up to me more and more. Mostly he'd talk crazy stuff about monsters and demons. But sometimes he'd make sense, start telling me about real people. A guy named Eddie. And a girl called Ellen. And a drifter.'

The shivering was taking hold of his whole body, now. Freezing cold sweat was trickling down his cheeks.

'He was sure it was the drifter who'd killed all those folks.'

Martin leaned forwards, above him, his bearded face screwed up with concentration.

'Did he mention a name?'

Jailbird's head began to whirl. Everything had been so clear, just a moment ago. Not now. He struggled to pull the memory out of the swirling morass.

Th— something. Thurber or Thorman or . . .

Abruptly, he heard a voice inside his head. Definitely inside his head this time. But not the man's hoarse timbre of this morning. It was a woman's voice, purring and unpleasant.

Feel my claws, little bird.

And before he could speak another word, the pain was tearing into him, from nowhere. Ripping through his stomach. As though something alive and razor-clawed was trying to tear his insides into shreds. He'd never felt such complete agony before.

The room blurred to absolute darkness, and streaks of red danced before his eyes, like deep slashes filled with blood.

13

Martin knocked over his chair, getting up. The file tumbled off his knees, its contents scattering on the floor, forgotten now.

He tried to grab hold of Jailbird's shoulders, but the man's big catcher's-mitt hands jerked upwards, closed around his wrists. They started tightening so fiercely he thought his bones would break. He yelped and struggled till he was free, stood back from the bed.

He gazed down numbly as the man continued to writhe. Jailbird was clutching his belly, pulling his knees up to his chest, rocking in agony on the mattress, the cords in his neck standing out like hawsers.

It was heroin withdrawal. It was the only thing it could be. The man was going into cold turkey. As he watched, the singer threw his head back wildly. His eyes snapped open, bulging and red veined now. And his mouth forced itself wider and wider until the joints started to make a creaking noise.

What was he supposed to do? He couldn't call a doctor. It would mean a trip to hospital, then a visit from the police, and Jailbird would be living up to his nickname again, back in the pen.

Before Martin's horrified gaze, dark smudges of red began appearing on the man's shirtsleeves, at the crooks of the elbows. They started growing, spreading. Blood was flowing, underneath the blue silk. The needle-tracks in his arms had opened.

The door creaked suddenly, behind him. Martin spun around, and found himself facing a tall, bearded mulatto.

Who did nothing. Leaned casually against the doorpost. His gaze flickered down to the man on the bed, then back, and regarded him coldly.

What the hell was going on here?

'Can't you see what's happening?' Martin stammered. 'Get help!'

But the mulatto just grinned.

'Man, you're looking at it. I'm the only help he'll ever need.'

*

14

By three in the afternoon, Martin was sitting in front of his office window – gazing down bleakly at a truck driver unloading crates of Coca-Cola bottles in the street below – when Lana came back finally from a meeting with the printers.

'How did it go?' she asked, dumping her purse on her desk.

He didn't turn to face her.

'The man's about as unreliable a source as you could look for.'

'Why's that?'

'He's a stone-cold junkie, for God's sake. He went into convulsions in his hotel room, right in front of my eyes.'

He sighed exhaustedly and rubbed at his temples, finally turned around. Gazed about the office and wished, for the thousandth time, that he was somewhere else. In Central Park West. In London.

Lana was motionless, her face pale and drawn. He'd never seen her look so discouraged before.

'I've got some notes,' he said, trying to cheer her up. 'Other people he mentioned, who might be able to help us. First names only, I'm afraid.' They were wadded in his pocket. He took them out and unscrewed them. 'I presume they're all from Yewlburg. There's an Eddie. An Ellen. They might still be alive. And something about a drifter, though we didn't have time to get into that properly. Let's give Denny a call.'

Lana picked up the phone and dialled, had a brief conversation with a receptionist in Butte.

'He's out with the lawyer all day,' she told Martin. 'He won't be back until this evening. Should I leave him a message to call us?'

Martin nodded.

CHAPTER FOURTEEN

1

Night fell as softly as a black gauze veil dropping over a lamp, breaking the city's glow into a million tiny squares of light. The sounds of the traffic became muted, and the air grew cooler.

Pashta shivered a little in the chill as she came out of the alley, and found herself, for a moment, longing for the endless, drowsy warmth of her homeland, far away. Her breath made a delicate mist in front of her face. The fine hairs prickled on her arms.

She glanced around quickly to make sure no one had seen her emerging. There was no need to worry. The cold had driven everyone indoors. There were no old women sitting on the porch steps, no children playing. A police car rolled by at the intersection, but the driver and his partner were talking about their wives – her sharp ears could pick out every word of their conversation – and they took no notice of her.

She glanced in the direction of the Village, smiled. And immediately sensed an annoyed stirring in her head.

It was her brothers, reaching out and touching her. It was unlike them to interfere, particularly Gorreq, who was normally so bold, so devil-may-care. But they were both growing impatient.

Go, their distant voices told her. *Go!*

She started moving west and upwards at a smooth, rapid jog, slowing only to cross the busier roads. Her feet made barely any sound on the grimy sidewalks. Her movements were as even and rhythmic as though her limbs were well-oiled machines. And she did not tire, though she passed block after block. There was a complete economy, a perfect balance and grace to her running. Her own physical perfection delighted her, as always.

It took her a bare handful of minutes to reach her first destination.

She came to a halt at a deserted corner under a broken streetlamp on Vandam. Raised her left hand and studied it intently. It already seemed as dim as a shadow.

She glanced up at the brightly lit office window of the Injustice Group, a mere hundred yards away. And a faint sense of regret overtook her. She hated to rush things. She loved to tease, torment. To play. It was her nature.

Go now! Tharman's voice chided, inside her head. *Enough of games. Do what you came for.*

Pashta hung back for just a moment longer, feeling the sublime strength coiling in her limbs.

And then she was moving again, like a released spring. Into a nearby alley. Up the rusting fire escape, almost faster than the eye could follow. Towards the fourth storey.

2

Martin and Lana shifted uncomfortably on their hard wooden office chairs, glanced at each other and frowned. It seemed impossible to feel so tired merely from inactivity, but they were both exhausted. The empty cartons of a take-away Cantonese meal lay scattered on Martin's desk, the smell of drying sauce fouling the already stuffy air. The window was open only a crack. He'd wanted to open it more, but the heating wasn't on in the building, and it had grown too cold outside. And there were times, such as now, when Lana just *hated* the cold.

'Perhaps Denny didn't go back to the office?' she suggested drowsily.

She'd been perhapsing for the last hour, and was beginning to get on his nerves. That hurt, to love her so much and still find himself irritated by her every so often. It made their relationship seem mundane and workaday, like a worn-out, conventional marriage, and he disliked the feeling intensely.

When the phone started ringing, they both jumped. Lana, as always, got to it first, snatched it up.

She smiled. 'And where the hell have *you* been?' she said into the receiver.

She held it out towards him. 'It's Denny.'

And Martin stood up and was just starting to cross the room . . . when the lights went out.

He stumbled into something. Denny's empty desk. Banged his shins and swore.

Ahead of him, in the sudden blackness, Lana was shouting, 'Hello? *Hello?*'

Martin's eyes adjusted slowly. There was still enough light coming in from the street to make out shapes and silhouettes.

He groped his way around the desk, said to Lana's outline, 'What's happened?'

She sounded puzzled. 'Phone's gone dead.'

Martin stood quite still for a moment, making sure of his balance. Then, he glanced towards the window and the building opposite. The lights across the street were still on. Maybe it was just this block.

But why had the phone stopped working? A shorted fuse wouldn't do that.

He could almost feel the darkness closing in around him.

'I've never mentioned this before,' he grinned stupidly. 'But actually, I'm a little afraid of the dark.'

He expected her to laugh at him, but when Lana replied her voice was understanding, soothing.

'My brother's got the same problem. Hold on, I've got some candles somewhere.'

She moved away from her desk and began hunting through the filing cabinets.

She found them in a bottom drawer, walked around the room confidently, lighting them one by one. There were four of them. They didn't cast much light at all, but they started letting out a cloying, fatty odour.

'What the hell is that stink?'

'They're cheap,' she said. 'What do you expect?'

'I think this is taking solidarity with the poor a little too far. I'm opening the window.'

He groped his way to the sash. The swollen, rotting frame made a grating noise as he started to push it up.

He'd only got it open six inches when he let out a yelp. Something warm and soft pushed past his hand and jumped into the office.

3

'It's a cat,' Lana said, the pitch of her voice rising with delight.

'Jesus! It scared the living daylights out of me!' Martin grabbed the window frame for support, his hands shaking. 'What the hell's it doing up here?'

But Lana wasn't listening to him. She was crouching down now, moving closer to the creature and trilling.

'Here, puss cat. Here, kitty.'

It was huge. Martin caught a glimpse of a long sinuous black shape and a pair of luminous green eyes before the animal vanished under a desk.

'It'll find its own way out,' he said. 'Let's see if we can get Denny back.'

He staggered towards the phone, picked it up. It was still dead, the line humming like a trapped insect.

'Damn it!' He glanced over his shoulder. 'Lana, will you leave that thing alone?'

The cat's eyes were visible again, brighter than before. It had climbed on to a filing cabinet right beside the door and was edging towards a candle Lana had placed there.

'No, kitty,' Lana was saying. 'Stay away from that. It's hot.'

Martin slammed the phone's cradle down several times, trying to get a clear line.

'What's the number of the office?' he asked. 'Maybe I can get a line for Butte.'

There was a sudden, angry hissing. Then a yell of pain that made him whirl around. Lana was clutching at the fingers of her right hand, backing away from the creature on the cabinet.

'It scratched me. Bad cat!'

'Lana, leave it *alone*. What's the number of the office?'

She spun around, to vent her annoyance on him.

But all of a sudden, Martin wasn't looking at her any more.

He was staring over her shoulder, at the cat.

Its eyes no longer seemed green. They had started to change colour, to a burning, glowing gold. And, as he watched, the creature raised one of its front paws and held it directly in the yellow candle flame. Keeping it quite still. Watching it coldly with those terrible, bright eyes. It turned the paw calmly, scorching it all over.

The telephone receiver dropped from Martin's limp grasp. He tried to say something, warn Lana what was happening, but it felt as though a sheet of ice had formed across his throat.

All he could do was stare, aghast, his own eyes widening and his knuckles turning pale.

The candle's flame broadened as the animal's paw caught fire.

Lana blinked at him bewilderedly, wondering what he was staring at. And then, she must have noticed the brightening glare behind her, because she swung back towards the cabinet and let out a shrill scream.

The cat took its blazing paw out of the flame, stood up on all fours, and arched its back. The fire was crackling across its fur, spreading all over its body, turning it into a living, blazing arc.

It didn't seem to be in any pain at all.

Why doesn't it start howling? Martin thought, his limbs frozen, his heart pounding. Why doesn't it hurt, or die?

Lana started backing away quickly. She collided with the edge of the desk behind her. Let out a gasp and stumbled.

The creature sprang at her, its claws outstretched. It

landed squarely on her chest and hung there like some massive, horrific brooch.

The front of her thin sweater began to smoulder. She let out a wail and scrabbled at the creature with her hands.

It was all happening so fast.

The cat jumped off her, bounded around the room, setting alight books, papers, desks . . . everything it landed on. A flickering glow started to fill the office. Smoke curled into the dim air.

Lana was burning now, the flames spreading rapidly towards her neck.

And finally, Martin unfroze. He leapt towards her. Beat at her sweater with his hands, ignoring the pain. Tried to smother the fire with his arms.

There was a swift, sharp agony between his shoulders as the cat landed on his back. It was gone before he could do anything about it.

He was burning, now. He tried to pull his shirt off, but was too frightened to manage it. The fabric wouldn't tear. The buttons wouldn't give. He began to howl as the skin of his back was scared.

He knew, through the panic, what he ought to do. Roll on the floor. Put out the fire that way. But not here. The whole room was going up. He clenched his teeth against the hammering pain, grabbed hold of Lana by the wrists, and began dragging her towards the door.

It was impossible. She was writhing furiously, wailing like a banshee now. All her hair was on fire, her face twisting to a charred ruin, the skin turning black, blistering and cracking.

Flame exploded abruptly from the cabinet nearest the door, setting the frame ablaze. Blocking their one way out.

Martin squeezed his eyes shut, spun around blindly, still clinging on to Lana as though his life depended on it. He started staggering in the direction he thought the window lay.

His own hair was on fire, now. And all his clothes.

His legs finally went out from under him as the agony, the incredible torment, swamped his body.

He hit the floor, without feeling it. Opened his mouth and sucked in hot smoke. There was a ghastly rattle as his lungs scorched. He couldn't feel Lana beneath his grasp any more. Couldn't hear her.

The flames moved in around them both, like wolves closing for the kill.

4

Exhausted and shaken, and still feeling a little dislocated from his body by the drug, Jailbird stood back stage of the Blue Horn's curtains while the support band hammered into their last number.

Lord, what was happening to him?

He wouldn't have come at all, this evening. Would have called the engagement off – the first time in his career he'd ever have done so. Except that character from last night, the one who'd banged on his door, had said he would be around after dark. And, crazy or not, he'd offered help.

The good Lord knew he needed help right now, and he wasn't fussy where it came from.

It wasn't only that, Jailbird realized, which had brought him here tonight. Not just that he wanted to confront the face behind the door. It was an attempt, on his part, to keep himself on the rails. On the straight track. Keep living the same way he'd done ever since he'd come out of prison. Everything seemed to have gone so quickly and badly wrong, in the past twenty-four hours.

It was as though he'd never really escaped his tangled danger-ridden past. As though it had been waiting for him here in New York. Had leapt out of the city shadows to grab him. 'Hey, you're that Jailbird Davis, ain'tcha, man? Don't I *remember* you from somewhere?'

No, dammit! This was *worse* than anything he'd known before.

Watkell hadn't dosed him up too heavily. The high had started fading soon after evening fell, and when he'd drifted out of it he'd found that the dealer had taken most of the money from his wallet, left a small cellophane bag of innocuous looking pale brown granules on the cabinet beside his bed. He'd been sufficiently in his right mind to flush it down the can immediately. He wasn't going to let *that* monkey climb on to his back again without a fight. But he could still feel the effects of the drug. The drowsiness. The gentle glow it lent to everything. Could still feel its presence, like an energy-sapping parasite, deep within his body.

He ought to have been filled with a dozen conflicting emotions. Fear, and bewilderment, and loathing, and anger. But he wasn't. Just a dull, passive unease. That was the heroin. That was what it did to you. It stopped you feeling. Anaesthetized you against the pressures of the outside world.

Tonight's was probably going to be a lousy performance, without emotion or soul. He hadn't even bothered to change into his stage clothes. But at least he was here, and persevering, rather than mouldering in that seedy hotel room. Try to stay with other people, that crazy man behind the door had said. Don't get caught on your own at night.

He was just about to peek out through the curtains when he realized the be-bop combo had stopped playing. The woman with the horn-rimmed glasses, Margie Hampton, came across to him and tapped him on the shoulder, reminding him that he was on next.

He tried to compose himself. But just as he was stepping out on stage, something else the man had said came floating back to him.

I can't come into the club tonight . . . because she'll *be there.*

5

He stopped under a spotlight, jolting with alarm. Practically stepped back into the wings. Only the residual numbness of the drug stopped him.

Quickly, frightenedly, he scanned the audience. The front row in particular.

The crowd was pretty much of the same composition as last night, but even denser. Word had obviously got out that his show was worth catching. The fat, miserable-looking girl in the polka-dot frock was there again, still wringing her handkerchief. And he thought he recognized some of the professor types.

But he couldn't see the woman with the cat eyes.

The air was filled with sidling blue layers of cigarette and reefer smoke, and in the dimness at the rear, near the bar, the tables had been removed and there was standing room only. The people back there were no more than tightly packed silhouettes, like a dark massive body with a hundred bobbing heads. It was impossible to tell who exactly was out there.

Jailbird started walking again till he reached the centre of the stage, his movements slow and deliberate. The crowd was applauding him wildly by now, but it made no impression on him. Didn't calm him or please him in any way. He cradled his guitar, cleared his throat, and, his eyes still scanning the audience furiously, drifted into his first number.

It went fine. And the next.

Where *was* the woman? It would have been bad enough if she'd been sitting in the front row, staring at him . . . but this was, somehow, even worse.

He sang 'Gaol Bars', and the crowd didn't notice he was unemotional and numb, seemed to think he was doing just fine. Perhaps his numbness was only apparent on the inside.

He tried one of his very first songs on them, 'Lyin' in the Sun', and they liked that too. The strange fat girl in the polka-dot frock got up halfway through and hurried out, making a commotion as she pushed between the crowded tables, but it seemed to be for reasons entirely of her own.

Look to the sun, he remembered the man behind the door saying, as he strummed the final chords. *Look to the sun*. What the hell did that mean?

How much time had passed now? Ten minutes? Fifteen? The set was gliding along like a boat on a river. He was going to get away with it.

So long as he didn't have to play—

'"Hanged Man Blues"!' shouted a drunken man's voice, from the back of the audience. 'Hey, daddio, let's hear "Hanged Man Blues"!'

6

Kellesh was leaning weakly against the wall of the back alley, a mere dozen yards from the stage door. He felt so tired and hungry he could barely stand. How long had he been in this city now? No more than a day. It seemed far longer.

The sun had almost caught him as he'd hurried out of the singer's hotel on 125th. He'd only managed to get two blocks downtown before he had been forced to take cover. Thankfully, there'd been a closed, deserted house near by, the front door padlocked and the windows boarded up. He'd used the last of his strength to conjure open the lock, and had slept the entire day on the grimy, mildewed hallway floor, the noises of the city rumbling past outside. He'd emerged as soon as night had fallen, but he hadn't had the chance to Feed, so far. The city was too busy, the crowds too dense. As though the mortals here lived like a pack of animals, afraid to wander the streets on their own.

Now, *he* was becoming afraid. Pashta was very close. He could feel her presence; it was like a rasping against his skin. And if he was going to fight her – if he was going to have any chance of slowing her down – he'd have to be as strong as he could get.

He looked up worriedly as another door, a fire exit, burst open further down the alley and someone hurried out.

It was no one to worry about, he saw. Only a large girl in a loud polka-dot dress, twisting something between her short, stubby fingers.

Kellesh sank back into the shadows, waiting for her to go away.

She didn't. With her back to him, she suddenly hunkered down, her dress brushing the filthy cobbles of the alley, and folded her arms around her head and began crying. It was a piteous wailing, like the crying of a bewildered child. Kellesh could feel the misery rising off her in waves. It seemed to brush against his lips, linger on his tongue. The hunger in him sharpened, became insistent.

Very gently, he reached out with his mind and touched hers. The taste of her sadness both sickened and excited him.

The girl was retarded, and her weight was glandular, not caused by over-eating. She'd never had a boyfriend. But, a month ago, one of her neighbourhood's most handsome young men had seduced her. She'd begun making plans, the moment he had gone, for the future, marriage, children. The crowd at the corner drugstore had delighted in telling her, later, that he'd done it for a bet. And she had been busting into tears, utterly miserable, ever since.

Kellesh's gorge rose at the thought of using this pathetic girl. It felt like scavenging, as though he were a jackal closing in on the scent of a rotting carcass.

But he had no choice. He increased his grip on her mind, holding her still and passive. And, moving very softly along the alleyway, he walked up behind her, placed his hands on the back of her head, and began to Feed.

*

7

For a moment, Jailbird thought he could see the woman with the peculiar eyes. Just her silhouette, moving through the crowd at the back. The same height, the same tied-back hair. But so many of these beatniks looked similar. He couldn't be sure.

She disappeared behind a tall man, and he lost sight of her altogether.

Several more people were taking up the cry, now. 'Hanged Man Blues'! 'Hanged Man Blues'! There was no way he was going to get out of it.

Jailbird scanned the rear of the club hopelessly, trying to catch another glimpse of that petite frame, but a lot of people were on their feet now, blocking his view.

A bead of sweat trickled along his eyebrow.

Screw it! He dropped his gaze.

Pressed his thumb down on the top string of his guitar. The calloused pad was so slick with perspiration it slipped away with a dull twang.

His arms were pouring wet. The sickness and the shakes were returning with a vengeance.

He looked up again. Couldn't see the back of the club at all, now. His sight was blurring.

He forced open his mouth desperately. Tried to sing.

'*Went—*'

He suddenly felt as though he were choking.

No. As though he were *being* choked, by invisible hands.

He couldn't breathe. Nor get his lungs to work.

Almost before he knew what was happening, the stage, the club, the dim blue lights, were spinning around him, whirling madly. He felt a sharp jolting sensation, then a pain in his right leg.

He'd stumbled, fallen on one knee. Dropped his guitar. Knocked over the microphone. The speakers to either side of him were ringing angrily with feedback. The crowd was gasping, now. He could feel his palms scraping on the rough wood of the stage.

He tried to look up, but could see nothing except a blur of jumbled faces.

Vaguely, he was aware of the girl in the horn-rimmed glasses hurrying out on stage and bending over him.

'Put some lights on!' he could hear her yelling. 'Put the damned lights on!'

He tried to climb back to his feet, but he just stumbled down again. Margie's hands were all over him, trying to restrain him. He pushed them away.

He could see one face now. Make it out very clearly. It was moving towards him smoothly through the crowd. Heart shaped and delicate, a gloating smile on the full lips.

It was the woman with the cat eyes.

Someone back stage finally threw a switch. All the spotlights, above and around the stage, flared on, hot and blindingly bright, like tiny suns.

The woman drew back a little. Bared her teeth.

He fancied he could almost hear her let out a sharp hiss. She raised one arm to protect her face.

Jailbird clambered to his feet and began to stumble, as fast as he could, through the curtains towards the stage door.

8

In the alley, the girl was nearly drained, and Kellesh was just beginning to release his grip when the stage door clattered open. Limping, and clutching at his chest, a wild-eyed Jailbird Davis staggered into the night air.

The man gazed at him terrifiedly.

Kellesh began to straighten, but it was too late. Davis had already seen him crouched over the girl.

The Lords only knew what he imagined was happening. But it seemed to make the big singer even more frightened than he already was. The man put his palms out in front of him, began to back away.

'Mr Davis, please.' Kellesh stretched a hand towards him imploringly. 'Listen to me.'

There wasn't much time. Urgently, he took a step towards the man – and the singer turned away and began trying to run, hobbling down the alley towards the street.

Kellesh began to summon up the Voice-that-whispers, quickly thought better of it. The enemy was almost on them, now. The singer would have more of a chance if he was allowed to run.

Jailbird reached the sidewalk, disappeared. Kellesh could hear his limping footsteps receding down the street.

He thought of following. But before he could start, there was another movement, at the mouth of the alley. A shadow, narrow and feline.

The priestess of Bast stepped into view.

9

She began sliding towards him, quickly, gracefully, one long-nailed hand upraised.

Kellesh felt his eyes glow hotly. Their golden brightness seemed to reach out, smother his palms. It coalesced there. Then leapt out, forming gouts of crackling flame which struck the woman squarely in the chest, knocking her backwards.

She let out a soft inhuman wail. Then recovered her balance, crouched.

But she didn't come at him again. Her green eyes slid away from him as she noticed the drained girl, still huddled where he'd left her. She smiled hugely. Her small needle-sharp teeth seemed to glitter luminously in the darkness.

Now, *her* eyes were glowing golden. She was using the Voice. The girl climbed obediently to her feet, and moved between them. She stopped, quite motionless, at the centre of the alley, with her arms spread; a barrier of human flesh.

'Use the flame now, idiot priest,' Pashta chuckled. Her

voice was soft, coaxing. Almost seductive. 'You'll kill her for sure. Do you want to do that, Traitor?'

Her shadow began creeping along the alley wall towards him. She was using the girl for cover. Her thin, feline shade and the obese form of the young woman merged into one.

He felt her try and probe his mind, find his weaknesses. He pushed her away.

And suddenly, she was rushing at him. Her arms were raised above her head, her fingers curled like talons. Her whole body was bent forwards, and her small feet barely seemed to touch the ground. And she was changing, even as she came. Her outline was blurring. Darkness was thickening around her like a shroud, masking her small, delicate features.

Before he had time to move, she was on him. And the moment their bodies locked, the alley seemed to fade. The walls became ink dark, receding. The cobbles drained into each other, became so black they might have been standing in empty space. Odd lights appeared to flicker in the sky above, like discoloured fork lightning. And every move they made set up its own muted reverberating echo.

Her thin arms clamped around him like a vice, her nails tearing through his coat and into the skin of his back. Her mouth stretched open wide, inches in front of his face. Her small dark tongue curled, and she let out an ear-splitting screech.

Kellesh concentrated, and he too began to change. Wide swaths of his skin contorted, hardening to dull, uneven scales. The front of his face pushed outwards till it formed a bulbous snout, with sharp jagged teeth protruding from the rigid lips. His fingers retracted, became sharp and angular, as his hands shortened to webbed claws.

He brought his stout scaly arms up and grabbed her around the waist, trying to pin her arms to her sides. He only managed to get hold of one.

Her other claw raked uselessly across his armoured snout.

The creature in his grip wasn't even vaguely human any more. Nor was it a cat.

Something in between. Something standing upright on its long hind legs, but with strangely jointed limbs, and covered with fur as black as a moonless night.

He tipped backwards and they both crashed to the ground. He tried to roll, pin her down with his superior weight, but couldn't manage it. He tightened his grip, attempting to crack the beast's narrow ribs. It kept swiping at his face. And now its gleaming claws were finding openings, drawing blood. The pain was terrible, but he still held on.

It was growing more and more difficult. She was easing her way into his mind again, now, making him relax his grip.

Her free claw flashed straight at his left eye . . . and though he'd shut it, though the hard, transparent scale slid down tight, the talons plunged straight through. He howled with pain, shoved her away, so fiercely that she skidded on her back and crashed against the dimly realized wall.

He staggered to his feet, clutching at his blinded eye. Blood was pouring down his cheek.

He turned away, and she landed on his shoulders, spitting and howling, her claws grappling for his face again. It was all he could manage to fend her off. Deep, bloody wounds began opening in his arms as she mauled him.

With the last of his failing strength, he flung himself back, slamming her into the alley wall. She let out a gasp as the air was punched out of her lungs, and fell.

The city came back sharply into focus. It was all the chance he needed.

He was running, to the end of the alley. Clambering over the wire fence. Escaping into the darkness.

He was beaten. There was nothing he could do, except find prey again, Feed again, and begin to heal his wounds.

*

10

A crowd of noisy kids, the boys in leather jackets and the girls in high-school sweaters and bobby sox, were making their way uptown towards Washington Square, and Jailbird tagged along on the kerb beside them, using them to block him from sight of the club. They kept glancing at him curiously, and one of the boys muttered something about 'spooks' beneath his breath, but they didn't pester him at all.

A subway entrance loomed up in front of him before long, and he left the small group and made his way quickly down the stairs.

There was something wrong with his breathing now. It was coming irregularly, and each lungful seemed to be filled with ice crystals, cutting like tiny chill daggers into the lining of his chest.

He reached the platform, slumped into a seat of the first uptown train and, ignoring the stares of the other passengers, closed his eyes and tried to calm himself down.

The carriage emptied gradually, around him. It was practically deserted by the time he reached 127th.

Climbing up a stairway proved to be a lot harder than climbing down. He was practically doubled over, now, with pain and a numb exhaustion.

The streets here were darker than they'd been downtown. And they seemed colder than ever. A wind had sprung up, pushing thin, dark clouds across the face of the moon.

He paused a moment, clinging to the subway railings. Then, he started hobbling towards Second and 128th, glancing behind him every so often as he went.

*

11

The voodoo shop was completely dark. But when Jailbird pushed at the door gently, he found it wasn't locked. It came open a little, and the bell above it tinkled.

He opened it fully, stepped inside. Stood as quietly as he could manage, letting his eyes adjust to the darkness.

There was a faint glow coming from beyond the curtain at the far end of the store, behind the counter.

He didn't know what to do next. The pain and the shaking were so bad he could barely think straight. He rocked gently on his heels, clutching his belly, feeling his breath hiss back and forth between his lips.

Suddenly, there was a faint scraping noise beyond the curtain, and an old, high-pitched voice called out, 'Washington? What're you standin' out there for?'

How'd she known it was him? But then, how did Madame Lapotaire know anything?

12

It wasn't so much a room behind the curtain as a deep, low-ceilinged corridor. It was only six feet wide, and about twenty long. Lined along the walls, on rows of battered metal shelves, was more of the produce from out front. Potions and herbs, and all the accoutrements of voodoo magic.

At the far end, a single candle glowed in a saucer on the floor, the wick sputtering angrily.

And sitting cross-legged on a blanket beside it, seemingly asleep, was the oldest-looking woman he'd ever seen in his life. It took him a moment to recognize her as Madame Lapotaire.

Her eyes were closed to narrow slits. Her bony, wrinkled hands were resting on her knees. She had a shawl draped around her narrow hunched shoulders, and a red-and-black scarf knotted tightly about her head. She seemed to have aged a hundred years since Jailbird had last seen her. He thought back hard, trying to remember how old she really was. She had to be in her mid-nineties now.

As he let the curtain drop behind him, Madame Lapotaire turned her head in his direction. Her eyes came fully open, and Jailbird gasped softly. They seemed to be glowing with a dull platinum light, in the candle's flame. They were milky and opaque, without pupil or iris.

Her eyesight had always been poor, as though it was the price she paid for her other gifts, her other forms of vision. But now, she was completely blind.

There was somebody else in the room, Jailbird realized. He heard a faint scuttling on the floor, and looked towards the far end of the passage, where another door led to a narrow flight of stairs.

A tiny pale face, white and skinny, returned his gaze from the shadows. It was a little boy, no more than eight years old, trying to hide from him and watch him at the same time.

Madame Lapotaire's face swung towards the boy, as though she was following Jailbird's gaze. She parted her withered lips, and let out a cackle.

'Oh, don't you worry 'bout him, Washington. That's Maurice.' She pronounced it *Maur-eece*, in the French manner. 'I found him wandering all on his lonesome, month ago, and he kind of thinks I'm his mama now. He can't talk, but he can listen good.' She waved a finger scoldingly at the boy. 'You go upstairs now, Maurice. There's grown-up stuff to be done here.'

The child pouted at her sulkily a moment. Then, on all fours, he scrabbled through the doorway and up the stairs.

The voodoo woman smiled and turned her attention back to Jailbird. 'He'll be on the landin', listenin', 'quisitive as a monkey. Some folks reckon that's a bad thing, but I don't. 'Quisitiveness is the root of all knowledge. I hope to teach him a trick or two, when he gets older.'

Her expression, beneath its tangled net of wrinkles, became quizzical.

'My granddaughter told me you called this morning,' she said. 'I'm sorry she turned you away like that. She's a good girl, but kind of stuffy. Said you were pretty sick. From what I can sense, you've got even sicker.' She stretched out both her hands towards him. 'Come over here, Washington. Let me touch you. Let me see what ails you.'

Jailbird stumbled towards her, trying not to fall. His own hands were still wobbling furiously. She took hold of them, very gently. Moved her bony fingers across his knuckles, touching and turning and squeezing, the way a doctor would inspect a patient.

Then, suddenly, she cried out, recoiled. As though she'd just been stung by a fierce electric shock.

13

She drew away from him, rubbing agonizedly at her knuckles. Her blind eyes had become wide, and her mouth was twisted with fear.

'Keep back from me!' she yelled, her voice suddenly shrill. 'Don't come any closer!'

All Jailbird could do was stare down at her confusedly, his head swimming.

She was pushing herself away from him, now. Putting as much distance between them as she could, the blanket underneath her scraping along the floor.

And she shrieked insistently as she moved.

'Stay put, Washington! Don't come *near* me, hear? You do, an' I'll throw you outta here, I swear it!'

Jailbird tried to understand what she was saying. Failed. He could barely think straight at all, now. Was reacting purely on instinct.

He reached towards the old woman imploringly. She seemed to sense the movement, and covered her head with her arms, let out an incoherent wail that brought him jerking back.

'Don't you unnerstand, fool?' The old woman's voice

was muffled, now, by the folds of her shawl. 'You've bin touched by the dark ones! Your soul is riddled through with their poison an' their evil.'

She was scaring him far worse than he'd already been. His legs were starting to go out from under him. Jailbird leaned towards one of the shelves, for support. Grabbed hold of it clumsily. A tiny clay figure of a squatting man rolled away from his fingertips and dropped to the floor, where it shattered.

He barely noticed. Fought hard to steady himself.

'I—' His dulled, jumbled mind tried to deal with what he was hearing. 'I've been *poisoned*?'

The voodoo woman's head shook furiously beneath her twisted elbows.

'You're under a spell, Washington. Worst I've ever seen. When I looked into your soul, just now, it was like gazing at a decayed cadaver. The dark ones have their hooks in you real bad – right through you an' out the other side.'

He still couldn't quite grasp what she was telling him. But he had the sense, at least, to take the old woman seriously. His mouth was suddenly extremely dry. His body had turned freezing cold all over.

'There must be something you can do about it? You *can* help me, can't you?'

Suddenly, the curtain behind him gave another rustle. There was the clack of high heels on the wooden floor.

'Grandma?'

Jailbird spun around.

Charlotte, the granddaughter, was standing by the doorway, staring at them numbly. She seemed to have just come back from an evening out; she was in a fawn-brown raincoat, opened to reveal a low-cut pink dress and a silver necklace at her throat. Her face was pale, her pencilled eyebrows raised.

She glanced past him, at the huddled old woman.

'Grandma, what's going *on*?' Her voice was quivering with fright. She'd obviously been listening outside.

Madame Lapotaire let her arms drop. She raised her

head a little, leaned towards the girl. Her withered lips curled angrily.

'You get out of here, child. Right *now*. There's nothin' you can do here.'

The girl stiffened, shook her head sternly. 'If this man's in trouble, I want to help.'

'You don't unnerstand. There's great danger involved.'

'For you as well as him?'

'Maybe.'

'Then I'm definitely staying,' Charlotte insisted, with a stubborn frown.

Jailbird gazed at her a short while longer, and then looked around worriedly at Madame Lapotaire.

The old woman seemed to have calmed down a little by now, a resigned expression slackening her features. She ran her tongue across her lips, shuddered, and then sighed.

Turned her blind face to Jailbird once again.

'I can't intervene in this directly. You realize that? If I could, I would. But when a dark one has a grip on a mortal this bad, how it ends is between them and them alone. No one else.' She frowned tiredly. 'I'm riskin' my immortal soul, even helpin' you a little bit. I hope you appreciate that?'

He still wasn't entirely sure what she was talking about, but Jailbird agreed quickly.

'Good,' she replied. She closed her eyes again, grimacing with concentration. 'So, if you're gonna fight, you have to know exactly what you're fightin', don'tcha? What does she look like, this dark one that's been givin' you such hurt? It *is* a she, ain't it?'

'Just like a cat,' Jailbird told her, instantly. 'A big pale cat, with weird green eyes.'

The woman tucked her head a little further down, and let out a soft moan.

'And when d'you see her? Day or night?'

'Night. Only ever.'

'And what's she bin doin' to you, Washington?'

'I think . . . she's been bringing back the old craving. For the stuff. The heroin. I haven't touched it in eight years, but since last night it's been like I never gave it up.' He was aware of Charlotte's startled gaze on him, and paused a moment before telling her the rest. 'And I think she's been talking inside my head.'

Madame Lapotaire nodded slowly, and gathered her thoughts a moment.

'It ain't voodoo stuff, or Christian,' she murmured. 'It's older than that. African.'

She drew her shawl tightly around her, as though the room had suddenly turned very cold. The candle spat again, and the flame grew shorter.

'Let me tell you what I know. My great-grandmammy was still alive, when I was a little girl. *She* was from Africa. Got brought over in a slave ship – all her life, she carried scars around her wrists and ankles from the manacles they put on her. Used to be a great witch-woman, back in her village. Knew everything there was to know about the night side of the world. All the legends, all the old tales. She told me about *them* back when I was four years old an' sittin' on her knee.'

She wet her lips, and her face grew slightly drowsy with the memory. Shadows from the flickering candle imparted a strange, burning alertness to her shrivelled eyelids.

'The animal-people, she used to call 'em. No, that ain't the exact translation. It was fiercer. More like . . . "*beast* people". They came originally from Egypt, so the stories went. From Pharaoh's land. But they loved the dark better, the shadows and the forests. They used to hunt for people all the way through Africa. They'd talk in their heads, and mess up their minds, and then devour 'em.'

'What the hell do you mean?' Jailbird stuttered. 'You mean, they're cannibals?'

The woman gave a dry chuckle, almost like a sigh.

'No, fool. They weren't interested in flesh. They'd devour your *soul*.' She shook her head sombrely, as though she was thinking of all the Africans who'd known that kind of fear. 'Finally, the people got on to 'em. Learned what they were, and how to kill 'em. So the beast people went away, into the lands where folks believed in Jesus

Christ and Mohammed and Buddha, and weren't wise to 'em. You unnerstand what I'm sayin'?'

Jailbird shook his head. He felt as though he were dreaming all this. 'No.'

'No, of *course* not. But that don't matter. The point is, Washington, they're scared of the sun. It makes them wither up and die, so they hate it, and all symbols of it. They call it *Re*, or *Ra*, somethin' like that. And it's the only way that we can hurt 'em.' She waved a hand towards her granddaughter. 'Charlotte, somewhere near the middle shelves there's an old disc. A bronze one with a picture of the sun on it. Get it, and give it your friend here, since you're so anxious to help him.'

The girl obliged immediately, scrabbling amongst a pile of masks and old pottery. At last, she drew out what must have been an amulet at one time – it was six inches across, and had a hole through the top edge big enough to pass a leather thong through. She reached over towards Jailbird, holding it out in her palm.

'Don't *touch* him,' Madame Lapotaire snapped. 'Do you want this cat-woman to know about you? Do you want the poison to spread? Just put it down and let him pick it up hisself.'

Charlotte set the bronze disc on the shelf and stood back. Jailbird hobbled past her gingerly, took hold of it with stiff, unfeeling fingers. It didn't look like much, just a scratched, tarnished piece of metal with a wavy sun, like a child's drawing, engraved into its face. But as he held it, he felt a little life come back into his hand. His sickness faded slightly.

'That belonged to my great-grandmammy,' Madame Lapotaire told him. 'A man tried to take it off her on the slave ship, and she killed him – that's how important she thought it was. It might just keep you safe till sunrise. But you gotta help yourself, after that. Buy the first ticket out of this city, an' get as far away as you can before night falls again.'

Jailbird blinked at her uncomprehendingly. 'I can't stay here?'

The woman gave her head a savage jerk. 'You stay *anywhere* for too long, an' she'll catch up with you, she'll *git* you. The only thing to do, now, is to keep on movin'.'

'For how *long*?' The singer could feel panic welling up in him again, like a swiftly rising tide.

'For as long as it takes. The one thing about these beast-people is, they're fickle. She might forget about you, find someone else to torment, after a while. Keep movin', and with good luck and the grace of the Old Ones, you might just rob her of a victim.'

Her wrinkled face was turned towards him once again, the blind eyes open. And the expression on it was of pain and intense pity. 'I'm surely sorry, Washington. I'd do more if I could. But there's nothing more that *can* be done. It's all up to you, now.' Her milky gaze flickered towards the curtain. 'She'll be lookin' for you, by now. You'd better get outta here, before she finds out where you are.'

CHAPTER FIFTEEN

1

She was a little stunned from her fight with Kellesh, and however much she cast around the city with her mind, Pashta couldn't find Jailbird Davis. She reached the Johnston Hotel, and went up angrily into the lobby. There were three aged men hanging around in the dimness, talking, in none too friendly tones, with a large woman behind a glass hatch in the wall.

Pashta reached out and touched all their minds, making sure they didn't notice her as she hurried past. She flitted quietly up the stairs to Jailbird Davis's room.

It was locked, but she simply pressed her flattened palm against the keyhole and the tumblers clicked. She let herself in, closed the door behind her.

One glance told her that the singer hadn't left. Or at least, he hadn't packed. All of his things were still here.

There was always the possibility, she realized, that he wouldn't return for them. Would simply flee the city and leave his belongings behind. He was not a stupid man by any means. She had to remember that.

She stood quite still in the mildew-smelling darkness.

Raised one hand towards her face – and realized it was shaking faintly.

That encounter with Kellesh had unnerved her badly. More than she preferred to admit. Far weaker though he was, he'd almost got the drop on her. Almost caused her harm. And where would her hunt, her little game, be then?

She walked to the window, drew aside the tattered blind, and gazed out grimly. This city, so busy, so overcrowded, was like a warren. A man might hide in it for years. She'd only been here once before, just at the turn of the century, when horse-drawn carriages had still clattered down the streets. It was infinitely vaster now. An overpowering milling termite-hill of a place.

Pashta cast her thoughts out, trying to find Jailbird amongst all the swarming, clamouring millions. It should have been easy. She'd touched his mind several times already – he was *linked* to her now.

But all she got—

She winced and dropped the curtain.

All she got, every time she tried to touch his mind, was a blinding yellow glare, like the glow of the infernal sun.

She couldn't read his mind. Couldn't see what he was thinking or doing, nor tell where he was. Every time she tried to probe into his thoughts, the intense light dazzled her.

Damnation! He had some kind of protection with him!

Don't lose him, sister, came Tharman's voice in her head.

She hissed at her brother angrily. She was trying to think.

If the singer had any sense at all, he'd try to get out, leave the city, right away. But how? And from where?

Pashta tried to probe him one last time, force her way through the searing brightness, but she couldn't manage it. She pulled away annoyedly, blinking several times. Her eyes and her face felt as though a blow-torch had been swept across them.

There was a noise behind her. The door, she realized, had come open again.

She whirled furiously, ready to strike out.

And found herself looking at a huge bearded mulatto. He was standing perfectly still, working a matchstick idly in the corner of his mouth, and staring at her with dark brown eyes which glistened with a mixture of aggression and puzzlement.

His gaze swept up and down her body, taking in her slim figure calmly, almost indolently. Then, a sudden, quizzical grin broke out on his face.

'Can I help you, honey?'

Pashta let her arms drop gently to her sides. She met his gaze with her own bright green one, held it. The way a cat fixates its prey.

She watched, satisfied, as his expression became blank. His lips grew slack, and the matchstick dropped to the floor.

Even after all these years, having power over people – greater even than she'd had in Egypt – was the most marvellous thrill.

'Yes.' And she smiled softly. 'Yes, I think you might.'

2

Jailbird stumbled through the darkened streets of Harlem, heading downtown, towards Broadway.

For the first ten minutes, he concentrated on nothing but his destination, putting one foot in front of the other, ignoring the pain all over his body, the cold sweat in his clothes. It was only when the outline of Central Park appeared, a few blocks ahead of him, that he stopped. In silhouette, at night, the tops of the trees looked like massed, dark clouds. Beyond them, high above the skyscrapers, he could make out the tiny flashing lights of two aeroplanes, one coming into Idlewild, the other soaring out into the moonlit sky.

He wished he were on that one, the one that was leaving. He didn't care what its destination was. Anywhere would do.

But he only had ten dollars left in his pocket, and he couldn't afford a plane. Christ, what was he doing walking? He'd never make it all the way downtown like this.

Clutching the amulet to his chest, he began searching for a cab.

There wasn't much activity at all, here in the lower Hundreds. Windows were bright, people were still up, but there was little traffic on the streets.

He reached the corner of Park Lane, just in time to see a lone Chequer Cab barrel towards him. He staggered to the kerb, began waving his arms. But the driver, a big, florid man with a blond crew-cut, just glared at him contemptuously and swept on past.

Desperation started closing in on him, but he fought it. The moment you gave up hope, he knew from years of bitter experience, was the moment you were lost. He crossed the street and kept on walking. It seemed his best bet. Perhaps the cat-eyed woman wouldn't find him if he just kept moving.

The muscles in his legs were beginning to ache dreadful bad.

Three blocks further down, the same thing happened again – a cab, a white driver. Except this time the hack leaned out of his window and flipped him the bird as he passed.

Jailbird hunkered down on the grimy kerb, and began to shudder violently.

He couldn't stop, however much he tried. It just went on and on. Perhaps the woman wouldn't kill him after all. Perhaps he'd kill himself . . . simply tear himself to pieces, shaking.

He finally managed to get it under control a little, calm his nerves.

When he looked up again, a huge, battered car, an aged black Dodge, was drawing up to the kerb in front of him. Its windows were all open, its radio on. A Dizzy Gillespie number, 'This Is The Way', was drifting out into the night.

It was full of kids, all dressed in beatnik uniform. Boys in dark shades, and slender young girls. For an instant, he thought he recognized the cat-eyed woman amongst them. He started drawing back, terrified.

The girl in the passenger seat, long haired and with a square jaw and bright blue eyes, leaned out and said, 'Hey, daddio? You OK?'

The driver, a thin boy in a beret, craned around her.

'You're Jailbird Davis, right? We saw you at the Horn last night. You were really cool, man. We'd be glad to offer you a ride, if you want one.'

Jailbird stood up painfully and stared into the back of

the car. The woman wasn't there. Smiling, pleasant young faces returned his gaze. They were passing a reefer amongst them, and didn't seem to have a trouble in the world. He considered their offer groggily, and realized it would be nice to ride with them for a while.

He looked back at the driver.

'You sure?'

'It'd be stone-cold honour, man. Where you headin'?'

'Greyhound terminal,' Jailbird mumbled.

The kids in the back squeezed over, making room for him as he got in.

The driver stared around at him curiously. 'You leaving? I thought you were here till the end of the week?'

Jailbird slumped back in the seat and didn't even bother to reply.

Exhaustion began to close over him. He couldn't shut his eyes, he was too frightened. But he felt that he could simply curl up and sleep for a week.

The car moved off unsteadily, with a loud grinding of gears and the stink of burning oil. Christ, it oughtn't to be on the road, in this condition. He could feel every bump on the asphalt, and there was an odd whining noise coming from the motor. The kids all began trying to talk to him, simultaneously, but he took no notice of them. Couldn't even hear what they were saying.

The reefer's smoke wafted around him. It made his head spin like a carousel. He let his arms drop exhaustedly into his lap.

And the amulet hit his knee, was knocked clear of his fingers, tumbled to the floor.

Instantly, the trembling and the chills, the agony of withdrawal, came rushing back at him, redoubled. He began scrabbling frantically on the floor for the bronze disc.

Something else hit him, right then. Something worse than the shaking and the gnawing pain.

For a moment, just before his fingers closed over the amulet again, he thought he could see eyes, staring at him. Great burning yellow eyes, with horizontal slits for pupils.

He clutched the amulet firmly to his chest. Felt the pain and sickness ebb a little.

Those staring eyes were gone, now. But he knew whose eyes they'd been.

The cat-woman's.

She'd seen him, he realized. She knew where he was.

3

By Fifty-First, the car had started to overheat. And several blocks further on, with the shifting, coruscating lights of Times Square drawing into view, the driver pulled over to the kerb and banged his palms angrily against the steering-wheel. Steam and a trail of black smoke were pouring from the hood.

Jailbird clutched the amulet as tightly as he could, threw his door open, and staggered out. Began hobbling away down the street as fast as he was able, ignoring the surprised, bewildered shouts of the kids behind him.

There were plenty of people out and about here, and that made him feel better. Nothing bad could happen to him, surely, with so many witnesses around. Stay with other people, the nut behind his hotel door had said. It seemed like good advice, right now.

Most of them ignored him. The few who noticed him at all glanced at his face alarmedly and then stepped around him, giving him a wide berth. They probably took him for a drunk. But he was glad they were there, all the same.

Forty-Second Street was churning, bustling, filled with couples who were emptying from the theatres or heading for the nightclubs. He grabbed hold of a passing man by the sleeve and asked, fiercely, where the Greyhound terminal was.

As he cut across town towards Seventh Avenue, Jailbird felt himself merge with the crowds; felt hidden amongst them, like a lone narrow tree in a great shadowy forest. The pain and the shaking had practically gone by now.

He was standing straighter, moving easier, his breath coming in long, heaving gulps.

At last, he reached Seventh. And the Greyhound terminal came in sight, just across the road. A bus, bound for Cleveland, rolled away as he watched.

He paused on the corner. Shifted his weight from foot to foot. Began to cross the road.

And saw her.

The woman with the cat eyes.

She was standing right beside the main entrance to the building, her arms folded casually across her chest, her head tipped to one side.

She was dressed all in black, as she'd been that first night. And now that he looked at her again, out here in the open, on the street, he noticed how diminutive she was compared to the other passers-by.

For an instant, it occurred to him that she was nothing to be afraid of. That maybe the heroin sickness was just that, a throwback to the old days. That Madame Lapotaire was just a crazy old woman who believed in fairy tales. That all the rest had simply been the product of his tired, fevered imagination.

Then, she realized he was there, and looked straight at him.

He couldn't see her eyes too well, from this distance. All that he could make out were tiny jade glimmers.

But he was afraid again.

He suddenly knew, without needing proof, how much he was in danger.

It wasn't human, the way she was looking at him. It was like a cat, staring at a bird.

He stumbled back a few steps from the kerb. Tried to turn. But he couldn't take his eyes from her. He was afraid that if he turned his back on her for just an instant, she'd be all over him, ripping at him, tearing him apart.

That was crazy. There were too many people around.

He forced himself to move away. Pushed his way into the middle of a jumbled crowd of people that was trooping along the sidewalk. He didn't know where they were going, but he followed them. The buildings and the neon lights seemed to whirl, around him.

Which way was Grand Central Station? Maybe he could get out that way?

Part of the crowd broke off and crossed the road, and he went blindly with them. Where was he heading? Uptown? Downtown? East or West? He didn't know the layout of the city well enough. But he didn't particularly care, either. The only thing that mattered was he kept on moving.

He glanced back at the terminal.

The woman was gone. He craned his head around frantically. She was nowhere in sight.

Then he thought he caught a glimpse of her. On the far side of the street. A dark, lithe shadow, that was all. Flitting behind the parked cars.

He sucked in a breath, and looked away, and kept on going. His legs were burning with pain again. But he couldn't stop. Didn't *dare* stop.

He didn't seem to be on Seventh any more. He glanced up, tried to find a street sign. But he was moving so fast that he couldn't focus on anything.

Four of the people he'd been walking with peeled off and disappeared into a doorway. A couple more stopped and went into a tobacconists.

The crowd around him was thinning, fast.

Perhaps he ought to turn round, go back the way he'd come. But he didn't *know* which way he'd come. And when he glanced sideways again, that dark, flitting shape was still keeping pace with him.

He must have kept walking for another four minutes before the crowd abandoned him altogether.

He was on a much narrower street now. There were only three other people visible on the sidewalk. There were far fewer streetlights. Huge flat-walled brick buildings towered up around him, most of their windows dark. The noise of the midtown traffic had become withdrawn.

Two of the three pedestrians suddenly turned a corner, disappeared.

There was only himself left on the street. And a thin man of middling build, about thirty years old, a dozen yards ahead of him.

The man abruptly stopped, took a key-ring out of his pocket, rattled it. Walked up a flight of shabby porch steps.

He had his front door halfway open before Jailbird started running towards him.

'Hey, man!' the singer called out, hoarsely. 'I need somewhere to hide! *Please!*'

The man swivelled around and stared at him, pale faced and aghast, for a moment. Then he quickly disappeared inside, slamming the door behind him. Jailbird could hear the lock rattling again, then a bolt being shot.

He whirled around, certain that the cat-eyed woman was moving towards him. But the street was full of darkness, shadows, and he couldn't make her out.

He pressed himself against the railings at the front of the house. Sweating. Shivering. Waiting for the attack to come.

And noticed heavy footsteps, moving in his direction.

He turned his head stiffly, looked back along the street.

It wasn't the woman. Loping down the sidewalk towards him, a dim silhouette in the poor light, was another man. A big man, this time. And, so far as he could tell, black.

Oh, Sweet Jesus. Thank God!

Jailbird let go of the railings, began stumbling towards the figure.

As he got closer, the bearded face resolved itself. And Jailbird recognized it. It was Calvin Watkell, the pusher from the hotel.

Jailbird skidded to a halt, began to back away. There was something weird about the man's expression. It seemed lifeless and frozen, like a corpse in rigor mortis. And the eyes . . . they didn't seem to be looking right at him. They were fixed on a point just beyond his head, staring blankly into the middle distance. The way he moved, too. There was something stiff and unnatural, almost mechanical, about it.

A hundred childhood stories came flooding back to him, all the way from the dim shanties of Louisiana. About zombies, dead men who rose from the grave and walked stiffly on the dark face of the earth.

Watkell kept on coming. He was only a few yards away, now. One of his big hands started coming up.

And Jailbird finally snapped out of it. Turned and ran for his life.

Down another street, narrower still. Around a corner.

He didn't dare look back. He could almost feel the man breathing on his neck.

All these streets were so damned straight! He'd never get away!

A dark alleyway loomed ahead, and he ducked into it. Hurried into the blackness.

It was a dead end. Jailbird let out a choking sob, fell to his knees.

He couldn't go any further. His age and his sickness had caught up with him at last. He could barely breathe, and he hurt all over.

He grasped the bronze amulet so tightly it dug into the skin of his palm, and looked back at the mouth of the alley.

Slowly, a shadowy figure stepped into view.

It wasn't Watkell but the woman. Her hands were on her hips. She moved without making a sound. He could see, again, the glitter of her eyes.

They weren't entirely green, now.

As Jailbird watched, they began to shine. Brightly, like hot coals.

She took a step towards him.

Jailbird held the amulet towards her, as far out as his arm could reach.

The bronze disc seemed to gather what little light there was, and shine.

The woman gave a gentle hiss. Stepped back.

But she didn't retreat far. She turned her gaze to the right.

Watkell lumbered stiffly into view.

Wordlessly, like an automaton, he began striding down the alley towards Jailbird.

He stopped in front of him. Reached down. Plucked the amulet from his fingers, grimacing with pain, and tossed it to the far end of the alley.

The woman started walking towards him again. Her eyes had become entirely yellow. Burning like huge golden stars.

She was holding something in her right hand.

A large syringe, with a glittering silvery needle poking from the end like the tongue of some bizarre metallic snake.

Jailbird opened his mouth to scream as she plunged it into his neck. But not a sound came out.

4

The news of his death was all around Harlem by the next evening.

The air had turned warmer with the promise of an Indian summer, and Madame Lapotaire, with Charlotte and Maurice, sat on next door's porch stoop, discussing it with their neighbours.

'*Weren't* no drugs overdose,' the voodoo woman scowled, the lids batting furiously over her whitened eyes. 'It were the beast-people. *That's* who killed him.'

Her neighbours smiled uncomfortably, but didn't say a word to contradict her. In her lap, the mute white boy squirmed and let out an unhappy strangled murmur, the only sound his unformed throat could make.

'You're frightening him, Grandma!' Charlotte scolded.

Madame Lapotaire smiled toothlessly, her old face wrinkling with affection, and reached out and hugged the boy, gathering him up in her bony arms.

'Don't you worry now, Maurice,' she cooed softly. 'Don't you fret 'bout nothing. Them beast-people won't git you. Not while I'm around. *Nothin's* gonna hurt you while I'm around.'

PART III

MAURICE

VIETNAM, 1969

CHAPTER SIXTEEN

1

The Chinook helicopter took off from Firebase Apache at 0950 hours and headed north, trailing its shadow across the Mekong delta like a clattering June bug on a string.

Maurice Lapotaire, two days' worth of stubble on his sunburned face, sat in the open hatch with his feet dangling in midair, snapping pictures. There wasn't much going on below him, but it was a habit he couldn't break. His colleagues in the press corps always laughed about it. This kid's keeping Fuji in business single-handed! Hate to be the guy who deals with your expenses, son!

He was dressed in sweat-stained military fatigues, and was still so young, a few months short of twenty, that people usually took him for a raw recruit, a 'cherry', until they saw the press credentials pinned to his breast pocket. That worried him a lot, the idea of being mistaken for a soldier. It was a pointless worry, he knew. The VC would kill any Caucasian, old or young, military or civilian, who they got in their sights. They weren't exactly famous for stopping and asking questions.

But he'd have been much happier, he always thought, if he could wave a six-foot white flag above his head with the word 'Press' emblazoned on it in Vietnamese. *Bao Chi*. He was always so scared, in-country. Always. Ever since the agency had given him the chance to come here, four months ago.

That was the trick, he realized. To be scared out of your wits, and still keep taking pictures. Almost by reflex, like the galvanic twitching of a dead frog. He wondered whether every other war photographer, down the years, had felt the same.

Probably. No, certainly. They were all human, after all.

And he *had* begged to come in the first place, though he regretted it every waking hour now. Here was where he'd make his name, he was sure.

The youngest pressman in the field. It ought to be a source of pride as well as concern.

He realized he was taking photographs of empty mud-flats, relaxed his grip, and let the heavy camera dangle around his neck.

The chopper shifted a little to the east, and was soon passing over a forest of petrified, colourless tree-trunks. He made some quick map references in his head, ploughing back through his sharp, persistent memory, and realized that the Man Bo Doi Woods ought to be down there.

'When did we clear them?' he shouted to the black Marine corporal behind him, his sole companion on this trip.

'Two weeks ago. Lots of Charlie activity coming out of there.'

Maurice gazed down sombrely at the shattered, denuded trees. This kind of thing always made him feel a little sick, deep at the pit of his stomach. It wasn't just that they had killed an entire wood. It was almost as though, with everything else they'd brought to Indo-China, their food and music and their way of life, they'd brought their seasons too. A New England fall had come to the Man Bo Doi Woods, courtesy of Western alchemy.

He shook his head glumly, then crawled backwards, on his rump, into the depths of the chopper. Rested his back against a pile of ammunition crates, and turned to face the corporal.

The man eyed his press tag sleepily.

'Lapotaire,' he said, getting the pronunciation right. 'You some kind of Cajun?'

'No, I'm a New Yorker. But my stepmammy came from New Orleans, before she moved to Harlem.'

The corporal's eyes narrowed for a moment, in that *Are you jiving me?* expression Maurice often got when he talked with black Americans. Then he shrugged, deciding to let it pass. Maurice felt relieved. He didn't feel inclined, right now, to explain his life story for the thousandth time. He couldn't stop thinking about his assignment. It was the most dangerous he'd had in all the sweating months he'd been here.

'What you going up to LZ Bravo for?' the corporal asked, on cue. 'Ain't much fighting up there.'

The big chopper yawed to the left for a moment, and then continued onwards with a monotonous shudder, for all the world like an airborne freight train.

'No fighting, but a lot of killing,' Maurice said. 'There's a Lurp unit up there which has a kill-ratio beyond belief. They're led by some Special Forces type – some kind of foreign mercenary.'

The corporal's eyes squinted again, but not with disbelief this time. With astonishment.

'Major *Gorrekan*?'

'That's right. Everyone round here's heard of him, I see.'

'You think you're gonna talk to Gorrekan's outfit?'

'I'm going to do more than that.' Maurice patted his breast pocket, and it gave a papery crackle. 'I've got authorization to go out on patrol with them.'

The corporal drew his knees up to his chest, as though he was trying to make himself smaller. 'You're out of your *mind*, dude! That albino fuck and his band of merry men? They'll shove that authorization where the sun don't shine. Not even the brass go near those mothers.'

Maurice tipped his head back against the crates. The motion of the chopper was making him a little sick, as usual.

'We'll see,' he murmured.

The corporal shook his head and looked away. He obviously took him for a madman.

They rode in silence for another twenty minutes. Finally, the Marine stared at him again and, for want of anything else to do, made a curious attempt at small-talk.

'How long you been taking pictures, anyway?'

Maurice smiled softly. 'Since before I could talk.'

'Don't you mean before you could walk?'

'No.'

The corporal's doubts seemed to be confirmed, and he turned his back on him again. But Maurice knew he'd told the truth.

He glanced out of the hatch again. The terrain below was changing, from grasslands, to scattered trees, and then to the edges of a dense verdant jungle.

I have both things to thank you for, stepmammy, he thought. Being able to take a photo. And being able to talk. I have *everything* to thank you for. Perhaps even my life.

2

As the chopper started circling the LZ, Maurice crawled to the hatch and leaned out, gazing down at the sand-bagged bunkers. He snapped a few shots, just to keep his reflexes tuned.

It was nothing special. Just a typical at ease off-duty landing zone, like a summer camp, but scruffier and with bigger kids. Washing flapped on sagging lines. Men lay sunbathing, bare chested, their heads propped on their helmets. There was the smoke of a campfire, and loud music playing from dugouts. And litter everywhere. The CO had obviously given up on military precision quite some time ago. Maurice was supposed to report to him the moment he touched down, but it hardly seemed worth the trouble.

The chopper hung suspended a few feet above the ground, then floated down the rest of the way as softly as a falling leaf. Maurice jumped out, made his way quickly through the cloud of hot dust the rotor blades were kicking up.

There was no one there to meet him. The sunbathers didn't even raise their heads to look at him.

He was already running over in his mind the few details he knew about Gorrekan and his unit.

Long-range patrollers, working behind enemy lines, at night. And the corporal had been wrong. The major wasn't an albino. He had some kind of rare skin condition – no one had been able to tell Maurice exactly what it was – which made exposure to the sun painful and unpleasant.

'Unable to determine' was a useful phrase whenever the subject of Gorrekan came up. Almost nothing could be learnt about the man. His dossier, if there was one, was buried in CIA files somewhere, away from prying eyes.

He wasn't American, that was for sure. So where was he from? The name sounded Balkan, or Greek, but it was impossible to tell.

The half-dozen men with him hadn't distinguished themselves in any special way before they'd joined his outfit. They should have fared no better or worse than any other Lurp patrol. But then the kill statistics had started coming in. And Command, at first, must have believed someone was making them up.

So far, the unit had accounted for something in the region of three hundred Charlie.

And their losses? *None.* Not one man. Not a single member of Gorrekan's patrol had suffered so much as a scratch.

As though they were invulnerable. As though they were made of armoured steel.

Maurice wanted to meet this major badly. Just talk to him, photograph him, that was all. He had to be a remarkable man.

He wiped dust from his eyes. Two grunts were lying not twenty yards from him, soaking up the morning sun. A cassette player beside their heads was blaring out the electric riffs of Jimi Hendrix. Maurice walked over to them, realized the music was too loud to talk across, thought of reaching down and switching it off. His few months of experience in-country stopped him. Some troops used the tiniest imagined slight as an excuse to start trouble, especially if they were bored. And some of them took exception in wild, unpredictable ways.

He stood over them and shouted.

'Excuse me?'

They either didn't hear, or didn't want to.

Maurice circled around them until he was standing between them and the sun, his shadow stretching over their faces.

That did it. One of them squinted, raised a hand to shield his eyes, then reached over and turned down the cassette player.

'What's your problem, man?'

'I understand there's a Lurp unit based here. Under the command of a Major Gorrekan?'

The grunt scowled. Said nothing. An apprehensive, almost frightened look had crept into his eyes.

'Where would I find them?' Maurice tried.

'You don't want to find them, my friend.' The soldier seemed nervous just talking about them.

'Wrong. Try again.'

Maurice waited impatiently for the man to answer.

'They're over there.'

The grunt jerked his finger unsteadily, as though he were afraid it might get bitten off. Maurice followed his gaze, to the edge of the clearing about two hundred yards away. There were no tents there. No signs of life. Just an impenetrable tangle of trees and lush, green undergrowth.

'Where, exactly?' he asked, puzzled.

'Right there, man. You're looking at them. Just keep walking in that direction. You'll know when you've arrived.'

He had the nagging feeling that the grunt was pulling his leg, but he crossed the parched, dried grass towards the perimeter. The quality of the air changed, as he moved closer. The odour of camp fires and cooking began to thin. The stench of the jungle seeped in to replace it. He'd never realized, till he'd come to Nam, how powerful it was. He'd always imagined a jungle would smell like an overgrown garden, but it didn't. It was best described as a mixture between a hothouse and a swamp.

The predominant odour was of rotting, of decay.

The jungle, he realized, smelled of death.

All but the really crazy types were frightened of it. Hated it. Perhaps for that reason.

You couldn't get that smell out of your nostrils for weeks, if you stayed there long enough. And he'd be out for several days, with the Lurps. Maybe this hadn't been such a good idea after all. It wasn't too late to turn around and get back on the chopper.

He reached the edge of the trees, and realized he *had* been kidded. There was no one here. Maurice glanced back, expecting to see the grunt and his friend sitting up and laughing. But they were sprawled on the ground, just as he'd left them. They'd turned the music up again. The wind was blowing in the wrong direction, and all that he could hear was its tinny beat, sounding very small, very distant.

There were no birds around here, he noticed. No insects either. That was odd.

Suspiciously, Maurice put a hand between two thin, supple branches. Parted them.

There was nothing in there. Only gloom and more shrubbery. The canopy, high overhead, was so thick barely a single shaft of sunlight reached down to break the dimness.

He hovered on the treeline jumpily, a moment. Then, he took a step into the jungle. And another. There was a loud rustle as the branches swung back into place behind him.

He took a third step.

And suddenly a hand reached down.

From above him. Directly above.

And, before he had time to move, it had fastened under his chin and was lifting him off his feet.

Suddenly, he was swinging in midair, kicking wildly. His neck felt as though it was going to break. He couldn't get free, couldn't breathe.

One of the fingers underneath his chin was moving, searching for a pressure point.

3

No, Bobby. Put him down.

4

Abruptly, the hand released him and disappeared. Maurice fell, stumbled, rolled. His shoulder scraped painfully against the rough bark of a tree. Twigs slapped into his face. His hands and knees sank deeply into the loamy jungle floor.

He looked up stupidly. He was alone once more. The silence had closed in around him. All that he could hear was his own rackety breathing.

It was as though he'd imagined it. It had all happened so fast, ended so abruptly.

He'd had dreams like that, as a child. Hands grabbing him. Usually after Madame Lapotaire had finished telling him some story of the night world, of the ghosts and demons and monsters that inhabited the dark.

He could feel something crawling on his arm, but he ignored it. Remained entirely still, peering into the filtered half-light.

A crazy image flashed behind his eyelids every time he blinked. Something that his memory had scrambled. Something that just couldn't be right.

It was a very brief glimpse he'd got, while he'd hung suspended, of the forearm that had grabbed him. It hadn't been white, or black. It had been green. Different shades of green, like the overlapping leaves around him.

As though the jungle itself had reached out and snatched hold of him.

He waited, letting his nerves steady. Nothing more happened. No one appeared.

He risked a quick glance at his arm. The thing crawling towards his elbow was a huge red-brown beetle, with a rounded body, like a scarab. He flicked it off, and it rolled on its back and scuttled away.

It took him two attempts to get back to his feet. The first time, his knees seemed to have no strength in them at all. Finally, wobbling, he managed it, and turned back to the treeline. He just wanted to get out of here. He'd sell everything he owned, just to walk into that scruffy camp again.

A twig snapped.

He almost yelled out as he spun around.

At first, he could see nothing but the dim shapes of the branches. Then he realized he was looking at a man, no more than five feet away from him, who was leaning against a tree trunk.

The man grinned, a band of unblemished whiteness appearing in his oddly coloured face.

Maurice stared at him dumbly. Realized he'd been right about the arm. The soldier before him was lank and muscular and over six feet tall, wore the usual camouflage pants, and a scarf of mottled parachute silk over his hair. But the area in between, the naked torso and the bare arms, the neck and face . . . the entire expanse of skin was painted with broad, twisted leaves, jade and olive and a dozen other shades of green.

The man wore no boots. His feet were painted too.

And he hadn't stepped on any twig. He was holding the two broken pieces between his fingers. He'd snapped it deliberately.

He was entirely still, like a frieze, a tableau. He didn't even blink. His eyes were dead and cold, and gave off no reflection whatsoever.

5

His name is Maurice Lapotaire, Bobby. He's a photojournalist. He has authorization to go out on patrol with us, but we're not supposed to know that.

Introduce yourself. Be nice to him. Ask him who he is and what he wants.

6

The green-painted man opened his fingers just enough to let the two halves of the twig drop. No other part of his body moved. His grin remained constant.

Then he blinked.

Maurice felt himself shy back a little.

The man straightened up, for all the world like some woodland spirit emerging from a tree.

And said, 'I'm Bobby.'

It was an odd way for a soldier to start a conversation. They usually asked who he was first, suspicion being the first rule of survival out here.

'Good for you,' Maurice scowled.

'Who are you? What d'you want?'

The accent was pure Kansas, and sounded incongruous in the middle of an Asian jungle.

Maurice asked, 'Can I reach into my breast pocket?'

The man seemed to think about that, then gave a nearly imperceptible nod.

As he was fumbling for the authorization, Maurice noticed for the first time that the soldier wasn't armed. There was no belt, no ammunition pouch. Not even the handle of a knife showed from his belt. That was weird. Most troops, anywhere inside the jungle, went about swathed in armaments like Barbary Corsairs.

This Bobby didn't seem to be worried by the jungle and the enfolding dimness at all.

He handed over the paper, and watched as the man scanned it with those cold, lifeless eyes. Found himself staring at Bobby's eyelids. When they blinked at all, it was few and far between.

The man handed the paper back.

'OK.'

Maurice frowned surprisedly.

'That's it? OK?'

'If you want to come with us, that's fine. It's your neck.'

It wasn't the reply he'd been expecting.

'Er – I'd like to see your CO, please?'

The soldier had become frozen into position again.

'Major Gorrekan?' Maurice tried. 'Where is he?'

Bobby jerked his head to the side, at what looked like a dense tangle of ferns. 'Over there.'

'Where?' This was getting crazy. 'I can't see him.'

Maurice started taking a step towards the ferns.

And never completed it. Suddenly, one of the man's hands was flat against his chest, shoving him back. Suddenly, the man was right on top of him. He towered over Maurice, staring down dully. This close he smelled of the jungle itself. Smelled as though he were made of rotting leaves.

He said, slowly, 'No one sees the Major before nightfall.'

'But—'

'No buts.'

Maurice went limp and backed off.

He almost jumped when another voice, in his ear, snapped, 'You're disturbing us, bro!'

He turned, and a second man, about the same height as Bobby but more thickly set, was standing by his shoulder. Like his comrade, he was naked from the waist and painted green all over. It took Maurice a moment to realize that, underneath the dappled paint, this one was black.

'We're sleeping now,' the man explained.

We? Where the hell were the others?

'You rest there.' The black man pointed to the ground at Maurice's feet.

There seemed nothing to do but comply. Maurice hunkered down, took the cameras from around his neck, and laid them on a dried patch of earth beside him. Then, just as he was trying to make himself comfortable, a question occurred to him. Which one of them had grabbed him around the neck?

He looked back up, to ask it.
But the men were gone.

7

The only insects which seemed to live around here were those big dark beetles. They had long barbed mandibles which curved out from their bulbous heads, but they seemed harmless enough. Maurice would find one crawling on him every so often, and flick it casually aside.

He ought to sleep, he knew. He needed to be alert tonight. He murmured one of the prayers Stepmammy had taught him, to protect him from bad dreams. But all that he could manage, lying on the jungle floor, was a fitful doze.

He'd often noticed how his dreams in half-sleep were more realistic than those of a full slumber. They had proper colour and proportion, and were usually composed of real people and events.

Madame Lapotaire's blind, wizened face leaned over him and said, 'Don' you worry, little boy. I ain't gonna hurtcha.'

He thought he heard something, and woke. He was too frightened to raise his head. But there was nobody around. The noise had been in his dream. The clatter of a trash can lid, falling in that alley in Harlem, all those years ago.

He closed his eyes again. The old voodoo woman was still bending over him.

'What's the matter?' She was smiling softly, talking very gently. 'Cat gotcha tongue?'

Maurice couldn't remember his own parents. Couldn't remember anything about his early life, except vague images of raised voices and violence. He'd never understood why that was. Perhaps his mind had simply blocked it out. Perhaps the opening chapters of his life had been too painful for him to bear. There were two long weal-like scars on his back, faded to a pale grey now, which supported that theory.

The only memories he had, of the time just before Madame Lapotaire had found him, were barely human at all. They were, he realized now, the memories of an animal. Running. Crouching. Hiding. Scrabbling for food. Always hungry. Always alert. Forever frightened.

Had he run away from home? Had he been thrown out? It seemed incredible that any child could exist on the city streets. But somehow, he had. And, somehow, he'd made his way up into Harlem.

Smelling chicken, going sour in a bin. Trying to reach over the lip of the too-high bin, scrambling. A door coming open in the alleyway behind him. A yellow wedge of light. Hide! Squirming in between the bins. The lid falling to the ground. Crashing.

Maurice bobbed back to consciousness startledly, a moment, sank down again.

'Grandma, we should call the police right away! He must have a home somewhere!' A name. Charlotte.

His clothes being pulled off. A bath, being filled to the brim. Off comes his undervest. The old woman's hands touching the weals on his back, very gently. A saddened moan.

So the police were never called. He couldn't have told them anything, anyway. The memories weren't there. He couldn't write. And he'd been born with his vocal cords tangled.

Madame Lapotaire had treated him like her own son. She'd taught him, in those first few weeks, the basis of reading and writing and arithmetic. She'd let him play with all the objects in the long corridor behind the shop. And when he'd found the old Box Brownie, in a cardboard suitcase filled with junk, and shown a special interest in it, she had sent Charlotte out to buy some film for him. And even though she couldn't see the pictures, when they came back from the developers, she had shared his delight in them.

'Perhaps if he can't talk,' she'd said to Charlotte, *'this is the way he can express hisself.'*

She fixed that for him a month later. After a consultation with the doctor, she took him to the hospital and he went under the gas. And when he came out there were nurses and men in white coats standing around him, smiling. And Madame Lapotaire. And real noises were coming from his aching throat.

How she'd got him into the public school system, how she'd got around the normal adoption procedures, he'd never found out.

She continued to teach him, in the evenings . . . and some of the things she taught weren't on any curriculum in the world. About spirits, good and bad. Voodoo gods. Demons. Creatures she called 'beast-people'. And he'd kept on taking his photographs. He sold his first to a newspaper on his fifteenth birthday.

Madame Lapotaire died two years later. In her will, she made Charlotte his legal guardian. And she left a trust fund for him, enough to get him through college. But by eighteen he was already working for the press agency. College could wait.

He felt like he'd aged another nineteen years, in the past few months.

8

It went on for several hours, the faint sleep and the dreams, the sudden waking.

Once, at about 1500 hours, he yelled sharply, jolted upright. And sat completely still for what must have been an hour or so. There were still no signs of life around him. A few more beams of sunlight slanted in thinly through the canopy now, at an acute angle. The jungle's leaves seemed to have closed in a little, around him. As though they had been steadily and quickly growing while he slept.

When he laid his head against the jungle floor again, he drifted off into a deeper blackness. He was fast asleep before he knew it . . .

His eyes clicked open. It was night.

Something – a bird, a monkey – was calling from the tree tops, far away.

Maurice lay perfectly still in the darkness, letting his eyes adjust. The moon, he realized, was shining brightly. For some reason, its cold white rays were making a better job of penetrating the jungle than the sunlight had. Everything around him was captured in dappled monochrome. Even the small space he was lying in, between one tree and the next, looked completely different now.

He could see perfectly well, after a while.

There was still no one around. Had they gone without him?

Maurice thought of calling out. But that, he knew instinctively, would be a bad mistake. The two Lurps he'd met so far had moved so very quietly. They seemed to live in a world of silence. It was best not to disturb them. So he sat up straight, and waited.

9

There was something moving near by. He suddenly knew it, could feel it, even though he couldn't see or hear it.

Something very close by.

His head swivelled to the left, his eyes scanning the shadows around him. They began to drift to the right, when suddenly there was a movement in the corner of his vision, just beyond his feet.

He clenched in a yell of fright.

No more than two yards away, by the twisted roots of a tree trunk, something was uncurling.

A large, round head moved. A pair of eyes came open, blinking dully.

It was another man, he realized. Painted all over with green leaves, just like the others.

A shudder went through Maurice's spine. He'd been sleeping almost within arm's reach of this soldier, had been next to him for hours. And he'd never even known the man was there.

The Lurp got up to his full height – they were all so huge in this unit – gazed down at him a moment, quite uncuriously, and then moved away into the undergrowth.

There were more faint movements around him now. He caught glimpses of other shadows drifting around him, flitting through the broken moonlight.

The overhanging branch, the one from which he'd been grabbed earlier, shuddered very faintly. A fourth man, naked save for a pair of shorts and painted like the rest, dropped down silently, landed on the ground on all fours. Hunkered there a moment, grinning at him. He was as thin and wiry as though his limbs were made from hawsers. His grin was knowing, gloating.

This one moved away into the jungle too.

There were faint, metallic noises springing up around him now. Maurice recognized them as the sounds of weapons being checked and loaded. But he'd never heard it done so quietly, so smoothly.

He wondered what to do. He wasn't even sure whether he was supposed to get up yet. He gathered up his cameras, slung them around his neck, removed the lens cap on the Nikon.

'Major'll see you now,' said a voice he recognized, directly behind him.

It was Bobby. The Kansas boy was holding a captured AK47, and there was something oddly shaped slung across his back that Maurice took a little while recognizing as a crossbow.

The Lurp motioned impatiently with one broad hand.

Maurice followed him between the trees. Almost tripped over the man in the shorts, who was stripping down a heavy machine-gun.

They left the rhythmic clattering behind them. Walked to a thicket where the overhanging canopy was very dense, the jungle almost completely lightless. Maurice could just make out a large pile of giant fern leaves. They weren't upright but lying flat. They'd been snapped from their roots, and piled into a rough pyramid about six feet across.

He watched them blankly for a moment, wondering what they were supposed to be, and where the Major was.

Then they moved gently. The top ones began to slide away.

A gap appeared between them, and a hand emerged.

CHAPTER SEVENTEEN

1

Asleep in the cool, perfect darkness beneath the ferns, Gorreq had spent the entire afternoon touching and probing Maurice Lapotaire's mind. Some of the things he'd found there worried him. The young man's upbringing by the old voodoo woman. The fleeting knowledge of magic and spells.

The idea that this child presented any kind of risk, however slight, infuriated him. He was, after all, the most awesome type of Incarnate, a fear-feeder.

It had been the natural choice for him, after he'd melded with his god. And it hadn't simply been down to his great size, which made people tremble. Nor the intimidating fire in his eyes. Nor his violent temper. It had been the time of the great battles against the Seleucid peoples and the Syrians, when he'd been a priest. The middle of the third century BC. The guidance of the war god Buchis had been much in demand. The generals of the Imperial army had visited Gorreq constantly, in his temple at Hermonthis. Knelt before him, clung to his every word. The Pharaoh, Ptolemy III, had treated him like kin.

And he had been allowed . . . special powers. Special privileges.

To increase Egypt's fortunes in the war, he'd been allowed to perform human sacrifices, eschewing the symbolic wooden models the priesthood had used in those days. Criminals had been brought before him. Beggars from the streets. Even children, snatched by night out of the hovels of the poor.

He could still remember the terror in their eyes. Their

piteous howls as they'd lain bound on the altar and he'd raised the knife above them.

And he had enjoyed it. Every moment of it.

Now? He'd never felt so empowered, so strong, as he had since the turn of this century. It was the wars, again. The blood-drenched conflicts, and the Feeding they provided him.

For the last couple of centuries, he had steered clear of battles, by and large. They had involved wearing a stiff uniform and marching like a clockwork toy on an open field, standing in a straight line and firing your musket at an enemy a hundred yards away. And all this in the daylight. Hardly ever in the dark. It had been out of the question entirely.

He had Fed on mortals one at a time back then. Kidnapping them, carrying them away to some dark, hidden lair. Toying with them and torturing them before slowly killing them. Gorging himself on their pain and their fear.

But everything had changed rapidly, since the nineteen-hundreds had begun. Technology had sped up, and the attitudes of the humans had altered. War was no longer considered a table-top game for the amusement of gentlemen. It was now a matter of skulking and hiding, and moving at night. And it was as though the doors of a grand banqueting hall, closed to him for so long, had finally been opened.

Often, he didn't even bother to take sides. In Korea, for instance, he had slept by day in a paddy-field or a deserted shelter, coming out at night to snatch Chinese and UN soldiers in equal measure. And in 1944, he'd used the 'skin-condition' story for the first time. He'd murdered an SS Colonel in Warsaw, taken the man's identity and transfer papers, and gone to Buchenwald for six months. None of the guards had dared awaken him before dark.

The prisoners had had a name for him, back then. 'The Golden Beast'.

But nothing could quite match this.

All year, he'd been drifting ever closer to this war. He'd been in a bar in Vientiane, just across the border in Laos a few months ago, when a CIA man, tired and slightly drunk, had wandered in. It had been an easy matter to take control of the agent's mind, set the man to work for him, falsifying records in the name of Gorrekan, getting him assigned to Special Forces.

And now, here was this Maurice Lapotaire.

Gorreq regarded the newcomer coldly.

2

An enormous head appeared, the blond hair cropped a millimetre from the scalp, the pale eyes blazing fiercely.

Then broad Herculean shoulders followed. A deep torso, and heavily muscled arms. A narrow waist. Maurice found himself struggling with his fear again. It was like watching some mythological creature arising, fully grown, from the jungle floor. He was looking at no such thing, he kept telling himself. Just a waking man.

The last of the ferns dropped away with a brittle rustle as the Major stood up.

Gorrekan looked a little shorter than his troops, but Maurice quickly realized it was an optical illusion. He stood over six feet tall, the same as the others, but was so broadly built it was hard to see that at first. The dimensions looked all wrong.

He was dressed in plain khaki uniform pants and a green waistcoat with insignia on the shoulders. Unlike the other Lurps, his skin wasn't painted. It was as white as chalk.

His movements were slow and deliberate. He brushed himself down, straightened his shoulders, then took a couple of steps towards Maurice.

Patches of moonlight began to flow across his face. It was flat, the nose squashed looking, the mouth wide, a glimmer of white, even teeth behind the lips. Not a handsome face, but strong, magnetic. It bore no lines or shadows. It was impossible to guess how old the man was.

Maurice had to fight down the impulse to get out of

the way as the man moved towards him. And Gorrekan seemed to understand that. He stopped and smiled – his teeth were squared-off, symmetrical – and extended a massive hand. He waited patiently until Maurice reached out and shook it. His grip was surprisingly gentle.

'Mr Lapotaire.' The voice was cavernously deep. 'My boys have been telling me all about you.'

From under there? Under the ferns? They talked to him while he was covered with plants? Well, he'd heard of much crazier things, he supposed, in his short time here.

Maurice tried to place the man's accent. It didn't sound eastern European or Greek at all. It was flat-toned, in an almost British way; but there was a deliberateness to it, as though Gorrekan had learnt English, but wasn't entirely comfortable with the language.

'Didn't I see some of your work last year?' the Major asked politely. 'In *Time*? Or was it *Newsweek*?'

Pleasant small talk, in the Indo-Chinese jungle, in the middle of a goddamned war. Jesus Christ, it was something he could never get used to. He found himself struggling for the right response.

'Er, *Newsweek*. On the Berkeley riots.'

'Those were the ones, yes. I was particularly impressed.'

Maurice wasn't sure if he was being kidded or not, but the man's smile didn't waver. He realized that their hands were still clasped. Tried to work his fingers free. Couldn't, at first.

Gorrekan let him go.

'So, the brass have decided you can come on one of our little strolls? Have you ever been on a night patrol before, young man?'

'Yes.'

'How many times?'

'Once.'

'Once ought to have been enough for anyone but a masochist, I would have thought,' the Major grinned. 'But at least you know some of the rules. Let me reiterate them.' He held up his fingers and began counting them off. 'Don't get in our way. Don't go wandering off on your own. If you do happen to get lost don't, whatever you do, call out. We'll find you. Do everything you're told the moment you're told it. And obviously,' and Gorrekan's smile became huge, ironic, 'no flashbulbs. Charlie isn't interested in posing for the press. No public relations skills, you see.'

'Right,' Maurice nodded. 'Absolutely.'

'You understand we only move at dark? How *are* you going to take your pictures, anyway?'

'I'll manage somehow. I always do.'

'I'm very pleased to hear that. I admire resourcefulness.'

The Major tipped his head to Bobby, who'd been standing quietly behind them while they talked. He let out a muted chuckle.

'You hear that, Kansas boy? This young man's pictures might turn out to be great art. Fabulous concoctions of light and shadow. You might find yourself hanging on a gallery wall some day. I'll bet you never reckoned on that, when you enlisted?'

'No, sir.'

Gorrekan's expression suddenly became grave. He stared fixedly at Maurice, and his pale blue eyes widened a touch.

'You still have a little time to back out. We won't think any the less of you for it. But once we start, you stay with us until the bitter end. Do you understand that, Mr Lapotaire?'

'I understand perfectly.'

The Major nodded. 'Brave boy.'

There was a faint rustle behind him, and Maurice turned. The other men were all around them now, moving in through the trees like ghosts.

He counted seven of them.

'Lock and load, if you please,' the Major told them.

They were ready to go.

*

3

Night mist drifted around them as they moved further into the jungle. It smelled faintly of marsh gas, left a thin patina of droplets on their skin, their clothes. Rods of silver light, pouring down through the canopy, made it glow coldly, like some primeval mangrove swamp. Dark tree stems appeared and vanished around them. The few animal cries which echoed through the branches were very distant, as though the unseen creatures were afraid to come too close.

The Lurps didn't say a word as they pressed on. Maurice wondered what their names were. Before an hour had passed, he was making them up. The man in the shorts who'd dropped from the tree he called Climber. There were two blacks, who he dubbed Bro 1 and Bro 2. Then there was Crouch, and Scarcheek, and Robin Hood, the last so called because there was a longbow and a quiver full of arrows slung across his back.

They moved as silently as big cats. Sometimes, when the mist gathered thickly around him, he wasn't even sure they were still there at all. They carried a strange variety of weapons. Crossbows, machetes, ironwood clubs. Bro 2 was fiddling with something as he walked, which turned out to be a wire cheese-cutter, perfect for slicing throats.

Maurice found himself searching their expressions for signs of fear, or enjoyment, or determination, or hatred.

There was nothing. They didn't even look at each other, let alone him. Just stared straight ahead and kept on moving.

And their eyes. Maurice thought, at first, they were the exact same eyes he'd seen a thousand times since he'd arrived in-country. Cold and withdrawn, from fear, from the horror of battle, from the pain of seeing friends killed. Eyes across which invisible shutters had fallen. He started to realize that was wrong, after a while.

These were different. Other soldiers' eyes had glimmers in their depths, some kind of repressed humanity. But these didn't. They were fathomless, lifeless, like the glassy, button eyes of dolls.

The idea stuck with him as he tried to keep up with them. They seemed like Gorrekan's personal toys, robbed of a life or ideas of their own. Since their first conversation, he'd nurtured an instinctive wariness of the Major, which had grown into a nagging dislike over the past couple of hours. There was a dreadful, cool arrogance to the man. Look at the way he was walking right now, up at the front of the group, like someone out on a country hike. But he'd never met a talented military leader before. Perhaps they were all like that.

They'd gone three hours, and the moon had practically crossed the entire sky, when the patrol abruptly stopped. There was no word, no signal. All eight men just froze in their tracks.

Maurice was painfully aware of the noise of his own footsteps as he stumbled on a few more paces and jerked to a frightened halt.

Gorrekan, several yards ahead, turned to him quickly and held out a hand, palm flat, then jabbed his finger towards a moss-covered tree trunk off to Maurice's left.

He understood immediately. Nodded, and slipped quickly behind it.

What had the Major and the others noticed? He couldn't see or hear a thing.

There was a low branch, at chest height, on which he rested his camera. He adjusted the settings by touch. There wasn't enough light to take a decent shot here, but there *would* be if a firefight started.

Then, he looked up. The others had disappeared.

Had they gone on and left him behind?

Maurice's heart began pounding sickly in his chest, but he had the sense to remain where he was.

After about a minute, the scene in front of him came into focus a little more sharply. He realized that the Lurps hadn't moved away at all.

They were still there. He could just make out their outlines.

They were so entirely motionless he couldn't think of them as human any more. They were more like paintings, of trees and foliage. He waited for one of them to move. Not one of them did. Not one of them gave the slightest tremble.

Gorrekan, who should have been the most visible with his white skin and blond hair, couldn't be made out at all. Where was he? And what the hell were they waiting for?

Another five minutes must have passed before he heard a crackling in the trees ahead. Very faint. Very cautious. Like a timid deer.

Then, a voice from the same direction. A whisper. He couldn't make out the words, but the tone, the metre, wasn't English.

Charlie!

Either North Vietnamese or Cong were coming gradually towards them.

Maurice felt a wave of panic take hold of him. His skin seemed to prickle and freeze, both at the same time. He could hear his own heart thumping. All of a sudden he didn't want to be here. He wanted to close his eyes, and find, when he reopened them, that he'd been dreaming. That he was back in the States, back in New York. Someone else should be here! The thought kept running through his head. Not me! I'm not ready for this!

He always thought the same thing, before the start of a firefight. He ought to have got used to it by now, but he never felt so vulnerable as when the enemy was drawing close.

Fifty yards ahead, the branches stirred and parted, and men started filing quietly through.

There were a dozen of them that he could make out, and they were regular NVA, not Viet Cong. They wore those curious pith topees that made them look like old-time colonialists; like the French they'd kicked out years ago. Short-sleeved tunics, knee-length pants. They moved in single file, about a yard apart, and their weapons, the bayonets fixed and gleaming, were held at the ready.

He calmed down a little, let his work occupy his

thoughts. Couldn't help but feel a tiny pang of pity for the men. A couple of them were smoking, and they were chattering quietly amongst themselves, glancing around nervously. They couldn't see what was waiting for them.

They looked so small.

The sympathy didn't last long. Maurice imagined what they'd do to him if they managed to get hold of him, and settled back to the job in hand.

The Lurps were still entirely motionless. The North Vietnamese could have walked right past them, never realizing they were there. For a moment, Maurice thought they were going to.

Wrong.

4

On a wordless signal, the seven green-painted giants swung their guns up, and began firing.

The silence was replaced by an agonized, deafening roar. Blinding light swept through the trees as flame poured from the muzzles. Maurice began snapping furiously.

It was all over in seconds. Almost too quickly. The North Vietnamese didn't even have time to react. They just screamed and fell.

And—

There was something wrong. Maurice's hands fumbled blindly over his camera.

The NVA were all down, but they were still yelling with pain.

His mind blunted with confusion, he tried to grasp what was happening.

They were still shrieking. Still thrashing. All twelve of them.

There'd been something wrong, he realized, with the way the Lurps had fired. Their weapons had been sloped low. The jets of flame had come out at a downward slant, lighting up the carpet of fallen leaves.

They'd shot the gooks' legs out from under them, but avoided killing them.

Where the hell was Gorrekan?

Maurice looked around wildly, craning his neck, trying to blink the flash of the guns out of his eyes. The Major was nowhere to be seen.

The stench of cordite was filling the area now. He looked back at the men on the ground, and felt sick with horror. One of them had stopped moving and was lying still, his hands clasped to his lower belly, blood oozing from between his lifeless fingers. But the others were flopping around like beached dolphins. Some of them were shrieking, bellowing. Others were making strangled, rattling noises, their faces screwed up with torment. One, a kid of no more than seventeen, was doubled up and clutching his thighs, crying and jabbering.

This couldn't be happening. It was all some horrible accident. They'd been shot from point-blank range, for God's sake!

He waited for a medic to move in. For the men at least, to fire again, put the gooks out of their agony.

When they didn't, when they stood there grinning, the truth finally sank home.

The Lurps had done it deliberately. Shot not to kill but to maim, aiming for the feet and legs and pelvis.

What had he got himself into? Was this some weird Special Forces gig? Some experiment in tactical wounding? Or the on-the-spot torture of hostiles?

He looked around frantically for the Major again. And this time, he saw him.

5

Gorreq could smell Lapotaire's fear as he moved back through the trees. Then see it. It was like a faint shimmering around the young photographer's body, dark and glowing at the same time. He stared at the boy and wet his lips hungrily.

But it was too early yet to Feed on this young man. They'd have to get deeper into the jungle, where the body would never be found, before he considered such a thing. Missing In Action. It was such a convenient term.

His attention returned to the North Vietnamese rolling and moaning on the ground. A strange little race. If only they'd had their kind back in Egypt, the Empire might never have fallen, the Romans and Byzantines and Moslems might have been driven away. They'd acquired an almost legendary reputation amongst the Americans for their stamina, their fearlessness.

But, in the end, there was no such thing as a truly fearless human. And thank all the Lords for that, or he'd starve to death.

6

The Major was standing in a tangle of near impenetrable shadow, where the moonlight barely reached.

Maurice stared at him astonishedly. As the man stepped out into full view, he could see that there was more than just a wide smile on his face. There was a look that was almost ravenous.

The lips were drawn back, the flat-edged teeth glinting behind them. The cheekbones seemed to hold cadaverous, hollow shadows. The nostrils were flared again, and the eyes were very wide. Staring, almost bulging. They seemed to be catching the moonlight in a peculiar way, throwing it back with a faint gleam of gold.

Maurice wanted to shout something at him. But what? This whole thing wasn't over yet. He could sense that. But he didn't have the first idea what was going on, and he was too frightened to do anything about it.

The Lurps were moving back amongst the trees, as entirely silent as before. If they felt any emotion, as the men on the jungle floor writhed and babbled, they didn't show it.

Maurice got the feeling that they hardly even realized what they'd done. Could barely hear the screams.

Drugs, that was it! Or some bizarre religious ritual, akin to Satanism. Some of the troops he'd met out here had got into some pretty weird stuff in their desperation to survive.

Jesus Christ, he was breathing too fast, hyperventilating. He looked back at Gorrekan, his head swimming.

The Major was advancing towards the writhing bodies now, making no attempt at caution, his steps falling heavily on the damp leaves. He drew a huge knife from a scabbard in his belt. The blade had to be fourteen inches long. Both its razor-sharp edges were serrated, and where they met at the tip, the moonlight seemed to break and scatter.

Maurice sucked in a gasp, but he couldn't find the strength to move. He remained hidden behind the tree.

As he watched, the Major gave a soft chuckle, brushed his thumb along the blade, and then advanced towards the closest of the wounded NVA.

The man became rigid with fear.

Gorrekan knelt over him and pressed a hand down on his brow, as though to hold him in place.

The *coup de grâce*, Maurice thought. He was going to finish the man off at last.

But that was wrong too.

The gook seemed barely conscious now, his mouth twitching spasmodically, his eyeballs rolling behind half-closed lids.

But when Gorrekan started pushing the knife, very slowly, into the side of his neck, he came awake with a sickening shriek.

He yelled something garbled and began trying to claw at Gorrekan's face. But the Major had a good six inches' reach on him; all that the man could do was scrabble futilely at one muscular shoulder. He tried twisting his body away, kicking furiously, but that was just as hopeless. The Major was pinning him down like a greyhound with a rabbit.

For God's sake! Maurice screwed his face up. Wanted to look away, but couldn't. For the love of Pete, *finish* it!

Blood sprayed into the Major's face, but that didn't seem to bother him at all. He simply pressed down a little harder on the soldier's brow, and began working the blade in carefully, twisting and turning it like a man whittling a hole in wood.

The gook let out another awful scream. His eyes were practically popping from his head, now. Blood-darkened saliva dribbled from his mouth, and his feet banged up and down spastically.

Only when the blade was a full inch in did Gorrekan move it towards the jugular. He took his time, cutting in an uneven, zigzagging pattern.

It must have taken a full two minutes for the man to die.

Gorrekan stood up. His face looked black now, under its mask of blood. His eyes still had that golden shimmer, brighter than before. He began moving towards the next victim.

This one was fully conscious, had seen precisely what had happened to his comrade, and as Gorrekan loomed over him he began reaching for his fallen rifle on the jungle floor.

Gorrekan kicked it away casually, and laughed.

The man started trying to crawl away on his belly, dragging himself with his elbows towards the nearest bush. It was pointless, but he kept on going. Gorrekan followed him a few yards. Then he bent down swiftly, turned the man over, clamped his hand across the furrowed brow, and moved the knife towards his chest.

And before Maurice knew what he was doing, he was screaming out loud and leaping from behind the tree and running towards the Major.

'*Stop* it! What in hell do you think you're doing? *Stop it!*'

He didn't get five yards.

He was suddenly knocked to the ground from behind. Hands closed around his ankles. A knee was jammed, savagely, into the small of his back. He managed to twist his head around, look up, and saw Bobby and Climber bending over him. Their faces were blank, expressionless; their eyes were as dark as coal pits.

There was a howl, ahead of him, as Gorrekan began working on his second victim.

7

It was getting close to dawn by the time the Major had finished. The quality of the light had changed. There was a faint, smoky greyness to the tree tops now and, every so often, a bird would clatter as it winged its way through the branches, some distance off.

Maurice felt empty and was trembling all over. He was crouched on his knees, Bobby and Climber squatting on either side of him. Cold sweat drenched his forehead, poured in rivulets down his arms, his chest. He wished that he could pass out, but unconsciousness wouldn't come.

Gorrekan had taken an especially long time with the last NVA, torturing the man until he twitched like a worm some malicious child had cut in half. When the gook finally lay still, the Major gazed at his slack, mutilated form for a while, then pushed him aside like a rag doll.

He stood up, his movements even stronger, more assured, than they'd been before. Then he turned, gazed down at Maurice. His face and the entire front of his waistcoat were thick with drying blood. His hands too, and his arms, right up to the elbows.

His grin was huge, in that mask of deep, glossy red-brown.

And his eyes—

For a moment, they seemed to have no pupils, no irises. For a moment, they seemed to glow incandescently. A burning gold.

Maurice knew he was imagining it. He wasn't thinking rationally any more. Strange deep shadows seemed to hang around the Major, as though another shape were trying to replace his huge muscular form. An even larger head, with horns protruding from it. Cloven hoofs, and a tail.

Look, Stepmammy, look! It's the Devil! Or one of your 'beast-people'.

He blinked, and the shadows were gone.

The Major took a couple of steps towards him, and Maurice stiffened and drew back, certain he was going to suffer the same fate as the North Vietnamese. But all Gorrekan did was peer down at him gloatingly.

'What's the matter, Mr Lapotaire? Can't you stand a little blood?'

Maurice struggled to reply, but his throat had dried up tightly and he couldn't catch his breath.

The Major glanced quickly at the lightness in the trees above him. Seemed to realize for the first time how close to dawn it was. He motioned urgently to the Lurps.

'We'll make camp west of here. Charlie's friends will come looking for them before long.' He jerked a thumb at Bobby. 'Mr Lapotaire is your responsibility. Make sure he doesn't try anything foolish.'

The Lurps slung their guns over their shoulders, and started moving away.

8

By the time Maurice and Bobby reached the camp, by the side of a clear stream half a mile away, the Major had washed his hands and face and was walking away into a deeper part of the jungle. Crouch and Robin Hood were following him like faithful dogs.

Bleakly, Maurice watched them through the trees.

It was just as before. They stopped in a dense thicket, where practically no light reached. A silhouette in the gloom now, Gorrekan sat down, took the groundsheet that Crouch handed him, and threw it over his head. Then, as he settled down beneath it, the two men set to work with machetes. They were cutting all the ferns within reach.

They piled them over the groundsheet until Gorrekan was completely hidden from sight.

The sun was rising. Through a gap in the trees, Maurice could make out a luxuriant ochre tinge to the sky. The temperature of the forest air was beginning to rise.

He sat down shakily beside the stream, splashed a handful of cold water on his face. Dried himself and looked around.

The seven other men had disappeared.

It occurred to him to get up and start walking, put as much distance between himself and these psychopaths as he possibly could. But he didn't know in which direction home lay. He wouldn't last a day, wandering around in the jungle by himself.

He was, he realized, the prisoner of a homicidal lunatic.

He curled his legs up and wrapped his arms around his chest. A chill was seeping into him that the warmth of the growing day just couldn't banish.

CHAPTER EIGHTEEN

1

You seem troubled, brother.

It was Pashta. Gorreq stirred, underneath the groundsheet and the ferns.

There is a newspaper man here.

The woman laughed. *So kill him. Or have one of your men do it.*

That is not the problem. He is here because of my unit's success. I'm afraid I am drawing too much attention to myself.

Brother Tharman said nothing but, from two continents away, Gorreq could feel his disapproval.

You are sad? Pashta asked.

Yes. Gorreq let out a deep sigh. *I have Fed well, in this war, and now I fear my idyll here is over. I am not far from the Cambodian border. Maybe it is time to cover my tracks and go.*

2

Maurice was woken by a kick in the shoulder.

God knew how he'd got to sleep. He'd been sitting bolt upright by the stream for hours, peering numbly at the surrounding jungle, when suddenly he'd seemed to hear the Major's voice inside his head. *Rest, now.*

He sat up sharply. It was night again.

The Lurps were clustered around him, gazing down. Gorrekan was at their centre, directly in front of him, his broad hands on his hips. He was scowling.

'You were shouting in your sleep, Mr Lapotaire.'

Maurice shook his head to clear it. Fought the urge to back away.

'I'm . . . sorry,' he muttered, trying to stare the man down. It proved to be impossible.

'That's quite all right. Fighting gets to us all in different ways.'

The Major said it so very lightly; as though nothing untoward had happened the night before. But there was, again, a mocking undertone to his voice.

A smile broke out on his face.

'Are you coming with us, or staying here?'

'I suppose I've got no choice.'

'That's absolutely right, Mr Lapotaire. No choice at all.'

As silently as the night before, the patrol turned and began to move into the jungle. Maurice sat there stupidly for a moment, watching them disappear, and then gathered up his cameras and hurried after them.

They progressed at a steady jog amongst the tree trunks and the winding creepers, never faltering, never pausing. The pace began to tell on him before long. What'll they do if I can't go on? he wondered. Leave me to die, or kill me? That thought alone kept him putting one aching foot in front of the next.

The Lurps moved in a direct straight line for most of the journey, heading unerringly north. Except for one occasion when Gorrekan, up ahead, abruptly stopped. The others did the same. The Major gazed into the undergrowth ahead for a short while, his entire body stiffening. Then, he found a track off to the left and began to lead his men away, in a wide circle.

Why'd he done that? Maurice hung back a little, and glanced into the dark, tangled foliage. There was something solid in there. Something tall, smothered with ivy and creepers. In a vagrant shaft of moonlight, he could just make out an exposed area of pitted, eroded stone, the symbol of a sunburst carved deeply into it.

It was one of those old ruined temples you came across in the jungle every so often. Khmer, probably. A temple to an ancient sun-god. He couldn't understand why Gorrekan had avoided it. Was it booby-trapped? Were there snipers in there?

Maurice realized he was being left behind again. Suddenly afraid, his whole spine tingling, he pursued them down the track.

The patrol spent a full ten minutes by-passing the temple, and then resumed its northward march, at the same merciless pace as before.

How much time had passed now? His breath was coming short, and every so often the jungle in front of him seemed to swim sideways.

He tried to keep his eyes fixed on Bro l's lurching back.

The men ahead were slowing again, drawing to a halt, unshipping their weapons.

They began to spread out through the darkness, till he could barely see them any more. He followed as best he could, trying hopelessly to make his tread gentle.

He went cold, and his skin began to crawl, when he heard a faint noise up ahead. It was a brittle, tinny clattering.

The Lurps pressed on with a quiet restlessness. The clattering noise came again. And, before long, he could hear the soft murmur of voices.

There were four of them, in a clearing twenty yards ahead. Viet Cong in black pyjamas and bush hats. They were sitting in a tight circle in a patch of moonlight, their guns across their knees. And they were eating. The clatter was their fingernails brushing against their tin-foil pans. They were whispering earnestly between mouthfuls, unaware of the danger they were in.

A fifth man appeared.

Maurice could just make out his head and shoulders. They seemed to be sprouting from the ground itself.

As he watched, the man bent down and disappeared from sight for a moment, then crawled out and joined the others.

It took him a few seconds to realize there was a tunnel down there. Perhaps an entire system of tunnels. That made him more frightened than he already was. Charlie by the hundreds could be hiding below the very ground they were standing on.

Gorrekan and the others must have realized it too, but they didn't seem in the least bit bothered. Almost casually, they moved in around the Viet Cong and levelled their weapons.

Maurice turned his head away, squeezed his eyes tightly shut, as the firing started. The horror of last night . . . he couldn't bear to watch it all over again. Nausea had already started welling up from his stomach.

The shooting was all over in a few brief seconds. His head rang with the noise. He waited for the screaming to begin.

It didn't.

The five Cong were sprawled across the ground, their heads thrown back, their limbs twisted into impossible positions. Their eyes stared, as though fascinated, at the narrow patch of sky above them; reflecting the stars; wide and unblinking in the filtered moonlight. Major Gorrekan was wandering amongst them almost disconsolately, prodding at them with the toe of his boot. They were all dead, had been killed instantly.

He should have been relieved, but he couldn't take his eyes from the Major.

Gorrekan stooped, picked up a fallen AK47.

And levelled it at his own men.

3

Maurice watched as the Major's eyes glowed golden again, and something happened to his troops.

One moment, they were stiffly upright, emotionless and placid, just as they'd been since they had left LZ Bravo.

The next . . . they were moving independently. Untensing. Coming properly alive.

Bobby reached up and clutched at his forehead.

'Jesus Christ,' he started mumbling. 'Jesus Christ almighty!'

'What the fuck—?' someone else said.

Maurice looked around. It was Bro 2 – the first time he'd ever heard him speak. The big black man was gazing bewilderedly around him, rubbing his eyes, as though he'd just woken from an awful nightmare. He looked dazed and frightened.

'What the hell *is* this . . .?'

It was another one. Robin Hood, the man with the longbow. He was staring at his arms, at the green paint. As Maurice watched, he began prodding at it with his fingertips. He was wondering how it had got there.

All of them were behaving the same way. Staggering as they moved around. Stumbling. Murmuring dazedly.

Maurice felt the hairs rise on the back of his neck, and sank back into the shadows. It wasn't drugs. It wasn't anything he'd ever encountered before, anything he remotely understood. What in all hell was happening?

It was as though Gorrekan had held them in a trance this far and, with that golden flash of his eyes, had suddenly released them.

He thought of turning, running. Glanced back into the jungle. It was too dark to see his way through the trees.

'Major? *Major?*'

It was Bobby again. The accent was the same, but the pitch of his voice was much higher now. Almost childlike. And petrified.

'Major, what're you *doing* . . .?'

Maurice looked in his direction, and saw the Kansas boy trying to back away, waving his arms furiously, as Gorrekan advanced on him, pointing the rifle at his chest.

Before he could fully take in what was happening, there was the crack of a gunshot, a spurt of flame from the AK's muzzle. Bobby fell to the ground, screaming, clutching at a ragged hole in his side.

Shock jolted through Maurice like an electric current. He floundered backwards, got his heels caught on a root and crashed to the jungle floor.

It didn't hurt. The ground was far too soft, yielded beneath him. He looked back up at the clearing.

Gorrekan was turning on Bro 2, and shooting him down too. Then Crouch. He was wounding them, just as they'd wounded the NVA patrol last night. All the men were armed, but they were too frightened, too confused, to put up any resistance. They were trying to stagger away, gaping at the Major as they retreated.

And the golden glow wasn't just a brief sheen in the man's eyes any more. It had taken them over, filling them, expanding from lid to lid. It wasn't any kind of optical illusion. It was real.

The shape of his body seemed to be changing. It darkened to the point where the waistcoat, the camouflage pants, the bare white chest were no longer distinguishable.

The whole of his face was becoming inhuman. Flat and savage, like the face of an animal. The lips were peeled back. Huge flat teeth gleamed ferociously. And there was the shadowy curve of horns above the brow, once again.

Maurice felt his mouth cracking open in a soundless yell. He fought to keep his mind clear.

God, he was going to be next. The Major was going to get him too. He had to *do* something.

He stayed down on his hands and knees, and began skirting around the edge of the clearing, trying to get behind the Major. If only he could reach the dead VC, lying with their weapons at the tunnel's opening.

Every so often he'd glance back at the carnage. The figure that had once been Gorrekan was taking its time, toying with the men. It seemed to be trying to make them as frightened as possible, before shooting them. It jerked towards Climber, feinting an attack, making the man trip over. Then it stood over his prone form, fired twice. Once in the groin – it laughed at the piercing scream of pain. Then once more in the shoulder, ripping away part of the man's arm.

Scarcheek was running blindly towards the undergrowth. The creature let him get most of the way, then cut him down with one shot through the lower spine, left him crawling and whimpering like a puppy a truck had hit.

It snorted, turned its attention to a frozen, jabbering Robin Hood.

Maurice's hand closed on something hard and cold. He looked down, saw that he was holding the wrist of one of the dead VC. He jerked back, then began scrabbling for the man's weapon.

It was some kind of machine-pistol.

He clicked the safety off – just as Gorrekan mowed down the last of the Lurps and swung towards him.

The moon had disappeared behind a patch of clouds, by now. The clearing had become pitch dark. All Maurice could see was that pair of gloating, bright eyes, bobbing as the creature moved towards him.

He fumbled for the machine-pistol's trigger.

Squeezed hard.

The gun roared, jumping in his hands. He held it as steadily as he could, aiming at a point two feet below the advancing eyes.

Everything seemed to be taking so long. Everything was happening in slow motion. The gun was growing hot in his grasp. Flames were spurting out, illuminating the surrounding trees and the shadowy form of the creature. But the creature wouldn't fall. Christ, when was it going to keel over and die?

The gun stopped bucking in his hands, and fell silent. Either it had jammed, or he'd emptied the whole clip.

The bright eyes paused for a moment. Stared down at him mercilessly.

And then began moving towards him again.

4

For a moment, Maurice froze completely; as though he were rehearsing death, and rigor mortis had already set in. Then, he rolled on to his side and, reaching the edge of the tunnel, let himself drop.

He'd only expected to fall a few feet, but it seemed to take for ever. The darkness whirled around him and, near the bottom, he banged his shoulder on something hard, clenched his teeth to hold in a shriek.

He hit the bottom in a cloud of dust. Earth pattered down on top of him. For a moment, he was terrified that the shaft walls would collapse and bury him alive.

The noise of falling dirt stopped, after a while.

It was pitch black down here. One arm was trapped beneath him, twisted at a painful angle. But the other was free. He waved it in front of his face, felt his palm scrape a wall.

For all he knew, the tunnel was crawling with VC. He'd almost welcome them, right now. Nothing could be worse than having to face that thing up there. He rolled on to his belly, tried to get up. Bumped his head against the roof immediately.

He was about to start crawling when, quite without warning, his mind started growing dull. Was he concussed? His hands went to his head, feeling for bruises.

Then he heard Gorrekan's voice.

5

Where are you going, my young friend? Come back up. Come back and take your medicine.

It didn't seem to be coming down the shaft. It was inside him, in his own head.

And before he could stop himself, his hands were groping through the air above him, closing around a ladder rung, pulling him upwards, towards the patch of faint grey at the tunnel's opening.

Maurice tried to let go, but the voice only grew louder, more insistent.

He fought to ignore it. Forced his mind to wander back, to the old days in Harlem. To Madame Lapotaire, and her stories of the beast-people. He'd thought that was all it was – stories – until now.

'They change their shape,' she was saying, 'and they

talk inside your head. They got golden glowin' eyes. An' the only way to fight 'em is—'

The memory tried to drift away from him, as though something were trying to dislodge it. But he clung on to it desperately.

'—the sun. Anythin' to do with the sun—'

It was night. And even if it hadn't been, he couldn't get any further away from the sun than here, below the jungle floor.

What do I do now, Stepmammy?

He'd have to make up a sun for himself, he realized. Or perhaps she told him.

Maurice thought of it as hard as he could. Visualized the burning globe inside his head. Concentrated on it so furiously that, within seconds, he could almost see a yellow disc, flaming before his eyes in the darkness. He battened on to that image, clung to it for dear life.

Believe in it, he told himself. That was the most important thing. Believe in it as passionately as his stepmammy would have believed.

Gorrekan's booming voice became weaker in his head, and then gradually faded away.

It was all the chance Maurice needed. He began crawling away from the shaft on his belly, dragging himself on his elbows, pushing with his knees. Above the noise that he was making, he could just pick out another sound. The creaking of the rungs behind him, as something large and heavy started to descend them.

Move! Just keep *on* moving! He sucked in a clammy breath, and redoubled his efforts.

The tunnel started bending sharply to the left. He was glad of that. Anything which put a barrier of solid dirt between himself and Gorrekan was something to be grateful for.

He wasn't sure how long he'd been blindly scrabbling when he finally saw a dull patch of yellow to his right. He froze, almost yelled, thinking, at first, he was looking at the creature's eyes. That couldn't be. He could hear the thing crawling in the tunnel behind him, by now, the noise of its progress heavy and rhythmic and all too fast.

The yellow was a light, some distance away.

He pulled himself towards the glow. And this time, he'd only crawled for half a minute when he came to a fork in the passageway. A narrower tunnel ran off to either side.

He chose the smallest one – the dark one – hoping the beast wouldn't be able to squeeze down it. And blind again, he moved like an exhausted swimmer, his feet kicking, his hands clawing desperately. Every muscle in his body was aching, now.

His outstretched right hand brushed against something thin. Something hard and cold. And he came to a halt.

Didn't want to do that. The noises behind him were growing louder. But some instinct stopped him from pressing on.

He touched the thing again. It was a wire. He ran his fingers along it carefully, sweating and shivering. It ran from one side of the tunnel to the other, about five inches above the floor. At one end, it was knotted to a stick. At the other, it was twisted around a metal ring, the kind you found at the end of a grenade. Beneath it, there was something large and metallic half-buried in the earth. It was a boobytrap.

The noise behind him stopped, and then a loud, uneven shuffling began. Gorrekan was manoeuvring himself into the narrow opening of the tunnel.

Panting furiously, Maurice raised his hand to the ceiling. There was a gap of about two and a half feet. Just enough room for him to climb over. Maybe. But if he stayed here, he was going to die for sure.

He got to his knees, stretched his arms over the wire. Pressed his hands flat against the earth on the far side. Then, raising his body into an arc, he began to struggle forwards.

He started to panic, before long. He couldn't remember where the wire was, and the shuffling noises were getting closer. He raised his left foot. Felt his toe catch the wire, just as it cleared the ground. Stopped dead, trembling savagely, all his weight on his arms and his right leg. He eased his foot back to the floor, backed up a little, tried again. There was no resistance, this time. He was over, safe. And, Christ, the creature was almost upon him by now. He had to get *out* of here.

He began scrabbling wildy, trying to put as much distance as possible between himself and the trap. Crashed into another wall. And, for a moment, he thought he'd come to a dead end.

He felt around. He'd come to a ninety-degree corner, that was all.

For one brief instant, he dared to glance back. The creature's burning golden eyes were moving steadily towards him.

The tunnel roof got a little higher here. Maurice raised himself to a crouch and, his elbows rasping against the walls, began to run.

There was a roar, louder than anything he'd heard in his life, piercing his eardrums like skewers, jarring his bones, pounding into his brain. He was knocked off his feet as a scorching blast of air hit him. Red-hot specks of dust burned deeply into his skin.

The commotion stopped, as abruptly as it had begun. The ground seemed to rock under him for a while longer, and a little more of the roof came down. Then . . . silence, except for the ringing in his ears.

He brushed the soil off him, got back up, and retraced his steps to the corner of the tunnel. Hunkered down, listening.

For the first time since he'd left the LZ, a grim, satisfied smile crept across his lips. The creature *had* to be dead. The bomb must have torn it to pieces.

He thought he heard a scratching noise. His ears were still buzzing furiously, and it was hard to be sure.

Then, there it was again! *Louder* than before. And as he listened, it became constant and repetitive, a slow, insistent scraping.

The creature, somehow, had survived. Was buried alive, but was digging its way out.

Maurice turned and fled.

6

He joined a far wider tunnel, after a while; a main passageway. Small electric lights, strung on loosely dangling cords, burned in the ceiling every fifty yards. There were cramped rooms leading off to the sides, oil lamps and cooking utensils and bedding scattered across their floors. A bullet-pocked steel helmet lay by a doorway like a dead turtle. The whole place was deserted, except for rats. But, God, it looked like an entire division had been living down here.

He pushed on down the corridor, but couldn't find any exits.

He'd been going for about five minutes when he heard another sound behind him. It was a loud thump, like a fist hitting one of the tunnel walls. And then, from far away, the resounding echo of footsteps.

He was rooted to the spot for an instant. Then, he was thinking of nothing else, just running.

A hundred yards further down, he found a ladder, riveted into the wall. There was a large round hole above, but no light. There *had* to be some kind of door up there.

He reached the top, pushed steadily. Heard the creak of bamboo hinges and a loud rustle of foliage. The trapdoor fell to one side, and moonlight streamed over him.

He emerged into an explosion of noise. The kind he'd always heard when he'd been in the jungle before. The kind of noises he'd missed for the last two nights. Monkeys screamed and birds shrieked all around him. Insects whirred, homing in on his face. The undergrowth crackled as small creatures pushed through it.

He'd come out into a tiny liana-wreathed clearing.

The high full moon overhead blinded him, after the darkness below ground. He blinked, rubbed at his eyes.

Above the jungle's racket, he could hear another sound. A slow, constant gurgling. He couldn't make out what it was, at first.

Water. There was a river close by.

He began stumbling towards it.

And that was when the ground suddenly slipped away from under him.

And an agony like all the punishments in hell drove its way through his left foot.

7

He hit the ground awkwardly, at a savage angle. His foot was trapped and for a moment he couldn't understand what was happening. He struggled wildly.

The pain simply grew ten times worse, and he threw back his head and screamed, almost passed out.

Nightbirds flapped away, around him. The jungle became entirely silent.

Then there was the horrible crunch of tearing flesh, as his foot came free.

He rolled into a ball, clutching at it. His fingers ran over it frantically, ignoring the terrible jolts of pain that greeted his every lightest touch. Trying to feel what had happened, trying to make out what was wrong. His hands became slick with blood immediately.

The sole of his boot had been almost entirely ripped away. He fumbled awkwardly with the laces, each tiny movement rewarded with a fresh quiver of pain. Finally, dribbling with gore, he got it off.

There was a deep tear in the sole of his foot. When he probed at it, very gently, lights exploded in his head and he blacked out for a second.

He shook himself awake again, leaned over the hole his foot had dropped into. The moonlight revealed something down there that was long and thin, and pointed at the top; which cast its shadow like a sundial. It was a *pungi* stick. A trap left by the Viet Cong. A concealed bamboo stake, razor-sharp at its tip.

He began to shake from pain and blood loss. Sometimes, the Cong poisoned these traps. Often, they smeared excrement on to the tips, to make the wounds septic. Thank God it hadn't gone all the way through. If it had, he'd probably still be trapped there.

He collapsed on to his back, faintness overtaking him. Gazed up at the tree tops, at the moon. His sight began to fade.

No! He had to stay conscious.

He could hear footsteps again, far closer than before, from the tunnel below. Heavy stamping treads. Maurice rolled on to his stomach, tried to get up. He couldn't. His legs were too weak and the pain too great.

There was a snorting noise, from the shaft.

Panic swirled over him. He began crawling, on his hands and knees, towards the river. Heard something crashing up through the foliage by the trapdoor, just as he reached its banks.

It was huge, the trees on the far bank as tiny as though he were looking at a photograph. The water was a dark and scummy brown. But when he looked out to the middle, he could see that the current was flowing much faster there. Rafts of matted leaves and fallen branches were being scurried along like strange, misshapen rowboats in their journey towards the sea.

It was a swim of about a hundred yards. For a moment, he was gripped with indecision. He'd never make it. For a moment, he considered lying low and simply hoping the creature wouldn't find him.

That was nonsense. He wasn't dealing with anything human, or even animal. He was being chased by something out of Stepmammy's dark magics.

There was no choice.

Maurice eased himself forwards carefully, his belly sliding on a thick bank of mud, and sank, as quietly as he could, into the waters.

He tried to side-stroke, keep the pressure off his left

leg. But he found himself being pushed back to the bank almost immediately – there was some kind of undertow here. He started to roll, got a mouthful of foul-tasting water. Struggled on to his chest again, trying not to cough or splash.

He attempted a crawl stroke, trailing his useless leg behind him. And that worked. Pure fear made it work.

He was halfway out, when he heard Gorrekan's voice booming in his head once again.

There was a chuckle. *Mr Lapotaire? Where are you?*

Maurice began swimming furiously. Didn't care, now, if he was making any noise or not.

Ah, there you are, in the river!

He tried to think of the sun again, but pain and fatigue were overwhelming him. He couldn't concentrate.

Why don't you stop swimming? Why don't you just rest? You must be a very tired young man. Let the holy waters embrace you.

He was almost at the middle. A cluster of twigs went drifting past his face, spinning like a top. But now, however hard he tried, he seemed to be getting nowhere. His strokes were far weaker than they'd been a moment ago.

He was still trying to understand it when the water closed over his head.

He kicked for the surface wildly with his good leg. Broke through, spluttering.

It was the voice, he realized. It had practically made him give up.

He could hear triumphant laughter in his head.

That's right, Maurice. Just relax. Let yourself go.

The water started closing over him a second time. Maurice clenched his teeth, ignored the voice. He kicked and pulled angrily, even made his injured leg work a little. And abruptly, he was in the middle of the river.

The current was dragging him along like a tiny cork. Except corks could float, and he just couldn't seem to. His head went under for the third time. Darkness enveloped him. He could hear a sound like a rushing wind. He grappled for the surface with his right hand. It broke clear, but that was all. The rest of him wouldn't follow.

The noise in his ears gave way to a high-pitched whining. His chest felt as though it was going to burst.

Then, his hand closed around something. It was only a twig, but he yanked on it and felt a heavier resistance.

He pulled hard, and his head and shoulders burst into the silver light.

In front of him was the massive tangled silhouette of a drifting tree trunk, like some bizarre ancient warship. Only its top third was clear of the water, but he'd caught hold of a slender branch and now the thing was pulling him downstream, faster than before.

The voice in his head became angry. *Let go, boy.*

He dragged himself towards the trunk with his last ounce of strength, grabbed hold of a trailing root, curled his arms around it.

Let go!

His grip began to weaken again. His eyes began to close.

Maurice took a deep breath and pulled himself up on to the tree, praying it wouldn't roll.

He heard a loud bellow. It wasn't in his head this time.

He turned his face towards the shore.

And caught a glimpse, in the moonlight, of a gigantic figure standing on the river bank.

The body was still that of a huge powerful man, except it was completely darkened, and seemed to have a tail, and legs that were angled the wrong way.

But the head. The enormous, oval head . . .

With long gleaming white horns curving from its brow, it was the head of an enormous bull. The Minotaur, he thought, dully. Look, Stepmammy, it isn't one of your 'beast-people' after all, just the silly old Minotaur from the old Greek legends. And, for a while back there, I was Theseus in its labyrinth.

He could see its burning golden eyes even from this distance. They blazed with outrage as they followed him. But as he watched, they began to recede.

The river carried him around a bend, and the beast was lost from sight.

Unconsciousness started closing over him, like a drowsy cloud of smoke.

8

When he came to, it was daylight. Brilliant sunshine burned down on his waterlogged skin, and flies buzzed all around him.

He'd been washed up on a muddy bank, how far downstream he had no idea.

His head came jerking up as something began rustling through the undergrowth near by, but it moved away quickly, and it only appeared to be small.

He squinted around and listened intently. Nothing was approaching him. There were no voices in his head any more.

And then it hit him and, despite the pain enveloping his leg, he smiled.

You can't come out in the daylight, can you? You can't get me now because you can't face the sun.

There was another rustle, behind his head, and suddenly a small Vietnamese face was bending over him, peering at him curiously. Maurice stiffened for a moment, afraid that the man was VC. But this one was wearing the uniform of an ARVN scout. A platoon of Green Berets brought up the rear, about five minutes later.

He'd been got into a stretcher, a dressing had been applied to his foot, and a Jolly Green was whirring down between the branches towards him, when he passed out again.

*

9

He awoke, in bed, from a dream in which blazing golden eyes were closing in on him.

He was in a white-walled hospital room. A fan was churning sluggishly in the ceiling, casting its shadows across the white-tiled floor. Slat blinds hid the windows, but the neon lights beyond them, the sounds of rock music and shouting vendors and puttering motorbikes, confirmed that he was in Saigon. Still in Vietnam, at night.

And Gorrekan was out there somewhere.

He began screaming for a nurse, for a doctor. Anyone. Whoever was in charge. And by dawn he was being wheeled across the airstrip towards a plane for Tokyo.

PART IV

THE MIDNIGHT CLUB

PARIS, 1972

CHAPTER NINETEEN

1

The overnight plane from New York cruised in above Paris at five in the morning, its undercarriage dropping as it approached Charles de Gaulle airport, and Susan Carroll woke at the double thump.

She wasn't quite sure at first whether she was still dreaming. It had been a long haul from Los Angeles, and she hadn't travelled, really *travelled*, in so many years. It had thrown her out completely, left her mind detached, her body feeling as though it didn't belong to her.

For a moment, she didn't move. Her head was pressed against the small scratched Perspex window, a tangle of her auburn hair drooping across her eyes. She shifted painfully in her seat – God, it felt as though it had turned into cast iron during the journey – and brushed her face clear.

And suddenly, she was looking down at the City of Lights.

She woke up quickly, her heart pounding and her breathing ragged. She could feel her skin flushing and tingling.

She felt more alive than she had in years.

The plane seemed to be moving over the heart of the city with an almost dreamlike slowness, as though to grant her a better view of the wide streets below. Her eyes flickered from one brilliantly illuminated point to the next, soaking it all in ravenously.

She could make out the Eiffel Tower from here, beacons flashing at its peak. *And* the Arc de Triomphe. The broad parallel rows of streetlamps leading from it, with the parkland at the end, had to be the Champs-Elysées. The building which looked like the winter palace of a

Holy Roman Emperor had to be the Louvre. And which was the presidential palace? There were so many choices, so many huge and beautifully ornate buildings.

The Seine snaked between them like a band of dark reflective satin. She could even make out the wrought-iron lamps on the bridges. Her lips drooped with amazement, the sticky, bad taste in her mouth forgotten.

The plane continued its gentle glide beneath the clouds, and Notre-Dame cathedral came in sight. Lord, she must have read the Hugo classic a dozen times, watched the movie twice as many. And now, here it was.

Her heart was still thumping fiercely in her chest, as though she'd just run up a steep hill. And at that moment, Susan felt that if it burst right now – right here on this plane – she'd die of simple, perfect joy.

A great passion flooded over her. She'd already fallen in love with Paris, she realized, before she'd even set foot on the ground.

'Purty, ain't it?' said a voice.

She turned to face the portly businessman who'd been sitting next to her since New York. His name was Hal something – he was from Clarksburg, West Virginia, and 'in plastics'. For the first half-hour of the journey, he'd tried cautiously to pick her up, even going so far as to drop a large be-ringed hand on her knee for a moment, while he spoke to her. When she'd shown no interest whatsoever, he had turned his attention to the youngest and most cheerful of the mini-skirted stewardesses.

He hadn't really seemed that interested in her, anyway. Had only tried his luck with her because, like a mountain, she was there. He'd be better off with someone half his age and undemanding, Susan thought. Her ex always had been, after all. And this man reminded her so much of Denny.

She forced herself to smile at him. That annoyed her. Why did she always have to be so friendly and polite to people, even when they were idiots or sheer nuisances? It was her parents' fault, she knew. Back in Santa Monica, she'd been brought up never to be rude or show anger; and now, at the age of forty-one, she simply couldn't change.

'Pretty isn't the word,' she told the man, as she let her eyes drift back to the rooftops. 'It's like . . . a great fantastic diamond, cut into a million facets.'

Hal chuckled admiringly. His big paw settled on her knee again, stayed there this time. So, he'd had no luck with Miss Twinkling Smile 1972.

'Lady, you sure do talk a treat. I can just *tell* you was married to a creative type of man.'

And Susan felt like bursting out laughing. Creative? Denny? He was a successful Hollywood producer, for sure. But the only thing he could ever have been accused of creating over the last few years had two arms and two legs and cried a lot, and was the result of a careless tryst with a six-foot-tall yellow-haired starlet called, believe it or not, Tiffany Jade.

Susan shivered a little, with anger. She'd been able to cope with his constant infidelities, over the two decades of their marriage. Been able to push them out of her mind, pretend they weren't happening, or at least that they weren't important. But a child? A paternity suit? It had been the last straw.

The hand on her knee shifted, then withdrew.

'I was wondering?' Hal said. His harsh accent had suddenly become muted. His eyes were wide and round. 'First time in a new city, for both of us. Nice to have a familiar face around, I would have thought. Maybe . . . dinner, this evening? I'm on a darned good expense account. I can afford somewhere real nice.'

Susan found herself surprised. Not by the question, she'd been expecting that. But by the way it had been asked, the slightly desperate, pleading manner. The tone of the man's voice was nervous, like a little boy's.

He was older than her, divorced himself. And perhaps, deep down, he wasn't just interested in a quick fling, whatever lies his ego told him. Perhaps, deep down, he truly needed someone who would care for him.

Don't we all, she thought. God, she more than anyone

needed someone to really love her, after all these loveless years.

Half a dozen put-downs had been dancing on the tip of her tongue until that moment, none of them her own. She'd got them all from books or movies, or from listening to friends. But she rejected them all. She'd suffered enough cruelty herself since the middle of last year. She didn't want to pass it on to yet another lost soul.

She'd let Hal down gently, she decided.

When she looked at him and smiled again, it was softly this time, genuinely.

'That's very kind of you, Hal. You're a nice man.'

'And . . .?' His bulbous red face was already taking on a disappointed expression.

'I plan to start work right away, I'm afraid. I'm on a deadline, and I'll never meet it if I start hanging around with you.'

He wasn't buying it. His lips became tight, scrawny.

'You mean to tell me you're going to spend your whole time in Paris tracking down this Maurice Lapawhosit?'

'That's right. Otherwise, I'd be happy—'

He pulled back from her sharply, as though he'd been stung. Leaned over towards the aisle. Looked away, and lit a cigarette, though the *no smoking* light had already come on.

He sulked, and didn't speak to her for the rest of the flight.

2

What was the French for faster? Kellesh settled for *vite*, leaned across the back of the cab and told the skinny, middle-aged Algerian driver it several times. The man shrugged, and made no attempt to speed up the battered Peugeot whatsoever.

Kellesh glanced frustratedly at his watch. He still had twenty minutes until dawn, and the apartment he'd occupied was only a short drive away. But being out of doors this close to sunrise always made him nervous. What if they had a breakdown, or a collision, or were stopped by one of the city's languid and officious *gendarmes*? He ought to have left the north-eastern suburbs much earlier. But wandering around the darkened streets of the African quarter, he'd felt such a thrill, such an electric sense of urgency.

He was near his goal, he was certain of that. In one of the slum tenements that crowded the shabby district was Maurice Lapotaire. He could feel the man's presence, strongly. But every time he'd tried to focus, he'd been blinded by the glare of *Ra* discs.

He would simply have to do the job on foot.

By all the Lords, was this journey going to take for ever?

He'd have harangued the driver if he'd remembered more of the language, but the last time he had been in France had been two hundred years ago. That had been during the Terror, and Gorreq had been here, serving in the court of Robespierre, revelling in the bloodshed, the screaming horror of the guillotine. Drinking deeply of the fear around him. Feasting, like a fat dark spider in its web. Growing ever stronger.

Kellesh had tried to hold him in check, but it had been hopeless. Perhaps, he reflected, if there was only *one* of them to deal with. Perhaps, if he was not forced to constantly divide his attention between the three. He remembered Tharman in Venice, at the time of Casanova. Gorreq in Toledo, with the Spanish Inquisition. Pashta in Morocco with the *hashshashin*. All that he could ever do was dog their tracks and try to slow them down. A futile task, whichever way you looked at it. They'd only find new games to play, a little further down the road.

He shook his head wearily, and swept out with his mind across the glittering drowsy city. The sky was just turning a faint lilac overhead. The insectile murmur of a thousand Parisian dreams filled his thoughts.

And, as he touched the Île de la Cité, something strange happened.

He felt only a blank.

A massive darkness, like a great wall of black stone.

He tried to probe it, drew back with a jolt.

They were there! All *three* of them, this time!

He hadn't even felt them arriving. Kellesh began to tremble.

Never, since his Incarnation all those centuries ago, had he faced all three at once.

They'd set up this barrier to stop him touching their thoughts, learning their plans. That was unnecessary. He could already guess. They were here for the same reason he was, hunting for the one man who'd ever escaped their clutches completely, who'd ever cheated them of their sport.

Maurice Lapotaire.

Kellesh had sensed the young man's pain and fear two years ago, in Vietnam, but he'd been too far away to help. He'd kept track, fascinated, as Lapotaire had got away and zigzagged across the world, always one step ahead of the dark creatures pursuing him.

It occurred to him, now, that perhaps he was helping them inadvertently. Perhaps he was leading them to the photographer. He'd have to be constantly on his guard.

The cab bounced over a pothole, and pulled up outside the front door of the grimy house behind the Gare du Nord where he'd moved into an abandoned studio. The driver turned around in his seat, pointed to the meter, and held out his palm, waiting to be paid. His face was drawn and haggard, exhausted. His deep brown eyes were watery and sad.

There were still a few minutes left till sunrise.

Kellesh felt his eyes glow as he fixated the man. He reached out, and placed his fingertips gently on the cabbie's greying temples. And began soaking away all his misery, all his pain.

3

Maurice Lapotaire lay in the taloned grip of a dream. Deep down, he knew it was only that, but it didn't stop him being terrified. He'd make a weak attempt to struggle back to consciousness every so often, like a fish flapping along a river bank. But Gorrekan kept dragging him down. The bull creature. The Minotaur.

Now, in his dream, it had finally caught him. Its face was pressed so close to his that he was suffocated by the hot stench of its breath. Its golden eyes blazed like molten iron, inches from his own.

It gripped him by the shoulders, and began tearing his arms off.

It wasn't alone, though. Not this time. Just beyond its hulking form, Maurice could make out two more silhouettes. They were creatures too, half human and half animal. One of them was like a great ape. The other, a slender, spindly cat. They glided towards him and helped the Minotaur finish off the job. Impossibly sharp claws raked down his chest, tearing open his belly like an over-ripe pumpkin to reveal the reddish pulp within. Powerful fanged jaws closed around his right leg, severing it at the knee. The ragged stump twitched, and the torn artery spurted.

Maurice let out a scream.

And suddenly, he'd woken.

He shifted uncomfortably on his damp, bare mattress. Gazed around cautiously, still shivering with fright. It took him a moment to remember he wasn't at home. He was in the basement of a tenement on the rue Albaiville.

The bare brick walls were lined with moss. Water dripped from the mottled ceiling on to the crumbling cement floor. There were scuttling noises from the darkest corners of the room.

He'd spent so many days and nights in hovels like this since he'd left the hospital in Tokyo. First in Manila. Then in Bangkok. Then Chad, Turkey, Bulgaria. Never going home. He could never go back to the States. He'd be too easy to trace, there.

The thing which had chased him through that tunnel, the night beast with the bull's head, was searching for him.

He knew it, from his dreams.

Maybe it was all the years he'd spent around his step-mammy. Maybe some of the voodoo woman's sensitivity, her psychic intuition, had rubbed off on him. Every time the thing that had called itself Gorrekan drew near to him, the nightmares would begin again. And it wasn't paranoia. He'd actually *seen* the blond giant, a year ago in Hong Kong. He'd been taking off from Kai Tak airport, looked out of the window, and there had been that unmistakable figure, standing beneath a light on the observation platform, staring up at him.

And now, this dream. It seemed worse than ever. He'd never had one like this before. Never seen the other two figures.

He'd have left Paris yesterday, if he'd had the money. But he hadn't been taking many photographs over the last couple of months, and his next cheque wasn't due until this afternoon. So he'd come here instead, as he always did when he felt threatened.

He shuddered, and looked up. A single dim lightbulb dangled from the ceiling. Around it, like mobiles in a child's nursery, hung discs of sparkling gold foil, suspended by fine threads. He'd filled this rotting basement with every symbol of the sun he could lay his hands on. There were more in his apartment downtown. Around his neck, he wore a bronze amulet with a flaming globe on it that he'd bought outside one of Thailand's opulent temples. On his finger was a ring with the same design.

He clutched it tightly, twisting it.

There was a sudden noise above his head. Footsteps, in the ground-floor hallway. Maurice sat up with a jerk.

They stopped, and were followed by a gentle knocking at the cellar door. It creaked open, admitting a shaft of thin dawn light.

Maurice relaxed. It was only Josh.

The old Cameroonian came hobbling down the narrow wooden stairs, peering at him anxiously. He was in his underwear and tattered carpet slippers, his white hair dishevelled, his lean grey face creased from lack of sleep. Joshua Makembe was the eldest of the thirty men asleep in the rooms above. Zaireans, Sudanese, and Senegalese, they all worked night shifts, sweeping streets or tending washrooms, except for Josh himself, who didn't work at all. He'd come to Paris thirty years ago, intending to stay until he'd earned enough money to return home and marry, and had never gone back. Now, he was a kind of 'house mother', cooking and washing for the rest, helping them write letters home, mending clothes, doling out advice.

They'd met, a couple of months ago, in a cheap café in the Latin Quarter. Maurice had been hunched over a cup of coffee, when Josh had simply walked across to his table, sat down opposite him and said, 'You are very troubled, my friend. Tell me, how can I help you?'

He'd turned out to be slightly psychic. His eldest uncle, back in Africa, had been a tribal shaman. His power was far duller and cruder than Madame Lapotaire's, but it was there.

The old man picked his way between the puddles on the floor and squatted at the end of Maurice's bed, for all the world as though he were home in his village near the Gulf of Guinea. He regarded Maurice evenly through hooded, bloodshot eyes.

'I heard you call out, M'sieu Maury. Are you all right?'

Maurice wiped at his slick face and nodded. 'Just another dream.'

But the old man didn't look reassured. 'Worse than before?' he asked softly.

'Yes.'

'I'm sorry to hear that.'

Josh shuffled on the spot. He looked uncomfortable and embarrassed, as though he had bad news. He couldn't meet Maurice's gaze directly now, kept glancing away, concentrating on the sun discs.

They were spinning in the draught from the open door, casting sparks of golden light about the room.

The old man ran his tongue over his worn, stained teeth.

'We were . . . talking,' he said at last, his voice a whisper. 'While you were asleep. The others, M'sieu Maury, they are younger than I. They are afraid. They say you will bring bad magic on us all.'

Maurice leaned towards him.

'Nothing'll happen in the daylight, Josh. You know that. The guys'll be at work, if anything comes for me.'

'Just you and me to face it,' Josh nodded. 'I do not mind that. I am an old man, and I cannot live for ever. The others, though.' And finally, he summoned up the courage to look at Maurice properly. 'They are not reasonable any more. They are too scared to listen to me. You must go by tomorrow night, M'sieu. They have agreed.'

Maurice took that in calmly. 'It shouldn't be a problem. I've money due, from a big magazine.'

The old man nodded, satisfied. 'I will be sorry to see you go.'

'But not entirely,' Maurice smiled.

Josh's face twisted. 'No.' And he glanced at the cellar walls, as though he was looking at something beyond them. Something only he could see. He hunched his shoulders, quivered. 'I can feel them too, Maury. The beast people.' His eyes fluttered shut, and he rocked gently on his heels. 'They are close, are they not?'

'Yes,' Maurice agreed. 'They are close.'

CHAPTER TWENTY

1

The phone rang by her bed, and Susan reached out groggily to answer it.

'Madame Carroll,' said a man's voice from the receiver. 'Your wake-up call. It is midday.'

For a moment, she was disorientated again. Thought she was in bed on Wilshire Boulevard, and that when she rolled over Denny would be grinning at her sleepily.

She ran her tongue around her mouth. Her teeth and gums tasted awful. Her eyes were stuck up and she could barely open them.

The man on the phone was waiting for a reply.

She mumbled, '*Merci beaucoup*,' painfully aware how bad her pronunciation was.

She could almost hear the man break into a grin at the other end of the line. 'My pleasure, Madame,' he said politely, before hanging up.

She rubbed at her eyes until they were clear, then sat up, looked around the suite. She'd barely noticed it in her headlong stumble to bed earlier this morning.

She was in a four-poster with a pattern of golden fleurs-de-lis on the azure drapes. The curtains on the huge windows to either side of her were the same. The walls were pastel green. There was an ottoman, a dressing cabinet, a large coffee table surrounded by three comfortable chairs, all in Louis Quinze style, shimmering dully with gold paint. An enormous mirror with a rococo frame occupied most of the far wall. A half-open door gave her a glimpse into the luxuriant bathroom.

Above her head was a bell-pull, a thick golden braid with a tassel at the end. Immediately she saw it, Susan felt like tugging on it furiously, just for the hell of it. It was like being a kid again, on your own in an enormous playground.

Her body, naked under the heavy blankets, felt clammy, over-ripe. She pushed a hand through her hair and it was greasy and lank to the touch.

She was dizzy when she got to her feet. She took two paces off the bedside rug, and yelped. The floor was marble underfoot, and freezing.

But the air against her skin was mild, and there was sunlight filtering in through the drapes. It was going to be a beautiful day.

She was just finishing her hair, beneath a shower-head in the form of a leaping dolphin, when the doorbell rang. Breakfast! She hadn't even unpacked yet. She had no robe.

Dripping, she wrapped one towel around her hair and another round her body. She went to answer the door a little embarrassedly, hoping there was a maid on the other side.

There wasn't.

The olive-skinned boy holding the laden tray was sharp-featured and handsome, and no older than twenty. Susan felt her cheeks flush. Began to edge backwards.

Then stopped, fascinated.

Within a second, the young man's gaze had flickered all the way from her feet to her face. And there it settled, fixing on her eyes.

It wasn't lust. There was heat in the look, but lust was too crude a word.

It was . . . admiration.

She hadn't encountered that for years. Since the mid-sixties, in Hollywood, an available teenaged girl seemed to be the only thing that turned men on. Now, she was face to face with a boy half her age, who found her beautiful in a special and exotic way.

How did that old French expression go? 'A woman of a certain age'? That was what she had become – she realized – the moment she'd stepped off the plane.

And she liked it.

She liked it a *lot*.

She took good care of herself, swam, jogged. Her face, give or take a few lines, hadn't changed much since her twenties. Her figure had filled out in all the right places, if anything.

Just because Denny had stopped noticing. Just because his floral-shirted, Gucci-shoed friends smoked dope on the lanai and talked of nothing but the hippy girls on Sunset—

Well, to hell with them all.

Her face was still tingling, but in a pleasant, comfortable way. And, to her own surprise, her lips pursed into a smile. Her hand went to the knot at the top of her towel – not to hold it closed, but to draw the boy's gaze there for a second.

He looked delighted, his dark eyes sparkling.

What was she doing, flirting with a total stranger? She was the mother of a nineteen-year-old girl, for God's sake. How would Casey react, if she saw her now?

Susan forced herself to stop it. Or at least, tried. But she could feel her hips swaying gently, as she led the boy into the room. She smiled ruefully and decided to enjoy it for what it was – a pleasant little thrill. Why not? Thrills had been noticeably absent from her life, of late.

She turned towards the window, the tray rattling down on to the table behind her. She could still feel the boy watching her as she moved. It was almost a gentle pressure on her skin, like the practised touch of a masseur.

She reached the drapes, pulled them back. Hot golden sunlight washed over her as she peered at the street below.

The avenue George V, just down from the Champs-Elysées. The roar of traffic met her. The cars below were jammed together solidly, beneath her tiny balcony. Horns were blasting, a miasma of exhaust fumes rising above the glittering carapaces of Renaults and Citroëns. Pedestrians were swarming on the broad sidewalks. And the scene shouldn't have been romantic at all. Should have been mundane, a disappointment.

But she simply couldn't see it that way.

Across the street, the names of shops stood out in

curling gilt letters. *Boulangerie*, and *Charcuterie*, and *Coiffeur*, said some of them. Butchers and bakers and hairdressers, but described with such beautiful and flowing words. Other names were familiar from Rodeo Drive, but they'd always seemed uprooted there, were entirely at home in this setting. *Dior. YSL. Pierre Cardin.* Tall trees lined the sides of the boulevard, their budding green-yellow leaves dappled by the unnaturally warm sun of early spring.

She was entranced.

There was another clatter behind her. The boy again. For a moment, she'd forgotten him.

He hadn't simply put the tray down on the table and left. He was in the middle of performing a small, intricate ritual, laying out a plate of croissants with butter and jam at the side, pouring milky coffee into a cup the size of a small soup-dish.

Was this part of the normal service? Or was he just using it as an excuse to hang around a little longer?

He looked up from his work. A lock of black, oily hair had fallen across one eye, giving him an almost roguish look.

'Is everything to Madame's satisfaction?'

She was surprised by his accent, which was almost perfect.

She started to nod, then looked at the cup again.

'Um – I normally take my coffee black.'

The boy raised an eyebrow, shrugged. 'This is the correct coffee for breakfast. Black is for later.' He smiled at her again. 'I can change it for you, if you like.'

'No, I'll try it your way.' She took a step towards him. 'Where did you learn your English?'

He straightened up, obviously delighted that she'd noticed. 'Miami. I was there for three years, working in all the big hotels.'

'Did you like it?'

'Oh, yes,' he beamed, pushing his hair back from his eye. 'It's a great city. And you are from—?'

'LA.'

He nodded approvingly. 'Nice too. And are you here on holiday or business?'

'The latter.'

'I *knew* it. I knew, the moment I saw you, you were not an ordinary tourist. A woman of your bearing – an executive for sure.'

'Hold it!' Susan giggled. 'I'm not representing IBM, you know. I'm a sort of – writer, I suppose.'

This seemed to puzzle the boy. His eyes narrowed a little, and he cocked his head to one side.

'To be a writer,' he said, slowly, 'is far better than an executive. But a "sort of" writer, Madame? What precisely is that?'

Susan crossed to the table, picked up the coffee and sipped it. It tasted sweet and wholesome, rather like chocolate.

'It's something I've just started. I've always had this big interest in photography. Done some myself, on an amateur basis. I've dozens of books on the subject at home. And I decided to write one myself.'

'On fashion?' the boy asked. 'Art photography?'

'No,' Susan said. She was hiding her face a little behind the cup now, suddenly nervous. 'War photographers. Unusual ones.'

The boy's face creased with surprise. She knew exactly why, and suddenly her attraction to him faded.

'War?' he blurted. *And, oh brother, here it came!* 'Why should a woman like yourself be interested in photographs of war?'

She'd heard similar reactions a dozen times, when she'd told people what she was planning. She'd even got some astonished remarks from her publishing friends in New York, when she'd first pitched the idea, though they hadn't put it quite so blatantly as this.

'Why on earth not?' she said, trying not to snap. 'They're just about the most moving kind of photos there are. And some of the people who took them were quite remarkable. Women like Margaret Bourke-White. Kids like Tim Page and Sean Flynn. People who shouldn't be within ten miles of a battlefield, in most people's opinion. Why shouldn't I be interested in them?'

She was partly annoyed out of embarrassment, she knew. She'd always harboured fantasies of being as brave as that.

The boy obviously realized that he'd put his foot in it, insulted her somehow, though he couldn't seem to work out why. He started trying to back-pedal furiously.

'Sure! You're right, why not?' he was saying. 'And there's a photographer like this in Paris? A woman?'

But the heat, the electricity of a few moments ago, was gone. The spell was broken.

The sound of traffic from the window was irritating her now.

'No,' Susan muttered, turning away briskly. 'Not a woman. A man. An American I think might be living here.' And it was going to be her hardest job, she knew, because it seemed as though he was hiding from the entire world. 'If you don't mind, now—' She glanced at the carriage clock on the dresser. 'I have an appointment in an hour's time.'

That was a lie. It was two hours. But she wanted to get rid of him.

The boy gave a small, stiff bow, completely bewildered.

'Of course, Madame. If there's anything else you need . . .'

'Sure,' Susan nodded. 'You'll be the first to know.'

She felt a twinge of regret as the door closed behind him. Let out a gentle sigh. The flirting had been so nice while it had lasted. She hadn't felt so coveted in years. Her spine still tingled with the pleasure.

She let the towel around her body drop to the floor, began rubbing at her hair until it became fine and downy to the touch. Then she picked up a croissant and nibbled at its corner, decided she wasn't all that hungry. She found a pack of cigarettes in her flight bag, lit one, wandered across the suite to a large cabinet with wires running from the back. A television was hidden inside. She switched it on, found herself watching the midday news. She couldn't understand a word the anchorman was saying, but within seconds footage of President Nixon in China flashed across the screen.

Her mind started humming as she worked over her routine for the day.

She'd promised Casey she would phone when she arrived. But it was only early morning in New York. Better to leave it until later.

She thought about the book again. She still had Maurice Lapotaire to see here, if she was lucky. The youngest and most remarkable on her list of photographers. Then on to England, to interview Page, provided he was still there. Then back to LA, for months of work transcribing her notes and tapes. And after that? Some photography of her own, perhaps. There were so many things she had to do, so many opportunities to catch up on. So much of her life to reclaim.

She opened her suitcase, and three copies of the American edition of *Decade* magazine fell out. She found a slip and put it on. Then she went across to the window again.

Stared out over the low, elegant rooftops of Paris.

The young photographer was out there somewhere, she was sure.

2

The offices of *Decade* magazine on the avenue de Rheims, just off the Champs-Elysées, made her feel as though she'd lived her entire life in some styleless clapboard house in the Valley, instead of Beverly Hills. It wasn't just that the odd but seamless blend of modernistic furniture and antique ornaments made her own home look as though it had been thrown together by a moron with a bric-à-brac shop. Far worse, she'd put on her smartest satin pants suit and her most fashionable Asian jewellery – and the stick-thin black-haired secretary who led her through to the back office *still* made her feel dowdy. Worse than dowdy. Like a bag lady.

The managing editor, Jean Valdurois, was sitting behind a large matt-black kidney-shaped desk. And, though he favoured her with the exact same admiring stare the boy at the hotel had given her, he didn't make her feel any better.

He was a pale man in his late forties, his midriff widening and his cheeks turning to jowls. But there was nothing of the middle-aged executive about him. He and the plastics salesman on the plane might have belonged to different species.

His hair was tied back into a flowing ponytail. He wore huge brown-tinted aviator glasses, an open-necked denim shirt, and bell-bottomed jeans. His fingers sparkled with rings, and there was an Indian *mandalla* on a heavy bronze chain around his throat. He was holding the unlit stub of a thick black cigar between his short, manicured fingers.

He used it as a pointer, indicating a red leather chair next to a cluttered bookcase.

She'd never seen a man with an air so casual, yet so regal, she decided as she sat down. This was someone who could get things done simply by clicking his fingers.

On the wall behind his head was a poster of the magazine's latest cover, a cartoon of Mao and Nixon in bed together. They'd never get *that* on the shelves in Orange County. A banner at the top read, *Soyez decadent avec Decade.* Be decadent with *Decade*, she translated roughly. To the left, a picture window looked out, through a gap between the buildings, at the Arc de Triomphe. The glass vibrated slightly with the rumble of the city's milling traffic.

Valdurois stared at her for half a minute, studying her closely, before he finally leaned forwards, thumped his elbows on his desk, and smiled.

'So, this is the Madame Carroll who's been so persistent with me? It's a great pleasure to meet you at last.'

His accent was harsh, unrefined. If she'd had to take a guess, it would be that he hadn't exactly risen from the cream of French society. That only made her admire him a little more.

'And you, Monsieur,' Susan nodded.

Valdurois jammed the cigar stub into the corner of his mouth, his eyes twinkling behind the tinted glasses. 'I confess, I wondered what you looked like, when we spoke on the phone last week. I'm far from disappointed.'

She said nothing. Valdurois glanced quickly at his gold Rolex.

'And now to business. Are you quite certain you wish to track down this Maurice Lapotaire – if, indeed, he is our mystery photographer?'

Susan felt her brow crease with a frown.

'I'm not quite sure I understand you.'

'Has it occurred to you, Madame, that if Monsieur Lapotaire has taken all this trouble to sell his photographs under an assumed name, to never show his face in public, to conceal his whereabouts, that he really may not *want* to be discovered?'

She couldn't quite believe what she was hearing. Had this man dragged her all the way across the Atlantic simply to lecture her? A hot flush began spreading across her neck, but she held her growing anger in check. Maybe this was some kind of European subtlety she wasn't familiar with.

She straightened in her chair, folded her hands in her lap. Didn't flinch from Valdurois' probing gaze.

'Yes, that's occurred to me, of course. But I'm never going to find out unless I ask him. That's all I want – the chance to meet the man, face to face.'

'Why should *he* want to meet you?'

Susan shrugged edgily. 'A man becomes successful so early in his life. Goes to Vietnam and takes two *Time* covers in a few months. Then he disappears off the face of the earth. Something happened to him out there, obviously. Maybe it'll help him to talk about it.'

'Ah.' Valdurois tipped back his head and gave a nasal snort of laughter. 'A purely American superstition. The absolute belief in the healing power of public confession. Perhaps you might convince him to appear on television and weep, Madame?'

Was he always this rude with total strangers? Susan was convinced by now that he was toying with her.

A phone started ringing in the outer office, and was promptly answered.

Valdurois reached behind his desk and pulled out a portfolio cover. Drummed his fingers on it for a moment, without opening it.

'Harry Bernstein,' he said. 'That's the name we've published all the photos under. So how did you suspect it might be Lapotaire?'

'The American edition of *Decade* came out a few months back. It had pictures of the demonstration outside the US embassy. The tone, the composition, were exactly like the photos Lapotaire took of the Berkeley riots. The same technique exactly.'

'I thought so too,' the man nodded, impressed. 'That's why I paid top rate and asked no questions.' He flipped open the portfolio and started pushing monochrome prints across the desk at Susan. 'These are new "Bernsteins", of the red-light district in one of our poorer suburbs.'

They were amazing. Light and shadow frozen into visions of a private hell. A girl in a tie-dye mini-dress, no older than fourteen, was injecting herself with a needle while a friend, the same age, watched. In the corner of an alley, a skinny pimp with hair down to his waist had his hand raised in the act of slapping a hard-faced, voluptuous woman. Her mouth was stretched wide open. Blood was running from her nose. You could practically hear her scream.

'How he took these without getting his throat cut,' Valdurois grinned, 'I'll never know. But I have no doubt – our "Bernstein" is a major talent.'

He sank back into his chair again, waited until Susan had finished poring over the prints.

'It may come as a surprise to you,' he said, 'that I was curious about "Bernstein" too. I did a little checking of my own.'

'Discreetly, I'm sure,' Susan replied. She was feeling a little numb.

Valdurois chuckled. 'Yes. *Touché!* Discreetly, exactly so. There *is* a Harry Bernstein. A Jewish gentleman, formerly of Vienna. He went to America after the war, where he changed his name from its original Heinz, but then came back here. He is a retired textiles salesman, and has never, to my knowledge, picked up a camera in his life. Yet every so often, for the past few months, he has been bringing portfolios of this quality into the outer office, unannounced. He always returns two days later for the cheque. He sees my secretary, Chloe, never me. And he comes and goes as though the hounds of hell were on his trail. You can find his address in the phone book. He lives near the Pigalle.'

Susan was tingling with curiosity now, shifting in her seat like an excited child.

'And you're *sure* he couldn't have taken these shots?'

Valdurois nodded firmly. 'I hung around the outer office, once, when he was due to pick up a cheque. He is a frail old man, in his late seventies. He – what is the word? – wheezes when he walks. And he has thick spectacles, and the beginnings of a cataract in his left eye. He could not possibly have done this work. He is a front man, that is all.'

'OK. So where do we go from here?'

Valdurois glanced at his watch again. 'He brought these photos in two days ago. And he normally shows up for his cheque in the middle of the afternoon. If you hang around the outer office, pretend to be a secretary, you will see him. What you do then, Madame Carroll,' he shrugged noncommittally, 'is entirely up to you.'

3

Josh was clattering around with a broom upstairs.

Maurice glanced at his watch, then swung his legs off the narrow mattress, slipping his bare feet into a pair of sweat-stained plimsoles. He kept his weight instinctively off his left leg as he stood up.

It was time to get going.

He looked around at the dank, crumbling walls of the cellar. Christ, he'd be glad to see the back of this place.

But Paris. He'd miss Paris deeply. He'd been here longer than anywhere he'd settled since Vietnam. He'd made no friends but Josh, no acquaintances but Harry. But there were days when the beauty of the city had so entranced him that he'd walked for miles, forgotten about the past for hours at a stretch.

He would miss *that* worst of all.

Harry would have left the Pigalle house by now, would be on his way to the *Decade* offices. He'd have his money long before evening started closing in.

And then? A cab ride to the airport, and he'd be on his way to . . . where? England? Too close. Scandinavia? Too dark.

There was time to decide that later.

The clattering above him stopped. The hiss of a scrubbing brush took its place. Josh began singing one of his favourite songs, an African tribal melody. The key sounded like beats on a marimba. The tone, like a whole tribe chanting softly, not one man. It was one of the most beautiful things he'd ever heard.

He'd stop here on his way to the airport, if he had the time. He couldn't leave without saying a last goodbye.

He pulled on his cotton bomber jacket and limped up the stairs towards the sun-washed street.

4

In the huge pitch-dark living-room of a salon on the Île de la Cité, the Incarnate stirred in their sleep.

They reached out across Paris with their minds, and smiled hungrily.

Brother, he is on the move!

Yes. I can feel it too.

He plans to leave the city while it is still light.

There was a hoarse chuckle from Tharman. *Then hurry,*

little Maurice. Hurry, race the sun! Dusk comes so very early at this time of year.

He'll never make it. We have him, brother.

We have him, dearest sister.

5

There was no mistaking Bernstein. He came shuffling into the office at a quarter before three, and looked as out of place there as a cleaning lady at a fashion parade.

He was bald, and old age had twisted his spine into a question mark. He walked with a silver-topped cane. Perched on his nose were a pair of spectacles that magnified his eyes so much they seemed to leap out of his face. The milky cataract was there, in the left one, just as Valdurois had said.

Despite the unseasonal warmth, he was wearing a thick tweed jacket and a grey woollen cardigan that dangled to his knuckles.

Chloe, the black-haired secretary, favoured him with a narrow, unfriendly smile as he approached the desk. She got a yellow envelope from a drawer and held it out towards him. He took it quickly, said a brisk, '*Merci, mam'selle*,' turned, and shuffled back towards the elevators.

Susan took the next one down. By the time she reached the lobby, he was struggling through the revolving doors. She followed him at a safe distance down the avenue de Rheims.

A bus came along the Champs-Elysées within two minutes, and Bernstein boarded it. Susan took care not to glance at him as she went past in the aisle. She sat well to the back, and fidgeted impatiently as the crawling progress began through the traffic. Her eyes wandered distantly over the passing crowds, the unfamiliar faces.

This was all like a fantasy in which she was a spy. She felt like pinching herself.

Bernstein got off at the corner of the place Pigalle,

wandered past a porno theatre and down the slope a hundred yards. He paused, looked around jerkily, then turned into a narrow side-street.

Susan reached the corner just in time to see him disappear through the entrance of a shabby-looking townhouse with a grey-painted façade.

There was a row of eight bell pushes by the letter box, with name cards underneath them. The fourth one down read, H. BERNSTEIN. DEUXIÈME ÉTAGE. Second floor. The fifth was blank.

She hovered by the porch for a couple of minutes, uncertain what to do. Then, her hand shaking a little, she pushed at the door. It swung open.

The lobby was dark and bare as she stepped inside. She heard the echoing bang of another door slamming, somewhere high above her.

There was no elevator, and the stairs were of a pebbly brown stone, worn to a shining smoothness. She took off her spike-heeled shoes before starting to tip-toe upwards. The only light came from a tiny, begrimed window at the top of the stairwell. She could barely see a thing, and felt nervous and vulnerable.

She groped around on the second-floor landing, and found a light switch. A twenty-watt bulb came on in a raffia shade.

There were only two apartments up here. The door closest to her had a *mezzuzah* – a Jewish prayer-box – nailed to its frame. A business card thumb-tacked beneath it read, *Harry Bernstein, Quality Textiles.*

The other door was completely blank.

Except that, just beside the lock, an odd little disc had been screwed into the wood.

It was the size of a saucer, was of polished bronze. Standing out in bold relief on its face was an engraving of the sun. Flames danced around its edges like twisted cogs on a fly-wheel.

What was it supposed to be?

Susan began edging towards it, when she heard scraping footsteps behind Bernstein's door, drawing closer.

She glanced around frantically, looking for somewhere to hide. The stairwell was the only decent bet.

She had the presence of mind to switch off the light again, then hurried up the next flight until she was out of sight of the landing. Bernstein's door groaned open behind her.

She crouched down, peeked out carefully.

The old man's silhouette was moving in the rectangular glow from his apartment. His back was to her, and he was bending down, with a painful, arthritic slowness. Stooping to reach the bottom of the neighbouring door.

There was another envelope in his hand, manila this time, not yellow. It was thicker than the first. And as he squeezed it between his fingers, it crackled. It seemed to be filled with money.

So that was how it worked. Bernstein took the magazine's cheque for himself, and gave Lapotaire cash.

As Susan watched, he slipped it under the gap, prodded at it with his fingers until it had gone all the way in. Then he straightened on his walking-stick, clutching his back and moaning. He disappeared once more into his own apartment.

She decided to wait a few moments, make sure the coast was clear. The faint, crackly murmur of an old gramophone record started up behind Bernstein's door. An orchestral piece, Mendelssohn perhaps.

Susan took a cautious step down, trying to find purchase on the bare stone with her stockinged feet.

Then another.

There was a hollow thump, far below, as the front door opened and shut.

She shrank back into the darkness again, as limping footsteps began coming up the stairs towards her.

6

Can you feel her, brother? The woman? She is looking for him. Can you feel her hunger and her fear?

More, sister. I can feel her heat. And her warm ripe skin. She is fine, this one. She has life and fire in her.

But the fear grips her, dear brother. And the fear will make her careless.

7

She started to grow alarmed as the footsteps reached the landing below. They paused a moment, then continued upwards.

That limp. Maurice Lapotaire had injured his foot during the war, hadn't he?

Here she was, on the point of coming face to face with the object of her pursuit. And what would she see, when he rounded the corner? What would he look like? Perhaps he'd been horribly scarred in Vietnam? Maybe his mind had been injured too, and she'd get a blazing, churning glimpse of it when she met his eyes?

And how would he react, when he realized he'd been tracked down? Violently? Weren't some men who'd seen the horrors of war supposed to grow brutal themselves?

The steps were almost upon her, by now. They echoed around her, resounding up and down the stairwell. She couldn't have moved a muscle if she'd tried. Her whole body felt dismembered, severed from her nerves.

And . . . one of her shoes slipped from her grasp.

She lunged down, trying to grab it. Her fingers closed on empty air. The shoe clattered on the step below, tumbled to the bottom of the flight, making a noise like a set of castanets.

The uneven footsteps stopped.

Susan jerked upright, tried to pull herself together. Her mind was racing in ten different directions at once.

Go down! Go down the stairs *now*! If it is him, he'll be gone in a few seconds!

She ran down to the landing, her nylon-clad feet skidding on the worn, concave steps. Swung herself around the corner.

And found herself looking, through the dimness, at a tall, thin man in his early twenties. Something, a large medallion, glowed below his throat. His blond shoulder-length hair formed a ragged halo around his features. His lower face was shadowed with stubble. His clothes were dishevelled, and he looked tired and feeble.

But she recognized him immediately from the pictures she'd seen.

A key dangled from his left hand, glittering. He obviously lived here.

He was frozen in a half-crouch, one arm raised in front of him as though to ward her off. His eyes were cold with fear.

Then, abruptly, he whirled around and began hobbling down the stairs as fast as he could go.

'No!' Susan reached towards him. 'Mr Lapotaire—?'

She tried to follow, too quickly. She'd only got a couple of yards when her footing finally slipped and she went over. Her hip cracked against an iron banister rung.

The sharp edge of a stair dug into her ribs, punching the breath out of her. She clenched her teeth with pain, blinded and dazed for a moment. Why'd she worn heels today? *Why?*

God!

She probed her side with her fingers, making sure she hadn't broken anything. She was suddenly angry, and that helped her fight back a little. She scrambled back to the landing and retrieved her other shoe, put them both on before heading down to the front door.

When she reached the open street, Maurice Lapotaire was gone. A couple passing arm-in-arm stared at her curiously from the far sidewalk.

Christ, she could *kick* herself!

Maybe if she hadn't been so scared. Maybe if she hadn't

gone so rigid. Maybe . . . if she hadn't, standing there in the darkness with the footsteps coming towards her, suddenly wished she was back in Beverly Hills, a quiet housewife again. And had someone else, anyone, even a swine like Denny, to lean on.

That was at the heart of it. That was the straightforward truth.

She'd been so full of herself, so sure of her self-sufficiency, until then. But the moment push had come to shove . . . she had folded like the proverbial house of cards.

She sat down on the porch stoop, put her head in her hands, and tried not to cry. It wasn't too difficult – she thought of Denny laughing at her, and refused to give him that satisfaction.

It was a few minutes till she realized she still had Bernstein.

8

'Mr Bernstein?'

The pounding on his door had been going on for a while before Harry finally noticed it. He'd been going steadily deaf, over the last few years. And besides, there was the music, his one remaining love. He'd been listening to Mendelssohn's second string quartet with the volume at full blast, allowing it to push him along like a leaf on a lazy river. Had practically fallen into a doze.

And now there was this knocking. And a voice, calling his name. An American voice. A woman's.

He jerked upright, his dim eyes blinking as they gazed around the dingy brown living-room and its dusty rosewood furniture. Who the hell could it be? All his friends were dead. He never had visitors.

He reached out for his stick, clambered out of his chair irritably, and began shuffling towards the hallway.

The pounding hadn't stopped.

'Mr Bernstein? Hello?'

'All right! All right!' he shouted. '*Ich komme!* I'm coming!'

Reaching the door, he leant his weight against it, wheezing. A lifetime of cigar smoking had left him with the beginnings of emphysema. *Nu*, he should worry at his age. With his free hand, he pulled back the tarnished brass cover of the peephole. He put his good eye to it.

The face of an auburn-haired woman, grotesquely distorted by the lens, peered back at him. Harry frowned with puzzlement. He knew no younger women, auburn haired or otherwise.

She seemed to realize he was there, leaned closer to the lens.

'Mr Bernstein? Do you speak English?'

'English, sure,' he grunted, 'English, French, Spanish. What is it you want, language lessons?'

'Could you open up?'

She looked harmless enough, but you couldn't trust anyone these days. At best, she might be some kind of loony evangelist. At worst – well, he understood, better than most, the worst people were capable of.

'Why?' Harry demanded.

'I'd like to ask a few questions about your neighbour.'

He stiffened with alarm. The wheezing in his chest grew fiercer.

'Neighbour?' He could hear how croaky and unconvincing his voice had become. 'I'm sorry, I don't know my neighbour.'

'I think you do. It's very important that I speak to you.'

Harry backed away from the door, the peephole cover sliding back into place with a metallic hiss.

'Lady, leave me alone!' he shouted, hoarsely. 'I'm just an old man. Leave me in peace.'

'But, Mr Bernstein . . .'

He turned, and retreated towards the living-room, the woman's pleading voice growing fainter behind him. By the time he'd reached his gramophone, she was pounding on the door again, insistently.

He reached out for the volume, tried to turn it up, and realized it wouldn't go any higher.

Then, he sat back in his easy chair. Stared at the picture on the television cabinet, of his wife, Zara, taken on her thirtieth birthday, the year before she'd died. He tried to let his mind float again.

It wouldn't at first, he was too disturbed. And when it finally did, it was back to the horrors of the past.

He rubbed vacantly at the faded, tattooed numbers on his wrist.

Back to Buchenwald. To the fear and the slaughter all around him. And the cold-faced SS guards. And the colonel with the blazing eyes. *Das Goldbiest.*

CHAPTER TWENTY-ONE

1

As dusk crept in, Paris dissolved into a million separate points of light, like yellow earth-bound stars, and Tharman woke.

He sat up on the *chaise-longue* and stretched, gazed around the darkened lofty salon on the Île de la Cité. It reminded him a good deal of Mildred Davritch-Dwight's apartment on Fifth Avenue, forty-odd years ago. The way the expensive furniture had been neglected. The way rare and priceless ornaments had been crammed together like second-hand goods on a jumble stall. It had the same scent of tasteless decadence, the same odour of wealth misspent.

He felt comfortable here; rested after all his travels. Pashta had chosen her new companion well.

He craned his head around and looked at the others. They were still asleep. Gorreq had rolled off the huge gold-braided couch and was lying on the scuffed parquet floor, a Persian rug with cigarette burns on it wrapped around his hulking form. And Pashta herself – she'd chosen the top of the scratched, stained mahogany dining table to the side of the room. She was motionless, curled into a ball, a peaceful smile playing across her shadowy features.

Pinned in her outstretched arms, her newest plaything – the young aristocrat who owned this grand apartment – shifted restlessly in a nerveless sleep of his own. He seemed to sense that he was being looked at, and gave out a feeble, high-pitched whimper, but he was too drugged to wake.

When shall we three meet again?

Tharman grinned. It was so good to be reunited, to hunt in company. He dearly loved them both, especially

Pashta, so small but so remorseless. He felt a special affection for her, almost like a father's for a lively, wayward daughter, though she'd be furious if he ever confessed that to her. Who exactly brought the Incarnate to who? she would snap.

Tharman stood up, straightened his clothes, crossed to the balcony window and pulled back the heavy blinds.

The apartment was situated directly on the north edge of the island, on the fourth storey of a grand old house. The Seine glittered below, just across the narrow road. He loved this city, almost as much as he'd loved Thebes.

There was the murmur of an engine from the river, and a brilliantly lit cruise boat started chugging past as he watched, a party of teenaged schoolgirls crowded along the rail. He studied them hungrily. Let his mind flicker over their thoughts for a moment. They were here on a trip from Dusseldorf, supposedly to see the art in the museums, but that was the last thing on their minds right now. A bottle of champagne was circulating amongst them, and all of them were tipsy and excited.

A few looked up suddenly, noticed him and waved.

It would be so easy to make the pilot bring them ashore here and . . . no! He drew himself up short. No excesses. He'd almost got into trouble that way before.

The boat had moved away by now, and the girls' attention had shifted to Notre-Dame cathedral. Their delighted squeals rang back across the water.

Tharman sighed and let his eyes flicker to the right bank of the city. He amused himself for a while watching the young women strolling between the trees in their crushed velvet hot pants and platform shoes. He was going to enjoy this era, he decided, just as much as he'd enjoyed the twenties. Drugs and sexuality were the order of the day again.

The minds of all these girls, though, seemed shallow when he touched them. He found his thoughts wandering back to that woman he'd noticed in his sleep. The one who'd been waiting outside Lapotaire's apartment, who'd scared the photographer away.

Susan Carroll, from Los Angeles.

She'd done them a great favour, without knowing it. And she was so warm and intelligent. So very strong, deep down, with such a ferocious lust to take her life in her own hands. She was just finding her own way in the world, like a child taking its first few steps. And she'd stumbled, fallen, this time. But she'd keep getting up for more – he was sure of that.

Again, he turned over the idea he'd started forming all those years ago, in Manhattan and that little Montana town. That maybe what he really needed was a companion.

Maybe her?

There was a scrape from the table behind him.

'Love sick, brother?'

Pashta had woken and sat up, her huge luminous eyes blinking amusedly. Her slender legs were curled beneath her. Her fingernails were resting on the titled junkie's brow, digging into the pale, sickly flesh beneath his greasy, curling hair.

Tharman smiled and nodded gently. She'd found him out, but he couldn't feel embarrassed.

'Perhaps, sister. Sick of lust and hungry for love, perhaps.'

'For the Californian mortal? She's older than you, by human appearances.'

Tharman turned back to the window, without replying. He could hear Gorreq stir and yawn obscenely on the floor behind him.

'She might lead us to Lapotaire,' he said.

'Oh, yes!' Pashta giggled. There was a sarcastic tone to her voice he didn't like. 'She could be of *great* use to us.'

She was being childish, Tharman decided. The best thing was to ignore her.

He waved a hand at her, without even bothering to look around.

'Wake up your friend, my sister. It's time for us to begin.'

*

2

The hotel suite had made Susan feel so free, when she'd awoken, but it looked like nothing so much as a dim, gilded prison cell this evening.

She'd never bothered much with drink, but she felt like bothering now. Felt like locking herself in with a bottle of gin and boozing herself to sleep. All her plans seemed to have crumbled, like a building that a wrecking ball had smashed to dust. Her confidence was gone, her spirit felt broken. She'd made such a *hash* of things.

Traffic still rumbled on the boulevard below. A car horn blasted, cutting across her thoughts. She sat up on the bed with a start.

She was forgetting something. Christ, she'd promised to phone Casey!

What was the time in New York? One in the afternoon? She couldn't remember the difference, or the international code, and had to get the desk to put her through. But the line, as the ringing started, seemed clear enough.

Someone picked up at the other end, and Susan found herself hoping it wasn't her son-in-law, Ted.

'Hullo?'

'Casey?'

'*Mom!*' Her daughter's voice came down the line in a high-pitched shriek of amazement. And, for a moment, it felt as though the girl was eight years old again. As though all the years in between had melted away. Susan felt that old, familiar rush of warmth in her belly she hadn't really known since Casey had become a teenager.

'Mom, are you *there*? In *Paris*? I can't *believe* it!' And Casey started laughing, perhaps at the idea that her *haus-frau*, stuck-in-the-mud mom had actually plucked up the nerve to cross a whole ocean on her own. 'Gee, I'm impressed! How *is* it there?'

'It's . . .' Susan fumbled for the right words, but they wouldn't come. Since that mess at the Pigalle, she'd been seeing the whole city through a funereal gloom, when she'd noticed it at all. There wasn't any point in telling Casey that. It would only make her sound inept and hapless. 'It's just great, darling. Really beautiful. I—'

'Mom, I have some tremendous news for you.'

Susan froze in mid-sentence, bewildered. Here she was, halfway round the world, and Casey was the one with news?

'Uh . . . OK,' she mumbled. 'What is it?'

'Mom, I'm pregnant!'

She gripped the edge of the bed, her fingers clenching till they hurt. Because, suddenly, she felt that she was dropping. Falling through space.

She was unable to think or even breathe for a moment.

She let go of the mattress, dug her nails into her palm. Her eyes squeezed tightly shut. The muscles in her jaw went rigid – and thank God for that, because Heaven knew what she might have said otherwise. Nineteen, for Chrissake. Casey was only *nineteen.*

She'd expected so much from her daughter. Her bright, beautiful girl.

And when Casey had married Ted Hammond – eight years her senior and an architect – last May, she hadn't given up hope entirely. A woman could be a wife and still make something of herself, these days. But a baby . . . it was history repeating itself all over again.

Her own history.

She too had married early. She too had chosen an older man, an established professional, who'd been too damned easy to lean on, depend on. And she too had fallen pregnant before the year was out.

No, dammit. A hot tear trickled from the corner of her eye and began crawling down her cheek.

'Mom?' Casey was saying at the other end of the line.

Susan shook her head, tried to catch her breath.

'Mom? You are happy for me, aren't you?' Casey let out an exasperated groan. 'Ted *said* you'd be like this.'

Susan yanked a handkerchief out of her sleeve and rubbed at her face hurriedly. Then, she forced a smile, tried to keep her voice calm as she spoke into the mouthpiece.

'That's crazy, darling.' Her words echoed hollowly in her ears. 'Of course I'm happy.'

3

An hour later, dressed up to the nines in her sequinned black dress and sable coat, she was out on the street again, marching briskly in her high heels towards the restaurant she'd chosen from her guidebook.

There was a whole reservoir of tears inside her still, trying to force their way out. But she held her chin up, kept her eyes fixed on the store fronts ahead. Wouldn't let them come.

As she turned on to the rue Pierre Charron, she started telling herself one thing, over and over. It's time to start living your dreams for yourself. Time to stop expecting other people to live them for you.

Casey had been a vessel for all her unrealized hopes, her unfulfilled ambitions, over these last nineteen years. She realized that perfectly clearly, now. And the vessel had just been shattered dramatically. It was time, long overdue, for her to do it all herself.

Tonight, she'd spoil herself, enjoy the town. And tomorrow, she'd get back to work, pick up the reins where they'd been dropped this afternoon. No more stumbling. No more freezing up with nervousness. No more sitting on porch stoops. Paris was a city of great opportunities and massive temptations, and dammit if she wasn't going to help herself to both.

She walked in through the revolving doors of the Café Maupassant. A glorious smell of *haute cuisine* washed over her immediately. A young, fair-haired waiter with bottomless green eyes gave her that now-familiar smile, and ushered her over to a small, round table by the far edge of the window.

It was, she realized, the first time she'd ever eaten out

alone. She ought to have felt uneasy. But, glancing around, she realized it wasn't an uncommon practice here. At three other tables people were working at solitary meals, reading newspapers or simply enjoying the view beyond the gilt-framed, steam-smeared glass. The Brotherhood of the Self-Confident, she decided. It was time to join them.

4

She was just starting to peck at the edges of her almond mousse, an hour later, when a shadow fell across the table. She looked up, and realized it wasn't the waiter.

The man standing above her was in full evening dress. He was over six feet tall and broad shouldered. Below dark collar-length hair, he had a tanned, aquiline face, rather like Peter Fonda's.

A montgolfier of brandy was balanced in his left hand. He put his right, very gently, on the edge of the tablecloth – he was making a cautious sortie into her territory.

He broke into a smile. It was warm and inquisitive, with nothing phoney about it.

And then he came out with a stream of French Susan couldn't begin to follow. She shook her head bewilderedly, and began to say *Je ne comprends pas*, I don't understand. She hadn't got halfway through the sentence when the man's eyebrows popped up with surprise.

'*Americaine?*'

'*Oui*, American,' Susan nodded, uncomfortably.

The man seemed delighted, though she wasn't sure why.

'I was wondering if you would like to join me at my . . . *table*?'

'Table. Same word.'

She felt nervous and suspicious, deep down. Was this what she really wanted? To go wandering off with a stranger, on her first night here? That might have suited Denny, but not her.

The man seemed to realize what was bothering her. He

quickly pointed to a large oval table near the back, with six other people, three chic, glamorous-looking couples, sitting around it, chattering.

'These are my friends,' he told her. As though in confirmation, a few of them glanced towards her, and one elegant woman about her own age gave a ring-flashing wave.

Susan looked back at the man, less wary of him now. He moved his hand a little further across the cloth.

'We would be very pleased to have your company,' he said. 'We are on our way now to the Royaume. You know the Royaume? It is one of the most famous night-clubs in Paris. *Très chic. Très élégant.*'

He started toying slowly with his brandy, waiting for her reply.

And this was exactly what she'd been hoping for. New friends. New experiences. New doors opening up to her. And she had to admit, the guy was pretty gorgeous.

'No,' Susan heard herself say. 'I'm sorry. I can't.'

She couldn't believe she'd said it.

But she seemed to have just heard a faint whispering, very close to her ear, almost as though it were inside her head.

Save yourself for me, my beautiful one.

The image of another man had sprung into her thoughts. Gaunter. Sharper featured. And with purple eyes. What the hell was happening? She didn't know anyone like that. It was a picture that simply seemed to have appeared, full-blown, out of the lightless depths of her own mind.

She rubbed at the bridge of her nose, trying to make it go away. But suddenly, her attraction to the real live man in front of her was vanishing quickly. Slipping through her grasp, like melting frost.

She couldn't understand why, but she couldn't stop it. Her gaze started travelling across his face, busily finding flaws in it.

His lips seemed too wide, now. His brow was too heavy.

The nose a little too long. He had a few deep pockmarks on his cheeks she hadn't noticed before.

The last of her excitement faded, leaving just an empty chill in its wake.

She glanced towards his friends again. They too looked gauche and ugly. She wanted all of them to go away.

She shook her head fiercely.

'I'm very sorry,' she intoned. 'I have a previous engagement.'

The man pulled his hand back from the table with a bemused frown. He seemed to realize she was lying. But, salvaging his self-respect, he bowed to her courteously.

'Then may I wish you a very pleasant evening, Madame. And a rewarding stay in Paris.'

He turned, and went back to his table. Didn't look at her again. His friends shrugged hugely and whispered amongst themselves. They called for their coats and left a few minutes later.

Susan, in her lonely corner, watched them go. Watched the tall, handsome man step out through the door and vanish. And wondered what on earth she'd just done.

5

Her heels clacked on the sidewalk again. The streets were emptier now, the night seemed to have grown darker around her.

And she wasn't quite sure of her bearings any more.

She fished her map of the city centre out of her purse, tried to consult it in the faint, yellow glow of a doorway. Normally she was good at reading maps. She'd had enough practice over the years, navigating on vacation while Denny drove.

But tonight she seemed to have gone – what was the map-reading equivalent of dyslexic? The thinly printed streets seemed to blur into a jumble. She could make no sense of them at all.

Perhaps she would go to the Royaume after all. Maybe

she could catch up with the crowd from the restaurant, and think up some excuse.

She looked around for somebody to ask directions. A *gendarme*, a cab-driver. But the few pedestrians around her seemed to be moving so fast. She'd start reaching out, to attract their attention . . . and they'd be gone.

After ten minutes, she began thinking that anywhere would do. A club. A bar. A café. Any port in the storm of confusion that seemed to be whirling around her.

She was near the Seine, now. She could see it winking magically, in the gaps between the buildings.

A wide doorway, lit up in vivid tangerine, appeared to her right. There was a commissionaire outside in a dark blue uniform. And as she watched, a limousine pulled up. A group of young people got out, laughing and shouting. The girls were in sequined hot pants and the boys in embroidered shirts. A pop song – she thought it was by a new British singer called David Bowie – hammered into the night air as they went in through the door.

This place would do. All she had to do was cross the road.

She reached the kerb. And suddenly, she couldn't move her feet. The muscles in her legs seemed to have gone numb.

She got another flash, in her mind's eye, of that hungry purple gaze. That gaunt, strange face. And words popped abruptly into her head. *No, not there. You'll be out of place and unhappy in there.*

Was she thinking to herself? Talking to herself? The voice didn't even sound like her own. This was crazy.

She found that she could back up from the kerb, but couldn't walk across it. So, with nothing else to do, she turned and moved confusedly away.

Was she really that afraid of trying something new?

The exact same thing happened outside a small mirror-windowed jazz club at a corner two blocks further down. When she tried moving towards it, she couldn't. When she walked away from it, and continued into the enfolding night, her feet seemed to patter along with a life of their own.

It was as though something were driving her onwards, to a specific destination. Something like a strong wind, or a hand dragging at her. But she couldn't understand what, or why. Panic began to overtake her. It was like being in one of those dreams where you kept on running and couldn't stop.

The river was hidden from view completely by now. The bright streetlights were vanishing behind her, giving way to thin, cold, old-fashioned lamps that made the surrounding buildings look dim and ghostly. Shadows clustered in their windows and doors.

She began to slow, at last, on a narrow, darkened street that was completely deserted. Halfway down it, a blue neon arrow was flickering.

It was pointing – she saw when she reached it – into a cobbled, musty-smelling alley.

At the end, beyond a clutch of garbage pails, was a narrow doorway, also lit in blue. A sign flashed on and off above it.

Le Club Minuit. The Midnight Club.

Susan hovered on the sidewalk for a moment, struggling against the forward movement of her limbs, trying to keep to the main street. God, this wasn't what she'd been looking for, when she'd left the hotel. She didn't want to go in *there*.

She'd been hoping for fun, experience, life. This place looked like death warmed up.

She tried to pull away, but this time her legs wouldn't let her. Her feet seemed to have taken root on the flagstones. She ought to have been terrified, she knew. Her heart was tripping furiously, and a strange, wintery chill was invading her stomach. But somehow, she wasn't half as scared as she ought to be. There was a little numbness to her reactions, as though someone had slipped her a tranquillizer.

Maybe this *was* what she'd been looking for, after all, she started telling herself.

Or maybe it was that odd voice in her head doing the telling.

Something very different. Something unusual and strange. Yes.

She drew herself to her full height, and went in.

6

Restless, Gorreq rode in the back of a cab towards the Pigalle.

Hunger was gnawing at his body like a nest of venomous ants. It would be so easy, he thought, to just reach across and grab the chattering, Gauloise-smoking cabbie by the throat, start to throttle him, and Feed. But Tharman had warned him against anything like that; anything that might draw the police in Lapotaire's direction.

Damn this city! He gazed out at the humming streets, the packed cafés. It was so busy here, so hard to find secluded places. He hadn't Fed since he'd arrived. His last meal had been – when? In Istanbul, two nights ago. He'd grabbed hold of a gypsy beggar girl who'd been squatting behind a pile of building rubble and dragged her down into the ancient Byzantine aqueducts. He'd toyed with her for practically an hour, drinking every last ounce of her fear, before ripping her apart like a fine muslin cloth and leaving her for the rats.

Now, in the airless confines of the cab, he could smell the driver. Smell the man's flesh, his heavy sweat. And Gorreq ached to make that flesh crawl, make that sweat run cold.

Later, Tharman had told him, before he'd left the salon. *You'll have to wait.*

Sometimes, he resented Tharman. So cool. So arrogant. So quaintly clever. But who was the strongest of them? Who, in a straight fight, would win?

Who was the priest of Thoth, to give out orders?

Gorreq's eyes glowed, faintly gold, and his massive

right hand began reaching, slowly, for the taxi driver's collar.

The cab pulled up with a shudder outside Lapotaire's apartment house. A crowd of Arabs, playing dice on the sidewalk, gazed up at it curiously.

Gorreq let his hand drop, frowned. Paid the driver, and got out.

It was completely dark inside the house, but that didn't bother him. He bounded up the stairs two at a time until he had reached the second-floor landing. There, he paused. He could still hear the Arabs chattering on the street below – their language had barely changed since he'd been human. The noise of a television echoed from the next storey. And music was seeping from behind the walls.

Lapotaire's door, he realized, was the one at the far end. He started towards it.

And was halfway there before he saw the *Ra* disc, screwed into the wood beside the lock.

Gorreq stopped, let out a bovine grunt of surprise and frustration.

Very carefully, he began edging towards it, one hand stretched out in front of him. Before he'd even got within six feet, his palm started to itch, then hurt.

By all the Lords, he could fight this. He was strong enough.

He pushed himself onwards, taking it inch by inch, step by creeping step. The burning sensation washed up from his hand all the way to his elbow. The fine blond hairs at his wrist started to twist and curl.

He clenched his teeth, forced himself forwards another pace. The pain surged to his shoulder, began to spread through his whole body. His arm felt as though it had been plunged in molten lead.

Blinding lights, as intense as the noonday sun, flashed behind his eyelids.

He let out a stifled moan of pain, and staggered back, furious.

*

7

At first, Susan thought the club was completely deserted. The desk, just inside the door, was empty. There was no one to take her money, and nobody appeared from the office at the back when she called out.

As she pushed her way through the blue velvet curtain at the end of the cramped white-walled lobby, she was met by total silence.

She wasn't used to nightclubs, hadn't been in all that many since she'd married, but this had to be the smallest and most dismal one there'd ever been.

Whoever had designed and decorated it had obviously gone for a cool, stylish atmosphere, and missed the mark completely. Over in the far corner was a tiny stage, no more than a rounded plinth, on which a microphone stood. A single, brilliant spotlight glared down on it. It was the only white light in the room. All the rest, as she picked them out, were faint and blue. They filled the room with a shadow-laden gloom, like a discoloured fog.

There were no more than a dozen tables, all of them small, circular, with room for no more than three chairs. Terrific planning, she thought, if two couples wanted to be seated together. Inch-long candle stubs in blue glass shades guttered at the centre of each.

There was a short row of booths beyond them, all but lost in the darkness.

Over by the far wall was a bar made of cobalt glass and chromium. It was art-deco, obviously expensive, but the ugliest example of the style she'd ever seen.

But worst of all were the walls and the high, dome-shaped ceiling.

They seemed to have been handpainted. Most of the colour was a kind of midnight blue, nearly black, and dismal, sucking in the club's weak light. On to this background had been painted stars. Constellations. Orion. The Big Dipper. Susan's gaze followed them upwards, and settled on a wan full moon in the roof over her head.

Midnight. That was what the fresco was supposed to represent. But it made the place look like a planetarium. Who the hell would come in here for fun? Who the hell would want to stay?

Then why had she just sat down at one of the tables?

8

She looked around alarmedly, jerking her neck.

One moment she'd been standing by the velvet curtain. And the next . . . she was here, seated. Her feet were neatly tucked beneath the chair. Her hands were folded on the smooth pallid blue tablecloth.

This was crazy. She hated the sight of this place. She had no intention of staying.

She tried to get up. Willed her legs to move. But, again, they wouldn't. She tried pushing herself upright with her arms, but that didn't work either.

She sat perfectly still, shivering. Afraid to even move her head now. She could feel goosebumps rising on her exposed skin.

It was cold in here, she began to realize. And damp, clammy. There was a faint smell of mildew in the air.

Was she having a nervous breakdown? A panic attack? Removed from her home and her secure, dull life, from bloated, boorish Denny, could she really not cope at all?

She heard a noise. A soft scraping, a shuffling, from one of the darkened booths.

And she realized she wasn't alone after all.

9

Harry Bernstein came awake with a frightened start. There was somebody moving around outside, on the landing.

He'd been sitting in his armchair, listening to Chopin's 'Winter Études' and gazing at the photograph of Zara, when he'd dozed off. And his dreams had been the same as they'd been for the past thirty-seven years. The death camp, Buchenwald, where all his family had died. In past years, he would have found tears on his face when he'd woken up. Now, God forgive him, there were no tears left. He'd run completely dry. That shouldn't happen to a man, should it? The ability to cry shouldn't be taken from him?

He shook his head groggily, looked down at his hands. He'd been scratching the skin on the inside of his arm again, even in his sleep, unconsciously trying to peel away the row of tattooed numbers. 677459. The skin around them was clawed to an angry red.

The soft thud of footsteps came from his front door again. And then a strangled grunt.

Had the young American finally come back? Herr Lapotaire? Was there something wrong with him?

Harry dragged himself painfully to his feet, and began shuffling towards the door. He was just about to switch on the light in the hallway, when something stopped him.

It was nothing concrete. Just an instinct.

He ducked his head and listened. Out on the landing, there was another thump, and then a muttered curse.

It was a man's voice. But not Lapotaire's.

The downy hackles started prickling on the back of Harry's neck. His liver-spotted, wrinkled skin suddenly felt even colder than it usually did.

He'd heard that voice before, he was sure of it.

Very cautiously and quietly, he made his way towards the door. There was no strip of light shining underneath it. The lamp was off outside. But he heard another shuffle.

Who on earth would be moving around in the dark? A burglar? Was someone trying to break in?

He eased himself gently the last couple of yards, taking care not to disturb the door, and slid back the peephole cover.

At first, he could see nothing in the pitch darkness beyond. He squinted desperately. Then a silhouette, no more than a vague shadow, slid across his field of vision.

It was a very tall and broad man. Harry couldn't make out any details, except the faint, glossy sheen of a leather jacket and an even fainter glimmer of blond hair.

Extremely pale hair. Almost white.

The strangest, most chilling feeling started creeping over him, and he began to shake. He'd seen that exact same silhouette before. Seen that flash of white-blond hair before.

But it couldn't be. It *couldn't.* Oh my God, not after all these years.

He was dreaming.

Unmöglich! Unmöglich!

It was impossible!

10

Gorreq tried to reach Lapotaire's front door half a dozen times before he finally gave up.

The last time, he'd practically closed his hand around the knob, his eyes clenched shut, his teeth grinding like millstones. He was so physically strong he'd been sure that he could do it.

But the sheer agony, the terrible brightness behind his closed eyelids, had got the better of him.

Now, he was slumped against the wall of the dingy landing, massaging his tortured wrist. It felt as though the bones inside had melted out of shape. His breath was coming in tattered whispers. He waited for the pain to fade before straightening up. This was hopeless. He'd have to find another way in. And it would have to be later. Right now, he *had* to Feed.

His hand stopped rubbing and he raised his head, suddenly aware that he was being watched.

He could see no one, looking around the darkened landing. Then, he reached out with his mind, and knew. The other doorway in this hall. The one directly opposite him.

There was a man standing behind it.

He could sense the human's old, decaying thoughts. Almost taste the senile stench of fear, as powerful as ammonia. It was like being ravenous, and standing in the aroma wafting from a bakery. It gave his hunger a new edge, a savage, sharp intensity.

Gorreq peered straight at the door. Saw the business card pinned to it. Saw the peephole, and the eye beyond.

He pushed himself away from the wall, began moving forwards. Inside, the man gasped and shrank back a little.

A grin creased Gorreq's broad, pale face. He was going to smash down that flimsy barrier and Feed. Right here. Right now.

No, brother!

Tharman's voice rang inside his head. Gorreq pawed angrily at his temple, but it wouldn't go away.

Brother, restrain youself! You'll turn attention on this house.

He was hungry almost beyond reason, by now. It was tearing him apart like a wild tiger, ripping at his nerves, dulling his brain. But what the gaunt priest said *did* make a kind of sense. He'd already let Lapotaire get away once, two years ago. He couldn't risk it happening again.

Impotent fury welled up in him. He let out an angry, cheated groan.

Then he walked right up to the door, stared in through the peephole at the old man. He slammed his palm, hard, against the wood, making it shudder on its hinges. Inside, the old fool stumbled to the floor and began moaning with fear.

Gorreq stood there for a few moments longer, watching him. Then finally he turned, and pounded back down the stairs towards the street.

11

As Susan's eyes adjusted to the dimness, she could just make out three figures sitting in the booth. Two slim men and a petite, skinny woman. Except that one of the men couldn't exactly be described as sitting. He was slumped face down across the table, as though in a drunken stupor. The woman had an arm resting on his shoulders, her hand folded around the back of his head.

Two pairs of eyes were lingering on her. She could see shimmers of sparkling brightness in them, almost golden. Susan stirred uneasily in her chair, but she still couldn't get up. Her legs felt as though they'd been turned to stone.

She ought to feel happier that there were other people in the club. A sense of loneliness had begun to seep into her body, like a cold invading virus, and their presence seemed to have banished it.

But what to do now?

She tried smiling back at them, found it easy. Nodded to their table – that was easy too. Only getting up was hard.

She turned her head away, looked at the tiny stage again. It was still empty, the spotlight bare. The microphone cast its thin shadow across the room like the mast of a deserted ship. Where was the entertainment around here? Where were the staff?

As though he'd read her thoughts, the slim man in the booth raised a finger, called out, 'A drink for the lady, if you please?'

He spoke in perfect English. His voice was very soft, refined. But his accent – she couldn't place it. German, perhaps? Or maybe she had noticed a tiny, guttural touch of Arabic? There were plenty of Frenchmen who'd been born in Algeria, she seemed to remember reading.

Her mind seemed to be moving so incredibly slowly. Like a swimmer in a muddy swamp. Something was bothering her. Who exactly had the man been talking to?

There was a rustle from the doorway.

She glanced towards it, saw that the curtain had been drawn part-way aside. A huge burly short-haired man in a tuxedo was standing there. He looked more like a bouncer than a waiter. But, as she watched, he lumbered silently over to the bar, took down a glistening green bottle from the chrome-edged shelf behind it, poured her a small glass of milky amber liquid. He brought it to her on a silver tray.

There seemed to be no intelligence in his eyes, as he set the glass in front of her. No spark of life, no light. Maybe there was something wrong with him. Perhaps he was retarded. All his movements were cumbersome and deliberate, like an automaton's. She'd been to a cabaret once to see a hypnotist, and the volunteers he'd called up on the stage had moved like that.

The man turned away wordlessly and vanished once more through the curtain. Susan picked up the glass, raised it to her lips. She got a whiff of aniseed, and almost choked.

This was Pernod or *pastis* or something. She hated the damned stuff. Years ago, Denny had got hooked on it, thinking it made him appear more sophisticated, more European, and the cloying stench of it had hung around his breath for months. Until he'd found a new fad. There'd always been a new fad, a new pose, a new girl, just around the corner, damn him.

She thought of putting the glass aside. But the gleaming eyes in the booth were still fixed on her. Watching her, expectantly. She didn't want to appear rude. This was the first real kindness anyone had shown her in Paris, after all.

Hold it, was that entirely true? Hadn't there been a friendly waiter at the hotel? And a man who'd asked her out to a nightclub with his friends? Susan thought about it, and wasn't quite sure. The memories seemed to scuttle away from her like tiny, nimble ants. It all seemed to have happened so long ago.

Go on, take a sip. Don't be a misery.

She raised the glass the rest of the way, forced a few drops of the sickly liquid down, trying not to gag. Then she smiled edgily, nodded her thanks to the couple in the booth.

They didn't respond in any way. They were quite motionless.

Until the slim man who'd ordered her the drink reached down for a silver case on the narrow table, took out a long black cigarette and clenched it between his teeth. A golden lighter glimmered in his hand. He raised it. Flicked at it.

The light of the dancing butane flame played across his face.

12

Susan almost dropped her glass.

The features illuminated by the lighter's glow . . . it was the exact same face which had popped into her thoughts in the café.

Her head reeled and she had to fight to concentrate. Tried to stop it spinning. What the hell was going on? She'd never seen this man before. Never in her life! She was positive of that.

She'd have remembered him. Even in the shifting, flickering jet of flame, even with shadows drifting and swarming across his face, she could see that he was striking. Masculine, but with an almost girlish quality you associated with young British actors or boys from Mediterranean countries.

She felt drawn to him immediately. It was like a hot, tight knotting in her stomach. And that scared her. The housebound, suburban part of her soul – the part she'd been trying to leave behind ever since she'd got on the plane – started curling up inside her with embarrassment. She'd been the object of plenty of admiring stares since she'd arrived in Paris, but given none back. Until now.

For a moment, she couldn't help herself.

She drew back alarmedly in her seat. Tried to look away, without success. This was getting too damned weird. This all seemed to be happening against her will.

Who exactly were these people? She'd no idea, but they had to be pretty odd, to be hanging out in a place like this. The drink had been a nice, friendly gesture. But that was as far as she was allowing things to go.

For Christ's sake, woman! she told herself. Get out of here!

The man puffed at his cigarette, the tip glowing like molten iron for a moment. He was still gazing at her evenly, smiling now.

Then he raised his left hand. It was ghostly pale in the blue light.

He crooked his index finger. Beckoned to her.

Thanks, but no thanks, Susan thought. Very kind of you and all, but I really have to—

She felt her legs start moving beneath her abruptly. Grabbed hold of the edge of the table, trying to stop herself. But she couldn't. Her grasp slipped away.

She was getting up, smoothly and quickly, and walking towards the booth.

CHAPTER TWENTY-TWO

1

Gorreq headed west from the place Pigalle, along the neon rainbow of the boulevard de Clichy, past the sex shops and the porno theatres, the peep-shows and the windows full of fetish wear; and the prostitutes in their short glossy leather skirts and thin tight cotton sweaters. He could make out the silhouetted blades of the maroon-painted windmill above the Moulin Rouge to his right. A coachload of tourists was disembarking in front of it, their flashbulbs popping.

The hookers had all clamped their eyes on him, and some of them called out, posing with their backs slightly arched, or leaning forwards to give him a better view of their cleavages.

'Hey, big boy, I like the look of you! Anything you want, for a price. And I mean *anything*.'

'You're a real man, yes? Well, I'm a real woman, if you'd like to find out. Come on, don't be stingy. I'll be so very wonderful.'

He understood their coarsened accents perfectly. A hungry smile crept across his lips, but he kept his gaze fixed straight ahead. Anything for a price, indeed. If only they knew the truth. There was no price high enough for what he wanted.

He'd Fed on prostitutes a hundred times before, but there were too many of them here. Take one of them, and they'd all remember him when the police showed up. Witnesses. He couldn't afford the risk. But, by the Lords, he had to Feed soon.

He reached the entrance to Clichy Métro station and descended into the bowels of the subway.

The tunnels were still busy at this time of the evening. The platform was liberally scattered with entwined young couples, noisy groups of boys, exhausted-looking businessmen clutching their attaché cases, a few older people nonchalantly dragging on blue-edged cigarettes. A long-haired wino in a filthy afghan coat was making his way towards the seats at the far end, bellowing the '*Marseilleise*' in a raucous, emotional baritone.

Gorreq made his way in the other direction, away from the signal lights, to the end where the last few carriages of the next train would stop. He leant against the scrubbed tiled wall, folded his arms across his chest, waited.

The train arrived a minute later, with a rush of warm air and a clatter like stampeding horses. It was packed full. Gorreq chewed back a curse, thought of waiting for the next one, but there seemed little point. That would probably be crowded too.

He made his way into the rear compartment. There were no free seats at all, so he took hold of a strap.

And immediately began feeling around with his mind.

It alighted, almost straight away, on a girl a couple of yards to his right.

Casually, he looked across at her. Sized her up carefully.

She couldn't have been much older than seventeen. Had a briefcase clasped upright on her lap, as though she were trying to hide her body behind it. She needn't have bothered, so far as the men sitting opposite her were concerned. She was a good twenty pounds overweight, with greasy skin and a florid rash of acne on her cheeks. Her red, centre-parted hair hung down in lank, oily strands to her hunched shoulders. She wore cheap shoes that were badly scuffed, and the ankles above them were chapped and swollen.

But – Gorreq probed her mind a little deeper – this was the first time she'd ever ridden the Métro on her own, so late at night. She was a secretary, had been forced to work late, putting right a mistake she'd made. And she was petrified of all the men around her.

There was something else. Something that forced him to suppress a grin.

She was travelling all the way to the end of the line.

2

At the next station, La Fourche, several people got off and a couple more clambered aboard, but Gorreq was able to drop into a seat directly across from the girl. He took great care not to look at her. Fought down the laughter that was bubbling to his lips.

As the train hissed into the tunnel again, he began risking the briefest glance at her – a mere dart of his pale blue eyes – every few seconds. She looked more pathetic and afraid each time. Her legs were curled tightly beneath her, the ankles crossed. Her elbows were clamped to her sides. Her head was bowed, quivering, her eyes downcast. As though she were trying to perform a feat of origami on herself. Fold her body in upon itself, until it was so small she'd almost disappear.

He thought of touching her mind, whispering in her thoughts, increasing her fear tenfold. But he decided against it. He didn't want her panicking and taking flight with everyone around.

A dozen passengers got off at Guy-Moquet, and only one got on. And at Porte de Saint Ouen, twenty departed. There were no new arrivals.

The train continued its steady progress away from the centre of town, out into the suburbs.

The girl began trembling all over.

Gorreq rolled his tongue around his mouth deliciously. He could smell her fear from here. See its faint, dim glow around the edges of her body.

By the time they reached Carrefour Pleyel, there were only three other passengers left in the carriage. Two of them got up and ambled out on to the platform. The alarm sounded, the doors clattered shut behind them, and the train moved off once more.

Gorreq sensed that the girl was looking at him.

He turned his head, met her stare coolly.

Her entire face had turned sickly pale, and there were droplets of sweat on her upper lip. Her eyes were wide enough to show the marbled veins at the edges of the whites. She was staring at him as numbly as a deer might stare at a cougar. As though she was somehow beginning to realize the danger he presented.

It wasn't that, he saw, when he glanced into her mind. She didn't know a thing. She'd be petrified, tonight, of anyone male and his size, his bulk.

He held her gaze for a moment. And then presented her with a calm, faintly teasing smile.

She suddenly remembered herself, and looked away. She glanced at the other man in the carriage, twelve seats down. Then towards the door. The train was slowing again, rolling into Porte de Paris. Gorreq consulted the map above the girl's head. It was the last but one stop on the line.

The flabby muscles in her legs bunched. Gorreq took another peek into her mind, and saw what she was planning. If the other man got off here, she was going to do the same.

He leaned back patiently.

The train pulled to a halt with a hiss of air-brakes. The other passenger suddenly seemed to realize where he was and jumped up, hurried out. The girl shifted in her seat, preparing to follow him.

And Gorreq spoke to her in the Voice-that-whispers.

No. That's foolish. You'll have a long walk home from here.

She didn't know why she wasn't moving. Her eyes darted around. Her hands began a resonant shaking. But her arms relaxed. Her legs untensed. She slumped back into her seat, as limply as a corpse.

She watched helplessly as the doors banged shut again. The adverts plastered along the station walls began to slide away.

Her mouth parted, and a bubble of saliva drifted down across her lower lip. Her fingers were twitching, by now. Tremoring spastically, of their own accord.

Her eyes went to a large red emergency button near the ceiling.

Gorreq didn't move. There was no need, yet.

But he let his eyes go golden.

And suddenly, she was jolting, and gaping, and looking straight at him. Her face was contorting. Her mouth was stretching open, so wide that it seemed its corners would split.

The clacking of iron wheels against the track grew louder as the train picked up speed.

The girl began shrieking. An insensate noise, rough-edged and braying, like some docile farm animal in pain. Her whole body spasmed, and the briefcase tumbled off her lap. It burst open as it hit the floor. Cheap magazines and a half-finished pack of biscuits slid to Gorreq's feet.

Her hands gripped the arm-rests of her seat, the knuckles turning white. Her legs shuddered uselessly, and she tried to burrow back into the coarse upholstery.

The emergency handle was forgotten now. Every sane, rational thought was being washed away in the spilling river of her fear.

He stood up, and as he towered over her the shrieking rose to a falsetto wail.

He grabbed hold of her by the hair, twisting it around his knuckles. His fingers brushed against her scalp, and he began Feeding deeply.

Then, she was up on her feet and scrabbling, trying to break away from him. Trying, hopelessly, to pull free of his grasp. Spots of blood began appearing, where the roots of her hair tore, but his hold remained solid.

He didn't even bother to knock her back down. Stood quite motionless, grinning, while she flailed and howled. Her blind, horrified panic filled him like a rich, dark wine. He could feel the power growing in his body.

The girl tried clawing at his face. Her short, jagged nails raked down his cheeks. But he was already too strong for that. They left no mark at all.

She could have tried going for his eyes. She might have hurt him slightly, if she'd dug a thumb in very hard. But Gorreq realized that his golden, burning gaze frightened her most of all. She wouldn't dare go near them.

She shuddered and passed out, just as the train was slowing for Saint-Denis. Gorreq caught her as she started to fall backwards. He cradled her slumped shoulders between his hands for a few moments, almost lovingly. Then, like a child disgusted with a broken toy, he dragged her across the carriage.

And smashed her head against the nearest window.

Twice. Three times. Four. Five.

There was a crunch and a soft sucking noise as the back of her skull crushed. Thick, viscous blood smeared the glass. There were tiny flecks of pink in it, and little white shards of bone. A few strands of red hair stuck to the pane.

Gorreq lifted her corpse, so that her slack feet dangled inches from the floor. He gazed, smiling, into her lifeless face a moment. She looked so astonished. So amazed.

Then he flung her aside, and strode out on to the deserted platform.

3

The thin, elegant man moved across to make room for Susan, and she slipped her coat off, sat down in the booth.

At first, she could barely see her new companions, it was so dark in here. But after she'd sat, nervously quiet, for a half-minute or so, their features began to resolve.

The man, she'd already had a look at.

The woman . . . was she a woman or a young girl? It was hard to tell at first.

Her face was heart shaped, all high cheeks and round sparkling eyes, albeit the pupils looked oddly distended. Her mouth, a wide slash painted with dark lipstick. Her hair was straight and black, cut short and swept flat across the brow, like a model in a Horst P. Horst photograph. She was wearing a cold, amused frown which seemed to suit her perfectly. For somebody so small, there was a haughty arrogance about her.

No. She was definitely not young.

The woman met Susan's gaze evenly for a while. Was it her imagination, or did those huge eyes never blink?

Then, languidly, her mouth twisted into a smile and she raised the knuckles of her free hand to her lips. The nails were painted silver, and were long and very sharp.

The other man, the one with his head down on the table, seemed entirely different to his companions. His hair was matted and unwashed, and he was going bald at the crown. He was dressed in a dinner suit, and she could just make out the corner of a bow-tie, like the crumpled wing of a moth, poking out beneath his throat. His jacket was dishevelled, the collar tips of his shirt askew.

She thought at first that he was unconscious; when suddenly he moaned, shifted a little beneath the woman's touch. His head rolled to one side, revealing a pallid, bloated face, a straggling red beard, and puffy eyes. He stared up at her groggily, his expression blank.

Susan jerked back as a faint touch of light caught his pupils. They were no more than tiny pinpricks. She'd seen eyes like that plenty of times, back in Beverly Hills over the last few years. He was out of his mind on drugs. Stoned to the point of subhuman pathos. She felt almost sorry for him.

'I'm being rude,' said the man beside her. It came so suddenly she almost jumped, but she managed to control herself. 'I am Lucius Tharman.' He indicated the woman with his cigarette tip. 'And this is Patricia . . .' He paused a moment, smiling thoughtfully, as though he was trying to conjure a name out of thin air. 'Patricia Felix.'

There seemed to be some kind of joke passing between the couple. The woman's smile broadened, her lips suddenly parted, revealing small, very bright teeth. They looked oddly pointed.

'And this,' Tharman continued, his voice a lazy drawl, 'is Patricia's friend, the viscomte de Raichlet. *Bon viveur*, disinherited heir, and the owner of this nightclub.'

Susan found herself struggling for a reply.

'You're – you're German, aren't you? Your name sounds German.'

Tharman shook his head condescendingly. 'I'm *Alsacien*, my dear. From Strasbourg, on the German border. And you – you're an American. From the west coast, probably. Is this your first taste of Paris nightlife?'

Either there was sarcasm in his voice, or she was just imagining it. She wasn't sure she liked this man entirely.

Susan nodded, and then gazed around at the empty room, the barren stage.

'It seems rather quiet.' She couldn't think of anything else to say.

'Not many people know about this place,' Tharman replied, 'and it's poorly located. The viscomte is not the most practical of businessmen.'

'That's a shame. And it's a pity about the stage, too. Isn't there any entertainment?'

Tharman's lips twisted into a crooked smirk. It was cruel, almost leering, the way he looked at her. Why did she find him so attractive?

'There was a singer, but he left.' He glanced enquiringly at the petite woman, his thin black eyebrows lifting. 'When was it Patricia? Two nights ago?'

'The same night we arrived,' the woman agreed, with a tiny shrug.

Why did she get the feeling they were toying with her? Why did she feel they were still playing a game, and that she was the ball?

She couldn't move again; though, strangely, that didn't seem to bother her too much. It was as though part of her mind had been closed down, put into neutral. The only thing she could think to do was stay put and be polite.

'Just my luck,' she said, quietly.

She could almost hear her own voice echoing in her head.

The man leaned towards her. 'Would you like some entertainment? Maybe Patricia could oblige?'

Susan glanced nervously at the woman, who was tapping her nails against her lower lip.

'I . . . no. There's really no need.'

'Nonsense. Patricia would be only too delighted. Wouldn't you, sister?'

Sister? Were they related?

The woman was already getting up, pushing the drugged viscomte back into his seat and sliding past him. Susan could see that she was no more than five foot tall, impossibly skinny. She was wearing a glossy black body stocking – and, despite her thinness, muscles seemed to flow and ripple beneath the tight fabric. She moved with a feral litheness.

But, just as she was climbing up on to the dais, the woman's grace seemed to desert her for a moment. She tottered back a couple of steps. Seemed to find that amusing, and giggled shrilly.

Was she on drugs too? Were they all?

Susan's heart had started beating faster now. She could feel it pounding in her numb, cold chest. The calm she'd felt a few moments ago was evaporating. Her mind was starting to clear, like a clouded sky being parted by a fierce, insistent wind.

It took a conscious effort, but she did it. Bunched her hands into fists. Pushed them down against her seat. Began to lift herself.

Tharman put a slender hand on the bare flesh of her shoulder.

'Wait.' He sounded hurt. 'Don't you want to hear Patricia? She's doing this especially for you.'

His touch felt more than warm. It was hot. Burning. Despite her fear, Susan felt a sexual tremor run through her lower body. It was as though she'd never been touched by a man before. As though he was the very first who'd ever laid a finger on her.

She found herself relaxing, settling back into the chair again. Tharman lifted his fingers from her shoulder – she almost whimpered as the heat vanished – and put them to the side of her chin, just beneath the smooth ridge of her jaw. Very gently, with only the slightest pressure, he turned her face towards him. And upwards.

Until she met his violet eyes.

How could so pale a colour seem so vivid? She felt that she was being drawn into them.

Behind her she could hear Patricia fumble with the microphone and begin singing in a deep, tuneless voice.

> *'Got jailed in Montana. Cha-boom.*
> *Got throwed in the slam. Scoo-dah.*
> *Met a kid named Joe,*
> *And that kid was gonna hang.'*

The woman was slurring the words badly, like a drunk. And every bar she sang was punctuated with a grunt or a giggle. It was only background noise, though. Susan could barely hear it.

She was vaguely aware she'd heard that song long ago, when she'd been young. But it didn't seem to be important. Only Tharman's eyes mattered. They held her attention completely.

She teetered on their violet brink a moment longer. Then fell, tumbling, into the abyss.

4

Susan, you are quite alone now. Quite alone, after so many years as a wife, a mother – completely on your own. And do you like it? Really? At the bottom of your soul? Free, yes. You are free. But are you happy, comfortable, content? Are you not afraid?

And is that truly freedom, to live the rest of your life bearing that hidden sadness within you, that awful fear? You will start to grow old, soon. Your beautiful face will wrinkle, crease. Your body will dry up like a dying tree. Not even the boy at the hotel will look at you any more. And what then? What then?

You are so strong, my beautiful one, my brave one. Deep down, there is such a fire in you. But you cannot find it on your own. The deep fear, the hidden sadness, prevent you. Only with my guidance can you find yourself. Only with my help can you fulfil yourself.

You can amaze the world, Susan. Startle it. Rock it on its heels. But only with me by your side. Only me.

5

Susan didn't know where the hissing words were coming from. But, for an indefinable while, they filled her mind. Invaded every corner of her thoughts, as she wallowed in those violet eyes.

For a while, they were all that she could hear.

And then, abruptly, startledly, she broke free.

Jesus Christ, what the *hell* was she thinking of?

She didn't need *anybody*. She was *glad* to be alone, for the first time in her life. All last year in Beverly Hills, she'd dreamed of nothing else!

She tore herself away savagely from the whispering voice. Thought— No, no, no! Let me alone!

And suddenly, Tharman's eyes seemed to shrink, diminish. Suddenly, she wasn't swimming in them any more. She was staring into his pale face, and blinking frightenedly.

He looked completely unappealing, now. Overly gaunt. Weasel featured. Skinny. His flesh was as colourless as maggots. And those eyes she'd found so fascinating a few moments ago – the pupils were minute. Concentrated spots of darkness. The irises were distant and baleful, like a reptile's.

Up on the stage, Patricia had stopped singing.

Susan looked towards her, and saw that the woman was clinging to the microphone stand and glaring down, her eyes blazing and her cheeks bright red with anger.

She felt Tharman's fingertips clawing at her shoulder again. But there was no heat this time. Only repulsion.

Susan recoiled, slid to the edge of the booth.

The man reached for her again, his sickly face rigid with surprise. His thin lips parted, and a whisper drifted out.

'Susan . . .?'

Shuddering with fright, she leapt to her feet. And then

she was pushing through the velvet curtain, hurrying to the door, and running away into the night.

6

The commissionaire at the hotel smiled and nodded to her, but Susan barely noticed him. She shoved her way through the revolving doors, hurried across the lobby to the elevators.

When she reached the door of her suite, at the end of the dim corridor, she practically fell against it. Her hands fumbled stupidly with the key. She couldn't seem to control her fingers, and it took her three attempts to work the lock.

The suite was pitch dark, when she finally got it open. She was afraid to go in. Clinging to the door-frame with one hand, she stretched the other inside and groped around until it brushed over a light switch.

She pushed it down. The room sprang into sudden, sharp relief, all glittering ormolu and solid regal furniture, exactly as she'd left it. But she wasn't pleased to see it. It was overbearing, cast strangely moulded shadows, like the rest of this damned city. She wanted to be back in LA, surrounded by modern buildings and brash, healthy people. Gone from this odour of decadence. Far from this smell of old corruptions and temptations.

She slammed the door behind her, leaned against it for a moment, panting heavily. Then, she turned around and locked it, put the chain on, shot the stiff bolt near the top.

It wasn't enough. She *still* didn't feel safe.

She clattered around the suite, making certain all the windows were locked and there was no way in.

Why was she doing all this? When she finally plumped down on the bed, gasping for breath and shivering, she realized that she wasn't quite sure. No one had threatened her all evening. No one had followed her. Tharman and that peculiar woman were unlikely to come walking into this room.

She was still confused about exactly what had happened in the Club Minuit. Maybe it was simply that she was unused to *pastis*, and the drink had affected her. Or the quietness of the place, and her own sense of loneliness, had gotten to her.

She pushed those ideas aside.

All she knew – *really* knew – was that she was scared out of her wits. And however much she tried to calm herself down, tell herself it had all been her imagination, the grasping, clammy fear just wouldn't go away. It was shaking her whole body, like a terrier playing with a rag-doll.

She put a hand to her chest, tried to steady her breathing. Lord, she was wheezing like an asthmatic old lady. There was little feeling in her arms and legs, and her meal of a couple of hours ago was threatening to come back on her.

For God's sake, stop it. Stop it! You'll tear yourself to bits if you keep this up.

What was she going to do now? What the hell was she going to do?

She tried to work out her options. But only one came to mind, pounding at her insistently, like a hammer against her skull.

Get out of here. Get out of here! For Pete's sake just get *out*!

Before she quite knew what she was doing, she was scrambling across the bed, snatching up the phone. Dialling zero for the front desk.

'Madame?' a bored voice responded. It was a different concierge, not the one who'd woken her this afternoon.

'Yes, hello? Can you help me? Could you tell me the time of the next flight to Los Angeles?'

The man sounded faintly bemused as he consulted a timetable. 'Nine thirty-five tomorrow morning, Madame. A Pan Am flight.'

'I'd like you to book me on it. Right away, if you please.'

The man's bewilderment gave way to concern. 'Madame, is there anything wrong?'

'Yes – n-no! Just make the reservation, please.'

She slammed down the phone before he had time to reply.

7

She began to calm down quickly after that, though the fear wouldn't entirely go away. Those weird characters in the club had left her feeling so raw nerved, so vulnerable. The man, especially. But at least she was able to think about going to bed, trying to get some sleep.

She felt exhausted, all of a sudden.

Susan lingered for an age in front of the bathroom mirror, wiping off her make-up, soaping her skin. She kept gazing, long and hard, at her reflection, her own eyes. Trying to detect any faint glimmer of madness in them. Perhaps she was going crazy. The face that stared back at her from the mirror was drawn and colourless, and seemed to have gathered a thousand tiny lines. It was the face of a once-beautiful woman on the brink of the inevitable downhill slide into old age.

She couldn't bear to look at herself, after a while. She was already shaking. Now, she felt like bursting into tears.

She padded back into the bedroom, packed most of her clothes.

God, she'd been wearing a coat when she'd gone out. Her expensive sable. She must have left it at the club.

Well, it was a gift from Denny anyway. Whatever it had cost, it had been a way of trying to buy her. And she was getting odd remarks from some people in LA these days, for wearing a fur. To hell with it.

She got a wide, flowing smock out of a panel in her suitcase and tugged it on. She'd slept in the buff every night since she'd left Denny. But not tonight.

She moved towards the bed, and then decided to check all the locks again. Like a silly old woman, she told herself. A stupid, paranoid old crone.

At last, she was satisfied. She went back to the door, clicked off the lights.

The fluorescent strip over the mirror in the bathroom was still on. A wedge of brightness streamed across the marble floor to the foot of her bed.

She decided to leave it that way. She couldn't bear to lie entirely in the dark tonight.

Like a child, she thought. Like a terrified infant. She hadn't slept with a light on since she'd been six years old. Which was she? Child? Old woman? Make your mind up, idiot. She was so confused. Couldn't seem to get her thoughts straight.

The sibilant, hissing words – the words which had whispered through her head in the club – came back to her again. Susan whimpered, tried to forget them.

The darkness seemed to bite into her like a November frost as she crawled into the huge four-poster bed. She pulled the covers up around her neck. And lay there, on her back, perfectly still.

A group of people went by on the street below her window, laughing loudly, drunkenly. She listened to them with her eyes wide open, staring at the black well of the canopy above her face.

8

Gorreq got to the club just after eleven. The scene which met his cold blue gaze was not what he'd expected. He'd been expecting to see the woman, the Californian, sitting beside Tharman, obedient as a doll.

Instead, most of the candles had guttered out. The spotlight on the stage had been switched off, and the room lay in a blue-tinged darkness.

And Tharman was sitting alone in the deep shadows of the booth. His elbows were on the table, his chin resting on his knuckles. He was gazing steadily into midair, smiling wryly to himself.

Pashta was more lively, busy at her latest game. She'd

swept one of the tables near the stage clear, and had bent the viscomte backwards over the polished wood. She was pinning him down with a knee in the middle of his chest. Her left hand was squeezing his jaw open, and with her right she was forcing a handful of pills – blue, black, red-and-yellow capsules – into his mouth. The man was struggling feebly and making sickening, gagging noises. The more he tried to fight, the more delighted Pashta seemed.

'Come on, baby,' she was murmuring, her face luminous with hunger. 'Swallow them. Eat them all up for Mama.'

The viscomte choked, spat out a few. Pashta slapped him on the face, leaving a row of bright red blood-spots on his cheek, and then started pushing another handful at him.

'You'll kill him like that,' Gorreq said, out loud.

The woman looked up at him suddenly, her eyes bright. Tipped her head to one side. 'Plenty more where he came from, my brother.'

She closed her hands over the viscomte's temples and began to Feed.

'What's up with him?' Gorreq broke in, waving his hand towards Tharman.

Pashta glanced across at the booth, and shook her head.

'He's suffering from a terrible sickness of the heart, and it's spread up to his brain. He let the Californian go.'

Gorreq stiffened with surprise, thought about that a little, and then moved over slowly to the booth. Tharman didn't even notice him at first. The gaunt man's violet eyes were glowing faintly as he peered into the dimness. A smile twitched at the corners of his lips, like a feebly twisting larva. He was muttering to himself, under his breath.

There was a black fur coat on the seat beside him.

You let her go? Gorreq asked.

Tharman looked up as his brother's shadow fell across the table.

He nodded. *She pulled away from me.* His tone was an

awed whisper. *The only woman ever to fight the Voice, and win.*

Gorreq studied him carefully. The thin, starved-looking face. The faintly trembling hands. He frowned, annoyed.

She broke away from you because you are weak. You haven't bothered to Feed.

Tharman seemed to turn that over for a while. And then, he let out a throaty chuckle.

No, not yet, my brother. But tonight, I shall feast like the Pharaohs themselves. Tonight, I shall gorge myself.

CHAPTER TWENTY-THREE

1

As the bus doors hissed open and Kellesh stepped out on to the darkened, grimy streets of the north-eastern suburbs, a terrible feeling of sickness swept over him, leaving him reeling and dizzy.

He'd felt Gorreq make a kill on the way up here. Felt the surge of power as the creature had Fed. And now Pashta was Feeding too. There was nothing new in that. He'd sensed their hunger and their greed many thousand times before.

But tonight, as never before, it nauseated him.

They'd always been barbaric, cruel, but now there was a new, ravenous edge, an almost desperate savagery to their games. As though, over the years, they had become ever more drunken on their power. And with Lapotaire so close, with the end of their hunt in sight, they were on a terrifying binge.

Kellesh steadied himself against a lamppost, rubbed his tired, sore eyes, and stared along the street. Most of the lights were broken. What little illumination there was came from windows with thin nylon drapes. The steely timbre of reggae music wafted across the mild night air, and somewhere in one of the higher apartments a man and a woman were shouting. A baby was wailing, trying to make itself heard above them.

A mangy stray dog rounded the corner and trotted angrily towards him, its hackles rising. Then, it stopped, peered at him more closely. It whined and turned away, scuttling into an alley.

Three men in flowing colourful robes were playing cards on a porch stoop halfway down the street, squandering their meagre handfuls of coins. They were so engrossed they didn't even bother to look up at him.

He could stay amongst these people for a century, it occurred to him, and never grow hungry.

But time was growing short. And he had work to do. He straightened up and walked slowly away from the card-players towards the corner of the rue Lafitte-Leard. Stopped there. Cast his mind around. He could hear the thoughts and see the dreams of the tenement dwellers clearly. But whenever he tried to focus on Maurice Lapotaire, a dazzling brightness hit him. Burning images of the sun whirled in his mind. He was forced to draw back again.

There was no way of telling where it was coming from.

He was sweating by now, his ugly brow drawn into a tight frown. What to do?

He could simply rely on luck, trudge the dismal streets and feel out with his mind until the brightness of the *Ra* discs became too much to bear. He'd know, at that point, he was near his goal. Or . . .

He stiffened suddenly as an idea came to him. Couldn't imagine why it hadn't occurred to him before.

If Lapotaire was hiding in one of these streets, then somebody had to be sheltering him. Somebody had to be helping him.

Someone – another mortal – had to know where he was.

A smile flickered on Kellesh's face, and faded just as quickly. There wasn't time to be pleased with himself. It wouldn't be long before the others came to the same conclusion.

He stood perfectly still, concentrating all his strength, all his energy, into his mind. Then, rapidly, he began to cast about the ghetto, like a fisherman casting a fly.

2

Maurice was sitting on his bed, his knees drawn up to his chest, his bloodshot eyes staring exhaustedly at the cellar wall, when he heard Joshua stop singing, upstairs.

He'd been lost in the turmoil of his own thoughts until that moment; too tired to move, too frightened to sleep. It would have been so easy just to pick up the money Harry had left, get on the first flight out of here, and leave Paris for good. Now, he felt imprisoned, like a rat in an ornate trap.

Who had that woman been, in the shadows of the stairwell this afternoon? His brain felt as though it was trying to leap out of his skull, as he turned it over for the hundredth time. Had she been one of *them*?

The abrupt silence from the hallway brought him back to his senses.

Josh had been running through that old African song again, and though Maurice had not been listening to it properly, it had formed a gentle, soothing backdrop to the racket in his head,

Now it had halted in mid-phrase, like a tune on a radio that someone had abruptly switched off.

Maurice's gaze shot to the door. There was something wrong up there, he was sure. He could feel it.

A chill flooded his body, and his skin seemed to tighten.

He remained perfectly still for a few seconds, listening intently. And then, when he could still hear nothing, cleared his throat.

'Josh?'

There was no answer.

'*Joshua?*'

His only reply was silence.

3

Kellesh hurried through the streets towards the rue Albaiville, his feet pounding on the cracked sidewalk. His breath was coming in fast bursts, and there was an air of urgency, excitement, like he hadn't felt in years.

This African he'd sunk his mental hooks into, this Joshua, came from an ancient people, from a race as old as the Egyptians. Had some magic of his own. Was strong.

And was fighting him. It would only be a matter of time before the old man broke away and warned Lapotaire. He had to hurry.

He turned another corner and the tenement house came in sight. It was no different from any of the others on the narrow street. Its walls were discoloured with soot, its stucco façade peeling. A broken window on the second floor had been boarded up from the inside and covered with plastic sheeting. The only light in the entire house was shining though the letterbox in the front door.

Kellesh paused for a moment, gathering his strength. Then he pushed on, towards the low, cracked porch steps. He cast a Spell of Opening ahead of him, and the front door rattled, then swung back, creaking.

Inside, revealed by a solitary, shadeless bulb, was a completely bare hallway. It was redolent of cooking smells and the flat, stale odour of rot. There was no carpet on the splintered floorboards, nothing but plaster on the damp-stained walls.

The African was trying to hide at the far end of the corridor, by the kitchen door, way out of the light. As Kellesh stepped inside, he grunted startledly. His hand went into the back pocket of his jeans, and came out holding something slim and smooth. His thumb shifted. There was a gleam of silvery brightness. He was clutching a straight razor.

Kellesh took another couple of steps forwards, and then stood perfectly still. He raised his hands in front of him, palms outwards, in a placatory gesture.

Touched the man's mind.

There's no need to be afraid of me. I mean you no harm.

Joshua's eyes grew wider in his wrinkled face. His lips parted slightly, showing a glimpse of his yellowed teeth. He shook his head, as though he were trying to rid himself of an annoying bluebottle.

His whole body was shaking, partly from fear, partly from confusion. The muscles in his arm slid together, bunching, and he swung the razor back. Tried to take a step along the hallway.

But their eyes were meeting now. It was easy enough to stop him.

Joshua, listen to me. Your friend is in great danger. I'm here to help him. Help, not harm. Kellesh glanced towards the cellar door. *Is he down there?*

The man let out a stifled moan, still fighting as hard as he could.

I must speak to him. I must see him. But I cannot go down there. The discs prevent me. Take them away, Joshua. Remove them.

The African began mumbling to himself. A prayer, maybe. An incantation. Something from his village. Something to ward off evil spirits.

He tried to move again, and this time Kellesh found it much harder to bring him to a halt.

He hadn't Fed sufficiently these last few days. He could stop the African from harming him, but could not bend him completely to his will.

The damp corridor seemed to be closing in around him. A truck went by on the street outside, sounding very faint.

Kellesh edged towards the cellar door, taking care not to reach down with his mind. The *Ra* discs would sear him, this close up. Blind him. Cauterize his thoughts. He stopped with one hand almost touching the cracked wood. Listened. He could hear nothing except for the faint stirring of the gold-foil discs.

His sharp ears couldn't even pick out any breathing. The man in the cellar had frozen completely. As though he sensed that something inhuman was close.

Kellesh called out, very gently.

'Mr Lapotaire?'

Suddenly, there were noises. A short, abrupt creak of bedsprings. A smothered whimper. Kellesh remained still and kept his tone as unthreatening as he could.

'Mr Lapotaire, please let me down there. Let me help.' He drew in a breath, remembering something. 'Do you recall, when you were a child in Harlem, an old, bald man with a scar on his face? A friend of your grandmother's? A blues singer? His name was Washington Davis. I offered to help him and he refused me – and paid the price. Please, don't make the same mistake.'

He regretted saying it the moment it left his lips. It sounded too much like a threat. But anything he said right now would sound like a threat. The man was scared senseless. Wouldn't listen to him. Probably wasn't even taking in what he was saying.

If only he could reach down and touch Lapotaire's thoughts, soothe them.

He turned back to Joshua. The African was standing like an ancient bronze figurine. Only his arms were moving, trembling faintly, imparting an electric shiver to the razor blade.

Josh, I'm his only chance. Please help me.

But all he sensed, when he looked into his mind again, was disbelief and anger.

It was no use. There was nothing he could do here, and he ought to go. But he'd run away once before, back in New York City, when the blues singer had died. He couldn't bring himself to turn away again.

Kellesh pushed his hair from his brow, combing it with his fingers. Sighed.

If we can't run, then we wait here. He favoured Joshua with a resigned smile, then glanced around the hallway and up the battered flight of stairs. *Then we fight, and probably die . . . but there is no other way. With any luck, they won't come here tonight. They seem busy with other matters. But I must be out of the light by dawn. Where can I hide, Joshua? Where can I rest?*

It was still no use. The man ground his jaw, refusing to speak. There were dense beads of sweat on his forehead, by now, and his bloodshot eyes were stark white with fear, but his resolve was as strong as ever. There was no getting through to him.

Kellesh had no option but to push his way deeply into his mind. He rifled through the old man's thoughts until he could see the entire layout of the house.

The cellar was out of the question. But next to the scullery was a second, narrower flight of stairs, running up to the loft. Beneath it lay a huge deep closet which was never used.

Perfect.

There was one more thing to do.

He whispered to Joshua a final time.

If I cannot make you do things, at least I can make you do nothing. Forget that I am here, old man.

Forget.

4

Somehow, Susan had fallen into a doze.

She was tossing and turning on her downy bed, small, agonized moans pushing their way up from her throat. It had taken an age for sleep to come. And now, she wanted to wake. And couldn't. It was as though a thick dark net had closed around her, tightening the more she squirmed. However much she struggled, she couldn't break free.

The nightmares were coming thick and fast. Most of them were set in the Club Minuit. Tharman was staring at her with those violet eyes again. He was smiling at her with those thin, pale lips. He was reaching out towards her, and suddenly that colourless slim hand was changing into something else. Something huge and heavy and dark, with thick blunt fingers and fur dangling from the wrist.

His voice filled her mind again.

Only with me beside you. Only with me.

Her legs flailed underneath the bedsheets, in the motion of running. But she couldn't get away from him.

The dream changed abruptly.

She was back in her room, on the bed. And her eyes were partly open, now. She was staring at the tall window, with the balcony beyond. And as she watched, the glass shuddered faintly. A shadow moved behind the drapes.

And then, by itself, the latch began to turn.

5

She wasn't properly asleep. Her beautiful eyes were open a faint glimmer, and she was staring at him drowsily as he moved across the marble floor towards her, trailing her sable coat.

Good. He was pleased.

Tharman reached out gently for Susan's mind; saw that she thought she was still dreaming.

Oh, my strong one. My brave one. You'll never have such dreams as these.

Her legs gave a final jolt, and she kicked all her bedclothes off, turned over on her back. The thin smock she was wearing was drenched with sweat. Tharman could see, quite clearly beneath it, the outline of her body, the swell of her breasts and the dark circles of her nipples. The hemline had ridden up. A triangle of shadow was apparent above her long, gracefully honed legs, a delta of blackness on her tanned flesh.

Tharman stopped at the edge of the bed and hovered over her. And immediately felt himself changing, as the creature inside him took over.

The woman's eyes came open a little more, and she let out a childlike whimper.

He touched her mind again, calming her, soothing her. Her whole body relaxed, and her eyes narrowed once more to thin, shimmering crescents. Then he reached out gently with his free hand, brushed the edges of his claws across her cheek. She shuddered, released a soft, breathy moan.

Again.

The sigh was deeper this time. Her tongue flickered along the edges of her lips.

His fingers began to follow the curve of her throat, as he settled down beside her.

CHAPTER TWENTY-FOUR

1

Susan woke, jerked upright on the bed and stared towards the balcony window. It was closed, the latch firmly in place. Bright sunlight was streaming through to an accompaniment of traffic noise.

It was morning.

Her head was blurry, and she couldn't tell if she was properly awake or not. She still seemed to be partly in the grip of the bizarre erotic dream she'd had last night. The one in which Tharman had come to her, made love to her. The one in which he'd changed shape until his body was huge and apelike, thick with fur. His face had been that of an angry dog, and his eyes had glowed a searing gold.

She could see them every time she blinked. She couldn't get their sheen out of her head.

Falling back on the pillow, she stared up at the canopy and tried to collect her thoughts.

There was an odd, musty odour all around her. A zoo-like smell. The stink of a wild animal. She inhaled deeply. It was all over the bed.

For a moment, she couldn't even move. Then she looked down at her body.

Her sable coat was lying at her feet.

She sat up again, gasping, and snatched at the garment. Turned it over in her hands. The same dreadful stench hung all over it.

Blind panic overtook her. Susan vaulted to her feet and ran to the door to check the bolt and chain. To the windows, to make sure the latches were in place. They were all as she'd left them when she'd gone to bed. No one could have got into the room.

Her mind was spinning like a top, now. She could hardly keep her balance. What had happened? She *knew* she'd left the coat at the Club Minuit last night.

The telephone began to ring, beside the bed.

Her hands clattered over it, practically knocking it to the floor.

Somehow, she managed to get the receiver to her ear.

'Madame Carroll?' It was the same concierge she'd spoken to last night. 'I'm afraid I must inform you of some bad news. There is a baggage-handlers' strike at the airport. All flights to America are cancelled.'

2

By midday, she'd emerged on to the street and had begun looking for a cab. Her hair was damp and frizzy and her skin dull, cold. How long had she stood under the shower? An hour? Two? She wasn't sure. She seemed to have lost all track of time.

All that she knew was she couldn't just sit in her suite all day, waiting for things to happen. She was the one who had to make them happen, now. The only lead she had was Maurice Lapotaire. He was connected with all this somehow, she was sure. She remembered the way he'd run away from her yesterday, the look of terror on his face. And the only lead she had to the photographer was the old salesman, Harry Bernstein.

A taxi, driven by a young stubble-chinned Arab, pulled over to the kerb, and she jumped inside and told him the address.

She snapped at him, a minute later, when she caught him staring at her in the rear-view mirror. She still felt frightened and overpowered. But she was getting angry too. It helped a lot, more than she'd ever have believed it would.

Porno theatres began to cluster in around her as they climbed the hill into the Pigalle district. There were posters outside each doorway with lurid, yard-high titles and garish illustrations. *Passion des Animaux*, said one. Animal passion. She felt sick, and had to turn away.

When the cab slid to a halt in front of the apartment house, Susan shoved a wad of bills into the driver's hand, without even bothering to count them, and scrambled out.

The second floor landing was as dim as it had been yesterday, but there was no music drifting from behind Bernstein's door this afternoon. She found herself praying he was home.

She held the bell-push down with her thumb for about a minute. There was no reply.

'Mr Bernstein?' She put an eye to the peep-hole, trying to see if there was a light on inside. It was covered up. 'Mr Bernstein, please open the door! I have to talk to you!'

She heard, very faintly, a shuffling noise from inside, then a groan.

'Mr Bernstein! My name's Susan Carroll. I was here yesterday. I *must* talk to you about Maurice Lapotaire. Please!'

There was only silence for a while. And then she thought that she could hear someone dragging himself very slowly towards her.

'The American lady?' a quavering voice called out.

'Yes, that's right!'

'Are you alone?'

'Completely. I promise.'

She was starting to grow afraid again. The old man's voice was different from yesterday. Very thin and weak and tremulous.

Locks and bolts began to clatter. She waited as patiently as she could. The door came open a few inches, held in place by a stout iron chain. Beyond it, from the darkness, a perfectly white face stared out at her, a pair of spectacles glinting blindly.

She was studied for what seemed an age, as though she might be carrying some fatal disease.

At last there was a final rattle as Bernstein slipped the chain. The door swung open under its own weight, and Susan gasped with shock.

3

When she'd seen him yesterday, he'd looked feeble and unsound, but not like *this.*

The rims of his eyes were an angry, swollen red, and his lips were tinged an odd grey-blue colour. The wrinkles on his face seemed to have come alive. Seemed to have turned into a dark, spidery growth which was eating deeply into his skin, distorting his features. His lower jaw hung slackly, and he seemed to be having trouble breathing.

His cane was lying on the floor behind him. He was swaying, finding it hard to stand.

As she watched, he clutched at his chest and his knees began to buckle. Susan darted forwards and grabbed hold of him.

For a moment, Bernstein grunted and tried to struggle. As though he'd forgotten she was there. As though he imagined someone *else* was grabbing at him.

He was heavier than he looked. She managed to get one shoulder underneath his arm, clasped him tightly around the back, and half-helped, half-carried him through into the neglected, cluttered living-room. Brown carpets and deep red wooden furniture surrounded her. Silver candlesticks gleamed dully on a long sideboard. The blinds were drawn and there was little daylight seeping in. She lowered him into a battered velvet armchair, then watched, alarmed, as his breathing became laboured and his chest heaved.

She ought to call an ambulance. She glanced around, but couldn't see a phone.

There was a sudden, faint touch at her wrist. Susan looked down to see that he was reaching for her, staring up at her imploringly. His pale, watery gaze had become a little brighter. His lips parted slightly, and he wet them with his tongue.

'*Meine Medizin, bitte,*' he whispered. 'My medicine.'

He jerked his hand towards a rosewood cabinet over

by the wall, under a massive, aged television set. Susan found a bottle full of tiny pills on the top shelf.

'Do you need water with these?'

The old man shook his head, accepted two of the tablets in his outstretched palm, and gulped them whole. Then he settled back, coughed. A little colour began returning to his cheeks.

Susan knelt down beside him and brushed a hand across his cheek. The skin was freezing cold. She took hold of his wrist, trying to find a pulse. It was faint, uneven.

Bernstein tipped his head back, sighed, 'Please, could you put the heater on?'

There was a dust-covered electric fire to her side. Susan switched it on, and the three bars started to glow a rosy crimson.

'You're an angel,' Bernstein murmured, nodding his thanks. 'All night, I've been out in that hallway. All damned night.'

She bent over him and began stroking his face again. It seemed to calm him down a little.

'Should I call a doctor?'

'No! No doctor. No nothing.' His hand went to his chest again, and he winced. 'If you call a quack, I know what will happen. I'll end up in an asylum . . . in a nuthouse, yes?'

'What exactly do you mean by that?'

'You tell me why you came back here,' he grimaced. 'And then – maybe – I'll tell you.'

4

'I have known Mr Lapotaire since he moved in here,' he explained.

The room had warmed up considerably by now and, though he could still barely move, the shaking was gone and Bernstein no longer looked so sickly. Susan was perched on the edge of his chair, listening attentively.

'A nice young man, but very quiet, shy. And in his eyes . . . you say that he was a war photographer? I could see that he had been through some terrible things. I was sympathetic to him, straight away.

'After he was here a month, he asks if I can do him a favour. He is taking photos for the magazines, but he wants to remain private. I never enquired why. It was none of my business. But we agreed that I should take his pictures to the magazines, pick up the cheques. For this, I got ten per cent of each payment, just like an agent. I didn't want it, but he insisted.' Bernstein made a weak attempt at a smile. 'And I got my name on the photos too. All of a sudden, fame, at my age.'

'Why put the money underneath his door?' Susan asked. 'Why not give it to him personally?'

'Sometimes I do. But he's not home, right now. He's been away for several days.'

'Where?'

'I've no idea. It happens every so often. He just disappears, and then returns a week or two later. He's always scruffy, in a bad shape, when he comes back. But like I said, I don't ask many questions.' He shrugged, and then seemed to remember something. 'A man visited him once. The only visitor I've ever seen. An African, though he spoke very good French, with a Parisian accent. I bumped into him in the lobby. Maybe Mr Lapotaire goes to stay with this fellow when he disappears.'

There were too many maybes by far. Susan was quiet, for a while. The old man seemed grateful for that. His eyes slid shut again, and his breathing became softer.

She didn't want him to fall asleep. But she didn't really want to ask him the next question either. What had frightened him so much? She was going to upset him all over again, but she had no choice.

She reached out for his shoulder, nudged him gently.

*

5

He reached down carefully and unbuttoned the cuff of his crumpled sweat-stained shirt. Rolled up the sleeve to reveal the row of tattooed numbers on his wrist. He held them up for Susan's inspection.

'Do you know what this means?' he asked.

'You were in a concentration camp during the war.'

Bernstein nodded matter-of-factly, trying to ease her discomfort. 'Buchenwald. Many Jews were there. Catholics too. Poles. Slavs. Gypsies. Intellectuals. Men who love other men – what is that word?'

'Homosexuals.'

'*Ja, so!* And you, young lady, probably know about the gas chambers, the ovens. But people don't talk much about the rest of it. How some of the guards behaved, how they took it on themselves to kill and torture.' His voice was croaky now, but very firm, as though he had an absolute duty to get the telling right. 'They would pick out a man from the barracks, do terrible things to him. The young officers were the worst. Some we were very afraid of. But there was one who was the most dreadful of all.'

The old man's hands clenched around the arms of his chair, as though he needed to steady himself.

'He was a colonel. We didn't know his name. A big man, huge, like an ox, with short blond hair and very pale skin. We only ever saw him at night, never by the light of day. He would let himself into the barracks and prowl amongst the bunks very quietly, like a hunting animal. And we'd all lie still, not moving a muscle, not even breathing, because we didn't want to draw attention to ourselves. No one wanted to be the unlucky one.' Bernstein frowned disgustedly. 'I think he knew we were doing that, and liked it. Whatever, eventually he'd choose a man, and take him outside. And there would be the most terrible screams, on and on, for more than an hour sometimes. Until finally they'd stop, and we'd be glad.'

He peered at Susan challengingly.

'Yes, glad. Glad that the man's agony was over. Glad that it was not us. That we'd been spared for a little while. And then, a few nights later, it would happen all over again. We never saw a corpse. We never found out what exactly he'd done to each victim. Everything was neatly cleared away by morning. I think the guards, too, were afraid of this colonel.

'But we had a name for him. We called him "*Das Goldbiest*". The Golden Beast. Do you know why?'

Susan was too horrified, by now, to even shake her head.

'His eyes.' Bernstein raised his fingers to his glasses. 'When he came into the barracks, his eyes would change colour. They would begin to shine a bright gold in the darkness.'

Susan thought her heart had stopped. She jumped to her feet, drawing back in horror.

In the dream, last night . . . in the dream of Tharman . . .

His eyes had changed too. His eyes had glowed bright golden.

Bernstein grabbed hold of her wrist. 'You think I'm crazy? I'm not. It's all true! And you want to know why I was out in the hallway all night? You want to know why I'm so afraid? I saw him again. He was trying to get into Mr Lapotaire's apartment. *Das Goldbiest* was here.'

Susan worked her wrist around, trying to break his grip. He was hurting her, frightening her, and she'd had enough of both, the past twenty-four hours, to last her a lifetime. Only his age, and what he'd been through, stopped her getting angry at him.

'That can't be, Mr Bernstein,' she blurted. 'You were imagining it.'

'No.' The old man was insistent. 'You think I wouldn't know him? You think I wouldn't recognize him?' His free hand went to his glasses again, tugging at them. 'I'm old, not blind.'

'But could you really see him properly? It would have been dark on the landing.'

The man shook his head adamantly. He wasn't going to be budged.

Susan eased her fingers free, at last, and cupped both her hands around his, trying to calm him down. 'Look, let's take it as agreed that someone was trying to get into Lapotaire's apartment. And whoever it was, we really have to wonder why. Do you have a key?'

'*Ja*. Maurice gave me a spare, in case of emergencies.'

It turned out to be in the same cabinet as the tablets, behind a bottle of Israeli *sabra*.

'You rest,' Susan told him gently. 'I promise I won't be long.'

6

Brother, the thoughts of your Californian bitch fill my head like the babbling of a noisy child. She is learning about us. She is discovering the truth. The old man too. Why can you not control her?

Be calm, sister. Brother. She is helping us. Tharman grinned in his sleep, on the Île de la Cité. *She is mine.*

7

Maurice couldn't remember the last time he'd moved. And God, he wanted so badly to just do something as simple as stretch out an arm, put a foot to the floor. He was drenched with perspiration, and his limbs were so cramped they felt as though they'd snap if he moved them too quickly. There was no sensation in them at all, except at the joints, which were painful to the point of bursting.

What time was it? The night was long gone – he'd been able to tell that by the change in the quality of light beneath the cellar door. But other than that, he had no idea. He'd pawned his watch a fortnight ago to pay an electric bill.

Maybe if he ran for it? Maybe if he bolted up the stairs and burst on to the daylit street?

But he couldn't bring himself to try it. He had no idea what was waiting for him up there, hadn't heard a sound for ages now. Nothing from the deep-voiced man who'd tried to plead with him. Nothing at all from Joshua.

He thought of calling out, but he was simply too afraid.

All he could do was wait now. And try to remember the few things about the dark arts Madame Lapotaire had taught him. Her blind, wizened face drifted before his mind's eye. She seemed to be smiling at him, trying to encourage him.

The names of the *obeah* gods came whispering from his lips before he realized what he was doing.

'Papa Legba. Mama Legba. Carrefour. Hear my prayers, I beg you.'

That's it, chile, Madame Lapotaire seemed to tell him. *Keep goin'*.

'Lords, watch over me and guard me.'

After a while, he almost seemed to be floating. Seemed to rise into the air, as though he were being lifted through a thin, indistinct mist. Then, he was dropping back, and the mist was thickening to a murky grey around him. He was falling into a drowsy trance.

A sudden noise brought him out of it. The sharp, hard rattle of a key in a lock.

His head jerked up, the muscles in his neck burning with stiffness. The cellar door hadn't moved. The lock was broken anyway, and there was no key that he knew of. And there was still no sound from the hallway.

It took him quite a while to realize what he'd heard. The noise had not come from anywhere in the house.

It had come from somewhere else entirely. He'd only heard it in his mind.

*

8

An hour passed before Harry found the strength to start getting genuinely worried. He sat up in his chair.

'Miss?' he called out.

There was no reply. He cleared his throat and tried again.

'Lady, are you all right?'

There was silence from the landing. All that he could hear was the murmur of traffic, the faint parping of motor horns, and someone shouting on the street, far below. He sat uneasily in the armchair for a while.

Had the woman gone? She'd been so scared, so confused, beneath the brave face she'd been putting on. Maybe she thought he was crazy, and had decided to put as much distance as possible between herself and this place. Who knew, perhaps she had the right idea.

But he couldn't be sure. He leaned forwards, straining to catch the faintest sound of movement. Anything.

Then he reached down the side of the chair, where he usually kept his cane. It wasn't there. It was still lying in the hall. He'd have to manage without it. Harry began climbing painfully to his feet.

His knees threatened to buckle, and he had to concentrate intensely on each step, as though he were a baby, learning to walk for the first time. Strange, how old age turned the body's clock back to infancy. He was grateful when he finally reached his silver-topped walking stick. He hunkered down and clasped it like an old and favourite toy.

The landing was empty. A little brightness filtered in from the tiny window upstairs, but that was all. Harry turned to his left – turning was always much harder than walking in a straight line – and gazed at Lapotaire's door. It was ajar only slightly. A glimpse of cracked linoleum on the floor was all that he could make out. But something was wrong with the door itself.

Something was missing.

That funny brass plate with the engraving of the sun on it that Lapotaire had screwed next to the lock the same day he'd moved in – it was gone. All that remained were a pale circular patch against the wood, and two jagged holes where the screws had been ripped out.

Had the Carroll woman done that? Why? He couldn't figure it.

He cleared his throat again, with far more difficulty this time. His Adam's apple seemed to have grown coarse and heavy, like a crude lump of rock.

'Miss Carroll?' It came out as a nervous whisper. 'Lady?'

He edged towards the door. Wasn't sure why he was being quite so careful. If there was any danger, he'd hardly be able to run away. The woman had seemed pleasant enough. Harmless. Was someone else in there?

His hands had begun shaking again, by the time he reached out and pushed the door open. All his dim eyes took in, at first, were the details of the apartment itself. He'd never been inside, in all the time he'd known the young American.

It was much smaller than his. The off-white walls were grubby. The pattern on the cracked, dirty linoleum had been black once, but had faded to a blotchy grey. It ran the entire length of a narrow room which doubled as a living area and kitchen. There were no pictures on the walls, no ornaments. Just a rusted gas stove and a fridge, and a tiny couch with horsehair pushing through the cushions. A mismatched set of chairs which looked as though they had been scavenged from junk shops stood on either side of a pine-wood dining table; which itself was piled with cameras and developing equipment.

There were no lights on, but daylight poured in through a huge sash window at the centre of the wall. Revealed in its bright gaze were two things Bernstein found odd.

The floor was scattered with what he took, at first, to be discarded foil from cigarette packets. Small golden glimmers. Except Lapotaire didn't smoke.

Awkwardly, his spine aching, he bent down and retrieved the closest one. Inspected it carefully.

It was foil, all right. But it had been cut into a circle. From its edge depended a fine length of cotton, with a piece of sticky tape at the far end. The rest were all the same.

Harry glanced at the ceiling, and saw the small tears in the paint where the tape had been ripped away.

What were they? Mobiles of some kind? Some kind of decoration? Maybe Lapotaire had picked them up in the Far East, though they looked hand-made and crude.

Whatever, someone had taken them all down and screwed them up.

The woman? Why'd she do that?

The other peculiar thing was the short battered metal filing cabinet next to the fridge. The bottom drawer was open, a large screwdriver lying beside it. It looked as though its lock had been jemmied, and the papers from inside were strewn all over the kitchen.

He peered at them intently, thought he could make out pictures on some.

Took a couple of fumbling steps towards them.

Then he noticed the American woman.

She was sitting in a straight-backed wooden chair in the far corner of the room; in the shadows where the sunlight failed to reach. She was tilted back against the wall, her legs pushed out in front of her, her feet wide apart.

And she was regarding him with a dreamy, semi-interested smile. Her lips were parted slightly, and her eyes were opaque, glossy.

He almost jerked back with shock. What the hell—?

He turned towards her, growing more puzzled by the second. He didn't know whether to be angry or scared.

'Lady, what do you think you're doing, huh? Did you make all this mess?'

He wasn't sure if she'd heard him or not. Her only answer was to give a little chuckle, her lips curling into a delicious grin, and arch her back.

Harry shook his head bemusedly. She was *crazy*. This was all he needed, at his age.

'Lady, what are you trying to do to me? This isn't my apartment, you know. I trusted you with that key.'

She squirmed again, her spine drawing as tight as a bow. Another laugh escaped her, a sparkling bubble of amusement. Her varnished-looking eyes were fixed on thin air.

She didn't seem to be squirming or laughing for him, he realized dully. It was as though, in her imagination, someone else was touching her. Someone was making love to her. And only she could see him.

Insane. She was completely crazy.

Harry was about to turn around and get out of the room when he noticed the slip of paper in her hand. It was a scrawled note, dusty with age. It fluttered limply between her fingertips, as though she'd picked it up and then forgotten about it.

He edged towards the woman until he was within arm's reach. Lunged out and snatched the note away. Again, she didn't seem to care. Harry scanned it quickly.

It was scribbled in hasty French, and its message was short and to the point.

Monsieur Maury,

It was good to meet you today and, yes, I believe I understand your problem. Come to meet me tonight at my home, 20 rue Albaiville, and we shall see what can be done.

Joshua

The rue Albaiville was north-east of here, in one of the immigrant quarters. So, Lapotaire *did* stay with the African when he disappeared.

Harry folded up the note and shoved it into his cardigan pocket. Then, his attention returned to the kitchen, the scattered files. The woman didn't seem to be a problem, however oddly she was behaving. She was still writhing gently, and crooning to herself now. Her gaze was as blank as though her eyes had been replaced with marbles. She was lost in her own little world.

Harry shuffled around one-eighty degrees, teetered towards the closest of the papers on the floor.

He'd almost reached it when the crooning stopped. The seat squeaked and its legs banged sharply on the linoleum, as the woman got up.

He tried to turn back again, couldn't manage it fast enough.

He craned his neck around as far as it would go.

Her face was rushing up at him, tight lipped and determined, her eyes burning with a cold, hard light.

She raised her hand, and there was something big and heavy-looking in it. A camera tripod she'd picked up from the table. He could only watch as it swung down towards his head.

Then, there was a terrible pain. And blindness, and falling. And the thought that he was, at last, going to join his family, his wife.

CHAPTER TWENTY-FIVE

1

That sharp metallic rattle – Maurice had a good idea what it had been. Somebody had opened his apartment door in the Pigalle.

He seemed to know instinctively, didn't even try to question it.

It must have been the chanting. Or else Madame Lapotaire was still watching over him, somehow. When he'd felt that eerie floating sensation, he had seemed to enter a place where the normal senses didn't count, where time and distance were meaningless, and things were known, discovered, entirely through the power of thought.

Had it always been this way for his stepmammy? Had she lived her blind, frail life connected to this world – and others – largely through her mind?

He'd shied back from the greyness at first, alarmed. The rattling in his mind had faded away, and silence had returned. But after a while, he'd begun to realize it might be his only hope.

He tucked his chin down, closed his eyes. Clutched the sun-amulet so hard the chain dug into the tendons of his neck. He tried to fall into a trance again. Nothing happened.

He concentrated furiously, mumbling the names of the voodoo gods once more, murmuring half-remembered snatches of the chants Stepmammy had taught him.

He remained in the dim cellar, on the mattress. Didn't float. Couldn't hear a thing.

*

2

The light below the cellar door was fading by the time he gave up.

His muscles were aching, as though he'd just run a marathon. He tipped his head back, exhausted, and tried to shift himself into a more comfortable position without making too much noise. He was too tired to be disappointed, too shaken to feel desperate. He rubbed at his forehead, his eyes, and tried to relax, a longing for sleep flooding over him.

And suddenly, he was floating again. Suddenly, he was drifting into a trance. He was in that grey, blinded place a second time.

And through it, he was touching the mind of the creature upstairs.

It was like closing his hand on a bare electric cable. His eyes snapped open, and he could feel the blood draining from his face. The soft hairs on his arms rose and prickled like a porcupine's quills.

Kellesh.

The name came to him like a great wave breaking on a stony beach.

He knew what the creature was, what it was planning; knew everything about it, all at once. So much was pouring into his mind Maurice felt, for a moment, as though he was drowning.

He fought to remain calm. It was difficult. The creature realized that he had touched it, and was stirring, coming slowly awake. He could see its ugly face quite clearly now, in his mind's eye.

Without opening its mouth, it began speaking to him.

At last. You see now that I mean no harm.

Yes. It felt odd, talking without sound. *But why couldn't you have spoken to me like this before?*

The discs stopped me from reaching you. Now, it's the other way around. You are reaching out to me.

Should I take them down?

No. The others will be coming soon, and the Ra *will protect you. We must fight.*

How?

Tell Joshua to trust me. I must Feed, and I need his help besides.

Yes, Maurice nodded.

And give him the amulet around your neck.

But there are three of them, and only one of you. Shouldn't we run? Shouldn't we try to escape?

It's far too late for that, the creature told him wearily. *They're already coming.*

The greyness faded. Maurice glanced up the stairs again. There was only blackness underneath the cellar door. The daylight was completely gone.

3

Tharman stopped at the corner of the rue Albaiville, with Pashta by his side, and gazed hungrily at the tenement house. No lights showed at the windows, and there were no sounds of movement. But there were other noises, of the type a normal mortal couldn't hear. Voices.

A gentle smile danced across his face. He could hear quite clearly what the photographer and Kellesh were saying to each other. It delighted him, like a kindergarten teacher listening to his class planning a make-believe war.

At long last, the Betrayer was going to stand his ground. This was a night they'd be talking about centuries from now.

The darkness thickening around him was a quiet one. Few cars passed this way. The rumble of the homeward-bound traffic was distant, unreal, and the sidewalks were empty of pedestrians. Despite the mildness of the last couple of evenings, the air was growing cold tonight. He watched as his breath turned to mist in front of his face. Not a single cloud was visible against the canopy of the blue-black sky. The stars and the full moon were unblemished in their pale chill brightness.

The few streetlamps around him strove vainly to compete. Their ochre glow was like a thin discoloured smoke that a vagrant breeze had blown between the houses. Long shadows, like faded stains, stretched across the chipped and broken flagstones.

Beside him, Pashta curled her fingers till the nails clacked together, and glanced at him annoyedly. Her heart-shaped face was puckered into an impatient frown.

What are we waiting for, brother? They're in there, all of them, so let's get this over with.

Tharman shook his head softly.

We're waiting for good reason. Why, sister, don't tell me you're jealous?

The woman's shoulders bunched angrily, and her skin grew a little darker, as though the night's shadows were seeping into her veins.

Of that soft cow? The green of her eyes gave way to gold. *She ought to be here by now.*

Tharman tipped his head to one side, listening.

She's on her way. And we cannot finish Lapotaire without her, remember that.

Pashta snorted, folded her thin arms across her chest, and turned away.

Before long, a faint clicking noise began drifting towards them from the far end of the street. The metronomic tapping of high heels on the sidewalk. Tharman raised his head, wet his lips unconsciously with his smooth tongue. A delicious sensation, velvety and warm, had begun flooding through his body. It almost startled him. He hadn't felt this kind of excitement for decades.

All his Feedings, all his couplings down the ages, had jaded him so very badly.

A shadowy figure was moving towards them on the far side of the street. All the lamps were broken, along that stretch. A human would only have been able to make out a pair of long striding legs, the fluttering hem of a brown skirt, in the faint glow from the kerb. But Tharman could see the whole woman, and his eyes widened with pleasure.

They turned golden as he watched. Almost seemed to burn.

Susan stopped at the kerb's edge, looking at him, and then marched across the crumbling stretch of asphalt, her feet crunching as she walked. He stretched out a hand towards her, and she accepted it graciously, like a fine milady at a Jacobean ball. Her face was blank, but her skin seemed to radiate an icy glow. Her eyes were fixed on his. On nothing else in the whole, churning world.

Tharman grinned with pleasure.

You were mine all along, my love, from the moment I saw you.

Pashta grunted.

'Can we go now?' she asked out loud.

Tharman nodded, without looking at her. He was gazing deeply into Susan's eyes, pushing thoughts into her blank, cold mind.

Wait here. Whatever happens, don't move until I call you.

Then he turned away and strolled towards the tenement door, with Pashta following closely. He didn't glance back. He needed to concentrate, now.

The walls of the house seemed to darken a little, as he approached. The rest of the street became vague and indistinct, like a painting seen through fogged glass.

He reached the porch steps, came to a halt, waiting for Kellesh to make his first move. It wasn't too long a wait.

The door burst open, sharply.

An old African was standing behind it, his arms outstretched, his feet set wide apart for balance. His expression was fixed and grim, and a straight razor glimmered in his right hand.

4

Harry Bernstein groaned and started to come around. He thought, at first, that he'd gone blind. All that he could make out was a shadowy, static murk when he opened his eyes.

Then he realized night had fallen. And he was no longer wearing his glasses. For how many hours had he been lying here?

He remained perfectly still, his cheek pressed against the cool linoleum. His whole body felt sore, and there was a biting, throbbing pain above his left ear where he'd been hit with the tripod. His skull was ringing faintly.

He was lucky to be alive, he knew. But it didn't bear all that much resemblance to luck.

Was the woman still here? Waiting somewhere in the darkness, to finish him off? It was difficult to make out anything without his spectacles, but he risked moving, turned his face towards the window. The moonlight slanting through it brought that part of the room into dim relief. Nothing he could see looked much like a crazy lady.

He listened intently, but all that he could hear was the weak pounding of his own heart.

That proved nothing. She might be hiding in the shadows, keeping quiet. But he couldn't just lie here all night.

His hands were shivering with cold, but he managed to grope around until he found his spectacles. He fingered the lenses. By some miracle, they were unbroken.

Harry slipped them on. Immediately, the jabbing pain next to his ear got worse, making him suck in a crisp lungful of air. He put his fingers to his head, and was rewarded by the feel of a loose flap of skin, and something cold and sticky running from it.

Congealed blood was matting the whole side of his face.

Harry shuddered, then steadied himself. He'd lived through the camp, for God's sake. Lived through that hell on earth, when so many others had died. If the Germans couldn't kill him, he certainly wasn't going to let a *meshuggah* woman do the job.

He started groping around again, but couldn't find his walking stick. Either it had dropped out of reach or the woman had moved it. He was left with no option but to drag himself across the floor till he reached the straight-backed chair next to the wall. He used it to support himself as he got up, then swept his hand across the peeling wallpaper until he found a light switch.

If he'd known pain before, it was nothing compared with the agony when the bulb came on. Shards of hot, red flame pushed their way deeply behind his eyelids, making his head pound. He whimpered, covered his eyes. Waited till the pain subsided.

Squinting between his fingers, he could just make out the dim shape of his cane. It had rolled into the kitchen, stopped beside the ransacked filing cabinet.

He made his way across to it, sweating and grumbling, fighting to keep his balance. Got down on his knees to retrieve it.

One of the scattered files caught his attention. He picked it up gingerly and studied it.

According to the heading, it was from the Simon Wiesenthal Institute, the organization that hunted down war criminals. There was a row of photographs, of Nazi officers in the black and silver uniform of the SS, with captions underneath. Emotionless, goggle-eyed faces peered out at him, their menace undiminished by the years.

Except . . . one of the pictures wasn't a photograph. It was a line drawing, presumably done from memory. Of a broad face above a bullish neck. Cropped blond hair. Eyes that were alive and hungry.

Harry let out a low moan of disgust, and studied the caption.

NAME: Unknown. No files exist.
RANK: Colonel, Waffen-SS.
AKA: 'Das Goldbiest.'
STATUS: Unknown. Has escaped any attempts at tracing him since disappearing from Buchenwald in 1944.

Good God, what was Mr Lapotaire doing with a picture of that monster? Were they connected in some way?

Urgently, his hands trembling, Harry rummaged through the rest of the files.

Some of them were newspaper cuttings. One of them read PENTAGON ADMITS CRACK LURP PATROL MISSING and carried a story about a long-range patrol in the Vietnam war led by a charismatic blond mercenary. MAURICE LAPOTAIRE WOUNDED IN JUNGLE, END OF TOUR FOR NAM'S YOUNGEST PHOTOGRAPHER, read another. And there were more photographs. One, aged and indistinct, was from the Sino-Japanese War back in the thirties, and had been taken at night. A large figure in the background, his cropped fair hair illuminated by an exploding shell, had been ringed with a red pencil. Another was labelled 'Korea, 1952'. Also taken at night, in a United Nations camp. And the blond, uniformed figure, walking below an overhanging lantern – his face wasn't visible . . . but could it be *Das Goldbiest*?

The front door opened and banged shut, in the depths of the house. Harry glanced out at the darkened landing. One of the other residents must have arrived home that was all. He returned to the files.

5

Pashta glowered up at the African and his slim razor.

He's mine, brother. Please, let me have him.

Tharman nodded pensively. He was hanging back a little, cautious and uncertain.

His sister drew herself up to her full height, her sharp teeth glimmering and her fingers arcing. They shortened to claws as he watched. Then her muscles bunched beneath her tight clothes, and she leapt up the stairs, moving faster than the eye could follow.

The African seemed doomed before he'd even started. He began swinging the blade towards her hopelessly. Far too slowly.

It couldn't be quite as easy as all that. Tharman watched carefully, interested now.

The man's hand suddenly opened and the razor flew from his grasp. Began spinning through the air, under its own power.

The brightly honed blade slashed across Pashta's outstretched palms, and she wailed and sprang back. She tumbled to a halt at the bottom of the stairs, sucking at her wounds and hissing furiously. Her eyes had turned completely golden now. The pupils had become thin vertical slits. Her head had changed shape slightly, the ears drifting up towards the crown and growing pointed.

Tharman gazed up at the African calmly. The man was entirely still again, in the exact same position they'd first seen him. And the razor had returned to his fist, like a small, glittering boomerang.

The Incarnate grinned, and pushed his thoughts past the man, deep into the house.

A good trick, Betrayer. But are you going to let this old man do your fighting for you? Show yourself.

There was no reply.

Very slowly, he put his foot on the first step of the porch.

The razor whirled upwards again, hovered a moment, and then came down towards him like some deadly toy.

Tharman kept his eyes on it. Reached up the split instant before it struck him.

Snatched hold of the handle.

It squirmed in his grasp, as though it were alive, but he tightened his grip. It couldn't break free.

After all these years of treachery, you still have so much to learn. Do you want to see a really good use for a razor?

Gently, he opened his palm again. The blade began to levitate, until it had risen a yard into the night air. He was controlling it now, however much Kellesh tried to take it back.

It drifted towards the African. Circled gently about the old man's face. Then it began to whirl.

Soon, it was moving so fast there was only a shimmering steel blur, a miasma of silver.

It moved an inch closer to the man, brushing his cheeks.

And blood began to spatter across the porch.

*

6

There were more photographs, and even a print of a painting. Harry recognized it as a Goya. It was one of his depictions of atrocities during the Peninsular War of 1808. Peasants were being burnt alive. At night. Of course at night.

And though the proof was inconclusive, though the faces were indistinct, each picture in the files contained a huge broad-shouldered man with short blond hair.

He'd thought the woman was crazy, but who was really going mad here? Himself? Mr Lapotaire? The entire world? Harry let the last of the papers drop to the floor, and pushed back his glasses exhaustedly with his finger and thumb. What was going on here? He didn't understand.

Footsteps had been coming up the stairs towards him for quite some time, but he'd been so absorbed in the pictures he had barely noticed them. He listened now.

He expected them to stop on the floor below. M. Bressay in apartment 4 was due home about now. But when they didn't, he stiffened. Drew himself upright on his cane.

He peered out cautiously at the landing again, for all the good that did. The light from the doorway barely reached halfway to the stairs.

Harry felt a nervous tic at the corner of his mouth, and called out anxiously.

'Mr Lapotaire? Maurice? Who's there?'

The footsteps kept on coming.

7

Gorreq walked slowly up the last few steps and made his way along the darkened landing, taking his time. When the light from the apartment finally struck his face, he came to a halt, relishing the moment the old Jewish salesman saw who he was. The man was leaning forwards, blinking with disbelief.

Yes, Harry, it's really me. Long time no see.

He tipped his head back, and felt his eyes glow with pleasure. His nostrils widened at the pungent scent of fear.

Bernstein had fallen to his knees when he looked back, and was clutching at his heart, whimpering with abject terror.

Harry, Gorreq chuckled. *Don't go dying on me yet. I've a little job I want you to do for me. We've all these annoying files to get rid of.*

He commanded the old man to his feet.

Go to the stove, Harry. Oh, it needs cleaning, doesn't it? Mr Lapotaire's a messy housekeeper. Never mind that now. Switch on all the rings, there's a good man. Now, you see that box of matches . . .?

He turned on his heel and began heading back towards the street.

He was careful to make his eyes blue as he emerged into the sharp night air. Strolled casually towards the main road, with its crowds of tourists and kerb-crawlers.

He was listening through Bernstein's ears, now. In his head, he could hear the steady hiss of the gas rings, up in the apartment.

And, as he reached the corner, the sharp rasp of a striking match.

He turned around just in time to see the second-storey windows blow out and the roof of the house erupt in a ball of flame. People around him gawped and began screaming.

The entire front wall of the house was collapsing now. Burning sheets of paper started floating from the blaze, swaying and twirling in the heat. They curled to grey cinders in midair, and drifted as gently as snowflakes to the pavement.

*

8

Still spinning idly, throwing off droplets of red, the razor sailed lightly back to Tharman's hand. He took it, gazed at it amusedly for a moment, and then flung it aside. With Pashta at his heels, he walked gently up the stairs towards the old man.

Somehow, the African was still on his feet. His neck and shoulders were drenched with blood. It was soaking into his T-shirt, flowing down his arms in rivulets.

His eyes were wide open, amazed, in a dripping mask of liquid. His face – it had a misshapen look, like a glove that had been pulled on crookedly. There were deep, streaming cuts all around the sides.

Tharman reached out. Pinched a fold of skin on the man's cheek. Pulled.

The whole face ripped away.

The African fell backwards, quivering, dying, the exposed muscles still working in his jaws. Tharman turned to Pashta, smiling.

You see how easy it is? Now go. And be more careful this time.

9

Pashta was halfway down the tenement's hall when the walls shuddered and the plaster cracked.

There was a sudden groaning noise, and a choking cloud of dust started to billow around her. A stout electric cable whipped out from the shadows to her left, swaying in the air a moment, while she gazed at it, surprised. Then, it lunged forwards, wrapped itself around her waist. It tightened painfully. Began to shift backwards and forwards, as though it were trying to saw her through the middle. Her clothing ripped, and a thin trickle of blood started running down her thigh. She struggled futilely.

There was a whistling noise from above, and another

cable arced down from the ceiling, reaching for her neck. She grabbed hold of it, and watched as it twined harmlessly about her wrist.

The wires began to pull, tugging her body in two directions at once. Trying to tear her in half.

Pashta threw back her head and laughed. Bunched her muscles, and yanked hard.

Both cables snapped like rotten twine, and fell away.

The ceiling began coming in above her with a reverberating, crunching noise. At the same time, the floorboards started cracking below her feet, driving up huge, jagged splinters. She jumped away nimbly, crossing six feet in one leap, landing on all fours at the foot of the stairs.

They too began collapsing, but she was too quick for the Betrayer. She hurried upwards, clinging to the banisters. Past the first floor. To the second.

Kellesh was hiding up here. She could feel him like an insect on her skin.

10

He was in the second room to her left. Pashta halted a moment, trying to sense if there was any danger, and then burst in through the door.

There was nothing more beyond it than a bare, dusty tool room, an empty light socket dangling from the ceiling. Rusty saws and boxes of nails lay scattered across the floor.

And there he was, trapped in the moonlight from the fly-specked window. The priest of the crocodile-god, huddled in a corner, motionless. Shadows swallowed the lower half of his body. He had his arms behind him, pressed against the wall, as though he were trying to burrow into it.

He had changed halfway into his godly form. His face had become elongated, his jagged underbite protruded, the teeth like short blunt daggers. His skin was unevenly patterned with dark misshapen scales, like a cancer on his white flesh.

Contempt and disgust filled Pashta. He looked like nothing so much as a sideshow freak at some down-at-the-heels carnival. His eyes were only glowing very dully, like a pair of tiny glass panes with a candle behind them, the flame going out. He seemed weak to the point of collapse. The few simple traps he'd put in her way had exhausted him completely.

She rubbed at the cuts on her palms again, and they vanished. Her arms turned black and took on a glossy sheen as they became covered with fur. Pashta gazed at Kellesh unblinkingly, considering the different games she could play with him now. The different ways to prolong his suffering, make him pay for all of his Betrayals down the centuries.

No. It was Tharman. He was still downstairs, dragging the African's corpse into the house. *This time we have him. And this time we'll finish him, quickly.*

What he said did make a certain prosaic sense, even if all her feline instincts rebelled against it. Pashta let out a low growl, then, padding very gently, made her way across the bare floorboards towards the huddled man.

He was gazing at her stupidly, no hint of fear on his ugly features. He had to know what she was going to do. He had to be terrified. But he was bottling it in.

It wasn't good enough. She wanted to look. Wanted to *see* the Betrayer's terror at the moment he died.

She reached inside his mind and probed.

It was blank. Completely silent.

Pashta stopped in her tracks, raising her claws defensively. However hard she pushed into the creature's mind, she could find nothing there.

It took her a few seconds to realize what was happening.

He was deliberately blocking her. He'd set up some kind of barrier in his thoughts, was concealing something. She pushed harder, trying to break through, but couldn't manage it.

He was hiding something from her.

A peculiar acrid smell was beginning to fill the room. Pashta sniffed curiously, her mouth tightening and her eyes widening with surprise. It was almost like the stench of burning flesh.

Her gaze darted about the room, then settled back on Kellesh. Something was happening to his face now. Drops of sweat were beginning to trickle down it, and the skin had turned a sickly yellow. His lips were clenched, the muscles twitching at the sides of his jaws, as though he were trying to hold in a tremendous scream of pain.

Pashta glanced at his arms. They were still behind him, the hands out of sight.

Was he holding something?

She was caught in a moment of indecision. Should she spring at him, finish him quickly? Should she move away?

He seemed to sense her hesitation. And suddenly began to move. He was raising his right arm into the filtered moonlight.

The hand had gone through its complete transformation. It was now a stumpy, armoured claw with webs between the fingers. But it had charred to black, the flesh smouldering like a burnt-out log.

A scale dropped off and vanished in midair as she watched.

Between his fingers was a simple golden chain.

And dangling at the end of it—

No!

She screeched and drew away.

At the end of it – a large bronze disc. An amulet. With the image of the *Ra* engraved on its face.

Pashta raised her claws to her eyes, trying to protect them. She stumbled backwards, in the direction she thought the door lay. But the disc was blinding her. Its glow started to fill her head.

She wailed silently for help.

Brother!

And heard Tharman pounding quickly across the shattered floor below.

Kellesh was watching her evenly, quite calm despite the terrible pain he had to be feeling. There was a look of grim satisfaction on his face. Then, his arm was swinging back. He was throwing the disc.

She lurched to the side, trying to dodge it. But it didn't travel in a straight line. It spun around in a wide arc, and struck her cleanly in the back of her head, embedding itself in the bone.

Her mouth stretched open wide. She let out a scream as the ghastly pain hit her. Scrabbled blindly at the amulet, trying to pull it free. But it burned so badly she couldn't get a grip on it. Her paws withdrew, charred and ruined.

There was a sharp, abrupt crack as her skull began to split.

The agony smothered her. She was whirling on the spot, now. Flailing. Spitting. Crazy and mindless as a wounded leopard. A terrible heat, like all the furnaces in the world, was filling her body. She could feel her insides melting.

The last thing she saw before her head burst open was the faint, dark bulk of Tharman, filling the doorway.

Too late.

11

It had gone completely quiet upstairs. After the crashing and the screaming and the howls, completely silent. Even Kellesh's voice, inside his head, had stopped, petered away. Maurice tried to reach out with his mind, but couldn't hear him any more.

He hunkered down beside his mattress, like a trapped animal, his back pressed against the wall. His eyes flickered to the door, then scanned the cellar quickly. The dim glow of the lightbulb, the bare brick, and the crumbling moss-green mortar had always made this place look like a dungeon. But it all seemed to be closing in around him now. There was no way out.

No way *in*, either. He clung on to that thought. Peered at the glittering sun-discs hanging from the ceiling. The creatures upstairs couldn't touch him here. And he could wait. Time was the one weapon he had. Come sunrise, they'd be powerless to harm him, and he could leave this house, flee the city. He'd never stay in one place for so long again. He swore it.

There was the sudden clack of footsteps on the floor above his head, picking their way carefully towards the door. His gaze flitted back. His teeth set, an involuntary whine pushing its way through them.

The noise stopped.

The knob turned, and the hinges creaked.

He expected it to stop. Expected the sun-discs to bring whoever was out there to a halt.

But the door swung open the whole way.

Framed against the blackness was a woman. Not the one he'd been expecting. He'd seen a skinny, cat-faced girl when his mind had linked with Kellesh's. Petite and fierce. Her name had been Pashta.

This one was auburn haired and in her early forties. Tall, and with the kind of hourglass figure you only normally saw in old movies. Her shape seemed familiar. Could she possibly be the woman who'd been waiting for him on the landing yesterday afternoon? Her features had been so enclosed in dimness then, he hadn't been able to make them out properly.

She was smiling down at him dreamily, the long fingernails of one hand scraping the painted red on her lips.

She was not one of the beast-people. He sensed that immediately. But she was alone. He could see no one else behind her.

Frantically, Maurice looked around for a weapon. There were none.

He didn't really need one, he told himself. If this was the best the creatures could send against him . . . she didn't look particularly strong, he could take her on quite easily enough, even with his bad leg.

As though she'd read his thoughts, she let out a throaty chuckle, took her first slow step towards him, her high heel clacking on the wooden stair. Then she halted, looked up curiously at the nearest of the *Ra* discs.

Her eyes narrowed sharply, and she winced.

Maurice thought at first she was going to tear it down. But she didn't. She simply moved around it as she took her next step.

She continued down the stairway towards him, her long-legged stride controlled and even.

Maurice rose to his feet, feeling a renewed surge of fear. She was moving so smoothly, so confidently. And with each step, he was becoming less sure he could handle her.

As she reached the bottom of the stairs, he lurched towards her, yelling. Wrapped one hand around her windpipe, knotted the other in her hair, tried to pull her head back, snap her neck.

It was like trying to bend an iron rod. She didn't budge an inch.

She stared at him coldly as he struggled to hurt her.

Until, suddenly, both her hands came up. Sharply, from her sides. Slammed him, palms flat, in the chest. And he was flying backwards through the air. Crashing to the damp cement floor. Sliding along it. Colliding with the wall.

Spots of light exploded before his eyes, and he couldn't breathe at all. He felt as though a car had hit him.

Somehow, he got up to a crouch and managed to scuttle to the side as the woman came at him again.

He was making for the stairs, hobbling quickly, when his bad leg gave way and he stumbled for a moment. He felt her grasp close around his ankle.

And he was yelling now, in a long high-pitched scream. The woman's grip tightened, and everything inside his head turned searing white.

He heard an ugly crunch as the bones in his ankle snapped.

*

12

Susan could barely hear his shrieks. All that she could think of was finishing her work and returning upstairs, to the slim arms of Tharman.

She dragged the struggling Lapotaire across the floor towards her, picked him up. He felt so pathetically light.

She carried him like a baby, over to the nearest wall. Pinned him against it, using just one hand, underneath his chin. His eyes were bugging from his head. He was twitching, crying. She knew vaguely, somewhere deep down, that she ought to feel sorry for him, ought to pity him his terror and pain, but the emotions wouldn't come. There was only a rich, sanguine delight. All she had to do was squeeze a little harder, and she'd crush the life right out of him. Tharman had been true to his word. She'd never felt such power. Never been so strong.

Was crushing good enough, though? She paused. Would that really please her master?

Susan turned it over coolly.

Who was this man? A photographer. And what was his crime? He had *seen* too much.

A determined smile lit up her face.

Lapotaire seemed to realize what she was going to do, because suddenly his body was wracked with a final burst of effort. He flailed in her grip, twisting like an eel, shrieking anguishedly.

It made no impression on her at all. She was simply too strong for him.

She shifted her grip a little, making sure his face was held very still.

Then she extended the middle two fingers of her free right hand, moved them towards his eyes.

He screwed them shut, but that made no difference. She simply pushed them through.

Blood started dripping to her elbow.

She increased the pressure a little, and was rewarded

with two soft, simultaneous pops, like a pair of tiny balloons bursting.

And then, her long, manicured nails were sliding even deeper, towards his brain.

13

Tharman was waiting for her when she went back upstairs to the ruined hallway. Seeing him filled her with an almost juvenile excitement. He looked so handsome, so elegant. She loved the way he seemed to devour her with his beautiful violet eyes.

But they were glistening sadly, now. He seemed distressed. She wondered why. Where, she pondered dully, was the cat-woman?

She raised her bloodstained fingers, felt a taut, vibrating nervousness as she waited for his reaction. Delight coursed through her as he nodded approvingly.

He moved closer towards her. She was deliciously transfixed, like a tiny, shaking bird. And then, he was reaching into his pocket and taking out a handkerchief. And softly, oh so charmingly, wiping her fingers clean.

Susan waited until he was finished, then embraced him.

They went out, arms locked, into the beckoning, enfolding night.

CHAPTER TWENTY-SIX

1

From his upstairs window, Kellesh watched them go. They reached the corner, turned it, and disappeared like phantoms.

He craned his head around, looked at Pashta's corpse on the floor. Her blackened head was split in two, and still smouldering, the bronze disc glinting in its ruins.

Darkness started closing over him.

It wasn't his normal sleep, he realized dimly. Instead, it was something that he hadn't known for eighteen hundred years. Not since he'd been fully human. Unconsciousness was claiming him, like an old, persistent debtor.

He tried to snap out of it. Tried to force himself to stay awake. But he was so weak. So utterly exhausted, and in so much pain. If he could only move away from the window . . . if he could only lie down it would help . . .

2

It must have been several hours later when noises from the street finally jerked him back to life. He gazed down helplessly, the scene below swimming before his eyes. A few people were emerging from the houses around him. Migrant workers, up early for their jobs in the city's hotels and restaurants, all moving with the detached weariness that was the hallmark of the poor.

Kellesh opened his mouth, tried to call out. But he could make little more than a weak croaking sound. If only they'd look in his direction. If only they could see him, spreadeagled against the glass. But their heads were lowered, they were paying no attention.

He writhed feebly, but couldn't free himself. Lifted his eyes from the street to his hands. Dried, clotted blood had completely smothered his forearms, so thick and dark he could barely see the long steel nails Tharman had driven into his wrists, pinning him to the window's frame.

He made one last attempt to tear himself away. Couldn't manage it.

He gazed, horrified, at the sky beyond the rooftops.

It was turning silver-grey at the horizon now. Kellesh set his jagged teeth, and tried to will himself free. But all his power was gone. He was completely drained.

The silver glow was brighter now, changing to purple at the edges. Kellesh moaned with fear and jerked his arms, was rewarded with a new jolt of agony.

All the centuries of his life. All those endless years. They began flickering before him, a tumultuous procession of countries, people, star-studded evenings.

He couldn't quite believe it was all coming to an end.

As the first shaft of light sprang up through the darkness, he became quite still.

The flickering rim of the sun appeared above the rooftops.

And suddenly, he was rigid, howling. He'd wanted to be brave, but couldn't help it. His head snapped back. His feet kicked. Every muscle in his body writhed, trying to crawl away from the deadly light.

The top layer of his skin started to bubble, a moment later. It charred to a crisp and flaked away, revealing the bleeding, raw tissue beneath.

Then the sunlight drove deeper, torturing his red, soft underflesh, heating his blood until it boiled.

Smoke began to envelop him. The fat and muscles in his body were smouldering.

He stared up at his arms again. Flaming tissue was sliding down them, exposing the clean white bones. It dropped to the floorboards with a sickening *plop*, and the room started to burn. He was blinded shortly after, couldn't hear, couldn't breathe.

It was a purifying fire, cremating the memories of half a million nights.

3

Can you feel it, my love? Can you feel him die?

No, Susan replied.

Hold me, then.

Susan slid a hand across the darkened bed of her hotel suite, and closed it around Tharman's limp, motionless fingers.

Now? Can you feel it now?

Yes.

Can you smell it? Can you taste it?

Her breath was coming in swift, excited hisses.

Yes, my love. It's glorious.

It will be time to leave, when the sun sets. There are so many wonderful things I have to show you.

She was firmly linked to his mind, and could feel how triumphant he was. But there was a terrible sadness in him, too. It made her wince, it was so intense.

It was for Pashta.

She rubbed his knuckles soothingly, and he shifted towards her in his sleep, his thin, angular face dark against the pillow. Susan watched it for a long, long time.

PART V

DARK CARNIVAL

NEW ORLEANS, 1979

CHAPTER TWENTY-SEVEN

1

Betty-Lou Turner, a stewardess for two weeks with Continental, went to the front galley of the plane as it descended over Louisiana to talk to her new friend, Geena Shaw.

'Have you had a good look at the weird one in First?'

'That gal who made all the fuss when it turned out she got a window seat? What's up with her?'

'I keep on thinking she's dead, that's what. She's kept her blind shut the whole trip, and she hasn't even taken her sunglasses off. She just sits there, doesn't move, doesn't talk.'

'Maybe she's tired. Maybe she's afraid of flying, so she just shuts herself off. You see it all the time, honey.'

Betty-Lou shook her head nervously. 'No. It's not that. I can't put my finger on it but . . . who is she, anyway?'

Geena picked up the passenger list and rifled through it. 'Susan Carroll. That mean anything to you?'

'Hold it. Yeah. She was in *Cosmo* a couple of months ago. Ain't she that photographer who takes all those dirty pictures?'

'All those what—? If you say so, I'll take your word for it, sweetheart.' Geena poked her head out quickly through the drape. When she pulled back, she was frowning. 'See what you mean. She is like a corpse, ain't she? Never seen anyone so damned pale.'

*

2

The muffled roar of the jets, the faint vibration of her seat, reached her only dimly.

On a plane again. Dozing, on a plane. Hadn't it all begun this way, years ago? Susan couldn't remember, however much she tried.

When she dug into her memory, there was a glimpse of a night-bound city rising up to meet her, but she couldn't think which. Images of other places kept overlapping it. Hamburg. Stockholm. Rio. Tijuana. Bangkok. Which had that first city been?

She always felt disoriented when she was apart from Tharman, even for a day. Felt less than human, a half-person, when he wasn't by her side.

But tonight, she'd see him again. Her lips curled slightly, with the pleasure of the thought. Tonight, they'd be reunited. And Gorreq would be there too.

When shall we three meet again—

'Miss?' said a young woman's voice, above her. 'Miss, are you awake?'

She opened her eyes a little, squinting in the white, reflected glare from Lake Pontchartrain. It was a stewardess, the young one with the lovely blue-black hair, who'd already tried to talk to her several times. The girl was peering down at her almost nervously.

'Miss Carroll, the seat-belt light's been on for quite some time,' she said. 'We're coming in to land.'

3

'*Damn* Mardi Gras!' snapped the woman to Casey's left.

She'd been lost amongst her sombre churning thoughts until that moment, oblivious to the bustle all around her.

Now, she turned around in her seat, in the arrivals lounge of International Airport, and looked at the person who had spoken.

It was a slim, elegant black woman in her late forties, strands of grey highlighting her thick neat hair. She was dressed in a simple red chemise with a gold brooch at the throat, and navy blue pants, and there was a little boy, no more than three years old, fast asleep on her lap.

The woman had obviously been talking to herself, to thin air. When Casey stared at her, she looked embarrassed for a moment, and then smiled, her nose wrinkling and her dark eyes becoming warm and lively.

'Sorry, honey. Just thinking out loud.' She pulled a face of mock alarm, cast her gaze around the crowded terminal in a fashion of exaggerated panic. 'Person could get lynched in this town, criticizing their damned festivals.'

Casey leaned forwards and grinned, glad, suddenly, of someone to talk to.

'You're not from around here, then?'

'Last couple of years, yeah. But before that I'm from Philly. Moved down here to be closer to my daughter and my grandson here.' She offered her hand. The nails were bright with glossy mauve polish. 'Ursula Smith, by the way. And this here is Edward. Haven't made up my mind what he's going to be yet – President of the United States or just the greatest brain surgeon.'

Casey laughed and shook her hand. 'Casey Hammond.'

'You're not one of these bozos, are you?' Ursula jabbed a thumb at the milling crowd. Another plane had just disgorged its passengers. Tourists were staggering towards the taxi ranks, weighed down with luggage, wearing mingled expressions of weariness, frustration, and a jangle-nerved excitement. Some of them had elaborate costumes in plastic covers thrown over their arm, and a couple of the more impatient were already wearing their Carnival masks. Mozart and *The Phantom of the Opera* loomed out of the crowd as Casey watched, then were swept away.

'Where you from, if you don't mind me being nosy?' Ursula asked her.

She shrugged and pulled a face. 'Seattle. By way of Washington, by way of New York. My husband's an architect, and his company keeps moving him around. I'm from the Coast, originally.'

'LA?' Ursula nodded her approval. 'Now *there's* a sensible town. Air ain't sticky. You can walk down a street without someone blowing a trumpet in your ear. And they don't have these damned festivals all the time.' She glanced at the crowd again, like a schoolmarm keeping an eye on a bunch of juvenile delinquents. '*Jazz* Festival. *Spring* Festival. *Crawfish* Festival. Damned *Frog-jumping* Festival! When do these people do any work?'

Casey gazed at her hands – the fingers kept twining and unfurling around her knees – and tried to smile again. 'At least everyone's having a good time, I suppose.'

'Are you?' Ursula squinted. 'You having a good time?'

She tried not to think about that. Simply shook her head. 'I've got a migraine coming on, I think. It's all this noise, and these fluorescent lights.'

'Oh, Lord, you get those? I've got something for that.' Ursula rummaged quickly in her purse, came out with a white tablet which she popped into Casey's hand. 'Best thing, though, is lie down in the dark and get some rest.' She suddenly looked up at the arrival gates and stiffened. 'There's my husband now. Gotta go. Nice meeting you.'

She offered her hand again, then got up quickly and hurried across the carpet, still carrying the sleeping child. Casey watched as a handsome black man in a grey sports coat embraced the woman and the little boy and kissed them both. The small group walked away towards the exit, chattering and laughing.

Happy families.

Casey felt a flat pang of envy. That was the way it was supposed to be. The way she'd always thought it would be, between her and Ted. But she'd come to realize, over the last few years, that dreams and reality rarely collided. Most people were lucky if the two even came close.

Christ, what a family we are. A husband and wife who bristle like porcupines whenever they get within three yards of each other, for no good reason they can think of. And a little boy who's never even seen his grandma.

She pushed back a lock of straw-coloured hair and reached into her embroidered denim jacket, took out the newspaper cutting, and unfolded it. It was from the *Times Picayune*, a small column from page seven.

CONTROVERSIAL PHOTOGRAPHER TO SHOOT CARNIVAL

Susan Carroll, author and photographer, will be in town for the last few days of Carnival, on which she plans to base a forthcoming book. Mrs Carroll caused widespread controversy two years ago with publication of her best-selling *Images of Darkness*, which offended many people with its blatant portrayals of human suffering and sexual perversion.

Casey gazed at it bleakly. She must have looked at it about a hundred times over the last few days, but that didn't stop her reading it again. Her eyes lingered, as usual, on the word 'controversy'. It was a term she'd never have associated with her mother, simply didn't fit the quiet, attractive Beverly Hills housewife she had known.

But then, it had been a full seven years since she'd last seen Susan.

That fact hurt her bitterly, deep down. Pained her more than she'd admit. Left her feeling dismal and rejected. It was as though, when Susan had obtained the divorce from Dad, the decree had included *her* as well; a separation from the entire family. The only word she'd received, since then, had been a hastily penned note from London, England, and a couple of cursory, warmthless phone calls. It was as though Susan had made them to reassure her she was still alive, and for no other reason.

Then there was the book itself. She'd had to go buy it in a Seattle bookstore, and had felt embarrassed doing so. *Images of Darkness*. 'Images of Sleaze', Ted had dubbed it, with its juxtaposed photos of S&M couples and drug addicts, orgies and bar-room brawls, leather masks and stabbings. She'd turned the pages numbly for an hour, and had decided to throw it away in the end, afraid that Petey, four years old back then, might get hold of it.

What on earth had happened to the woman? What was going through her mind?

A rather drunk businessman in a crumpled grey suit staggered past her, then plumped into the vacant seat. Casey realized the Tannoy was booming again, announcing the arrival of the flight from Chicago.

She got up, and worked her way to the front of the crowd, scanning the emerging passengers anxiously.

Felt a cold, hard knot of panic tightening in her throat.

What was she going to do, when Susan appeared? What was she going to say?

The bobbing head of a woman, the right height, with that so recognizable auburn hair, moved into view. Was that *her*? Casey's whole body stiffened. She could feel her skin prickling, the way it used to do when she was a little girl and something exciting or scary was happening. Part of her felt like drawing away, shrinking back, going home and forgetting the whole business.

But she resisted it. Took a gulping breath.

'*Mom?*' she called out.

And, as the crowd parted slightly, the woman turned.

She was dressed entirely in black, a colour she'd never worn in Beverly Hills, and looked like some seductive Russian agent in an espionage movie. Her narrow skirt stopped just short of the knee, giving way to sheer dark stockings. She wore a broad-lapelled jacket with a silk blouse underneath, and a patent leather purse, as glossy as a sealion's hide. Most of her face was hidden by large opaque sunglasses, and a wide-brimmed hat with a black sequinned band.

She was carrying an over-stuffed pigskin suitcase, and had a bulky hold-all dangling from one shoulder, but they didn't seem to be weighing her down at all. And what had happened to her tan? The one luxury Susan had always allowed herself was a long bask, every day, in the Californian sun, toasting her skin to a deep, even brown. Now, it was as white as goat's cheese. She looked like a photographic negative in those clothes. Her hair and her coating of dark red lipstick were the only touches of colour.

Casey almost stumbled with shock. When she'd moved to New York with Ted, she'd left behind a woman who was beautiful, for sure, but soft and sad, passive. To be confronted with this . . . this changeling. So bold! So aggressive-looking! So – Casey found herself recoiling from the word with a childish, wounded horror – so utterly *sexual*. It was like looking at a total stranger.

She'd made a mistake, she decided. This wasn't her mother after all. She'd only turned around because the yell had surprised her. Maybe she was someone else's mom, though she didn't look it.

But she wasn't turning away again. The dark glasses were peering at her blindly.

Casey took a wobbling step forwards. It was hard to avoid being jostled, right now. Other people were rushing towards the gate, laughing, squealing, wrapping their arms around loved ones.

'Mom?'

Susan's face, what little she could see of it, was blank. The lower lip hung slackly, and Casey could make out a glimmer of white teeth.

'Mom?' She was aware how very small and reedy her voice had become. 'Don't you recognize me?'

Susan seemed to come around, as though out of a trance. She squared her shoulders, straightened her neck. A pale hand came up, adjusting the hold-all strap at her shoulder.

'Of course I do. How are you, darling? I thought you were in Seattle.'

There was no smile. The voice was deep and toneless.

Casey felt a terrible injured rage well up inside her. She'd imagined a thousand different greetings over the last few days, ranging from delight to confusion, but nothing like this.

You didn't know I was here, did you? she thought angrily. What were you planning to do? Spend the rest of your life avoiding Washington State?

She held the words in, puzzlement replacing her annoyance. What was wrong with the woman? Was she on drugs or something?

She struggled to think of something to say, but Susan beat her to it.

'I have a limo waiting for me, dear. I can't keep it waiting for ever. We can talk while we walk, if you like.'

Suddenly, she had turned on her heel and was pushing her way through the throng towards the exit, her bag swinging from her hand. Casey froze a moment, aghast, and then hurried up behind her.

'Aren't you going to ask how Pete is? You remember Pete? Your *grandson*? He'd actually like to meet you, you know.'

Susan didn't break her stride, but gave a brief, stiff nod, her gaze fixed straight ahead. 'That would be very nice.'

Oh, *good*, Mom! Oh, great! How pleasant! What the hell have I ever done to deserve this?

'Wh . . . where are you staying?'

'The Grand Royale, in the Quarter.'

'You could come and stop with *us*, you know.'

'I'm afraid that won't be practical. I'm busy tonight, and all next day. I'll come and see you for dinner tomorrow evening, if that'll please you. Phone my hotel and leave them your address.'

Still, her mother wouldn't slow her pace. *Still*, she wouldn't look around.

They were passing through the airport doors now. The morning's dank, grey sky had burnt away, and cars and rows of taxis glittered in the bright afternoon sun. This had all gone far enough, Casey decided. She'd allow it to go no further. She was going to grab her mother. Shake her. Scream into her face, until she got some kind of reaction that was recognizably human.

She reached out to snatch hold of one black-clad arm.

And suddenly pulled back, shocked for the second time in a minute.

Because her mother looked in pain the moment the sunlight touched her. Looked twenty years older, her pallid face screwed into a mass of wrinkles. Her body hunched over, and one hand went to her brow, to protect her eyes.

Except she was already wearing dark glasses.

Before Casey could work out what was happening, the woman was scuttling away towards a stretched black limousine, a few yards further down the kerb. A huge, fierce-looking black chauffeur, in a peaked cap and Ray-Bans, was standing next to it, holding a placard reading *Carroll.*

Casey watched dazedly as the man held the door open and her mother scrambled inside.

The chaffeur slammed the door shut, marched around quickly to the driver's seat.

The limo slid off towards Airline Highway a moment later, leaving her with nothing to do but stand like an abandoned two-year-old and watch it go.

CHAPTER TWENTY-EIGHT

1

From his office window near the river, Ted Hammond could see across his drafting-board all the way to Lake Pontchartrain.

The lake itself was a grey, hazy blur tinged with dark blues and faded greens, the Causeway an indistinct rippling scar across its cheek. The Louisiana sun was dropping low towards its western edge, huge and orange and boiling, like a gout of flame spat out by some gigantic fire-eater. Further towards him, within the bounds of Lakeshore Drive, he could make out quite clearly the treetops in City Park, the white, irregular shapes of the above-ground tombs in the cemeteries, and the massive flying-saucer outline of the Superdome. To his right were the picturesque roofs of the French Quarter and the high, white spire of the cathedral. Closer, the tall modern buildings of the Business District – 'Fat City' – sprawled. New Orleans had acquired a skyline, of recent years.

His gaze drifted to Canal Street, far below. Another parade was going past, down there. He'd lost count of them, in the last few days.

He was too far away to make out this one's theme. All that he could see were the rectangular shapes of the dozen or so floats, the tiny colourful dots milling around them. It was so alien to anything he'd known before, and he still couldn't get quite used to the way Carnival worked. Each parade was financed privately by a club, a secret society, which called itself a Krewe. They had strange names – the Krewe of Momus, the Krewe of Rex – each with traditions older than the United States itself. They organized the masked balls too, spending an entire year in the planning.

And here he was, sitting in his sound-proofed office

above all this activity, this gaiety. He'd never felt quite so alone.

Ted leaned back in his seat, glanced towards the outer office. The desks were empty, the phones silent. There'd only be a skeleton staff manning the place these next few days. There was no real reason for him to be here at all.

Except that it was better than going home.

He ran a hand through his dark curly hair, then fingered his moustache, thinking glumly about Casey. Christ, she was so beautiful, so dear. He cared for her so much, deep down. Why had he been so angry with her, this past year? Why did every gesture she made, every word she spoke, seem contrived to irritate him?

She seemed to feel the same way about him. He couldn't understand it. They'd tried talking about it, and it hadn't helped much. He felt that he'd missed out on a lot of the excitement of the early seventies. And she hated moving every couple of years – she wanted stability, perhaps a career of her own.

But their problems went a good deal deeper than that. They both knew it.

Maybe they were simply falling out of love. That seemed cruel and unfair, simply because there was no reason for it. He'd be happier, he often thought, to come home and find her in bed with another man. Then, at least, he'd know why he kept getting furious all the time.

He blinked at his reflection in the plate-glass window. A tall, slim man with a long square jaw gazed back at him. There were shadows underneath the eyes that hadn't been there a year ago, and a fixed downward droop to the corners of the thin-lipped mouth.

He felt like he was looking at a total stranger. Closed his eyes.

There was the tap of knuckles on the door behind him.

'Sleeping on the job?' came the rich drawl of his boss, Joe Deck.

Ted shifted around in his swivel chair and forced a smile. He didn't like Deck, not one little bit, but he always tried to hide it in the presence of the man. Deck was like a big, muscular dog, who could smell hostility from miles away.

'What the hell're you doing here anyway, huh?' Deck enquired, pushing his huge face towards Ted, his lower lip protruding and his bushy eyebrows bobbing sarcastically. 'I'm glad you are, though. Come into my office, would you?'

2

Deck's office was about three times the size of his own, with a good view of the wharf-lined river. The Mississippi, sluggish and mocha-brown, twisted into the distance like some enormous shifting highway. It was full of traffic today, freighters and smaller fishing boats.

There were houseplants by the window, and along two of the walls, but Ted knew Deck never lifted a finger to take care of them himself. They were all looked after by his secretary, Pam, in the moments when she wasn't hammering at her IBM Selectric.

All in all, it was hard to tell what the boss *did* do with his time.

In his huge black leather chair, his feet up on the desk, Deck smirked at him and waggled a finger, ushering him in. There was a poster behind his head reading *King of Fat City*, with a picture of a coronet floating above his short tawny hair. He was the archetypal big broad-shouldered Texan, with massive hands, jowly cheeks, and tiny squinting ice-blue eyes. He was from Houston originally, but over the five years he'd lived in New Orleans he'd adopted a fey theatrical manner which would have gotten him a beating, at the very least, back home. Today, he was resplendent in a lavender suit with matching boots, and a polka-dotted bow tie. A neatly folded handkerchief protruded from his breast pocket.

He waved a hand airily at Ted. 'Shut the door, good buddy. Come and sit yourself down.'

What the hell is this? Ted thought. Was he in some kind of trouble?

Deck squinted at him, as though trying to fathom his mind. Then, he fished in a desk drawer, took out a thin green cheroot, lit it. He puffed foul smoke into the cool, conditioned air.

And smiled mischievously.

'Teddy? Can I ask you something?'

'Sure, Joe. Go ahead.'

'Why ain't you having fun?'

Ted felt his throat tighten a little. His hand went unconsciously to the knot of his tie. The question made him uncomfortable, though he wasn't quite sure why.

'There's a whole city out there having a good time, boy.' Deck jabbed a thumb in the direction of the French Quarter to emphasize his point. 'Passed a beggar on the street this morning, one leg, one arm. Even he was whooping it up. And yet you ain't. Why is that?

'I'll tell you why,' he continued, without waiting for a reply. 'You haven't got into the swing of things yet. You haven't got that northern stiffness out of your body and let N'Orleans take hold of your soul. You and your good lady been invited to a ball, this year?'

'Our landlady did ask,' Ted heard himself saying. 'But Casey's a little protective of Pete . . .'

'Uh-huh.' Deck's eyes glazed over boredly. 'Troubles at home. I thought as much.' He leaned across the desk, and his voice dropped to a hushed, conspiratorial drone. 'Let me offer you an invitation, then. Just to you, you understand. *Not* your lady wife. You see, not long after I arrived in this burg, I realized what was needed was a *special* kind of ball. All those masks and crinolines are very nice – but something a little more fun and a little less formal, that's more my style. We've a regular society going every year now. Call ourselves the Krewe de Chat. You understand what that means, Ted?'

'It's French for cat.'

'Or pussy.' Deck leered, the cheroot wedged between his teeth. 'A few close friends and their wives. A few junior execs and their girlfriends. A couple of secretaries from right here in this office. And a few of those nice working ladies from down on Bourbon Street, just to add a touch of spice to the occasion. We get together every year and have ourselves a regular hoe-down. It's at my place, tomorrow evening after sunset, if you're interested.'

Ted couldn't quite believe what he'd just heard. And then, when he *did* believe it, he didn't have the first idea how to react. Would refusal offend? Was this, so far as Deck was concerned, some kind of requirement of the job?

He sat there stiffly, a dozen replies running through his head. And one of them, he was alarmed to note, was *Yes, sure.*

Was that just weakness on his part, or had his marriage really gone that sour?

Deck noticed his hesitation, began to chuckle mockingly. There were few things more dangerous, Ted realized, than a brutish, vicious man who was perceptive with it.

'Worried about the little lady, Teddy? Oh, she needn't know a thing. I'll vouch for you.' The hand with the cheroot waved lazily. 'Don't you get it yet? This is the Big Easy. You can throw away the rule book, because anything goes. Especially during Mardi Gras. You know what "Carnival" means, Teddy? It's from the Latin – *carnisvale*, "farewell to flesh". We just like to give it a very fond farewell, that's all. Promise me you'll think about it?'

Ted managed a jerky nod, feeling ridiculous.

'That's just grand!' Deck exclaimed. He jabbed a thick finger towards the door. 'Now get out of here, you damned Yankee, and have yourself some fun.'

3

The streets around the French Quarter were clogged solid, and the cab, when Casey finally managed to get one, had to take the long route along the lake shore and down Paris Avenue to reach the Faubourg Marigny.

Casey felt her usual prickle of annoyance as the aged, fading suburb came in sight. She hadn't wanted to move to New Orleans in the first place – she was sick and tired of dragging Pete all over the country, breaking up friendships he had just begun to form. But Ted's firm had insisted he come here, and she'd retaliated by doing some insisting of her own. If they were going to live anywhere in this city, it was going to be the beautiful and airy Garden District, a couple of miles uptown. She'd taken it as settled. It was only when they'd got here, and been met by that pig of a man Deck, that they'd discovered every decent apartment in town had been rented months in advance for Mardi Gras. This was the only place the company had been able to find.

The cab slowed to a weary crawl as it reached Frenchmen Street. Carnival revellers had spilled out from the Quarter, just across Esplanade, and were dancing in single file along the middle of the road.

Casey ignored them, turning her glum attention to the townhouses around her. The Faubourg Marigny must have been a marvellous area in its time, and could be again if someone really put their mind to it. But these days, it had been neglected and had gone rather to seed. The plaster on the houses was ragged and torn, the old slate rooftops shaky. Soot lined the intricate wrought-iron work of the balconies, coating them with an uneven black. A few of the residents had tried brightening things up, setting little gardens outside their windows to add a dash of colour, but it was a feeble resistance against the decay. Most of the store-fronts were begrimed and shabby-looking, and there was a bar, right on the corner of their street, which catered to a noisy, uncouth clientele.

If this had been her first year with Ted, and they'd both had the licence to be irresponsible, she might have found the place exciting, darkly glamorous. But they had a child now, and this was no place to bring him up.

If it wasn't for Audrey, she wasn't quite sure what she'd do.

*

4

When the huge mahogany door of the ground-floor apartment swung open, Audrey Charbonne was revealed in what – Casey recognized immediately – was her natural state.

An ivory-white taffeta ballgown spread all the way from her bare shoulders to her heels, whispering on the cracked mosaic floor of the hallway every time she moved. Her dyed red hair was piled up Marie Antoinette style, and seemed to be largely held in place by the sparkling diamond tiara she wore. More jewels glittered at her wrists and throat. Her thin, high-cheekboned face was overly made-up, but then it always was.

In the few weeks that Casey had known her landlady, she had never seen the woman unkempt, or without her rouge and eyeliner. Never seen her lose her poise or forget her manners, either. Audrey Charbonne was in her late fifties, and bore the title 'widow' like a medal of honour. She was pure Creole, and claimed that she could trace her ancestors all the way back to Franco-Spanish aristocracy. She could talk the hind legs off a whole procession of mules, and at first Casey had thought that was going to be a problem. But she'd quickly developed an affection for this tiny, birdlike woman. The airs and graces weren't a sham. They sprang from a code of behaviour long forgotten in the rest of the States. And though Audrey looked as though a vagrant gust of wind might blow her away at any moment, she was strong and wilful deep down, a true ally to anyone lucky enough to call her a friend.

Her smile, as she inspected Casey, was warm and dazzling.

'Why, hi there, cher! How did it go with your mama?'

Casey shook her head tiredly. 'Not too hot, I'm afraid, Audrey.'

The woman frowned with disappointment.

'Well, I'm truly sorry to hear that. Come on in and tell me all about it.'

Casey followed her into the wide, cool hallway, and started recounting the meeting at the airport. She talked about how brief it had been, how her mother had treated her so distantly, so coldly. But she left out Susan's peculiar appearance, and her aversion to sunlight. She still hadn't absorbed all that herself. Couldn't quite believe what she had seen.

Audrey looked sad and puzzled by the time she'd finished, her mouth pursed and her eyes a little hurt. She seemed to be trying to find the right thing to say.

'Just give it time, cher,' she murmured softly, at last. 'Perhaps your mama needs a while to get used to things again. Divorce does all kinds of strange stuff to folks – I've seen it myself, plenty of times. Why don't you find out how it goes tomorrow evening?'

'That's just what I was planning to do,' Casey nodded.

'I feel sorriest for your little boy, I must say. A child should have a grandmama.'

Audrey led the way into the huge antique-cluttered living-room. The french windows at the end were open on to an equally jumbled garden. Two huge elms stood out there like sentinels, and bougainvillaea, honeysuckle, and ivy fought for room between them. Pete's tousled, dark head was just visible amongst the riot of flowers. He was watching a bumblebee drifting along the back wall.

'How's he behaved himself?'

'Oh!' Audrey beamed. 'Like an absolute angel. No trouble at all.'

Pete must have heard their voices. His head suddenly whipped around, and then he was sprinting towards them.

He stopped dead, just inside the room, when he realized that Casey had returned alone. Like the brave little soldier he was, he tried not to look sad or bemused.

'Grandma's coming tomorrow evening,' Casey told him quickly, before he could reach the wrong conclusion. 'For dinner. Won't that be nice?'

He nodded, rather gravely.

Casey hurried towards her son, scooped him up in her

arms. Was about to plant a kiss on his cheek when she noticed a powdering of sugar around his mouth.

'I let him try a few of my home-cooked beignets,' Audrey said.

'No *wonder* he was good. You know I'm trying to keep him off sugar, Audrey.'

The older woman looked disgruntled. 'All these silly new ideas. It'll give him a sweet disposition, cher. And it *is* Mardi Gras.' She suddenly glanced at her tiny jewelled watch. 'The cab will be here in a few moments. Are you and Ted quite sure you won't come to the ball?'

'Thank you. I'm not sure it's practical.'

'You can bring the child. Nobody'll mind.'

Casey shrugged apologetically. 'I'm not sure when Ted'll be home. And besides, I'm not dressed for it.'

'You're my *guests*,' Audrey said, firmly. 'Doesn't matter how you dress, no one'll dare object. And I can make the cab to wait.' She gazed at Casey expectantly for a few seconds. Then, recognizing defeat, she flapped her hands and sighed. 'OK, cher. I'm not going to nag any more.'

There was the blast of a horn from the street outside.

'There's the cab now,' Audrey muttered, snatching up her purse from a gold-and-scarlet ottoman in the corner. 'You're welcome to stay here, if Pete wants to play in the garden a while longer.'

'No, it's getting late,' Casey smiled. 'We'd better go.'

She was still carrying the boy as she made her way up the curving flight of stairs towards her own apartment, on the first floor. God, he was getting so heavy, these days. She wouldn't be able to keep this up much longer. She could hear the cab moving away. The house became echoingly quiet around her.

She let herself in awkwardly, put on Fleetwood Mac's *Rumours*, and started getting her son ready for bed, wondering all the while when Ted would be coming home.

*

5

Ted had fully intended to forget his troubles, put his work behind him, and simply breathe in the festive air along Canal Street. But as he pushed his way through the jostling throng, the reason for his move to New Orleans came in sight. On a lot that had been cleared of its old buildings – not without resistance from local conservation groups – the Courtenay Tutton Building was in the first stages of erection. The ageing, eccentric shipping magnate had commissioned the design himself, and had insisted on something grand and tapering, like the TransAmerica building in 'Frisco. Accordingly, the building had quickly taken on the nickname, around Ted's office, of 'King Tut's Pyramid'. He wasn't sure he appreciated the joke. He was very proud of his design. It had won out, after all, in a fierce competition with six other firms of architects.

The Tutton was a bare skeleton at the moment, naked steel girders hanging against the low, dimming sky. Work on it would not resume until the Carnival was over. The thought of the delay almost had him grinding his teeth with frustration.

He started patting the site keys in his pocket.

So much for enjoying the celebrations! Here he was, in the heart of it all, and he was impatient to get back to work.

Ted wondered, rather numbly, whether he'd lost his capacity for enjoyment altogether.

Joe Deck certainly had fun, in his own perverse way. Ted's thoughts wandered back to the offer he'd made. And suddenly, he found himself conjuring up the scenes in the Texan's house tomorrow evening. The whisper of flesh against flesh. The press of strange bodies against his own. Even during this nightmarish past year, he'd never felt any genuine inclination to cheat on Casey. The thought of other women, mindless sex, didn't really attract him that much. It was simply the idea of . . . *letting go* for once in his adult life. Just once! Throwing off the yoke of parenthood and marriage. Stripping himself bare of scruples and morality for a couple of hours.

That was what this whole festival was about, in a way. Was there really anything so terrible in that?

There was a roar from the crowd, further down towards Baronne Street. Another procession was coming.

He heard the wail of sirens half a minute later, and the flashing of blue lights formed patterns against the cooling air. An arrowhead formation of police motorcycles was leading the parade. Those revellers who'd strayed beyond the kerb jumped back, and the press of bodies around him immediately tightened. His arms were pinned to his sides, and his chest felt constricted and painful.

A few feet away from him, a little girl began to wail. She was hoisted quickly on to her father's shoulders, and the profound cry of fright transformed to a delighted chortle.

The motorized escort had passed, by now. After them came masked Krewe members on horseback. Then a uniformed marching band. And then the torch-bearers.

The first of the massive floats trundled into view. The theme was ancient Egypt, the Pharaohs. The costumes of the Krewe and their fluttering satin masks were lined with sequins and paste jewellery and feathers, breaking up the torchlight. It seemed to give them an almost spectral glow.

Seated on a huge gilded throne, a sceptre in his hand, the King of the Parade waved to the crowds with a drunken regal flamboyance. The girls to either side of him began to throw handfuls of souvenir doubloons towards the sidewalk. A massive cheer went up, and the people at the back jostled to get closer.

The little girl on her father's shoulders shrieked, and windmilled her arms, trying to catch one of the aluminium coins.

Ted watched it all, and couldn't feel a thing.

After a while, he managed to shoulder his way back through the throng, and went to find a cab.

*

6

When he turned the key and pushed the door open on to the darkened hallway, Casey's voice drifted out from the kitchen.

'Where've you been so long?'

'I just thought I'd go and look at the parades.'

'Oh, that's just great, Ted.' A blender whirred sharply. 'You haven't found the time to take your son to a parade yet, but you manage to go yourself.'

He took his jacket off, his movements stiff and jumpy. 'I thought you took him yesterday?'

'I did, but he wants *you*. He wants to share . . . Christ, do I have to explain everything to you?'

He ignored her and went into the broad, high-ceilinged living-room, cluttered with the ageing furniture Audrey had provided; most of their own was still in storage. Thought of settling into his recliner – but then he'd probably retreat into a doze, and that would provide Casey with yet *another* grievance. He moved some toys off the black leather Chesterfield, wedged himself in its corner, and reached for the remote.

Casey brought him a TV dinner after a while, dumping it down on the coffee table in front of him.

They sat on opposite ends of the couch, and for want of conversation watched an old re-run of *Laugh-In*. They'd always loved *Laugh-In*; it was one of the first things that had brought them together. But neither of them so much as smiled, all the way through the show; as though it were a challenge, to see which of them could keep a straight face the longest.

CHAPTER TWENTY-NINE

1

Susan stood at the open, darkened window of her hotel suite, gazing along St Louis towards Bourbon. It had started raining gently, but no one down there seemed to care.

She was perfectly still, and her eyes barely blinked. Her face was slack and sad.

The crowds swirling below her in the gaslight, the clamorous music drifting up towards her from the clubs and bars, might as well not have been there. All she could think about was Casey.

How long had it been since she'd thought of anyone but Tharman? She mumbled to herself, trying to recollect, but the memory wouldn't come. Her past seemed nothing but a dark, shadowy blur. There were a few fleeting glimpses of a house with a swimming pool, somewhere sunny. Los Angeles? And of a man who might have been her husband once. But the rest was lost, like a dream you snatched at upon waking, and which melted to a pale mist in your grasp.

A *daughter*, though! She'd barely been aware, until that meeting at the airport, that she even *had* a daughter.

Something inside her – something that was purely instinctive – had wanted to reach out and take hold of that young woman. Hug her. Squeeze her very tightly. Kiss her and croon to her.

But she hadn't been able to. She'd felt so numb and confused. And, though she'd managed to hide it, so deeply afraid.

It pained her now, her inaction. Hurt like a knife in the ribs.

Casey. She turned the name over again and again.

Casey. So soft and pretty. Like looking at a picture of a younger her.

Except she couldn't remember ever *being* young.

There was a tickling on her cheek. Perhaps an insect had landed there. This was mosquito country, wasn't it? She raised her hand, touched the smooth skin of her face. And her fingers came away warm and damp.

She was crying.

How long had it been since she'd cried?

Tears, my love? came a familiar voice inside her head.

She felt a soft, shifting sensation as Tharman reached inside her thoughts. He was caressing her troubled mind, smoothing away the anguish of those half-formed memories. Normally, they'd vanish entirely. But tonight, they clung on just a little, at the edges of her consciousness.

No matter. She could ignore them. She smiled happily at the thought of seeing the thin man again. Turned away from the window, as a knock came at the door.

2

There were three figures standing around the doorway when she opened up. Two of them, Tharman and Gorreq, were entirely familiar. They'd arrived here last night, a day ahead of her, and had obviously kept themselves busy.

The third was a teenaged girl, about nineteen, in cut-off jeans, white high heels, and a skimpy, printed T-shirt, a leather jacket thrown across one shoulder. She was vacant eyed, and had a can of Bud clutched in one hand, unnoticed now. Tharman must have picked her up on the street outside.

Her presence didn't bother Susan in the slightest. Her love had to include other women in his Feeding. He'd drain her entirely, if he nourished himself exclusively on her. But his couplings with strangers were brief, matters of necessity, of hunger, nothing more. He always came back to her in the end.

He smiled at her now. Reached out, and wiped her face dry with a slender thumb and index finger.

Never do this, my beautiful one. You'll get lines under your eyes, and how will you look then?

The three of them filed past her into the room.

Susan took a better look at the girl in the light from the window. Nineteen was a bit on the long side, she realized. Young women had such mature figures, these days. An early eighteen was closer to the mark. She had flaxen hair and pink thighs, and full, heavy breasts. The legend on her T-shirt read UNIVERSITY OF IOWA. She was down here for the Carnival, obviously, and had to have come alone, or Tharman wouldn't have bothered with her.

A long way from home. She wouldn't be missed for quite a while.

Tharman took the girl's hand and led her straight through to the bedroom. There was the sound of ripping cloth, a moment later, and a stifled giggle.

Then silence, suddenly, from the young woman.

There was the creak of bedsprings, and a suppressed animal growling.

Susan glanced over at Gorreq, but he ignored her. He was waiting impatiently, standing in the middle of the suite, his arms folded across his chest. He'd take the girl somewhere isolated, quiet, when Tharman was finished with her. And there he'd Feed, himself. The police might find her body, a few days from now, floating in Lake Pontchartrain or some distant bayou.

Susan sat down in a chair and waited for her lover to return, feeling a pricking impatience of her own.

3

It was an hour before Gorreq went to fetch his prey from the bedroom. He emerged with one hand clamped tightly about her tanned brown wrist. Her face was still entirely blank, she was staring at him witlessly. She was wearing her leather jacket, zipped up now, with nothing underneath, and Gorreq had the remains of her T-shirt in his other fist. He was being careful – as Tharman always reminded him – about leaving evidence.

Susan watched idly as the young student was trooped out through the door. There ought to be a twinge of pity for her, she knew, but she'd seen this whole routine so many times before. And besides, she had other things stirring at the corners of her thoughts.

From the lightless bedroom there was a rustle, then the gentle tread of feet across the carpet. Tharman appeared in the doorway, framed in silhouette, his eyes still glowing a dull bronze. He gazed at her evenly for a few seconds, then crossed the room towards her.

He bent over her and cupped his hand under her chin, turning her face towards him.

What is this, beautiful one? What is it that so troubles you?

She didn't want to look at him, kept trying to pull away. It was hopeless. She couldn't fight him.

'You know what it is. I can't help it.'

Your daughter? You're thinking of her now, aren't you? And your grandson – you're wondering what he looks like.

She nodded stiffly, her nerves jangling. Tharman crouched down in front of her, and fixed her with a smile.

Does it really mean so much to you? More than I do?

'No!' The idea unsettled her terribly, made her squirm frightenedly in her chair. 'Of course not.'

Haven't I given you everything? Everything I promised? Haven't you seen the world and left your mark on it? Haven't you revelled in the glory of your new life? Haven't you been reborn?

She felt ashamed, closed her eyes. Her nose blocked up and she started to whimper.

Tharman took hold of her by the elbows, lifted her from the chair, and led her, very gently, over to the big silvery mirror above the dresser. He turned her around to face it.

Look. He shook her. *Look at yourself. You are forty-eight, but you look no older than the day I met you. I did that for you. Would you turn your back on it now? Would you turn wrinkled and grey for the sake of a woman who doesn't care for you, a child you've never known?*

Susan gazed at her reflection. Her colourless face was as flawless and smooth as expensive bone china. It had a terrible, cold beauty that almost frightened her.

She shook her head jerkily.

That's right, my love. How sensible you are. Now let go of these thoughts. Let me think for you, a while.

The reflection of his face was directly behind hers, looming over her shoulder – gaunt, and shadowy, and grinning. She looked at him for a while, stared into those bottomless eyes, then inclined her head passively.

A deep, quiet bliss began slipping over her.

4

Since there was no excuse to go into the office, Ted had agreed to take Pete uptown to St Charles Avenue today, to watch one of the early-morning walking clubs troop by. And since Casey had no reason to stay home, she'd promised to come with.

Happy families, Ted thought grimly. They were going to spend the whole morning using Pete as a buffer between them. That wasn't fair on him, but he couldn't see what choice there was.

At least Casey seemed to realize the problem as acutely as he did. They moved around each other silently and cautiously at breakfast, like a couple of strange dogs locked together in an empty room. But they took care not to lose control and start snapping or shouting. Thank God, Pete didn't appear to pick up the bad vibes between them. He was too excited, wide eyed and jittery, gobbling down his breakfast and then yanking on his new long-coveted cherry-red baseball shoes.

When Casey went into the hall to phone her mother at the hotel, Ted grasped the opportunity to tell Pete a joke he remembered from his own schooldays. It was a silly gag, about a mermaid and a frog, but they both found themselves giggling hysterically, the little boy's face turning pink and tears forming in his eyes. And, for that moment, Ted was happier than he'd felt all year.

It faded, and his whole body went cold again, the moment he heard Casey put the phone down.

'The Queen of England's actually deigning to come and see us?' he called out.

His sarcasm was perfectly reasonable under the circumstances, he felt. It shouldn't have annoyed Casey. But by the tone of her voice, it had.

'She's asleep. She's left instructions not to be disturbed. But I gave the hotel our address, and they said they'd pass it on.'

She sounded jumpy and uncertain of herself. She was going through a small and private hell, Ted knew. He only wished she'd let him reach out, talk to her, help her. That seemed as impossible as trying to touch the moon, these days. They'd grown so far apart.

Pete scrambled off his chair and ran to the front door, jumped up and down on the spot and shouted for them both to hurry up.

'OK, OK! Don't rush me!' Ted grinned. 'Let your old man put his jacket on, at least.'

He went into the bedroom, and was halfway to the closet when the telephone on the wall started to ring.

'Teddy, boy!' came Joe Deck's voice. 'Glad I caught you. I'm waiting for a decision, remember? About this evening?'

Ted glanced into the hallway, where his son was still bouncing and yelling.

'Sorry, Joe.' God, his voice had dropped almost to a whisper. He felt like a goddamned spy. 'I can't make it.'

'And why the fuck not?'

'Casey's mother's just arrived in town, and she's—'

He was cut off abruptly by a raucous gale of laughter from the line.

'You mean to tell me,' the Texan managed to choke

out, 'that you're turning down some of the best gash in Louisiana because your mother-in-law's coming to visit?'

Ted could hear Casey's footsteps on the tiles of the bathroom. He turned the phone away from her, as though he was trying to hide it with his body.

'That's the situation, Joe. I'm afraid I can't discuss it any further, right now. I'll see you in the office after Mardi Gras.'

Deck's laughter faded altogether. 'Oh, I'll see you, all right,' he replied sternly. 'But not in the same light, Teddy. I thought better of you than this. I am *severely* disappointed in you, boy.'

There was a loud clatter as the man hung up.

Ted put the receiver down, then heard a noise behind him, swivelled round. Casey was standing stiffly in the doorway, glowering at him.

'What's all the whispering about?' she hissed, keeping her voice down, so Pete couldn't hear.

Ted tried to look blank and unbothered, but he knew from bitter experience how hopeless that was. He was no good at lies at all. However hard he tried, his face always gave him away.

He could feel it stiffening right now, his eyes widening slightly.

'It was Deck.'

'Oh, great. What did *he* want?'

'He asked if I'd come into the office today. I told him no.'

He'd unconsciously started rubbing his palms together. Stopped it. But Casey had already noticed, and her gaze darkened.

'You can *go*, if you like. I'll take Pete on my own, yet again.'

'Christ, didn't you hear what I just said?' He was starting to raise his voice, couldn't help himself. 'Didn't you *hear*?'

Out in the hallway, Pete stopped jumping.

Casey said, 'Now look what you've done.'

*

5

Susan woke unexpectedly, at about ten o'clock. She tried to close her eyes again, but couldn't get them to shut.

She lay peering at the cross-hatched moulded ceiling bemusedly, listening to Tharman's shallow breathing on the pillow beside her. She never usually woke this early unless there was a good reason. A plane to catch. An interview. Normally, she slept right through till dusk, just like the others. Why'd she woken now?

After a while, the weight of Tharman's arm across her chest became uncomfortable. She lifted it away. His smooth brow furrowed as she did so, and he mumbled something from between his gently parted lips. Maybe he had fixed his dreams, again, on Pashta, the seven years since her death being no more than an eyeblink to him. Then she got up and padded, naked, into the living-room. The blinds were drawn, throughout the suite, and blankets had been thrown across them to provide an added barrier against the sunlight. And the door, of course, had been sealed with a Spell of Fixing; proof against nosy chambermaids. She felt claustrophobic, suddenly. As though she were in a locked cell.

Her eyesight, these days, was almost as good in darkness as the others'. Golden wallpaper and white, smoothly lacquered furniture met her gaze. There were so many potted palms and succulents the place was like a greenhouse.

She looked at Gorreq, who was sprawled across the couch, sleeping like a well-fed tiger. There were dark crescents underneath his fingernails, the dried blood of the girl last night. She hadn't heard him come in again, and almost resented his presence. But he was lying so still, he was easy to forget after a couple of minutes.

Her thoughts were blurred, and moving sluggishly, but they seemed to be her own for the moment. Tharman wasn't touching her mind at all. Whatever he *was* dreaming, he was engrossed in it. She'd often wished that she could sift through her past like him, for moments of delight and splendour.

But now she was free, for a while. If you could call this free.

The face of the golden-haired woman, her daughter, Casey, resolved itself in her head again. She thought she could hear muted snatches of the conversation they'd had yesterday. She'd promised to visit them this evening. And there had been something about an address. Yes, that was it. Call the hotel, she'd said.

Very quietly, she tiptoed over to the phone. She picked up the receiver, trying not to make a sound, dialled zero, and the clerk at reception answered quickly. Sure, her daughter had called. She scribbled the address down on a pad of hotel notepaper as the man read it out.

'Will there be anything more, ma'am?' he asked cheerfully. 'Breakfast, perhaps?'

She hung up without answering.

The clock on the mantelpiece said ten fifteen, now. God, she wished she could go back to sleep. What else was she going to do?

Susan moved about the dark suite gently, peering at the furniture and the pastel, abstract prints on the walls. They all looked peculiar, alien, to her. The noise of revelry still drifted from the street below, not much quieter than the night before. She could almost feel the sun, beyond the heavily cloaked windows. It was rising above the rooftops like a fire out of control. Just thinking about it hurt her a little.

Get back into that sumptuous bed, all her impulses told her. Snuggle up against your love and forget all this.

Something stopped her. She wasn't quite sure what.

She got her Japanese silk robe from the bathroom, slipped it on. Sat down in the armchair opposite the couch, and gazed dismally at the blanket-smothered drapes. Nothing moved, in the room. The only sound that was being made in here was the ticking of the clock.

Daytime was dangerous, she knew. Daytime was a hateful thing. Yet . . . she couldn't stop thinking about all those people down there, moving about freely, enjoying themselves in the sunlight. Perhaps Casey was out there too, letting the *Ra*'s heat warm her body. Maybe Pete was with her, squinting blissfully in its glare.

She'd enjoyed the sun once, she seemed to recall. Spent hours lying in it. Was that right?

She found herself envying the people on the street. It was only a faint prickling of jealousy, but it was there.

After a while, she got up again and crossed to the furthest window. Took hold of one edge of the drape.

Gorreq moved suddenly, behind her, and let out a hoarse grunt. She froze, terrified. Glanced around at him. But he was still asleep.

Very carefully, she pulled the drape aside a fraction of an inch. A thin shaft of yellow fell across her wrist. It felt like a whiplash. Burned. Stung. She immediately wanted to pull away, jump back. Let the curtain drop and forget the whole thing. But she clenched her teeth and forced herself to hang on.

Slowly, she eased her free hand into the gap between the fabric and the glass. Pushed it through, until it was fully in the sunlight. It hurt badly at first. But after a while the pain subsided to a dull, throbbing ache. Look, she could do it. She felt a little closer to the world, now. To the other humans out there in the city.

Her fingers shifted, like pale writhing insects, in the revealing light of day.

6

Audrey knocked on the Hammonds' door a little before dusk, and waited, smiling nervously, until somebody answered. It was Casey in a stained red-and-white apron, a wooden spoon clutched in her hand. Her hair was tousled and damp, her cheeks red and sweaty. Behind her, a grim-faced Ted was just disappearing, pushing a vacuum cleaner through into the bedroom. The roar of cartoon music coming from the living-room had to be Pete, watching the TV.

'All ready for your mama?' Audrey asked.

'Getting there.' A tired grin creased Casey's mouth and eyes. 'I decided to attempt a crawfish bisque. Attempt, as in an assault on Mount Everest. I'm beginning to wish I'd never started.'

She led Audrey through into the kitchen, where two pans were bubbling on the stove.

'Can I be of any help, cher?'

'No,' Casey said. 'Thanks very much, but I'd like to do this myself.'

'Of course. You're quite right.' Audrey sniffed at the pan with the shellfish and nodded approvingly. 'Well, this is a real *occasion*, isn't it?'

'Oh, absolutely,' Casey chuckled. 'One way or another, it promises to be quite some evening.'

'How was the marching club this morning?'

Audrey realized immediately she'd asked the wrong question. Casey's eyes went very sad for a moment, and she turned away quickly, pretended to be rummaging through the cutlery drawer for something.

'We didn't go. Or rather, we got halfway there and Pete decided he wanted to come back.'

The noise of the vacuum cleaner stopped abruptly. Audrey thought she heard Ted step out into the hall. Was he listening? There was obviously a great deal of tension in the air, and it made her feel uncomfortable, like a stranger in her own home. She'd heard shouting from up here before, but her code of manners had prevented her from interfering, until now. It was such a crying shame. They seemed such a nice couple, if only they'd give it a chance.

'Well, there's always next year,' she said, brightly. Then she raised her voice a little, so that Ted could hear. 'And I think you're very lucky, having a man who helps out around the house. Mr Charbonne was a fine husband in many ways, but I never so much as saw him make a slice of toast, in all the years we were married. I admire Ted.'

'Well,' said Casey, drily, 'at least he's good for something.'

There was the swift pounding of footsteps, retreating down the hall. Then a clack as the front door opened, and a deafening bang as Ted slammed it shut behind him.

7

Gorreq smiled viciously as he followed the architect in his mind's eye.

Down the curving stairs of the house – almost stumbling – out through the door and on to Frenchmen Street – off towards the Quarter – shouldering blindly through the crowds – thoughts whirling—

He could see, through Ted's eyes, the sun dropping towards the rooftops, the sky turning bronze and red.

He's mine, he told Tharman. *You take the daughter and the little boy.*

But there was no reply from his brother. He could sense only anger and dismay. It took him a little while to realize why.

It was the woman, Susan Carroll.

8

She was still awake when the sun finally set and the light beyond the curtains vanished. She was sitting in an armchair near the window, staring at the frame, a tear drying on her cheek.

As Gorreq roused himself and sat up, she jumped frightenedly, like a child who'd just been caught stealing. A guilty expression spread across her face, under his golden stare.

Just look at her, brother. Look what she's thinking. You're losing control of her.

No, Tharman replied, casually. *I chose her in the first place because she's strong.*

Too strong.

Gorreq stood up, and began moving angrily towards the woman. She cowered back a little in her chair, staring at him helplessly.

Brother, there is no need for that. Tharman's voice, inside his head, was drowsily persuasive. *It's thoughts of her family, doing this. And after tonight, there will be nothing left but distant, fading memories.*

CHAPTER THIRTY

1

Ted marched down the gaslit expanse of Bourbon Street through the gathering night, his chin tucked down and his hands thrust into his pockets, the plant-lined balconies and high, arched windows and the flags of nations outside the hotels sliding obliviously past him. He was barely conscious of the crowds swirling along the sidewalks, the tourists and the beaming locals, the rowdy groups of students and the staggering drunks. On the odd occasion he glanced up, he couldn't seem to focus at all. They all seemed to merge into one shifting, amorphous, many-legged body. Their smiling faces, whisking by him, were indistinguishable.

All he was really aware of was that every single one of them was having fun. *Fun!* A party atmosphere reigned, block after block.

And, in the middle of this all-smothering celebration, he was as unhappy and alone as ever. He felt like a visitor from another world, surrounded by a race whose language he couldn't understand, who were performing a ritual he didn't know how to take part in.

It made him seethe with anger, after a while. How could they be happy when he was not? Why didn't they take any notice of his misery, his pain? He wanted to grab hold of them, rattle them, slap their faces.

No, more than that he simply wanted to get *out* of here. But how? He couldn't seem to find his bearings. The only plan he managed to come up with was to keep on walking, putting one foot in front of the other. If he walked for long enough in a dead straight line, he'd leave the Quarter eventually. Leave the music and laughter behind, and dissolve into the darkness.

He lost his concentration completely for a moment, and suddenly crashed into an ageing black man in a silver lamé suit, who'd been tightrope walking along the kerb, twirling a striped umbrella. Practically got his eye poked out by one of the spokes.

'Hey, you all right?' the old man said. Ted only heard him distantly. 'You oughta watch where you're going, feller.'

A hand brushed across his sleeve, but he shook it off annoyedly, moved away. Took a good look at his surroundings for the first time in . . . he wasn't sure how long. Time had melted into the same grey blur that was swallowing everything else.

He was near the corner of Conti Street, on the three hundred block of Bourbon, right in the heart of the red-light district. Neon swirled around him like an electrical storm gone berserk, like a rainbow that had been shattered into a thousand swirling fragments.

He stood quite still, gazing at the flashing lights, the crowds moving around him as though he were a fixture on the street.

All that was on offer, for as far as he could see, was human flesh. The flickering signs were advertising it as though it were a brand-new discovery, some kind of miracle drug that would cure all ills.

It was all of the look-but-don't-touch variety, he knew. A fantasy mimicking substance. He found himself thinking again of Joe Deck's invitation yesterday. Of the real, hands-on pleasures that were waiting in the Garden District. He toyed with the idea a moment, then pushed it away. It would be better if he cooled down a little before jumping to a decision like that.

He started walking again, much slower this time, ambling across the intersection at Conti, gazing at the clubs and bars on either side.

There was another tug at his sleeve, as he stepped on to the far kerb. He looked around, into the face of a smiling frizzy red-head in her late thirties. Her clothes were too skimpy for her mature figure, and her face was overly made up in a feeble attempt to hide the dry thin lines.

'Hi, honey,' she simpered. Her voice had a throaty Cajun twang, harshened with cigarettes and booze. 'You looking for someone nice? You've found her. I'm as nice as pie.'

He pulled away, without answering her, and continued slowly on.

The doors of the strip joints were wide open, so that the shows could be seen from the street. Like baited traps, he realized.

Glancing inside, he could see red and purple lights in some, flickering, retina-jarring strobes in others. And, in all of them, women twisting and shimmying on the stages. They were wearing sequins, feathers, G-strings. All of them gyrated to the pounding beat of rock music, their movements so in sequence they looked completely unreal, like puppets. The bassline in each club was turned up so high it thumped against his eardrums, even out here on the sidewalk.

There were grinning men in shirtsleeves beside each doorway, calling out hoarsely to the passing crowds.

'In here, fellers! Right in here! The girls of your dreams, and they're shameless!'

'The most disgusting show in all Louisiana! I'm ashamed to be associated with it! Step right in and see for yourselves!'

Every time one of the hucksters noticed he was interested, Ted moved on quickly a few yards, like a pawn being nudged along a chessboard. But he hovered for a longer while outside each club. It wasn't the shows themselves that were beginning to attract him. He'd never cared much for striptease, even in his single days; it had always struck him as a tawdry and juvenile way to spend an evening.

But he could see more than the stages and the dancers, from out here. He could make out the audiences too. The men, sitting at their tables in the coloured, distorted light. Some of them were wide-eyed and smiling, bouncing in their chairs to the rhythm of the music, clapping and whistling. Others were hunched and silent, clutching their drinks in both fists, gazing, dull-faced, at the shows. But they all seemed remote from the outside world. No happy families in there. No laughing parents with their children. No students, no young couples hugging each other and smooching as they walked. None of the things that made him feel so much like a freak, an outcast, in his present state of mind.

Clustered in the smoky atmosphere, shoulder to shoulder at the tables, the men were like a huddled congregation at a neon church, shielded from the grim realities of life.

God, he needed to escape this damned Carnival. Needed to get away from these revellers, before he suffocated.

He moved towards the door of the nearest club. Didn't make it. A skinny, grey-eyed man, with elastic bands holding up his shirtsleeves and a dead cigarette in the corner of his mouth, jerked towards him quickly.

'In you go, pal,' he gestured. 'Just stroll on in. You'll have yourself a whale of a time.'

It was too sudden, too indiscreet. Too damned seedy, as though Ted were just another mug who could be hustled about and relieved of all his money. Ted grimaced uncomfortably and started backing away.

'Just looking, that's all.'

'Oh, come on friend!' The huckster seemed to realize he'd blown it, and his gaze hardened with contempt. 'What've you got to lose, your virginity?'

He said it so loudly that a few passers-by turned and stared.

Ted felt his neck grow hot. He spun on his heel and marched away. God, how many people had heard? What were they thinking of him now? A group of co-eds were strolling towards him, giggling, and he was sure they were laughing at him.

Jesus, he had to get *out* of here.

When he came to the next club, the Pink Bayou, he

didn't even think about it. He was sick of thinking. He just took a deep breath and, staring straight ahead, walked right inside.

2

Gorreq slowed his pace until he came to a soft halt outside Joe Deck's house on Carondelet.

He gazed at it for a while, studying it carefully. It was much smaller than its grand rococo neighbours, set well back in the depths of a tree-filled yard that hid most of its green-painted frontage from the street. He could hear the faint boom of a stereo, and the sudden high-pitched laugh of a young woman. One of the downstairs windows could be made out, through a screen of narrow branches. The blind was drawn, but flickering light was being thrown against it, from the inside; the sputtering, jerky light of a movie projector.

He reached out with his mind, and could feel eighteen, maybe twenty people in there. But Ted Hammond was not amongst them.

Gorreq looked around quickly, making sure he wasn't being watched. There was little need to worry about that – this close to Mardi Gras, the District was unnaturally quiet. Everyone was out in the Quarter or down on Canal Street, joining in the festivities.

He smiled to himself. Opened the wrought-iron gate and walked smoothly through the shadows to the front door. There was a shiny brass bell-pull to one side of the porch. When he yanked on it, everything went abruptly quiet inside. There was the squeal of a needle across vinyl, as someone killed the music.

'Who the hell's that?' he heard a woman say, in a nervous whisper.

'Shit, is that that moron Hammond?' came a Texan drawl. 'Don't worry, folks. I'll have this sorted out in no time.'

There was the bang of a door in the depths of the

house, a moment later, then the scuffing of bare feet across carpet.

'Who's there?' came Deck's voice, a little agitatedly.

Gorreq remained silent.

'I've got friends here, bud, and you're disturbing us. Now tell me who you are or go away.'

'Ted Hammond sent me.'

There was the rattle of a lock, and the door came open halfway. Behind it, trying to keep out of view of the street, was an absurd-looking Joe Deck. He was dressed in a makeshift Roman toga, and had a tinsel crown perched lopsidedly on his head. A half-smoked green cheroot was clamped between his teeth, and he shifted it with his lips now, staring at Gorreq curiously.

'Ted Hammond did what?' He squinted, aggrieved and puzzled. 'Look, buddy, I think there's been some kind of misunderstanding here. Teddy had no business to go inviting guests. Sorry to waste your time and all, but this happens to be a private party.'

'Are you sure?'

The man frowned with exasperation. 'Of course I'm sure!'

A door further along the hall swung open, and a woman stuck her head out. She was attractive, olive complexioned, and in her early thirties. Gorreq caught a glimpse of her bare shoulders through the floral see-through kaftan she was wearing. She was high on something. Her pupils were huge and sparkling black, and there was an infantile grin on her face that seemed entirely out of place under the circumstances.

She took a moment focusing, then looked him up and down. Her smile broadened admiringly.

'Oh, a big, *big* guy. I like the look of him. Be a sport, Joey cher. Let him in.'

Deck glanced at her annoyedly, his broad face growing fraught and sweaty.

'Get the hell back inside, Fleur. We don't have the first notion who this feller is.'

He was turning back, and Gorreq could already see

the words forming in his head. *No offence, good buddy, but I'm asking you to leave.*

He reached out and touched the Texan's mind. Very gently. Just enough to change it.

Deck relaxed suddenly, and chuckled.

'Well . . .' He puffed at his cigar. 'If Fleur likes you, I guess it's OK by me. Welcome to the Krewe de Chat, good buddy.'

3

The Pink Bayou was jam-packed. There was no room left at the big round tables to the darkened rear of the club. They were entirely taken up by a group of men who looked like they'd come from a convention, all in rumpled suits, their ties askew. They were wearing paper hats, and some had party streamers draped around their necks. All of them were drunk, red faced, and most were shouting obscenities at the stage.

Ted turned away, and eased through the crimson light just in time to see a man at the very front vacate a bar stool. He moved in before anyone else had the chance. Felt grimly pleased with himself.

He ordered a vodka from a harassed-looking topless waitress and glanced up, only to see the dark-haired dancer on the narrow stage finish her routine and stride off quickly into the wings. All he caught was a flash of her bare skin, but it set up peculiar tremors in his nerves, his muscles. The rock music faded for a moment. There were sardonic applause and cat-calls from the back of the club.

Then, the lighting changed colour to a sickly orange. 'Jungle' by the ELO came booming out of the crackling speakers, so loud it made his stool rattle, and two new women appeared.

They were both peroxide blondes, their hair throwing back the glaring light like mirrors. And they were both dressed as jungle animals, a leopard and a tiger, with costume ears and fake fur outfits, and flossy tails dragging behind them on the floor. Dark blue make-up turned their eyes into slanted triangles, and they had mascara whiskers painted across their cheeks. It made them look cruel and dangerous, but Ted found himself following their every move, enrapt.

To hell with Casey. To hell with the whole damned charade. He'd tried playing the good husband long enough. This fantasy unfolding before his eyes – why shouldn't he enjoy it for a while?

He found himself rocking gently to the music's beat. Gulped carelessy at his vodka, and spilled a little down his chin. It made him feel dizzy immediately. He hadn't eaten a thing since breakfast, was drinking on an empty stomach.

So what? Sooo fucking what?

He wiped his mouth, took another gulp, and concentrated on the dancers' gyrating hips.

'Having fun? I am,' a deep, faintly accented voice said.

It seemed to come from right beside his ear.

But when he looked around, he saw that no one was paying any attention to him; no one seemed to have spoken to him. The voice had sounded so close. Had he imagined it? Or was someone playing games with him?

He peered annoyedly at the men on either side, then decided to forget it, and returned his attention to the stage.

4

Casey was just putting the final touches to the table when the doorbell rang downstairs.

She jerked upright, her hands clasping together and her fingers knotting for a moment, and was just about to head down when she heard the faint clatter of a lock, then voices. Audrey had gone to answer it. Thank God for that. It gave her a minute or so to prepare herself properly.

She glanced around the living-room, and winced

uncomfortably. It looked unfamiliar, odd. Why'd she arranged it this way? Normally, it was conventional and rather sloppy, but had a homey, welcoming feel. Now, it was not only neat . . . she'd made an effort to transform it into something special, something a little arty. She'd arranged all her coffee-table books where they could be spotted instantly, when normally they'd be stacked beside Ted's reclining chair. And she'd draped the hand-made native tapestry she'd bought in Seattle over the back of the couch – something she'd been meaning to do since she'd bought it.

From the closet in the hall, she'd retrieved the perfumed oil-lamp – a confection of polished brass with a carved, frosted glass bowl – she had bought in the French Market the first week they'd arrived here. It was the first time she'd lit it since Ted had complained that the smell was gagging him. Well, screw him. It sat in the middle of the dining table, now, sputtering gently, the scent of jasmine filling up the room.

But why'd she done all this? Why'd she tried to make her home look a touch bohemian?

She felt intimidated by Susan, she realized. By this new and unexpected incarnation of her mother. For all her strangeness, there was an air of sophistication about the woman she'd never seen before. And she didn't want to be sneered at, looked down upon.

'Pete?' she called out. 'Are you ready?'

Pete came hurrying through, dressed in his best shirt and short pants. He'd combed his hair, slicking it down with a wet palm, and looked the perfect cherub. Casey made him turn around on the spot, inspecting him, then grinned and kissed him on his forehead.

He looked up at her sombrely, his eyes a little damp and puzzled.

'Isn't Dad coming back?'

She'd been trying to put that out of her mind ever since Ted had gone slamming out. 'I don't think so. But you know what *that* means? You get to sit at the head of the table.'

She gave him a wry smile, wrinkling her nose, then glanced out through the living-room's huge windows, past the curving balcony to the street below. Where had Ted gone? Of all the childish ways to behave. But . . . perhaps it was a blessing after all. She didn't really want Susan to see the tension between them, realize the marriage wasn't working. She remembered the arguments she'd had with her mother, all those years ago, and hated the idea of being proved wrong.

Of all the ways that life could fail you, this seemed the worst, the bitterest.

'Where *is* he?' Pete insisted.

'He had to go to the office.'

The lies came so easily these days, didn't they? Pete, however, wasn't buying this one. He shook his head, frustrated. 'But he—'

'I know, I know.' She crouched down in front of him, folding her hands gently around his shoulders, staring at him determinedly. 'But there's nothing to worry about. We'll tell Grandma he's at the office. No point upsetting her the moment she arrives.' She pecked him quickly on the cheek. 'OK?'

Pete nodded, but his eyes went a little cold and stern. Poor kid. He was frightened, deep down. Scared, because he didn't really understand what was going on.

There was the slow clatter of footsteps on the stairs. Audrey's voice drifted up. She was chattering away like a machine-gun, putting Susan through a polite, but thorough, interrogation. Casey grinned. It served her mother right.

She stood up, went to the big round mirror above the marble fireplace and made sure that she looked presentable. Christ, the corners of her eyes were slightly wet. She rubbed at them, and only succeeded in making the lids red. Then she took Pete by the hand and went out into the hallway, just as a knock came at the door.

Audrey was beaming like a homecoming queen, with Susan close behind her. Still in that wide black hat and tailored suit. *Still* in those damned sunglasses.

She was stiffly upright, like a carving that had come to life. Her expression was completely blank, bored-looking. Her mouth was slack and dead.

'Cher, you never told me your mama was so *beautiful*,' Audrey jabbered, barely able to contain her excitement; she seemed to have quite forgotten the earlier upset. 'And guess what? She's brought with her a most charming gentleman friend.'

A gaunt man, in a black tuxedo and bowtie, stepped into view from the shadows of the landing.

He looked Casey up and down smoothly. Glanced at Pete. Gave a swift bow of his head, then extended one pale, slender hand.

'Lucius Tharman,' he introduced himself.

There seemed to be a faintly sardonic tone to his voice. He wasn't American, though she couldn't place his accent.

Casey stared at him numbly for a moment. How pale he was. He and her mother looked like two porcelain statues. And those eyes. Violet, rather than blue. She'd never seen eyes that colour before.

As she reached out to shake his hand, she felt Pete grab hold of her skirt and let out a barely audible whine.

He hadn't done that for years, she realized. Not since he'd been a tiny child in New York, and a passing wino or a crazy had suddenly made him nervous.

5

She didn't like this Tharman herself, she realized a few moments later. Not at all. There was something arrogant about the way he strode in and began glancing around, as though he owned the place.

And what the *hell* was wrong with her mother?

She was following the man stiffly, keeping those blind-looking glasses fixed on him. Not even bothering to look down at her own grandson.

She seemed to realize her mistake after a moment, glanced at the boy and said, 'You must be Pete?'

A stiff, unconvincing smile fluttered across her lips. There was no emotion in her voice at all.

Are you on drugs? Casey thought, peering at her coldly. Is that why you're hiding your eyes?

Pete shifted uncomfortably and clung on to her skirt a little tighter.

Audrey was going, now. Audrey was saying, 'I'll leave you be. You all must have so much to catch up on.'

Casey felt her nerves twitch. *No*, she thought, *stay*. But she could only nod and try to smile, as Audrey wished them all a pleasant evening and went back down the stairs.

The door swung shut behind her. The latch clicked.

She followed the couple as they wandered through into the living-room. Tharman peered around again, and grinned superciliously.

'Charming.' The timbre of his voice was the precise opposite of Susan's, rich and full and purring. 'How very cosy.' His gaze alighted on the table, and the flickering oil-lamp at its centre. 'And that is a beautiful example of the local craftwork. But you're wasting its effect.'

Without even bothering to ask her permission, he went over to the dimmer switch and turned the lights down.

6

The lamp's deep, flickering glow spread out, like water in the burning ochre of a sunset. The whole room seemed to change in an instant. The big couch, and Ted's reclining chair, and even the dining table itself, became mere silhouettes, insubstantial and wavery. They looked as though if you tried to touch them your hand would pass right through.

Casey had familiar ornaments scattered all over the room, collected from the different places they'd lived, but she couldn't even see them now.

And the faces of Tharman and her mother . . . they had become indecipherable. Shadows danced across them, making their features shift. The glow of the oil lamp limned their edges, but that was all. They were both turned towards her, studying her, and she felt an uneasy tingle of menace.

Pete let out another whimper, louder than before.

And Casey, a sudden anger boiling up inside her, marched towards the switch, the boy hurrying behind her.

'There's no need for that,' she said curtly. 'You're scaring Pete.'

She took care to avoid Tharman's gaze, for some reason she couldn't quite understand. Grabbed hold of the dimmer switch, twisted it clockwise.

Nothing happened.

She turned it back the other way, then tried again. The lights stayed down.

'Hell!' She glanced accusingly at her mother. 'Now it's broken.'

'I'm so terribly sorry,' came Tharman's voice. He said it politely, but didn't sound at all sincere. 'I thought the effect might be pleasing.'

Yeah, right. If you liked Halloween in March. Casey bit the retort back, turned around. And this time she did meet Tharman's gaze. She peered angrily into those strange, pale orbs.

They, like his voice, were calm and faintly gloating. He was watching her admiringly, the same way he'd looked her up and down at the front door.

Jesus, what a creep. What the hell was Susan doing with this guy? Surely she realized he was gawping at her. But, if she did, she didn't seem the least bit bothered. Perhaps she'd fallen in with some pervy, arty crowd since the success of her last book.

Casey stared the man down fiercely, the way she would a masher on the street.

'Do you have any children, Mr Tharman?'

He shook his head. 'No. I'm afraid not.'

'Then maybe you don't understand. What's pleasant for adults isn't necessarily the same for kids.'

He seemed to consider that, pursing his lips. Then, he

did something that surprised her. He suddenly crouched down on his thin, angular knees, and reached out towards Pete.

'Nonsense. Children love a touch of excitement, a hint of mystery. It's only grown-ups who lose that innate sense of adventure. Isn't it, Petey?'

She was suddenly terrified of him touching the boy. She didn't want him laying those bony hands on her son. Again, she wasn't certain why she felt so anxious – but it was there. Thankfully, Pete edged a little further back behind her skirt.

Tharman didn't seem in the least put out. He simply straightened up again, and glanced at the place settings on the table.

She felt the urge to move them all into the kitchen, serve the meal in there, under the bright fluorescent strip light. How could she manage that without looking ridiculous?

She began to feel rather afraid. And for the first time in months, she really wished that Ted was around.

CHAPTER THIRTY-ONE

1

The dancers were edging closer to the front of the stage, and the men around Ted were getting five and ten spots out of their wallets, when everything suddenly faded. The first of the images floated into his mind.

A Mediterranean-looking woman. It was Fleur, from the office. She was in some kind of flowing, transparent gown. And moving closer to him. Wetting her lips. Reaching out a long-nailed hand towards his face.

A larger colourless hand moved out from the edge of his vision and pushed her roughly away. A hurt look came into her eyes. Her lips moved, but he couldn't hear what she was saying . . .

Ted blinked, and the club returned.

God, what was that?

It wasn't like the fantasies he'd had, about the wild party at Deck's. It was almost as though he'd just taken a look at the actual thing, through a camera. Or through someone else's eyes.

He shook his head, trying to concentrate on the strip show.

The girls had both dropped to a squat now, just within reach of the audience. Cheering, laughing men were shoving money into their bikini pants.

A white-painted room. The living-room of Deck's house. He'd seen it before. The lights were turned down. It was filled with sprawling people. Deck was sitting at the centre of them all, in a toga. Grinning. Laughing. There was a woman on either side of him. And a movie projector turning. Grainy images were being cast on to a bare wall, of a woman and a man wrapped around each other . . .

The dancers on the stage had stood up again, and were

starting to remove their tops, but Ted barely noticed. He couldn't fathom what was happening inside his head, where those weird pictures were coming from.

He clutched both hands to his brow, half-covering his eyes. His thoughts didn't seem to be entirely his own any more. The blaring music from the speakers was fading away to a dull murmur around him. He couldn't even hear the yells of the convention crowd at the back, now.

Look, but don't touch, came a deep voice.

It was the same one he'd heard a few minutes ago.

This time, he didn't even bother to look around. It seemed to be coming from right inside his skull.

That's all you'll get if you stay there, Teddy. There's more fun to be had than that. You know what I mean, don't you?

He thought of Casey. Thought of Pete. Battened to their images as hard as he could. But even as he tried to picture them, they seemed to dissolve, vanish. He couldn't quite remember what they looked like.

The scenes from Deck's house filled his head again. *Look at Fleur*, the voice said. *Isn't she gorgeous? Don't you want her? Look at the other women. That young blonde. That red-head. They're all here for the taking.*

He was easing himself off the stool now. Couldn't stop himself. He could barely make out the strip-joint any more and, his thoughts whirling like a carousel, he stumbled towards the exit.

2

'Hey, boy, what are you?' growled Joe Deck. 'Some kind of voyeur? You just gonna sit there all evening and watch?'

Sitting against the living-room wall, his back straight and his legs folded beneath him, Gorreq met the man's gaze coolly. He was a couple of yards back from the rest of the crowd, and had pushed away each of the women who'd tried to get up close to him. An old Velvet Underground album was booming out of Deck's expensive stereo system. Lords, this was a man who *really* lived in the past.

The party hadn't started in earnest, yet. Most people's attention, up until now, had been focused on the stag movie flickering across the wall, and on the joints that were being passed carefully around the room. It was as though they were all waiting for a signal to begin.

Gorreq stared at Deck unblinkingly, not saying a word, until the big Texan coughed and looked away.

'Well, different strokes for different folks,' Deck muttered to the rest of the crowd. 'We're a tolerant bunch here at the Krewe de Chat, now ain't we?'

Then, his mood changed abruptly. A broad grin split his face, and he reached behind the couch. His hand came out clutching a plain golden pill-box.

'Oh my Lord,' he chuckled. 'What in the world do we have here? I do believe it's party time!'

He flipped it open. Gorreq could see that it was filled with tabs of blotter acid, and breathed an inward sigh of relief. The marijuana they'd been smoking until now would only have kept them calm, and he didn't want them placid when he started to Feed.

It had to be a mild variety, or they wouldn't be able to do much once they'd taken it.

The box started passing from hand to hand.

It took a while getting to Fleur. She picked out a pink scrap, studied it a moment, then popped it in her mouth. Most of the others had already swallowed theirs and, even as he watched, the drug began to take effect. Dark pupils were widening. People were staring around the room as though it was the first time they'd ever seen it.

A blond, slim couple near the corner were peering at him curiously. Drugs sometimes did that, he remembered. Allowed people a closer look at him, at what he really was.

The couple both seemed worried now, glancing around anxiously at their companions, then back at him. And Fleur was staring at him as well, biting her lower lip and squinting, as though she wasn't sure what she was looking at.

He decided to reward their efforts. Let his eyes turn golden.

It got a different reaction from different people. The couple over by the corner let out amazed gasps and leaned towards him. Fleur moaned with fright, and started to wriggle backwards across the deep-pile carpet, on her ass. A balding man beside a huge cane chair looked around, gawped for a moment. Then, his whole body stiffened. He jumped to his feet, began to shriek.

Gorreq stood up briskly, walked over to him, and grabbed his smooth head in both hands. Lifted him off the floor.

He could feel waves of the man's blind terror surge into his body, filling him like rich, pure honey poured into a jar.

The man kicked and jerked, tried to swipe out with his fists, but couldn't reach him. Gorreq let him hang there for a moment, writhing, while everyone else in the room watched dazedly.

Then he squeezed, increasing the pressure until the skull burst.

'What the hell—?' Deck began mumbling, over by the couch. Some of the man's blood had spattered across his face. He was dabbing at it with his fingertips, goggling at it stupidly. 'What the goddamn *hell*—?'

Gorreq caught a glimpse of himself in a chrome-framed mirror, as he advanced towards a cowering woman with short black hair. His shape had changed entirely, without his even willing it. His massive body was as dark as pitch now, his golden eyes blazing in his gigantic horn-topped head.

The woman began shrieking, trying to scramble away. Who knew what she was seeing, under the influence of the drug?

He grabbed her by the ankle, hauled her towards him. Snatched hold of one of her flailing wrists, and lifted her. Twisted at her arm, working it free of its socket.

It came adrift with a ripping, sucking noise.

The others looked horrified, but they weren't moving. They were not sure – Gorreq realized with a nasty satisfaction – if he was real or hallucinatory.

Then the young blond couple – the ones who'd been so fascinated by him – staggered to their feet, babbling with terror. They began stumbling towards the hallway.

Gorreq threw a quick glance at the door. And it slammed shut, under its own power. The couple banged at it, struggled with the handle, but it wouldn't give. They couldn't get it open again, however hard they wrestled with it.

A second glance, in the direction of the stereo, brought the level of the music up, to hide their rising screams.

3

He saved Deck until last, and was rewarded with tears. The Texan knelt down on the floor as he approached. Clasped his hands in an attitude of prayer. Pleading, sobbing, all dignity gone.

Gorreq made the last moments of his life very slow indeed, concentrating on the ears and fingers, plucking them like daisies. The man was twitching like a dismembered frog by the time he finally killed him.

Gorreq let the pieces drop. Quickly resumed his human form. He went through into the kitchen and rummaged through the cabinets until he found a can of Bar-B-Q Kwik Lighter Fluid. Returning to the lounge, he sprayed the contents all over the furniture and the mangled corpses.

A cab drew up outside. Its door clacked open.

Casually, Gorreq stepped back to the hallway and fixed his gaze on Deck's movie projector. The film had reached its end, but was still running, the loose celluloid tail spinning around and clacking like a child's toy windmill.

The Incarnate's eyes flashed golden one last time. The machine shuddered, and toppled off its stand. It burst open as it hit the floor, showering the room with electric sparks.

The fluid caught light, and fire began to spread rapidly, washing the room with a leaping orange glow.

Gorreq reached out of the house with his thoughts, touched the cabbie, stopping him from driving away. Then he turned his attentions to Ted Hammond, taking control fully of his mind.

You're too late for the party, my boy. But what say we go elsewhere, and have a little celebration of our own? Just us two musketeers, huh?

4

Pete didn't like the bisque, but it seemed to go down well enough with everybody else.

Casey could barely taste it at all.

She hunkered over in the fluttering glow of the oil-lamp, feeling less and less at ease. Kept glancing at her mother, who was drinking her soup like an automaton, with her head bowed low.

There was plenty of dinner-party conversation, but Tharman was making all of it. He would ask her questions about her life and Ted's – no one had even remarked on Ted's absence, and that was odd – then wander off at a variety of tangents. He seemed to be much travelled and well read, knew an awful lot about history and geography, and spoke fluidly and interestingly. But he kept his eyes fixed on her, the whole time.

It ought to have repelled her. Yet she couldn't help falling under the spell of his deep, soothing voice every so often, returning his gaze intently.

She fought against it. But it was getting harder by the minute.

Cut it out, stupid. He's your mother's boyfriend, and besides, he's a creep. You don't like him. Keep telling yourself that.

But that insistent, inner voice – the voice of her own conscience – seemed to be growing fainter.

Pete, for his part, was taking no notice of the man. He kept glancing up at Susan's face, and squirming uncomfortably in his seat, the way he always did when he wanted to ask a question.

He took advantage of a pause in the conversation, and finally came out with it.

'Is there something wrong with your eyes, Grandma?'

An uncomfortable hush fell across the room. Casey stared at Susan pointedly.

'He's right, Mom. Here we are in the dark, and you've still got your shades on.' She smiled inquisitively. 'Is there some kind of problem?'

Susan stiffened in her chair, her spoon halfway to her mouth. Then, she looked at Tharman, as though she was seeking his approval. He nodded, his manner indulgent.

It practically gave Casey the screaming heebies. She had to struggle just to keep her temper in check. Did her mother need permission to take her *sunglasses* off? What kind of sick scene *was* this?

She only just managed to stop herself exploding. Pete had heard enough rows for one day; there was plenty of time later, when he'd gone to bed.

She watched as Susan reached up gingerly and removed the shades. Blue eyes suddenly glittered in the dim glow of the lamp.

Casey froze, all anger forgotten.

The woman's face was as slack and expressionless as it had been all evening. But the eyes themselves – red-rimmed and shining – there was a look of ghastly misery in them. Of deep, terrible pain.

Her lips moved, very gently. She was trying to say something.

Abruptly, Tharman cast her an angry glance. And something very peculiar seemed to happen to his own eyes. A thing so quick Casey was barely sure she'd seen it.

They seemed to glitter, for the briefest instant. Shine a brilliant yellow colour.

Susan's mouth clamped shut again.

Whatever was going on here, she'd had quite *enough*. Casey began pushing her chair back, getting up. Reaching out for Pete's arm, to hurry him out of the room. She managed neither.

There was a voice in her head, now. A whispering.

She felt her fear and anger drift away like wisps of firecracker smoke on a gentle breeze. Her body went limp and she dropped back into her chair.

Her eyes sought Tharman's face, and halted there.

She could see how wonderfully handsome he was, now that she took the trouble to look at him properly. And he was staring at her with such fierce adoration. His eyes were reflecting the lamp, but looked as though they were throwing out a drowsy light of their own.

She favoured him with her warmest smile, and he returned it.

5

The crowds around Canal were so dense that Gorreq had to abandon the cab on St Charles and walk the rest of the way. Ted kept pace beside him, trotting along like a marionette. His face was dead and his movements stiff, and he seemed oblivious to the chaos all around him, even when some passers-by bumped into him.

Another parade was edging down the broad straight thoroughfare. Everyone was pushing in to get a closer look. Gorreq could see the first of the floats. A woman in a sequined costume was perched on top of a huge model elephant. She was beaming and waving, a firework sparkler in each hand.

How many people were there here? he wondered. How many thousands? And not a single one of them realized what he was. To be alone, entirely self-contained, amongst all this surging humanity. To Feed, within an arm's reach of this throng. The idea of it amused him greatly.

He shouldered against the flow of the crowd, forcing a

path through it, until he reached the site of the Tutton Tower. It was entirely surrounded by a high corrugated-iron fence with barbed wire at the top. You couldn't see the lower floors from here. But the bare iron skeleton of the upper storeys loomed above them like a fossilized dinosaur in a museum, the girders criss-crossing the dark, overcast sky.

They stopped beside a door in the fence. Ted reached slowly into his pocket, got out his set of keys. He gazed at them dull-wittedly for a moment, then selected one, undid the padlock.

Once they'd stepped in, Gorreq locked the door again. The noise of the crowd dimmed a little.

He gazed around, inspecting the place. It looked exactly like a field after a battle. The earth was scarred and mangled, heavy gouges running through the loam. Earth-movers and diggers lay off to the sides, silent now, crouched like animals in a heavy sleep. There was a drainage pump beside the girders, to remove the water from the saturated New Orleans soil.

The naked Tower presided at the centre of it all. The wire cage of a construction elevator sat idly at the ground floor.

He could only see one way out, and that was through this door. Good. Very good.

He stepped behind Ted and, for the second time that evening, felt the change come over him. Felt himself transform into his godlike shape.

And then he let go of Ted's mind.

6

Ted blinked, alarmed, and gawped at the fence. Was he dreaming? One moment he'd been getting out of a cab on Carondelet, and the next . . . what was he doing here?

He glanced at the padlock. Shook his head bewilderedly. Fumbled through his pockets, but couldn't find his keys. Maybe the strain of this evening had got to him. Was he losing his mind?

He could hear the crowd roar, out on the street. Stepping back a little, he could see lights going past, their glow making the barbed wire at the top of the fence glisten like lights on a Christmas tree. God, he had to get out of here. His shoes slithered on the mud as he moved towards the door.

Then he stopped, his scalp stirring and prickling.

He suddenly felt sure that there was someone else in here. That there was someone behind him, staring at him.

There was a faint noise from back there. Something was scraping, very gently, across the soil. His whole body went rigid and icy, and he couldn't find the courage to turn. But what else was he going to do? Stand here all night, until he was attacked, hurt? A dozen ideas spilled through his head. Perhaps it was a thief. Or maybe it was just some wino who had got in from the street.

He squared his shoulders, and quickly spun around.

7

Gorreq waited for him to react, and felt a swelling disappointment when he didn't. Lords, how weak, how feeble, this man was. Hammond's eyes were widening, and the blood was draining from his face. But he could not so much sense fear from the man as numbness. As though Hammond's mind was trying to shut itself down, blank out what it was seeing.

Another float was going by, beyond the fence. The roar of the crowd rose to a crescendo.

As Gorreq watched, Hammond's knees began to fail him, began to buckle. This wasn't good enough at all. He had expected this to be a grand feast.

Gorreq walked forwards smoothly, his hoofs digging into the loamy earth. And, with the back of one hand, slapped the man's face, just hard enough to hurt him.

The man's eyes closed for a moment, and blood trickled

from the corner of his mouth. But when his face swung back he looked just as numb as before.

Anger surged through Gorreq. He grabbed hold of the fool by his jacket, lifted him. Flung him through the air. The man landed on his back against a pile of white sand and rolled to the bottom, gasping and coughing.

And then, at last, he broke out of his stupor and began to howl with terror.

The Feeding had begun.

8

There was someone yelling with fear. It took Ted a prolonged instant to realize who it was. *Him*. They were his *own* screams.

He scrambled quickly to his feet, his eyes fixed on the huge figure that was staring at him from the gate. What *was* that thing? For a moment, his mind tried to retreat again, but he wouldn't let it.

In stark black silhouette, the figure was perfectly still, regarding him calmly through a pair of burning golden eyes. It seemed neither man nor animal, but a strange mixture of both.

He realized what it had to be, after a moment. Someone in a bizarre Carnival costume. Some huge man in fancy dress.

Some kind of psycho.

How'd he wound up here, though? Ted still couldn't figure it out.

He was shaking all over, vibrating and sweating, as though he'd contracted sunstroke in the depths of the night. There was a tight ball of pain in his chest, and he couldn't swallow properly. But maybe, if he showed no fear, this lunatic might just go away.

His eyes darted about quickly for a weapon, saw nothing he could make any use of. Returned to the figure. It had clenched its right fist now, as though in a moment of decision. It took a heavy step towards him. Then another, its brush-ended tail dragging along the mud behind it.

It was staying between him and the door. There seemed no way to get around.

Ted paused a moment, then came to a decision of his own. Spun round, and bolted for the fence. Began running along it, banging his hands against the corrugated iron.

He shouted at the top of his voice.

'Hey! Out there!' He could hear people shrieking and laughing on the other side. 'Hey! Help me!'

Another roar from the crowd drowned him out. There was a high-pitched blast of trumpets, and the beat of marching drums. He waited helplessly for it to stop.

'Help me, someone! Please!'

He slammed so hard that the whole fence shook, but no one on the other side seemed to be taking any notice. And he could hear the madman coming up behind him once again.

A gleam just ahead caught his eye. It was a short length of scaffolding pole, half buried in the mud. He lunged for it, dragged it free. Struggled to keep his balance as he tightened his grip on the cold, tubular steel. He swept around, holding it point outwards, like a lance.

Drove it, as hard as he could, square into the middle of the costumed man's chest.

It was a blow that ought to have done some real damage. Broken a rib. Punctured a lung. But the man didn't even seem to feel it. He simply came to a halt, reached down, and snatched the pole out of Ted's grasp. Flung it to one side. An instant later, he was trundling forwards again, his arms outstretched. And Ted was backing away frantically, his arms flailing. The ground had turned to a quagmire beneath him.

He only got a few steps before he slipped. Landed on his back, the mud sucking at him. And the next thing he knew, the figure was towering above him.

Reaching down.

He rolled away just in time. Terror was driving him now. The pure force of adrenalin was pushing him on.

He scuttled to his feet, and ran in the direction of the skeletal tower.

The elevator cage . . . it was his only hope. He scrambled inside, not daring to look back. Punched the button that switched the power on. Threw the control lever. There was a rasping mechanical whirr.

And suddenly, he was being hoisted sharply upwards.

His sweaty, dripping fingers clung on to the wire mesh. Wheezing with relief, he stared at the receding ground. He could see the crazy man beneath him, his arms hanging limply at his sides, the great head tipped back to watch his ascent. Those weird golden eyes grew smaller, the higher he rose. Finally dwindled and seemed to wink out. And the figure was lost in the shadows.

Ted fell to his knees on the shaking metal floor, clutching at his chest. He was safe; even if he had to spend all night on top of this damned tower, it was better than going another few rounds with that costumed maniac down there. He could see the people on Canal clearly now, a pack of milling, brightly hued dots. He thought of calling out to them again, but they wouldn't hear him from this distance.

A breeze ruffled his hair, cooling the perspiration on his face. Ted looked up at the night sky. It seemed very close now.

As he watched, the clouds parted and a huge ghostly moon began edging out.

There was a bang, a shudder, as the cage stopped at the top storey. Wide steel girders, laid out in symmetrical patterns like a massive cobweb, stretched before him through the darkness.

He stood up, took a deep breath. Hit the big red knob which switched the power off, and then stepped out of the cage, his shoes clanking on the flat, cold steel. The height didn't bother him at all. He'd been on taller constructions than this.

He paused a moment, making sure his balance was steady, and then leaned over the edge and peered towards the ground again.

The figure was entirely gone from sight.

Got you, you bastard, he thought. Just try and get me here.

He teetered a little. His nerves were still shot. It would be a lot wiser if he sat down.

He yanked at his filthy, sweat-soaked clothes, trying to unglue them from his skin, then settled down, his feet hanging over the edge. Wild shudders started running through his body, as the ordeal he'd just been through began to sink in properly. He gripped the edges of the girder tightly with both hands.

And was just starting to calm down a little, when there was a sharp whine from the elevator cage.

The power had come on again.

That couldn't be! There were no other controls!

As he watched, it shuddered, ready to move. Ted panicked, grabbed out for it wildly. Almost fell.

The cage began to drop away.

CHAPTER THIRTY-TWO

1

The elevator pulleys were spinning inexorably, a mere three feet from his reach. Whirring counter-clockwise now. Rising, now. They'd barely paused at the bottom. Maybe he could stop them. Shove something into the main wheel and jam the cable. But there was nothing to do it with.

God Almighty! He climbed to his feet, hanging on to an upright, and looked down again. The cage was drawing closer by the second. He couldn't make out the madman himself, but a pair of golden eyes was blinking up at him from its depths.

His gaze slid to the girders of the storey below. They were too far down, too widely spaced, and there was no way of reaching them.

Ted began backing away, moving carefully on the high steel. Then, he turned and walked faster, dropping to a slight crouch. The girder took him past one of the site's enormous floodlights. The dead eye of the lens stared at him greyly as he shuffled past.

There was a switch up here somewhere. He was sure of that. But he couldn't remember where.

A dull boom resounded through the night air as the cage reached the top. A moment later, he heard the man step out on to the steel. It struck him as peculiar immediately . . . the tread didn't sound like shoes. Much harder and heavier than that. Almost like the stamp of hoofs. He spread his arms out to his sides, and made his way off the main girder at a right angle, along a narrower span.

Halfway across, he caught a glimpse of the ground, far below him. It seemed to rotate a little as he watched, swivelling clockwise. It appeared unreal, from this distance. Looked as though it couldn't hurt him. And for a moment, he was almost overtaken with the impulse to jump, get out of danger with a single leap.

That alarmed him badly, brought him sharply to his senses. Don't look down again, he told himself. The urge to jump from a great height was all bound up with vertigo, and that was something he'd never suffered from in his life.

His heart was pounding so fiercely it felt as though it was going to burst against his ribs. He reached one of the broader central girders, let his arms drop a little, and began making his way towards the western edge of the tower. He had one advantage, he realized, over the man behind him. He knew the layout of the building as well as he knew his own home. If only he could circle around, draw the man *away* from the elevator, and then double back—

The steady, even clack of footsteps was coming up behind him, far closer than it ought to have been. The dark figure had followed him along the girders easily.

He glanced back. Caught a glimpse of its huge bulk moving towards him between a pair of uprights. He let out a soft moan of dismay, and kept on going, the night breeze tugging at him as he moved.

2

Pete had gone very still. That was nice. It was good to be quiet and calm.

Casey watched, a soft smile on her face, as her mother put her sunglasses back on. That was good too. Those eyes of Susan's, so pained, so sad – it was ridiculous. There was nothing to be unhappy about. This Tharman was such a marvellous man. So impressive. So very charming.

Her eyes drifted back to him. She felt as though she were being wrapped up in light, warm sheets of golden satin, as he leant across the table towards her.

She reached out a hand. And he began to brush it

gently with his narrow fingertips. Her skin seemed to vibrate like a tiny chiming bell.

3

Ted reached the second floodlight before long. He didn't have to edge his way past, this time. It was set out on a platform, bolted to the main girder, with railings around its edge. He could make out a switch back there. And something else. Lying by the rail was a big chrome-plated spanner that some careless idiot had left lying around.

The whole structure juddered as he stepped on to it. He glanced over the railings at the mud below, and frowned. It took him a couple of seconds to recognize what he was looking at.

Clearly illuminated in the moonlight was a forest of closely set metal spikes. They were steel reinforcing rods, standing twelve feet high around the building's portico, waiting to have concrete poured over them come the end of Mardi Gras. From this height, they looked like a fakir's bed of nails.

His pursuer's tread was drawing closer. He crouched, picked up the spanner. It felt reassuringly heavy in his grasp. Then, he reached up with his free hand, closed his fingers on the light switch. If he could only blind the man for just a moment, get the drop on him.

He could see the silhouette quite clearly now, the bulky head, the curving horns, and the man's size made him shiver. The shoulders were wider than any he had ever seen. Wrestlers didn't have shoulders like that. Weightlifters didn't. The arms looked unnaturally short only because they were so broad. Those burning golden eyes were fixed on him intently. How did the man *do* that? He couldn't work it out.

He gripped the spanner tightly, his whole body trembling furiously. His head began to swim again. He couldn't stop it this time.

Curiously, he thought he could hear the madman

breathing. Perhaps he was imagining that. It was a heavy snorting, like an animal's.

A few more steps – and the figure was almost on top of him. He waited until it reached the edge of the platform.

And he threw the switch.

4

He'd meant to leap forwards with the spanner, strike quickly, in that frozen moment. But, as the blinding light poured out and washed over the figure, he found he couldn't move.

Couldn't believe what he was seeing.

There was *no* mask. It was *no* Carnival costume.

Captured in the circle of electric brilliance was a man's body, shadowy and dark, with parts of a huge beast grafted on. The legs were angled backwards at the knee. They ended in glistening cloven hoofs. Thick, oily hair lay matted from the waist to the ankles. The torso was human, and so were the muscular arms and the long-fingered hands. But the head, twisting away from the light now . . . it was the mighty head of a bull, rising seamlessly from the human neck. Saliva dribbled from its cleft lip. Steam billowed from its nostrils.

Ted let out a scream, certain he'd gone completely mad.

Before his astonished gaze, the creature's golden eyes squinted shut. The light seemed to be hurting it, somehow. The paler parts of its hide seemed to redden slightly, as though they were being scorched by an intense roasting heat.

It teetered on the girder and, for a wild, delirious moment, Ted felt sure it was going to fall.

Then it righted itself. Gave a furious, agonized howl, and came charging at him blindly.

There was no escape. No room to dodge aside. Ted straightened up alarmedly, and lashed out with the spanner as the creature closed on him. It struck uselessly against the side of the great head – there was a clunk of dense, impenetrable bone – and spun out of his hand, whirling away into empty space.

And then the whole platform was lurching dangerously. And the beast was crashing into him.

The impact knocked all the air from his body. He didn't even register the pain. He was being driven backwards, towards the railings.

Ted grabbed the creature by the throat with one hand, helplessly trying to shove it away. Snatched at the rim of the spotlight with the other, for support. It swung around, following him. Blinding him. Even when he shut his eyes, the glare was as bright as the sun.

The creature let out another yell of pain. More intense, this time. More highly pitched.

Ted's back slammed into the rails. But still he didn't stop. They were both moving too fast, too hard.

Everything was whirling. The world was flipping upside-down. They began to topple over the side, the searing light still following them.

The creature bellowed sharply, with alarm.

Ted suddenly forgot everything but the will to live. Grabbed at the topmost rail. Missed it. And missed the second. But his hand closed around the third and final one. Fastened around it like a vice.

He let go of the creature with his other hand.

It was sliding past him now. Pawing at him, trying to get a grip. It had been so strong before, so fantastically powerful. But now, it couldn't even manage to hold on. He felt its grasp slide down his leg. Had the light weakened it, somehow? The blazing yellow-white circle, which was still playing down on them?

They both seemed to hang suspended in its brightness for a second.

And then, with a sickening abruptness, he couldn't feel the creature any more. It was dropping away from him. Falling like a stone.

Ted watched it go.

It thrashed with its massive arms as it plummeted

downwards. But it didn't make a sound, all the way to the steel rods. The impact drove it on to them impossibly hard. The spikes exploded through its back and thighs. And then, it was sliding down them, impaling itself still further. It writhed furiously. Tried to struggle free. Ted could see it all perfectly clearly in the bright circle of light. Watched, as the creature's movements slowed. As the massive body became still.

Then, before his eyes, its shape became confused and indistinct. He couldn't make it out properly, for a moment.

When it resolved itself again, the bull-headed animal wasn't there any more. In its place was a huge, pale man, blond hair glimmering coldly in the moonlight.

Whatever it was, it shuddered one last time. Tried to raise its head.

Slackened.

Lay entirely motionless, pinned like a butterfly, at the exact centre of the bright circle of light. It was starting to dissolve now, but there wasn't time to watch that.

Ted looked up alarmedly, just as his grip on the rail slipped a little. His body swivelled to the left, his shoulder flaring with pain.

Canal Street swung like a pendulum below him. The people massed beyond the fence – he could see their tiny faces lifting towards him now. They'd finally noticed what was going on. A police motorbike, its red and blue lights flashing, was jockeying its way towards the kerb.

He set his teeth and, grunting, tried to swing himself the other way, get his right hand to the railing. But he couldn't manage it. Couldn't quite reach.

It was starting to bend under his weight. His feet kicked hopelessly against empty air, trying to impel him upwards, as he reached again.

His eyes screwed shut. He was almost crying now, breathing with heavy sobs. His palm, around the cold steel, was becoming drenched with sweat.

One more try. Come on, *do* it!

He lunged, too violently.

His grip slid from the railing. And then, he was following the creature, down towards the spikes.

Two words screeched through his head, as he fell. Two names. *Pete!* And *Casey!*

5

The change from her numb trance to alertness was so sudden, Susan almost yelled out loud.

One moment, she was watching through her darkened glasses as Tharman started getting up and moving towards her daughter, through the flickering lamplight. He disgusted her completely, at that moment, but she couldn't act.

None of her thoughts were more than half-formed. They were dim and blurred, and slipped easily from her grasp. She seemed to be watching the events unfold around the table from an enormous distance. There was nothing she could do about them; she was too far away. And she couldn't seem to draw any closer, however much she ached to.

She watched the hapless smile on Casey's face. The hungry leer on Tharman's. The room had become entirely silent, as though the night itself were holding its breath.

He had started reaching out towards the young woman.

And the next moment . . . it all changed.

Susan was still connected to Tharman's mind. And so she *felt* the tremendous wave of fear, then pain, rush through him.

She realized what had happened in an instant.

Gorreq had just died.

She didn't know how, but she was certain of it. It was as real as a gun going off beside her head. As a bomb exploding.

Somewhere out there in the surging, torchlit darkness, the priest of the war-bull Buchis had met his end.

She was still reeling with profound shock, when the link between her mind and Tharman's vanished. He'd let his grasp on her thoughts slip, like a leash dropping, unnoticed, from his hand.

Then she was unfreezing. Her head was clearing. She was rising startledly to her feet, like a sleepwalker awaking.

She was herself again, she realized. Her mind was entirely her own, for the first time in seven years.

It was like being hurled from a moving carousel. Her head spun, and she teetered wildly. Gripped the edge of the table to keep her balance. Looked across at Casey and Pete.

They'd broken out of their trances as well. They were both shaking their heads, their eyes hollow and their faces gaunt with fright.

There was a howl from Tharman.

Who was . . . clutching the sides of his face. Tipping back his head. Screwing shut his eyes and stretching his mouth open.

He let out another yell . . . a bellow of misery and pain so vast no human could ever have made it.

'*NO, MY BROTHER! NO!*'

It was loneliness, Susan realized. A terrible, bottomless loneliness, devouring him like acid. There were no familiar voices in his head now.

He was the last of the Incarnate.

6

His face started to grow shadowy and dim. His white, even teeth began lengthening, giving way to curving fangs. His features distorted, broadening and stretching.

They were all frozen with disbelief and horror, for a second. And then, everyone was moving.

Casey was edging away from the table. She almost stumbled as she backed into her chair. Susan reached out for Pete, trying to pull him out of the way. But he was screaming too, now. Wailing terrifiedly, insensately. As she touched him, he twitched back, not even seeing her. He dashed away, running to the couch. Disappeared behind it.

'Pete, *no*!' Casey started yelling. 'Pete, come *here*!'

Tharman had stopped howling now. Susan looked back at him.

The transformation was complete. A massive dog's head, with a huge ridged brow and tooth-lined jowls, met her frozen gaze. Matted black fur dangled from the crouching simian body. The eyes came open, burning furiously.

Susan heard her daughter start to shriek, but she took no notice. The creature's eyes were boring into her.

No! She steeled herself. If he took her back, Pete and Casey would be finished. She was the only thing that stood between them.

Tharman snarled viciously and stretched out a paw towards her. She backed quickly out of his reach.

Don't fight me, his voice croaked, inside her head. There was none of his usual suaveness. His smooth tones had harshened. He sounded shaken to the core. *Come back to me, my love, or I will kill you all.*

Bullshit! He'd been planning to kill her daughter and her grandson anyway.

She took another backward step. He started shuffling towards her, his tread very soft on the carpet. He was looming up again, filling her vision. In a moment, he'd be on her, at her throat. Running would do not the slightest good.

Her gaze flitted across the dinner knives – they'd be worse than useless – and settled on the oil-lamp.

She snatched it up, and flung it savagely at his face. But he was too quick for her. He raised an arm, knocked it aside as it swung through the air.

It crashed at his splayed leathery feet.

The glass shattered and the oil spilled out, igniting. Formed a circle of crackling flame.

Tharman grunted and backed away. The fur around his wrists had begun to curl and smoulder.

He tried to lunge at Susan, desperate and enraged now,

but couldn't get past the ring of flame. His canine features twisted, and he yelled with agony.

He paused a moment, his whole body shifting in the dancing ochre light. Then he was moving with its flow, turning, bounding away.

His shadow fell across the couch. There was a petrified shriek from Pete.

And now Casey was leaping forwards, yelling.

Too late. Tharman's shadow sped towards the windows. Crashed through them, to the balcony beyond. Swung over the railings, and was gone.

He'd been clutching something underneath his arm. Something that had kicked and struggled. Susan couldn't find the strength to move. She gazed at the shattered panes, a cold, dry horror swamping her.

Casey had stopped hunting behind the couch, and was now crunching across the broken, twinkling glass, out on to the balcony, shrieking her son's name.

She could yell all she liked. It would do no good. It wouldn't bring Pete back.

Footsteps were scuttling up the stairs. It had to be the older woman who'd let them in – Audrey – alerted by the noise.

Susan went over to the dimmer switch and turned it. The lights came up easily this time, and she peered about the smoke-filled room, her eyes starting to fill with tears.

She almost imagined she could hear Tharman laughing, in her head.

CHAPTER THIRTY-THREE

1

She drove slowly along Tchoupitoulas Street, late the next afternoon, her gaze scouring the docks which lined the north bank of the Mississippi. The sun was already dropping beyond a wide bend in the river, and she didn't have much time left.

She was exhausted and shaken, and handled the wheel of the rented Mazda uncertainly. Every so often, a passing car would swerve around and hoot at her, but she took no notice. Everything around her still seemed distant and unreal, as though she'd been newly born into the world of normal mortals, and her eyes hadn't quite focused yet. She still could feel her head reel, once every so often. Felt that she was losing balance, falling. And the sun – however low it sank – dazzled her, making her squint, she was so unused to it. Its light caused her soft white skin to itch uncomfortably, as though it were being rubbed at with a scouring pad.

It was a miracle she'd managed to get away from the apartment at all. The horror of Pete's kidnapping had been quite bad enough. But when, forty minutes later, a couple of uniformed patrolmen had turned up at the front door with the news about Ted . . . all hell had broken loose. Casey was in a hospital room now, under sedation. And Susan had spent all morning and most of the afternoon fending off questions from bewildered, angry detectives. They'd been hostile towards her throughout their interrogation. They knew that something quite out of the ordinary had happened in the apartment, and that she was part of it. But they couldn't work out what.

The entire NOPD would be hunting for Pete, by this

time. It would be no use. She was the only one who had the slightest chance of getting him back safely.

A short gravel track came up to her right. A few yards further back from the road, she could see a huge overgrown lot, beyond a rusted wire fence. She slowed the car and pulled off the asphalt, her tyres rumbling as she braked. There was a massive low-framed warehouse behind the mesh, its doors shut and its windows boarded over. A wharf lay to its left, edging out into the river. The whole place was littered with trash, smothered with weeds, and looked as though it had lain abandoned for years.

Susan let the engine idle. Perfect. This was exactly what she'd been looking for. Somewhere abandoned, isolated, where she could draw Tharman to her without being disturbed.

The gates were padlocked, but the chain looked nine-tenths rust. She got a tyre iron from the trunk, and snapped it easily, drove the car inside. She parked it behind the warehouse, out of sight of the road, then went back to the trunk and hefted out the three steel cans of gasoline she'd bought at a filling station down the road.

A shiver ran along her spine as she carried them towards the wharf. She was taking the worst risk of her life. But what choice was there? Leave Pete to die?

She simply couldn't do that.

It looked as though the place had been a lumberyard at one time. There were broken sun-bleached planks of timber strewn amongst the weeds, and the ground crunched beneath her feet as she walked. It was liberally strewn with wood shavings and sawdust.

All the better to burn with, she thought grimly.

Traffic hummed by distantly on Tchoupitoulas, like a swarm of busy insects.

She opened the first can and began walking backwards along the edge of the wharf, pouring the gasoline carefully, trying to make a perfect circle. The pungent, sickly odour of the fuel made her head reel, but it would fade before darkness closed in entirely. She *hoped* it would. There was a slick of engine oil lapping along the side of the dock, letting out its own putrid, rotten-egg stench. With any luck, it would cover any residual smell, and Tharman wouldn't even notice.

If a small ring of fire had driven him away, last night . . . then maybe a larger one could destroy him. She hoped to God that she was right. The alternatives didn't bear thinking about.

The last of the fluid dribbled out. She shook the can and tossed it aside, started on the next. She completed the outer edge of the circle – it was at least ten feet wide, she judged – and then began working quickly, taking less care of accuracy, filling it in.

It was getting a little easier to see straight, by the time she'd finished. The dazzling sunlight was almost gone. She walked away from the gasoline, letting the fumes disperse, and glanced towards the west.

Only the top rim of the sun was visible, wavering and rippling above the edge of the far bank. It had turned a brilliant crimson, and looked distant and strange. But oddly – however much it pained her – she didn't want it to disappear. Didn't want to lose sight of it altogether. It served to reassure her she had returned to the normal world. Was the only thing that did. She felt like reaching out and trying to grab hold of it, stop it sinking. Once it vanished, she'd be trapped in the dark realms Tharman inhabited, once more.

Calm down, for Pete's sake. Quite literally, Pete's sake.

She shivered, took a box of matches out of her jacket pocket. Her hands were trembling badly.

This wasn't going to be easy. There was one possibility she'd already considered a hundred times. That if she managed to lure Tharman into the ring of flame, she might get trapped in it herself.

There wasn't much option, she realized.

Images kept flooding into her thoughts. Photographs, taken by those war journalists she'd studied all those years ago. Of people roasted in fires, blasted by napalm, their skins a flaking, blackened crust, their corpses hideously twisted; jaws stretched open in a final endless shriek of torment. She started thinking of herself that way. Felt ill. Tried to push the idea from her mind. Pete's safety was the only important thing, now.

There was a low bellowing noise from the direction of the city. She almost yelled as she whirled around.

It was only the horn of a big grimy freighter, sitting low in the water, plying its way smoothly along the dusk-shadowed river towards the Gulf of Mexico.

The sun had practically set by now. A dwindling shard of ruby red was all that remained. Lights had begun sparkling through the gloom, from windows, from streets. White electric lights, everywhere she looked. It was as though the constellations had dropped from their high perches and settled around New Orleans.

The air was cooling quickly. Goosebumps started rising on her arms and neck. She took a deep breath, straightened herself, and then walked back into the ring.

To its direct centre.

Stopped, rigid.

She stared back at the gates, the fence. Could see nothing. Absolute darkness had settled over the lot.

A car went by with its radio blasting. Inside, a bunch of kids were shouting, laughing. They were probably on their way to the Carnival, and were already excited at the prospect of the evening that lay, stretched out, before them.

And her? Might this really be the last night of her life?

Something else drifted into her mind. Tharman's face, the lips moving. Tharman's voice, telling her that she would live a very long while, that nothing would harm her, that the world was hers. It was only a memory, she knew, but it pained her terribly. It was so very tempting. Didn't she want to go on living? She thought of all the places she had been, all the things she had done. The excitement and the luxury and the sensuousness of it all. Didn't she *still* have so much to do?

No choice, she kept telling herself, reciting it like a mantra. No choice. No damned bloody cocksucking choice.

She was holding the matches out in the open, where they could easily be seen. Dammit, she was doing this all wrong. She hid them quickly behind her back.

Tharman would be up by now, she realized. And he'd be reading her thoughts. He'd know about the trap long before he reached her, if she wasn't careful.

She tried to block it out. Thought about other things. Two times two is four. The Presidents of the United States are, in ascending order . . . She stared towards the clustered lights of the city, wondering where he was.

I'm here, my Tharman, my love. Come to me. Please.

She pushed out the thought insistently. Knowing he would hear it. Hoping it would draw him towards her.

I'll be yours again. I'll always be yours, till the day I die. No need to use the Voice on me, my love. No need for that. I'll go with you of my own free will. I'll go gladly. I promise.

It was all a lie, but she hoped he didn't realize that.

From the darkness, there was no answer at all.

2

The night's coolness had been working its way into her body for some time, making her bones feel hollow. Her fingers had grown stiff around the matchbox. There didn't seem to be much feeling left in them. Perhaps she was gripping it too tightly. She wasn't sure how long she could keep this up.

The stars had come out, glittering distantly, by now. And the sallow moon had begun to rise above the warehouse roof, like a swelling, white balloon.

She swung her gaze towards the gates, once more.

And suddenly, the shadows moved. She twitched violently. Waited for something to happen. Nothing did.

Her eyes had started playing tricks on her. The harder she stared, the harder she tried to make sense of the shadows, the more they appeared to shift and slide.

There was a faint murmur behind her on the river. It

was drawing closer as she listened. Her whole body went stiff. Her neck felt so tight she could practically hear the vertebrae grate together.

There were several noises now, and they became jumbled. She couldn't make out what they were. It sounded as though a crowd of people were hurrying across the water towards her.

When she finally turned her head, a sparkling brilliance met her gaze, gleaming on the darkened, reflective Mississippi like some huge back-lit jewel. The regular thrum of an engine, the slap of blades, and the brassy timbre of a jazz band drifted to her ears. It was a large boat, a paddle-steamer, out on a night-time cruise. A party was under way on board.

Her gaze remained fixed on it, mesmerized, for a while.

Then she remembered herself, and turned back towards the fence.

A pair of golden eyes was staring at her through the darkness.

3

Susan forced a smile, hoping it looked genuine.

Was the thing behind the eyes still in the form of a man? She couldn't tell.

'My love,' she whispered, keeping her voice as sweet and even as she could. 'I'm so glad you've come. I was so alone, without you.'

He didn't move at all. His eyes hung suspended like a brace of tiny lanterns in the blackness. The rest of his body was lost in the deep shadows that crawled about the lot.

Where was Pete? She couldn't see him either. Susan's blood ran cold at the thought that he might already be dead. But somehow, she kept calm. Managed to keep the warm, adoring simper plastered across her face, like a thin rubber mask.

God, she could still smell the gasoline.

'Why are you standing there, my love?' she asked. 'I'm completely yours. Come, take me.'

She felt an odd prickling sensation, like a beetle crawling across her scalp. Tharman was trying to probe her thoughts. No. She had to keep her mind clear until he was inside the ring. She resisted him, concentrating furiously.

'There's no need for that,' she insisted. 'I promise. I'll come with you willingly.'

She could hear her voice growing higher pitched with every syllable. The smile was melting from her face, now. She couldn't stop it. How could she ever have imagined she could trick him?

She made one last, desperate try.

'I'm . . . I'm sorry for what I did last night, but I was frightened, confused.' Tears began to prickle at the corners of her eyes. Her whole body seemed to be vibrating gently. The skin. The bones. The muscles. As though she were beginning to shake herself apart. She couldn't hold the question back any longer. 'Where's the boy?'

He's here.

Tharman's drowsy voice, in her head, made her jerk. She fought hard to compose herself again. Drew herself up straight.

'Show him to me, please. I want to know he's safe.'

Have I ever lied to you? Ever? His voice resounded angrily inside her skull. *The way you're lying to me now?*

Susan felt her teeth grind. He *did* know what she was up to. He *knew* what she was planning. She'd been an idiot to have ever believed she could get the better of him.

His eyes started growing larger as they drifted gently towards her.

4

The starlight gradually revealed him. He was dressed exactly as he'd been the night before, in the black tuxedo and bow tie – but they were rather crumpled now. His dark hair was unkempt, a few strands dropping lazily across his forehead. He was carrying Pete, a slim hand beneath each arm, as though the boy weighed next to nothing.

Her grandson was completely stiff, his face hard and lifeless, his feet dangling limply. His eyes were glossy and unblinking.

Let him *alone*, you bastard monster, Susan fumed. Let go of his mind. He's just a child!

Tharman chuckled coldly, in her head. He'd heard the thought, as though she'd spoken it.

He reached the edge of the ring, stopped. Looked down for a moment, at the damp gloss on the blades of grass. And when he raised his head, the grin on his face was bare toothed, a skull-like rictus, bitterly annoyed. His eyes seemed to widen, and their golden glow grew brighter.

Susan squared her feet, held her ground.

Tharman set the boy down idly, at the edge of the ring.

Then, he lifted his right hand, the upraised palm held flat. He curled his fingers a little.

The box of matches suddenly jerked in Susan's grasp. It started shifting, twisting from side to side, its edges rasping against the skin of her palm. She tried to get her other fist around it. But before she could do so, it was free, drifting into the air. She snatched at it, almost over-balancing, but it had already sailed out of her reach.

It alighted gently in Tharman's hand.

He stared at her a moment, registering her surprise, and then studied it coldly.

5

Did you really think that you could kill me? he asked, very quietly. *I, who have seen a thousand armies march into oblivion? A thousand emperors rise, and wane, and return to the dust?* He rolled the box into his fingers, where he clutched it tentatively. *I, who gave you everything.* His smile relaxed a shade, becoming calmer, the annoyance draining away. Being replaced by something else. *Do you really want to kill me, Susan?*

Still holding the box, he started walking into the ring.

Susan tried to back away, but found that she could barely move. It wasn't that he was stopping her. More as though her body had given up. Stopped trying to run because there was nowhere left to go.

Dimly, she could hear the music from the paddle-steamer, out on the dim river. It might as well have been coming from another universe.

Tharman stopped, so close to her his face blocked out the lot. He lifted a hand, brushed it gently along her cheek. It wasn't thin or pale any more. It had transformed into a large dark claw, the thick, blunt nails scraping her as they travelled across her skin. Strands of fur hung from the cuff of his shirtsleeve, shifting idly in the cool air.

Susan shuddered, and bit her lip, fighting back a groan.

Her gaze darted towards Pete. The boy was still standing exactly where Tharman had left him. As rigid as a mannequin, his eyes bright with a damp mirrorlike veneer.

Run! she begged him silently.

Please, while you've still got time!

She looked back at Tharman, afraid he'd notice. But he seemed too intent on her. His hand had reached her cheekbone now, and was moving up towards her brow.

It stopped there, the cold, dry flesh pressing against her temple. She was growing more surprised by the second. She'd expected him to kill her, tear her limb from limb. This was almost as though he were trying to Feed. Almost, but not quite.

He *still* wanted her back, she realized with a shock.

His eyes started growing so hot looking into them was painful. His voice started cutting through her brain like a razor-edged knife.

Do you honestly believe you can go back to the way you were? Do you want that, deep in your heart? There was none of the usual dry sarcasm in his tone. He sounded . . . almost sad for her. *Besides, do you think they'll* have *you back? The humans?*

She peered at him stupidly, her heart turning over like a chainsaw engine. What was he trying to do? Twist her mind around? *She* knew what she wanted. And that was Pete. And Casey. She wanted their warmth, their love, their closeness, their affection. Not that she was going to get it, now. He'd never let her, would he? One way or another, she'd be denied all that.

Tharman's smile became as downcast as his voice. He almost looked as though he pitied her.

You have been so strong up till now, my love, he said. *But are you strong enough for one last thing, I wonder? For the truth?*

What kind of insane game was this? she thought. If he wanted her back, despite everything, why didn't he just use the Voice-that-whispers? But she had no option but to play to his rules, at the moment. She clenched her lips, and gave a stiff, sharp nod.

His palm shifted position slightly, on her forehead. His glowing gaze became faint and distant. And suddenly – as she'd done before – she could see through his eyes, feel through his mind.

She could feel him reaching out across the packed, glittering city. Feel him reaching into Casey's room, in the hospital. Susan jerked as he touched her daughter's mind.

And, abruptly, she could hear the young woman's thoughts.

Casey was just coming out of the sedative she'd been given. It was like bobbing to the surface of a milky, troubled sea. Her mind was still scrambled, and every time she tried to clutch on to a fully-fledged idea it disintegrated in her grasp. But there was a formless anger, swirling deep inside her, that made Susan jolt with fright.

Ted's dead. Pete's gone. God, let this be a nightmare! But it's real, isn't it! Thought I was unhappy before. Thought I was living in a bad dream. But this! *If only I'd known.*

Her fault. The bitch's fault. She brought that thing *into my home. The thing that took my son.* She *brought it. Let it touch her. Let it love her. Followed it around like a dog.*

Sick bitch! Ted was still alive, before she came. Pete still had a father. I still had a son.

What's she turned into, that sick bitch with her photographs? She left us alone, all these years. Why did she have to come back?

'Stop it, please!' Susan heard herself gasping. Her voice seemed to be coming from a great distance away.

Tharman's touch drew back slightly, and the contact with Casey was broken.

Thank God.

Susan's head began pounding. Her own thoughts were descending into a bottomless, swirling morass. She might have started crying again – but she wasn't sure. She felt entirely disconnected from her body.

No, Casey couldn't hate her that much! That couldn't be the truth, could it?

'She'll . . . snap out of it,' she mumbled hollowly. She was talking to herself more than Tharman, she realized. Trying to reassure herself. She lowered her head slightly, shook it, as though in an attempt to loosen the grip of the pain. 'She'll realize it wasn't my fault . . . in time.'

Will she? Tharman asked. *Are you certain of that? Or do you need more?*

His grip tightened again. And abruptly, she was travelling with his mind once more. It was sweeping further still across the city, to a precinct house in the French Quarter. In a scruffy room with fluorescent strip-lights on the second floor, the detectives who'd interviewed her were hard at work. Some of them were on the phone. Others were going through thick files of old cases. But whatever they were doing, their thoughts were all the same.

Dig that Susan fucking Carroll! I don't believe a word she says. She's up to her eyeballs in this.

What is it with that weird broad? She's in league with her boyfriend, that's for sure. Some kind of hoodoo black-magic thing, I'll bet.

Her own grandson! Jesus! Let's pull her in again, and book her. Accessory to kidnapping. It'll stand up in court.

Susan blinked, and the shadows of the wharf returned. Tharman had let go of her altogether.

She stumbled back a couple of paces, as though she'd just been smacked in the centre of her forehead with a hammer. That was exactly how it felt. As though her brain had been struck. Jarred, so that the grey pulp had become dislocated and jumbled within her skull. It was barely any use for thinking any more. Not for rational thoughts. A terrible violent panic was starting to rush over her, like a breaking tidal wave.

She was drenched in its cold ferocity for an instant. Couldn't move. Couldn't breathe, in or out.

Tharman was still gazing at her, his shoulders slumped a little wearily, his thin arms hanging limply by his sides. And . . . something strange had happened to his eyes. Something she'd never seen before, in all the years she'd known him. They weren't bright any more. Their glow had diminished to a faint diluted amber, tinged with just a smear of red. It was as though the intense, cruel fire behind them had finally burnt itself out. All that was left were the embers.

Do you still, he asked sombrely, *want to go back to them?*

It was all a deception. *Had* to be. She *had* to keep telling herself that. She didn't know quite what his motive was, but he'd made up all that stuff about Casey and the cops. Made it seem real. That was the only *possible* explanation.

She began moving away from him, her legs practically giving way beneath her, her shoes scraping awkwardly across the ground. Began moving around him, towards the little boy. Tharman didn't follow her, except with his face, his faded eyes.

Finally, she reached Pete. She hunkered down in front of him, gripped him by the shoulders. Shook him. He didn't respond. He was as stiff as a board, his eyes wide, his face pursed into an unmoving frown.

'Pete?' His name husked out of her throat like a sob. 'Petey? Wake up! Look at me!'

She gave him another shake, harder than before. Got nothing in return.

Glanced back at Tharman, who was still at the centre of the ring of gasoline.

Let him go? Please?

The words formed themselves inside her head. But before she had the chance to speak them, the priest of Thoth raised his left hand slightly. Clicked his fingers.

The rigidness beneath her palms turned into living, moving flesh. The boy was squirming, trying to get away. She turned back to him alarmedly.

His eyes widened to circles, and he howled with fear.

'*No*, Petey! Be brave! I won't let him hurt you!'

One of his small hands flailed up and hit her, just beneath the nose. It didn't hurt, but it stunned her all the same.

Because suddenly – she realized.

Realized the truth.

The boy wasn't looking at Tharman. He was looking at *her*.

Her head swam, and her grip relaxed. Pete wriggled away from her, still shrieking with stark terror. Started moving backwards. Tripped and fell. Even then, on his back, on the ground, he kept on trying to push himself away from her.

She didn't want to make him more frightened than he already was, so Susan remained still, watching him numbly. Her hands were outstretched towards him – but all her fingertips were touching, now, was the empty air.

She heard the quiet, even crunch of shoes as Tharman moved up behind her.

Now do you believe me? His moonlit shadow fell across her arms. *He associates you with me. With bad, terrible things. With the horrors of last night. With monsters. With disaster. They all do. All the humans who know you.* His touch alighted, like a huge delicate insect, on her shoulder. *You've spent too long in the night, my love. You belong to it, now.*

The words sank into her mind at a snail's pace. Like

pebbles in a tar pool. She wanted to reject them, but they wouldn't stop. It took what seemed an age before the surface closed around them and they were absorbed.

And when they finally were, she ought to have cried her heart out. Really wanted to.

But there were no tears left. Not in her heart. Not anywhere else.

All that she could do was watch – coldly, drily, as though from a great distance – as the little boy tried to get up to his feet, and tumbled down again. Still moving back, away from her. Was Tharman making him fall?

She'd come to save him, hadn't she? Any way she could? Whatever the consequences to herself?

She came to a decision.

'Let him go.' She said it quietly, but with great determination. 'Let him go now. Let him and Casey live, unmolested. Do that for me, and I'll be yours until the end of time.'

She raised her left hand and, very slowly, closed her fingers over Tharman's. He let them rest there. Didn't demur. She knew why. He was just as alone, tonight, as she was.

Now she understood why he'd let her make her own mind up, and hadn't used the Voice. Having a vacant dummy by his side, down all the years that lay ahead, would be worse than having no one.

The boy had managed to get up now, and was running with all his infantile might towards the open gate, his feet scampering furiously. He didn't look back once.

Susan gazed after him, wanting to follow, knowing that was hopeless. As impossible as flying to the moon by flapping her arms. And, as his tiny form diminished, the whole world seemed to pull back from her. Draw away. Recede. Contract.

The darkness covered everything, and her body became as cold as the night.

Goodbye, sweetheart.

She closed her waterless eyes for a moment.

Try to have a happy life.

When she looked up at the gate again, Pete was just scrambling through it. He hurried up the gravel track, reached the sidewalk, and a moment later she could see his tiny silhouette bobbing along behind the wire fence, in the direction of the city.

He'd only got a couple of dozen yards when a blue-and-white patrol car eased up alongside him, flashing its red lights briefly. The passenger door clacked open.

Susan got to her feet.

6

'Hey, kid, what's your name?'

'Jesus *Christ*, it's the Hammond boy!'

Susan could hear the cops' voices perfectly clearly, drifting across the river-quiet night air. She huddled back against Tharman a little, glanced at his face. He'd let his eyes go back to their normal violet, and looked entirely unconcerned.

One of the cops was on the radio now. Within ten seconds, a second patrol car was speeding towards them along Tchoupitoulas. Its lights were ablaze, its siren wailing. It skidded to a halt and both the men inside jumped out.

'They're in there?' one of the first cops was asking Pete. The boy was pointing at the fence. The cop followed his gaze, and stiffened.

He could *see* them. Jesus Christ! Susan looked at Tharman again, who had started to smile. Do something! she thought. Use the Voice!

'Get him out of here!' another of the cops was shouting. 'Get the kid out of here! Ray, call for more back-up!'

Holsters were being unclipped, guns drawn. Pete was bundled into the first car. Susan watched desperately as he was sped away, hoping to catch a last glimpse of his face through the windows. She got none. She ought to have registered pain, at that, but there wasn't even time.

She could hear more sirens now. They were distant,

but closing fast. Both ends of Tchoupitoulas looked as though they had started burning with a dancing scarlet flame.

She unconsciously pushed herself harder against Tharman, as though she were trying to burrow inside him. He was smiling faintly, now. Why?

'For God's sake, stop them!' she snapped. Her voice was quavering with terror. 'They can't hurt you, but they can damned well *kill* me!'

His only response was to swivel round a little, and toss the matchbox back to the centre of the gasoline ring.

This was unbelievable! She truly *needed* him for once, and he was doing nothing.

A third car pulled up, then a fourth, a fifth, each with a squeal and the stench of dust and rubber. Then an unmarked Lincoln, with a flashing red beacon stuck on to the roof, arrived. One of the two plainclothes men who got out went back to the trunk. Susan heard the loud, unmistakable clatter of a pump-action shotgun being loaded.

She grabbed at Tharman's sleeve with her fingernails. '*Do* something!'

There was another noise now, below all the others, coming in along the river from the direction of the sea. She glanced to her right, and saw the black speck of a helicopter scurrying towards them, its spotlight playing along the wharf-lined bank.

'Let's go!' she heard the detective with the shotgun say. The others started following him along the gravel track.

What was this? Had Tharman been playing with her all along? Had he *intended* her to die? His smile had grown still broader on his narrow face, as though the whole thing were an enormous joke.

She could hear the policemen's boots coming towards them, and the rattle of the handcuffs and nightsticks on their belts. She stiffened with alarm. Their silhouettes began emerging from the shadows. They were spreading out, as they approached.

The moon was far higher by now. Its light caught the

furious, glinting eyes of the detective with the shotgun, making them seem huge and silvery. He was a balding, squarely built black man, in a three-piece suit. His face was damp with perspiration. His bushy eyebrows were drawn together angrily.

He had his massive gun levelled directly at Tharman's chest, his aim unwavering. And he got within twenty yards of them before he stopped, glowering balefully.

'Stay exactly where you are, both of you! Put your hands on your goddamn heads!'

Her whole body was shivering again. She wanted to try and explain, knew it would do no good. Susan started to do as she was told.

Except Tharman ... wouldn't let her. He simply reached out, very smoothly, and took hold of her left hand with his right, gripping the heel of her palm between his thumb and fingers.

Her face whirled towards him. Her mouth started opening around a protest. But he wasn't looking at her. Nor taking the slightest notice of her. His attention was focused completely on the cops.

'You two *deaf*?' she could hear the black cop shouting. 'I said put your *hands* on your goddamn *heads*!'

Most of the uniformed men had lined up around him, their feet splayed and their knees bent, their revolvers held out in front of them in both hands, arms extended. A couple more were circling cautiously around to the sides, staying out of the line of fire.

There was an ear-splitting roar as the helicopter began to hover overhead. A few of the men's eyes flicked up to it, then jerked back down again. It was so loud, it seemed to make the ground tremble. Or was that her, trembling? Susan wondered. Its spotlight washed over her, brilliant and blinding. The downdraught from its rotor blades made her clothes flap. Locks of her hair shifted across her face like seaweed. Like tendrils, suddenly alive.

The grass and weeds began to hiss, around her feet, and the air started to fill with flecks of sawdust.

The black cop was still shouting at them. She could see

his mouth snapping open and shut, but she couldn't hear the words. Several of the uniformed men had joined in. She couldn't hear them either. The helicopter was drowning them out. Their eyes were becoming wide with panic and anger. They couldn't understand why they were being ignored.

What are we going to do? *What?* Stand here like this all night?

As though in answer, Tharman's steadying grip changed to a gentle pressure on her hand.

A forward pressure.

Her mouth came open in a perfect zero of terror.

NO!

He relaxed a moment, then tried again. He wanted them to start moving towards the cops.

Susan's entire body seemed to have frozen to a block of ice. Except for her stomach, which was churning, boiling. This was crazy. It would be like taking a step towards a firing squad. The cops were so keyed up by now, they'd shoot the moment she and Tharman moved.

This was downright insane! But the pressure on her hand wouldn't go away.

It wasn't the Incarnate who finally made her mind up, though. It was – after a few seconds' more thought – herself.

She finally . . . gave up. Just . . . quit. Stopped trying to resist. She was so scared, by now. So numb. So confused. She'd lost everything. Become the toy of an irrational monster. And to hell with it. To hell with it all. Hadn't she been prepared to die tonight, anyway?

She couldn't take this a moment longer – trapped in this searchlight like a moth, with all these yelling cops around her, all these guns.

To hell with it. She readied herself. Felt her throat tighten. Felt her insides contract. Felt a strange, bulging pressure behind her eyeballs, and a squeezing like an angry hand around her heart.

She took a shaky breath.

Tipped her head back a little, exposing her throat, and let her eyelids flutter shut.

To hell with it all. The whole damned lot of it.

It's better, this way.

What would it be like, when the bullets plunged into her chest? How would it feel? Would it hurt, or wouldn't there be enough consciousness left for that?

Anyway, to *hell* with it.

Keeping time perfectly with Tharman, she took her first step forwards.

7

Nothing happened.

She wasn't quite sure which was worse – the crack of gunfire, or this.

She stopped again, sharply. Opened her eyes, just a tiny gap.

Beyond her quivering lashes, she could see the cops, exactly as before, still pointing their guns at her and shouting. As though that step had not been taken.

There was another tug on her hand.

She took her second pace forwards.

Now?

Something very strange was happening. She realized it the moment she took the third step. She could see the detective's eyes quite clearly. And they didn't seem to be focused properly on her. Rather, on something just behind her. He seemed to be looking *through* her body.

She glanced questioningly at Tharman, then tried to look back over her shoulder. But he gave her a quick, discouraging tug, and kept on leading her forwards.

They passed right in front of the detective. So close that Susan could have reached out and brushed her hand along the barrel of his gun. But it was only when they'd walked right past him, and stepped outside the ring of cops, that Tharman allowed her to turn her head.

Her sight wavered for a moment. Then, she could see precisely what the cops were seeing.

Her. And Tharman. Still standing, motionlessly, at the edge of the circle of gasoline.

They were not real, to her eyes. They looked wraithlike, slightly transparent, the white beam from the helicopter passing through them like torchlight through frosted glass. But she knew that they appeared solid enough, to the cops. When Tharman planted an image in a human's mind, it could seem clearer than reality itself.

Tendons were standing out in the black detective's neck. Sweat was dripping down towards his collar. He was howling wildly, now.

'Do as I *say*, you two! Right now, or I'll *blow your goddamn heads off*!'

Tharman smiled at her conspiratorially, raised a finger to his lips. Then he closed his hand fully around hers, and led her up towards the street.

More patrol cars were arriving, disgorging their occupants. They hurried past Susan, without even noticing anyone was there.

Tharman waited till they'd reached the far end of the lot before he stopped again. Susan followed his gaze through the wire fence. There had to be twenty or more police down there, by now. Some of them had started moving, at a feral crouch, towards the images. The helicopter had dropped a little lower, and was circling the wharf, keeping its spot fixed on the translucent man and woman. A sharp-shooter in a harness was leaning out of one side. And the detective had brought the shotgun up to his shoulder, and was squinting along the barrel.

Beside her, Tharman whispered, 'Goodbye, Susan Carroll.'

His eyes turned bright golden again.

Susan's gaze darted back to the wharf. Just in time to see her and Tharman's images raise their arms, and start to lurch forwards, as though they were attacking the massed policemen.

There was a roar of gunfire which rivalled the noise

from the chopper. The air started to fill with cordite smoke and orange sparks.

Tharman nodded satisfiedly, then dabbled at the air with his fingers, muttered a few words of a spell.

And the ring of gasoline exploded.

It should have just caught light, with a dull thump. But Tharman's magic made it far more impressive than that. It went off with a resounding blast, sending most of the cops flying. An enormous gout of flame soared up into the air. Kept on rising, for all the world like some biblical pillar of fire. Susan watched her own image and Tharman's being destroyed. Watched her own face twist with agony. Her hands scrabble blindly. Her hair and clothes catch fire. Blinked, as the figure was swallowed by the blaze.

She even thought she heard a thin falsetto scream.

She drew back a little, nervously. It was ghastly and unsettling, watching something that looked like her perishing that way. But she understood why Tharman had done it. No one would come looking for either of them, now.

They were gone. Lost in this painful brightness, flowering at the core of the night.

It was chaos, down there. She took it all in numbly. A couple of the uniformed cops were rolling across the ground, yelling with pain, their shirts on fire. Sparks were falling all over the lot, amongst the dry grass, on the warehouse roof. The other men were desperately trying to dodge them. Embers started hitting the river, embroidering its surface with wisps of smoke and steam.

A chunk of blazing wood sailed high into the air, came crashing down through the windshield of one of the police cruisers. It started burning, and within seconds the gas tank exploded, spreading a licking tide of fire to the other cars.

She watched it all as though it were happening a thousand miles away.

Finally, her eyes lifted to the helicopter, above a river now washed with shifting yellow and red. It had been caught by the blast, and was spinning wildly, chasing its own tail. She tried to imagine the pilot's horror, as he fought to regain control. Tried to imagine the sick terror of the men inside, trapped in that whirling, fragile piece of metal, high up in the air. But she couldn't.

They all seemed so very far away, now. As distant as the stars.

Shall we go? asked Tharman.

She gave a tiny, brittle shake of her head.

'Do one last thing for me?'

He knew what it was, without her even having to ask. Turning to face her carefully, he laid his hand on the side of her temple again, and touched her memories of Casey and the child.

Forget, he told her, smiling quietly. *Forget.*

They faded from her mind. As though they'd never existed.

PART VI

THE TRAVELLERS

1979–?

CHAPTER THIRTY-FOUR

1

There was an evening in LA when a platinum-haired woman – very rich, very tanned, all tennis muscles – approached her in the Polo Lounge, laid her hand on Susan's wrist, and invited her to a 'little soirée' at her beach-house in Malibu. There were five other women there when she turned up, each in various stages of undress. They weren't exactly pleased when they saw that she'd brought Tharman with her. Until his eyes glowed, and the Voice-that-whispers stilled their protests. Susan went through to the back, let herself out through the glass patio doors. Sat on the edge of the rear porch, wiggling her toes in the sand and watching the foam-capped waves of the Pacific crash against the shore until almost dawn.

There was a night in Hamburg when Tharman insisted she accompany him to the Reeperbahn, the city's red-light district. There, they made a game of picking out the most delicious and attractive of the streetwalkers, for him to Feed on. The same happened in Amsterdam and Copenhagen, Manila and Jakarta and Mexico City.

Sometimes, she thought of trying to run away. Simply sneaking out, during the daylight hours, and getting on a plane. It wouldn't have done any good. He'd have found her again as soon as darkness fell.

There was a night, in their hotel's lobby in London, when she bumped into an old school friend who'd thought that she was 'dead or something'. And Tharman had had to touch the woman's mind, to make her forget the meeting. But he didn't have to take her back up to their suite. Susan begged him not to, but it did no good, as usual.

She'd have had problems getting away in the sunlight, anyway. She even had to wear dark glasses in a brightly lit room these days. And her skin had become *more* than pale – it was practically translucent, like the flesh of a white fish. Occasionally, staring in a mirror, she practically imagined she could see her blue veins pulsing, just beneath the surface. She still hadn't aged a day since Paris. If anything, she looked slightly younger.

2

There was a night . . .

And then another night. And then another. They trailed away behind her almost a decade. Marched away, ahead of her, into eternity.

There were the days, too. They, if anything, were worse.

3

He'd been able to control his dreams, up until that fateful Mardi Gras. But after New Orleans, after Gorreq . . .

'Brother—?'

The first time it happened was in Puerto Rico, in a little fishing village on the lush Atlantic coast.

'*S–sister—?*'

Susan came awake in the narrow hotel bed, thinking that the sun had set. She realized her mistake after a moment. The windows were completely covered, but she could tell – from the noises outside – that the god *Ra* still ruled the skies.

But if it was still day, why was Tharman talking?

He gave a groan, and mumbled something.

Susan looked down at his gaunt, shadowy face, almost expecting him to stare back at her. His eyes were firmly closed, though. He was definitely asleep. But, beneath the thin, membrane-like eyelids, there was frantic movement. A fluttering. A jerking, to and fro. Whatever he was dreaming, it had taken hold of him completely.

As she watched, he shifted on the bed. His lips parted,

and he exhaled an anguished sigh. Then, he started shouting.

'Brother! Sister! Where are you? *Speak* to me!'

He dropped into Egyptian, muttering the alien-sounding words loudly.

He'd always talked to Pashta and Gorreq in his sleep, Susan remembered. Now, they were gone. Now, there were no voices in his daylight hours. There was only silence in his head, now.

His voice began to rise, louder still. She was afraid the people in the neighbouring rooms would hear. Susan pushed herself up on to her knees, reached across. Laid her palm against his cheek, trying to soothe him.

His left hand came up suddenly, the thin, bony fingers clamping around her wrist. His grip was so tight she practically yelled with pain.

A gentle smile worked its way across Tharman's twisted features.

'. . . Sister . . .'

He raised his other hand, and began brushing it along her arm, as lovingly and gently as you'd touch a newborn child.

'Sister, I'm so glad you're here. I was – worried. I dreamt that you had died.'

He did not let go of her till dusk. When the sun finally disappeared, dropping behind the jungle's vegetation, his eyes came open slowly. They were unfocused at first, their violet almost cloudy. But – as they grew sharper, as they steadied on the ceiling of the room, as he remembered where he was and how he'd got here and what had gone before – a lonely sadness filled them that was almost unbearable to look at.

The last of the Incarnate. The last, solitary god, trapped in a world of mortals. It was an expression Susan would see more and more of in the coming year, even when he was moving through the night, even when he was hunting.

He realized he was still holding her wrist, and released it uncomfortably.

*

4

Montego Bay, Jamaica; January, 1981: In a bikini and silken gown, Susan stepped out on to her balcony on the fourth storey of the Blue Reef Hotel. She leant against the railings, gazed down the gradient of the hill first, towards the distant glittering lights of Gloucester Avenue. Then she looked more sharply down, at the floodlit grounds of the hotel, and the curving shore beyond. A few determined revellers were still partying down there, their dancing no more than a drunken swaying to the rhythm of the ever-present reggae. As she watched, one of them collapsed. People started laughing and went over to help him.

Banners slung between the palm trees proclaimed HAPPY NEW YEAR, PEACE AND LOVE TO ALL THE WORLD.

It was five in the morning by now. Sunrise would be coming in less than an hour's time. She enjoyed the scene while she could. The happy, dancing people. The beauty of the flower-filled gardens. The soft white crescent of the beach, and the gentle lapping of the Caribbean surf. There was a splash and a squeal of delight from the water. A red-headed woman and a local boy were out there at waist depth, wrapped around each other, oblivious to everybody else.

She wanted, quite suddenly, Tharman beside her. Looking at all this with her. It was not the kind of scene you watched on your own without a twinge of pain.

But it wasn't going to happen. The noises from the bedroom reminded her of that.

Tharman had picked up the two Milwaukee girls just after midnight – neither of them could have been older than seventeen, and they were both stoned out of their minds on the local *ganja* – and had been Feeding on them all this time. Savagely, with a demented abandon. He Fed increasingly on strangers, these days, rarely came to her. And each time was more frenetic than the last, as though he were trying to lose himself in a tide of unfamiliar flesh.

It had been this way for months, now. Susan frowned and went back into the room.

The moans from the bed were subsiding, the shadowy figures on it becoming still. She ignored them as best she could. Strode through into the bathroom, without switching on the light, and began to run a tap into the basin.

The face which gazed back at her from the mirror on the medicine cabinet was still beautiful. But there were a few lines around the eyes that hadn't been there a week ago. She switched off the faucet, and studied them curiously, angling her chin first to the left, then the right. Very odd. They were tiny lines, no more than thread-marks, but they oughtn't to be there.

There was the rustle of fabric from the bedroom as the girls pulled their clothes back on. Susan waited, brooding, until the door closed behind them. Then she went back in and sat carefully on the bottom corner of the bed. Brushed one of Tharman's bare feet with her palm.

He didn't seem to notice her at all. His violet eyes were milky, wet, and he was staring vacantly into space. Listening to the silence in his own head, yet again.

She took hold of his big toe, pinched it, and his gaze flickered to her dully.

'I've aged a little. Aren't you working the magic on me any more?'

He sighed, shook his head numbly. *I forget, sometimes.*

'Will I die?' she asked.

He blinked, bewildered. She'd never asked him such a question before.

'Eventually?' Susan insisted. 'Will I die?'

Tharman shifted his head on the pillow, closed his eyes. He let out an exhausted moan, and didn't answer her for a while.

I can slow it down, he said, at last. *But I can't stop it. Not even I can do that.*

Susan felt an unease, a chill, beginning to overtake her. She tried to fight it down.

'And you? What will you do when I'm gone, when you have no one?'

Tharman rolled over on to his stomach, refusing to look at her.

Maybe . . . step out into the daylight. It's been such a long time since I last saw the sun.

Her face stiffened with shock.

'Is it wise to joke about such a thing?'

No joke.

She straightened, in her seated position. Mumbled her lower lip between her teeth. The chill was taking hold of her bones, now, making them feel stiff and old. She didn't like the sensation one little bit, she realized. The idea of becoming older had grown alien to her. She hadn't even thought about it, all this year.

There was a slight quaver to her voice when she spoke again.

'There must be something we can do?'

What? Tharman snapped. *You cannot change anything. You are not Incarnate.*

5

It occupied both their minds, most of that week. Susan couldn't take pleasure in the Caribbean any more. Even on the clearest, most starlit of nights, shadows seemed to hang over every shore, every wave, every tree.

Tharman was quiet, night after night, and barely Fed at all. As though the twin shadows of loneliness and death were occupying the full compass of his thoughts. As though the hanging shadows were obsessing him.

6

It was near midnight, the following Friday, when Susan marched the last half-mile towards the isolated beach. She was tired and dusty, sticky, and her feet hurt in the flimsy sandals she was wearing. But she didn't care. Tharman's voice had started calling to her insistently, an hour ago. He'd been gone since dusk, she hadn't been sure where. But now, he was summoning her, in a tone that could not be disobeyed. All she'd have to do was follow the direction of his voice, and she would find him.

She'd left Montego Bay far behind by now. There were no other pedestrians on this narrow road that ran parallel with the shoreline. And no sidewalks. Every so often, she had to pick her way across a tangle of tree roots or a pile of large stones. Once in a long while, a passing car would whisk by, its headlights sweeping brilliantly across her for a fleeting instant before vanishing. And – more frequently – she sensed eyes peering at her through the darkness, from the hillside shanties concealed amongst the trees on the far side of the road.

She kept expecting somebody to burst out from the foliage at any moment. Or a car to slow and roll up alongside her. But nothing like that happened. Tharman, she realized, was watching over her.

His voice was much louder, now.

Come! Hurry!

She increased her pace, startling some land crabs in the undergrowth.

Rounded a bend.

To her right, the hill grew steeper, its incline so sharp that no one could possibly live up there. To her left, there was a massive rocky outcrop. A great pile of boulders that had pushed its way out through the island's parched soil. It must have stood a good thirty feet wide by twenty high, and she couldn't see beyond it. But she could hear, behind it, the low, repetitive hissing of the tide against the sand. She was much closer to the shoreline than before. Susan pressed on.

It was, indeed, a beach. A beach of pure white sand, completely deserted. Not a sign of human habitation was in sight; not a light winked in a window anywhere. It was in the shape of a perfect quarter moon. At its far end, where the tide went flat and the water oily, the gnarled, insectile outline of a mangrove swamp began. Closer, there were more rocks, more boulders. None of them were as large as the outcrop beside her, but they dotted the colourless strand at irregular intervals.

Tharman was waiting for her beside one of the largest and the flattest, a narrow, erect silhouette against the paleness. The moon was coming up directly behind him and, unlike the crescent shape of the beach, it was full, swollen. It looked enormous, big enough to swallow the whole island. And yet . . . thin, two-dimensional. Unreal. Reach up and touch it, and your fingertips might pass right through that dimly mottled surface the way they'd pass through vapour.

Tharman stared at her a moment, his eyes burning goldenly. Then he stretched out his arms towards her.

She started running. Dodging the smaller rocks ahead of her. Kicking off her shoes as she went. And he grew larger in her vision until . . . ten yards from him, she stopped.

Came to an abrupt halt, the sand grinding painfully against the bare soles of her feet.

There was someone lying, tied up, on the even surface of the boulder. She took a moment realizing who it was.

Eli, the seventeen-year-old boy who sold conch shells and lumps of coral from a stall just outside the grounds of their hotel. He was stripped of his shirt now, a length of strong cord wrapped around his chest and waist, and fastened to his wrists. And perfectly motionless. He didn't try to struggle or escape. His eyes were gazing straight up at the canopy of stars above his face, as though he were trying to see beyond them.

What was going on? Why was he tied up if he was mesmerized? Unless it was – some form of ritual.

She stared questioningly at Tharman, but his expression was deadpan, his glowing eyes gave away nothing.

Susan forced herself to speak.

'Wh—what are you doing with him?'

For an answer, the Incarnate reached into his pocket and pulled out a long, curved knife in a leather scabbard.

He unsheathed it slowly, the razor-sharp blade flickering like a white flame in the moon's glow. And then, grasping it carefully by the point, he held it out towards her, handle first.

Susan shook her head, drew back a little.

'I don't understand.'

It is the only way. His voice was urgent as it echoed through her head. *Take the knife. Do everything I tell you. You will understand soon enough.*

Still, she didn't reach towards it. She peered at it as though it were a snake.

Until Tharman took hold, extremely gently, of her mind. Wiped away her fear, her anxiety. Wiped away her doubts, and her sharp feelings of revulsion.

The problem is, he explained to her, *you are not Incarnate.*

7

When she stepped up to the boulder, she found that she was moving in a way her body had never moved before. Perfectly upright, stiff-backed. Her arms hanging by her sides. Each motion of her legs, each pace, each footfall, so smooth and calculated she might have been on a parade ground. It was a ceremonial way of moving, she realized coldly. A ritual way. As though she were . . . some kind of *priestess.*

She stood over the bound, unseeing boy a moment, then raised her arms out to her sides, her spread-eagled shadow falling across him. He didn't even blink, not even when the knife glittered again, in her right hand.

Tharman was guiding her every step of the way, by now.

She muttered a few words he put in her head. They were in Egyptian.

Then she reached forwards with the blade. And, with the detached precision of a surgeon, drew it across the boy's throat, slitting his jugular. There was no protest from Eli. He shuddered a little, and his bound feet gave a few stuttering kicks – that was all.

She watched, with lifeless fascination, as his blood started spurting into the air. And noted, equally detachedly, that when it dropped on to the surface of the rock, it wasn't dropping naturally. It was falling in symmetrical patterns on either side of his motionless head. Spirals, and curlicues, and shapes like the broad primary feathers at the tips of eagles' wings. And it was soaking in and drying the moment it touched, so that the flat top of the boulder became etched with dark red.

More words started pouring from her mouth. A whole torrent of them. A chant. She didn't understand them individually; they were all in Egyptian, as before. But she understood their combined meaning, almost as though she sensed it. Knew what they were supposed to do.

This was called . . . the Incantation of the Door. Its purpose was to open a portal into the *Duat*, the Underworld, the habitation of the gods. Just as Tharman had done sixteen hundred years ago. Just as all the others had done.

She couldn't stop mouthing the words . . . but she *still* didn't understand! Tharman was the *last*, wasn't he?

Susan was vaguely aware that the gaunt man was moving, now. Her gaze was still fixed on Eli's throat – the pulsing jets of blood were growing further apart, and weaker. But she realized, from the corner of her eye, that Tharman was climbing up on to the rock himself. He knelt, just above the Jamaican's head.

And, pressing his fists side to side, extended his wrists towards her.

'Now me.'

She was so surprised to hear him use his normal voice, she whirled around sharply, practically losing her footing on the sand.

He was staring at her with an odd expression, part impatience, part querulousness, part regret. And his eyes were not burning or golden, now. They'd returned to their soft, beguiling violet.

She became intensely aware of the knife in her hand. Its hilt seemed to dig into her palm. She wanted to let her fingers uncurl, let the blade drop, turn away. But Tharman's insistent gaze didn't allow her to do that.

He jerked his wrists towards her.

'Now *me*! Do it!'

Then, he held them very still.

As slowly as though in a dream, Susan raised the knife. She set its edge against his skin precisely where he directed her, where the delta of veins and arteries and tendons met.

And she jerked it backwards savagely.

Normally, the sharpened steel wouldn't have left so much as a faint red graze. It sliced deeply into his flesh, this time, and the thick blood started pumping, because he was *allowing* it to happen.

She was starting to feel scared, again. But staying put. The Incantation continued to roll from her lips.

She noticed she was saying one word more and more frequently. Thoth. *Thoth.*

Now she was really frightened, bewilderment swamping her, like a cold, dark storm inside her head. What, by all the Lords, was going on? Thoth, the moon-god, was inside Tharman. Part of him. She couldn't summon him, could she?

The rock began to shake. The stars overhead, the moonlit sea, the beach around her, seemed to dim.

Tharman—

—wavered.

His whole body went faint and misty for a moment. Rippled like a pool a tiny stone had been thrown into.

When he became whole, solid, again, there was a point of brightness at the exact centre of his chest.

Which began to expand.

The light, as it grew broader – Susan saw – was not perfectly white. It had a grey edge to it, a cold, dull tinge. Like the light from a mortuary window. It reached the outer edges of his chest.

And – *somehow* – kept on spreading.

She was still intoning the chant. Running through the last few lines as though her life depended on it. But it wasn't opening a Door into the *Duat*, she knew now.

Tharman's body suddenly went limp, behind the spreading paleness. His head tipped back. His mouth dropped open. He tumbled backwards on to the rock. Lay there, his limbs twisted. An empty shell that had once been a man.

Susan barely noticed. Something was emerging from the circle of brightness now.

The last word of the Incantation died on her lips.

The creature that was climbing out was darker than all the nights of the world compressed into one blackness. It had the body of a massive ape, the head of a great savage dog. But it didn't have hot, glowing eyes. Its gaze was violet.

Tharman was in there, too.

Susan fell to her knees, shaking furiously. Bowed her head.

The Lord's shadow dropped across her shoulders, as it stooped towards her.

CHAPTER THIRTY-FIVE

1

Montana; July, 1982: The ancient pink T-bird bumped down the narrow heat-cracked road with a rattle of loose fenders and springs, and a faint clanking from the engine. It was a noise that stilled the crickets in the surrounding fields for a moment, as the automobile passed. The car's off-white top was folded down. A sad country-and-western ballad, from the radio, drifted out towards the canopy of stars.

Susan sat behind the wheel at a lazy slouch, steering with one hand and tapping her long painted nails against the dashboard to the rhythm of the music with the other.

It was eleven at night. The tune on the radio subsided abruptly, and the news came on. None of it was good, the Middle East in flames. The shelling of Beirut was still under way, and the two-year war between Iran and Iraq showed no sign of abating.

She reached across, thinking of switching the radio off. Then shook her head, smiling ruefully.

What an unholy mess the old desert lands had become. How Gorreq would have loved it.

She often thought of him and the cat-priestess, but with affection more than sadness these days. They hadn't *really* gone. They'd be alive as long as she remembered them. Besides, she had more pressing concerns right now. This truly was the middle of nowhere. She had to find somewhere to rest up before dawn.

She progressed another half-dozen miles without seeing so much as a distant light. There were so many hills and forests around this part of the world, it was impossible to see to the horizon anywhere.

She'd been on the road for the past four months now

– making her way through the small towns of the Midwest, stopping briefly at Kansas City and St Louis – before deciding to head north-west. It was an area of the States she'd never visited before. Now, she was becoming convinced she had made a mistake. The yawning emptiness of the big car niggled at her. The night sprawled around her, a shadow-filled vacuum. She could almost hear a noise from it – the flat, dreary hissing of static, of nothingness. For a moment, she toyed with the idea of turning back, heading for the more densely populated states. But there wasn't time. She had to keep going.

A half-mile further on, the road came to a fork. She braked, the T-bird's motor idling badly, and then followed her instincts and turned right.

Five minutes later, she realized why. WELCOME TO YEWLBURG, read a sign caught in her headlights. POPULATION: 27,938.

Well, well! Tharman chuckled, from inside her head.

She started passing wheatfields to her right. That had to be the old Danvers ranch. The cattle were obviously gone. Susan craned up in her seat, gazed northwards, trying to see the great house itself. But there was just a copse of trees in that direction. It was nowhere in sight.

The road suddenly widened. Lights gleamed ahead. She had reached the outskirts of the town, much sooner than Tharman's memories told her she ought to. Street upon street of wooden houses, with stores and gas stations and fast-food joints along the edges of the incoming road, met her gaze. Half the place still seemed to be awake. Teenaged boys, leaning against pick-up trucks, wolf-whistled at her as she passed.

She adjusted the low neckline of her pink halter-neck top, ran a hand through her hair, which was tied back into a ponytail. Grinned hungrily.

You should see the legs, fellers.

Main Street, when she reached it, was still called Main. But that was all she recognized. Bob Nyman's store had become a 7-Eleven. The *Gazette* offices, a Dairy Queen.

A combined TV and hi-fi showroom had replaced the burnt-out shell of Johnson's Hardware.

The town had its own cinema now. A double-bill of 'Rocky' movies was showing.

Eddie's Bar was gone.

But Meacher's Hill was still there, though the lower half of its wooded slopes had been ripped away to make room for more houses. Susan slowed the car and gazed up at the pine-topped crest for a while, her thoughts full of old conquests and adventures. They weren't hers. They were Tharman's. But he was part of her, now. She could recall it all as clearly as she could remember what she'd done yesterday.

Finally, she tore her gaze away. Drifted the T-bird up to the kerb outside a new bar with a neon Budweiser sign, and the legend *Double Horseshoe* in red lights above the phoney-looking Western-style saloon doors.

A Willie Nelson song and babbling voices and laughter drifted from inside.

2

She got out of the car, her auburn ponytail dropping almost to her waist. Popped on a pair of sunglasses. The frames were the exact same pink as her halter top, the lenses opaque black.

Below the waist, she was dressed in faded denim cut-off shorts – the legs sheared away as high as decency allowed – and a pair of white, embroidered cowboy boots, with silver toe-caps and leather fringes at the back. She could already feel eyes on her, from windows across the street. Ignored them.

Advanced towards the bar doors, and pushed them open.

She'd seen places like this a thousand times, in her travels. There was a bare wooden floor. A mechanical bull over at the back, silent now. A pool table. Steer-horns and moose heads on the walls. And dozens of farmhands clustered around the bar, their attention focused on the few available women.

Her practised eye swept across them, didn't alight on a single one.

Susan's gaze drifted across the room until it settled on a couple at a table in the far corner. Lords, they were so beautiful! Both young and fit and tanned. Both tall and blond, with gleaming white smiles. They wore matching chequered shirts and identical blue jeans, and were holding hands, staring into each other's eyes. Obviously very much in love. Behind her darkened glasses, she could feel her eyes glow golden with a hunter's satisfaction.

Perfect, the pair of them.

There was so much of herself to Feed, now. A man, a woman, and a god. Tharman and Thoth and Susan, all wrapped up in one warm body.

But—

The heat in her eyes began to fade. That prickling sensation of unease she'd felt in the car began to creep over her again.

These two looked so wonderful. Perhaps she'd take them up to Meacher's Hill, and relive old triumphs. Yet she knew exactly how it would be . . . the same way it had been since the beach. She would make love to them very gently, very tenderly, without a hint of roughness, as she always did. And they'd respond in kind. But their smiles would be those of the mesmerized, the barely conscious. Their expressions, a blankness with a rictus drawn across it. Their adoring eyes would be as hollow as empty wells. And she'd feel as alone, amongst them, as a person in a graveyard.

As she always did.

Perhaps, one day, she'd find someone she could truly care for. Someone special. A long-term companion.

Just as Tharman had found her.

She felt her heart flutter and her spirits lift at the very thought. Forgot all about the bar, the couple, for a moment. Just because she hadn't found that person yet, didn't mean she never would.

But not tonight.

One of the clustered men noticed her. Then another, and another. They gawked at her, like fish staring from a bowl.

'Hey, foxy lady!' called out someone from the back.

Susan wet her lips – and went inside, letting the doors swing shut behind her.